Praise for *USA TODAY* bestselling author Delores Fossen

"*Always a Lawman*...includes plenty of thrills, romance, suspense and a hot cowboy/lawman hero."
—*RT Book Reviews*

"This is much more than a romance."
—*RT Book Reviews* on *Branded as Trouble*

"Nicky and Garret have sizzling chemistry!"
—*RT Book Reviews* on *No Getting Over a Cowboy*

"Clear off space on your keeper shelf, Fossen has arrived."
—*New York Times* bestselling author Lori Wilde

"Delores Fossen takes you on a wild Texas ride with a hot cowboy."
—*New York Times* bestselling author B.J. Daniels

"You will be sold!"
—*RT Book Reviews* on *Blame It on the Cowboy*

"This...series...has gotten better and better with each new installment."
—*RT Book Reviews* on *Holden*, part of The Lawmen of Silver Creek Ranch miniseries

Also available from Delores Fossen and HQN Books

A Wrangler's Creek Novel

Lone Star Cowboy (ebook novella)
Those Texas Nights
One Good Cowboy (ebook novella)
No Getting Over a Cowboy
Just Like a Cowboy (ebook novella)
Branded as Trouble
Cowboy Dreaming (ebook novella)
Texas-Sized Trouble
Cowboy Heartbreaker (ebook novella)

The McCord Brothers

What Happens on the Ranch (ebook novella)
Texas on My Mind
Cowboy Trouble (ebook novella)
Lone Star Nights
Cowboy Underneath It All (ebook novella)
Blame It on the Cowboy

To see the complete list of titles available from Delores Fossen, please visit www.deloresfossen.com.

DELORES FOSSEN

LONE STAR BLUES

Recycling programs for this product may not exist in your area.

ISBN-13: 978-1-335-63199-2

Lone Star Blues

This edition published by arrangement with Harlequin Books S.A.

For questions and comments about the quality of this book, please contact us at CustomerService@Harlequin.com.

www.HQNBooks.com

Printed in U.S.A.

CONTENTS

LONE STAR BLUES 7

COWBOY HEARTBREAKER 321

LONE STAR BLUES

CHAPTER ONE

THE FIRST THING that Dylan Granger saw when he opened his eyes was the woman's naked butt. It was impossible to miss it because he'd been using it for a pillow.

Hell, not again.

It was one thing to face an unfamiliar butt when he was twenty, but he was thirty-four now and too old for this.

He glanced around, trying to get his bearings. He was in his own bed. Well, sort of. He was in his own *room* anyway at his family's ranch, but only the bottom half of his body was actually on the mattress. The rest of him was angled off the bed, his arms dangling, and his face was squished against the woman's left butt cheek.

At least it was soft.

Groaning and grunting, Dylan lifted his head. It wasn't easy. He felt every one of the tequila shots he'd downed the night before. All for a good cause—it had been his brother's bachelor party. At least it'd seemed like a good cause when the celebration was in full swing. Right now, Dylan could just add it to his *too old for this shit* list.

He managed to scoot back on the mattress so he

could sit up, and that's when he realized he was fully clothed. In fact, he still had on his cowboy boots, and his jeans were even zipped. Those were good signs.

The naked woman on the floor, however, wasn't a good sign in any way, shape or form.

She was on her stomach, her face turned away from him, and she was snoring. He couldn't tell who she was. But she was blonde, and there was a bumble bee tat on her lower back. That was hardly enough info for Dylan to make an ID so he gave her arm a little shake to wake her so he could ask her name.

"Go away," she grumbled without moving, and within seconds she was snoring again.

Not exactly a friendly reaction, but maybe she, too, was feeling the effects of multiple tequila shots.

Dylan made himself stand up. Again, there was nothing easy about it. All the livestock in the entire state of Texas were clomping in his head. The room was spinning, and every strand of his hair was hurting. That's why it took him a good minute, maybe more, to make it a couple of steps to the other side of the woman so he could get a look at her face.

And after that look, he still didn't know who she was.

It was hard to tell with her cheek squished from her awkward sleeping position. At least there was no wedding or engagement ring, thank God.

He forced himself to try to remember what had happened at the party. It'd been at the Longhorn Bar here in his hometown of Wrangler's Creek. There'd been strippers and skimpily dressed cocktail waitresses. His brother Lawson had been there, of course, since it was his bachelor party, and plenty of their friends had shown up, as well.

Dylan's other brother, Lucian, had even made an appearance. The only other things Dylan could recall with any accuracy were the tequila shots and the limos he'd hired to make sure everybody got home safe and sound. That included him. He remembered coming into the house. Even recalled staggering into his bedroom, but there sure as heck hadn't been a naked woman when he'd arrived.

Dylan blinked hard a couple of times to get his eyes to focus, and he glanced around the room, looking for the snoring woman's purse so he could find out her name. But no purse. No clothes scattered around, either.

That was another bad sign.

He went into the bathroom, took a quick shower, and after he dressed, he headed downstairs to go all Sherlock Holmes and look for clues. He soon found one, too. The housekeeper, Marylou Culver, was in the hall heading toward his room, and she had a heap of women's clothes gathered up in her arms. Dylan saw a devil-red lace bra and what appeared to be a strappy black dress. Two equally strappy silver shoes dangled from Marylou's fingers. Since Marylou was in her sixties and usually dressed like a 1950s schoolteacher, the clothing probably didn't belong to her.

"Uh, these things were on the stairs and on the front porch," Marylou said. "I'm guessing you have… company."

It was no guess, and Marylou's slightly disapproving look told him that. The woman had only worked at the ranch for a month or so, but Dylan knew his reputation preceded him. It wasn't the first time a housekeeper had found women's clothes on the stairs. Or even the porch. And that kind of information wouldn't have stayed secret for long in a small town like Wrangler's Creek.

"There was a pair of panties, as well," Marylou went on, "but the dog got to them before I could."

Great. The dog was Booger, the persnickety Yorkie that his mom had left at the ranch while she went to a yoga retreat in Costa Rica. Booger had failed multiple obedience programs, and he was finicky about what food touched his mouth. Everything else was fair game, though. Manure-caked boots, table legs, toilet paper. He'd probably chewed the panties to shreds by now.

"How did the dog get out of the house?" he asked.

"Beats me. Maybe he got out when you and the naked woman came in."

That was possible. After all, if he couldn't remember the woman, then he might not have noticed a dog the size of his foot making an escape. "Was there a purse or wallet with the clothes?"

Marylou shook her head. "I can keep looking, though. What do you want me to do with these?" She tipped her head to the clothes.

"Just put them outside my bedroom door for now." Best not to have Marylou actually witness the bare butt for herself. She already had enough gossip to fuel the town for a week or two.

Dylan started down the stairs on a mission to find some strong coffee, the naked woman's ID and perhaps a large rock that he could use to hit himself on the head for drinking too much.

"Oh, and your brother wants to see you," Marylou added. "He's not in a very good mood."

Before she'd tacked on that last part, he was about to ask which brother, but Lucian was the most qualified for the bad mood award. That meant Dylan would avoid him. At least until he'd tanked up on coffee and got the naked woman clothed and wherever she should be.

He made a beeline for the kitchen, hoping it was empty. No such luck. But at least it wasn't Lucian, Booger or another naked woman. However, it was a female.

Lucian's assistant, Karlee O'Malley.

She was pouring herself some coffee, but she took one look at him and handed him the quart-sized mug that'd been meant for her. "Are you already regretting the vow of celibacy you took last night?" Karlee asked.

Since Dylan had been in midmumble to thank her, it took him a moment to hear what she'd said. As bad as he needed the coffee—and he needed it—he didn't gulp any down just so he could say, "Wh-what?"

Karlee whipped out her phone from her pocket and pulled up a video. Of him.

"I, Dylan Granger," he slurred on the video, "do hereby take a vow of celibacy for the next month." He'd only pronounced two of those words correctly. "No form of sex whatsoever. If I fail, then I agree to carry out the donation."

"I'm guessing lots of alcohol was involved in this," Karlee said. It wasn't a question. "Especially since you sent it to me shortly after midnight."

Oh yes, alcohol had been involved. He'd been drunk, and Lucian hadn't been, which meant his turd-head brother had likely been the one to come up with this stupid idea.

"Do you remember doing this?" Karlee pressed.

Unfortunately, he did. Now that his head was clearing some, more of what'd happened was coming back to him. But it was coming back as impaired, jumbled memories that Dylan wasn't especially eager to remember.

"The last time you got drunk was what…three years ago?" Karlee went on. "That's when you ended up staying in a hotel in San Antonio, and you called me to come and get you. You didn't remember much of anything then."

He had indeed ended up in a hotel after a party and had called Karlee the morning after when he couldn't find his truck. But that hadn't been because of tequila shots but rather a bad reaction to some prescription cold meds. The pills had knocked him on his butt.

"What's the donation?" Karlee, again. Her forehead bunched up. "It's not like to a sperm bank, is it?"

No, thank God. This didn't involve anything that would require him to lower his zipper. "Fifty grand to be donated to the Wrangler's Creek Charity Rodeo."

Karlee's mouth quivered as she fought back a smile. She lost that fight. Smiled. Then, she laughed. And she kept on laughing until Dylan glared at her.

"Sorry," she mumbled, but she was clearly still trying to hold back a giggle. "But you've never come close to lasting a month. What will the rodeo committee do with all that extra money?"

Dylan wanted to believe that was a dilemma that the committee would never face, but Karlee was right. He'd never lasted that long. Still, it was probably time he took on this challenge. Time he gave up booze completely, too.

"Where's Lucian?" Dylan asked after he got some more coffee in him.

"He's here at the house, in his office." Karlee checked the time on her phone. "He wants to see you, but he'll be leaving in about a half hour for San Antonio."

There was nothing unusual about any of those three things she'd just told him. Lucian only lived part-time at the ranch, which meant he was always coming and going. Though there'd likely be no going today until he'd seen Dylan. Which was fine because now that he had seen the video and had some coffee, Dylan wanted to confront his big brother about what part he'd played in that vow.

"When I came in earlier, I saw what appeared to be bits and pieces of a pair of shredded red panties by the back porch," Karlee added. "Should I ask about them?"

"Only if you can tell me who they belong to." He saw the concern flash through her eyes so he added, "There's a naked woman in my bedroom."

The concern vanished, and she had a fight with another smile. "Your celibacy didn't last long."

"I think it did. I woke up like this." He fanned his hands over his fully clothed body, and then pointed to his closed zipper.

Of course, if Lucian knew about the naked woman, and Dylan was betting he did, then there was no way his brother would believe that sex hadn't happened. That meant Lucian would try to hold him to the stupid celibacy agreement.

And to that rodeo donation.

Lucian might have even planted the naked woman in Dylan's room. Though this kind of prank seemed more suited to a teenager than a grown man.

Dylan didn't mind giving the money to the rodeo. It was for a good cause since they used the profits to fund the hospital library and such. In fact, he made an anonymous donation every year. He just didn't want the money tied to his sex life or a drunken vow.

Karlee gave his arm a pat. "Have you actually thought about the wacky notion of giving up on all this frat boy behavior and settling down?"

Even though Karlee hadn't meant for it to happen, that gave him some instant bad memories. He'd tried settling down, once, and he had the wedding band in his dresser drawer to prove it.

Since there was no way Dylan wanted to talk about that, he just flashed Karlee one of his grins. The kind that made men smile back and women blush. Karlee didn't blush, but she did shake her head.

"Just hang in there," she said. "Once Lucian is back in San Antonio, I'll try to keep him as slammed as I can with meetings and such so he'll get his nose out of the ranch business."

Dylan wanted to kiss her. Not in the way he wanted to kiss most attractive women. And Karlee was indeed attractive. But he didn't feel that way about her.

Plus, she was also in love with Lucian. Or in strong "like" anyway.

She had felt that way about Lucian for as long as Dylan could remember. Why, he didn't know. Apparently neither did Lucian because Dylan was positive that his thickheaded big brother had no idea whatsoever how his assistant felt about him.

"Oh, and when you see Lucian," she added, "it's okay to talk about the celibacy-donation pact, but it's best not to bring up anything about the rodeo itself."

Since that was an event Lucian looked forward to every year, her words surprised him. "Has he actually decided not to compete since he loses every year anyway?"

Karlee shook her head. "Not a chance that he'd drop out of it. But first thing this morning, he was practicing his bronc riding skills and got thrown hard. His family jewels and pride took a bruising."

Dylan would definitely rub that in. It was the brotherly thing to do.

He topped off his quart of coffee, thanked Karlee again and made his way to Lucian's office, which was at the other end of the house from Dylan's. Instead of feng shui, Dylan had gone with the "out of sight, out of mind" approach when choosing his work space. He got along best with Lucian when they weren't in the same general vicinity.

Lucian's door was open, and before Dylan could even step inside, he heard his brother growl, "There was a bra and a dress on the front porch this morning."

Obviously, Lucian had missed the strappy silver shoes. "They're mine." Dylan said it with as much cockiness as he could manage. It also had more than a smidge of anger since he wasn't especially happy with Lucian right now.

"You've started cross-dressing?" Lucian managed some cockiness of his own.

"Yeah, I started it right about the time you decided to get me to take a vow of celibacy when I was drunk."

"A vow you've already broken. There's a naked or seminaked woman in your bedroom, isn't there?"

Since Lucian almost certainly knew the answer to that, Dylan went with the truth. "Yeah, but I don't know who she is, and I didn't have sex with her. I'm figuring you planted her there. Maybe even paid her."

Lucian gave him a flat look. "I wouldn't have to plant or pay. Naked women gravitate toward you and your bed. I've even heard there's a Dylan Granger Sex Bingo Game being played around the county."

Sadly, that last part was true.

Tiffany Kelly, a cocktail waitress at the Longhorn Bar, had indeed started a bingo game that involved sex categories—specifically sex categories with Dylan—and she had distributed variations of the cards to women around town. The one card he'd seen had things on it like give Dylan a BJ, Dylan gives you a thigh hickey and a double orgasm from Dylan to you. Apparently, once a woman had her card filled, Tiffany would give them a drink on the house.

So far, there'd been four winners.

Okay, there were five, but one of them had cheated. No way had Susan Finkley had two orgasms since he'd had to work for nearly an hour to give her just one.

While Dylan wasn't especially proud of those winners or the game itself, it was obvious Lucian was only bringing it up to take the attention off the fact that he'd been a dick. A busy one. Because while he was riling Dylan with this conversation, he was also answering an email. And ignoring the three lights that were flashing on his office phone. Apparently, Dylan wasn't the only person who wanted to have words with Lucian this morning.

"I didn't have sex with the woman in my bedroom," Dylan repeated once he got his teeth unclenched. "But even if I had, there's no way in hell I'd let you hold me to a promise that I made while I was drunk."

"You didn't just make the promise to me. You sent a copy to Mom and your lawyer."

Well, shit. Dylan didn't care about his lawyer knowing. He'd sent her drunk texts before. Heck, he'd had sex with her, too.

But their mom, Regina, could be a problem.

She was always nudging him to quit sleeping around and find Ms. Right. This was despite her own failed marriage that'd happened nearly two decades ago. Apparently, his mother wore a pair of massive invisible rose-colored glasses when it came to love and such. Dylan tended to see things a lot clearer than she did. Ironic because her marriage had been to an asshole. Dylan's had been to, well, a woman who wasn't an asshole.

Jordan.

Dylan hated how she just kept popping into his head. Even the remnants of the booze-haze didn't stop it. Neither did sleep. Time. Or anything else he'd tried.

He went closer to Lucian's desk and leaned in so that his brother wouldn't miss a word or any of the ice-ray glare he was giving him. "I don't care if I sent that text to Santa Claus and the Tooth Fairy, it's not a binding agreement. And it was pretty low-down and dirty for you to come up with it."

Lucian quit typing on his computer keyboard only long enough to spare him a glance. "It wasn't my idea. It was yours."

Dylan just rolled his eyes because there was no way he would believe that.

"It started off as a friendly conversation between Lawson and you," Lucian continued after he huffed. "And Lawson mentioned your reputation around town and the sex bingo. Folks call you the cowboy rake, you know?"

Yeah, he was well aware of that, too, though Dylan always tried to make sure that a commitment was never on the table, or in the bed, when it came to sex. He always hoped that would lessen the chances of a broken heart, but he knew it had happened a time or two.

"How the heck did all of this lead to my celibacy?" Dylan pressed. He actually remembered snippets of the conversation from the night before, but the logic behind it—if there had ever been logic, that is—was lost in the clomping stampede that was still going on in his head.

"I tried to convince Lawson that you could give up sex if you really wanted to do that," Lucian went on. "He laughed. Actually, everyone in the Longhorn laughed. *A lot.* That's when you got mad and said you'd show them, that you'd make a celibacy vow. Lawson's the one who pressed for the vow to have consequences when you failed."

Clearly, he needed to have a chat with Lawson for egging him on to do something this stupid.

"So, who came up with the charity donation?" Dylan demanded. "And are there any other specifics that I don't know about?"

Another shrug. "You'd have to ask Lawson. That's about the time I left, and Lawson and you were still hashing things out." Lucian's huff was louder and more impatient this time. "Look, I've got three hours of work that I need to do in the next twenty minutes. Just finish sobering up, deal with the woman in your bedroom and don't miss the meeting you've got first thing tomorrow morning with the new feed supplier."

Oh, he was sober all right, and Dylan didn't need a reminder about the meeting since he had been the one to set it up. Lucian never seemed to remember that he didn't run the ranch 95 percent of the time. Dylan did. But that was an annoyance for another day. Today, he needed to deal with the naked woman right after he spoke to Lawson.

Dylan took out his phone, called Lawson, but it went straight to voice mail. Not really a surprise. After all, it was the morning after his bachelor party, and Dylan was betting Lawson had gotten as shit-faced as he had. Also, it was possible Lawson would be unable to recall what'd actually happened. If so, Dylan might never discover if the rodeo payout held some other special level of hell he didn't know about. He wanted any and all specifics that he could pass on to his mother when she called.

Which she'd already done.

That's when Dylan saw the five missed calls from

her on his screen. He'd had his phone on silent, but it had only been three minutes in between the time when he'd sent out the celibacy video and her first call.

"Remember, you'll need to apologize to Walter Ray," Lucian threw out there. "Maybe send him a bottle of scotch to smooth things over. He favors single malt."

Dylan only knew one Walter Ray. "*Judge* Walter Ray Turley?"

"That's the one," Lucian verified with a layer of smart-assery in his tone.

Dylan got a jolt of more memories, and these were the clearest yet. Walter Ray had shown up at the bachelor party, but things had gotten a little ugly when the subject of the Dylan Granger Sex Bingo had come up.

Because Walter Ray's daughter, Melanie, was one of the winners.

The judge hadn't approved. Dylan hadn't approved of the threats that Walter Ray had doled out. Threats involving neutering or a shovel to the head if Dylan didn't "put a ring on it." His brother Lawson and his cousins Garrett and Roman had broken things up before they got ugly, and Walter Ray had stormed out.

"We do business with plenty of Walter Ray's friends and family," Lucian went on. "Best not to let this sort of thing fester."

It was already past the festering point. About three months ago, Dylan had gone out with Melanie, and they'd run hot and heavy for a couple of weeks. Longer than most of Dylan's relationships. That length of time was probably why Melanie, and therefore the judge, had got the notion that it was serious between them.

It hadn't been.

And even though Dylan had long since ended things with Melanie, he wasn't sure that she truly believed it was over between them. Walter Ray certainly didn't believe it.

"Oh, and you might have to take Booger to the vet," Lucian added just as Dylan headed for the door. "He might have eaten the elastic from your guest's red panties."

Great. Now, he could add possible canine intestinal issues to this already-shitty day. But there was a silver lining in this. At least there was if he believed in the old wives' tale that bad luck came in threes. Booger was number three since Dylan had already gotten the naked woman and the riled judge. So, maybe the bad luck was all finished.

"Where's Booger now?" Dylan asked.

"The sunroom. Karlee chased him down and left him with Bertha, the housekeeper."

For a man with his pulse on the business, Lucian didn't bother keeping up with the daily workings of his family home. Bertha had quit weeks ago, during Lucian's last visit, and now they had Vera and Marylou. Dylan knew Lucian hadn't meant Marylou because Booger hadn't been with her when she was upstairs. So the dog had to be with Vera.

Since it was obvious Lucian already had too much on his plate, Dylan would keep the family jewels' injury ribbing for later. Instead, he tried to call Lawson again, but when he got no answer, he decided to drive over and see him in person. His house wasn't far, less than a half mile away, but he wasn't going to walk there today. Best to get back here fast and take care of getting the naked woman home.

He walked the maze of halls that zigged and zagged through the house and came out the back door where he kept his truck. When he stepped out onto the porch, Dylan spotted their cook, Abe Weiser, who was stretched out, napping, in one of the wicker lounge chairs. He was a lousy cook, not especially good at managing the house, either, but he tolerated Lucian. That was Abe's sole asset and the reason he'd stayed employed at Heavenly Acres for the last twenty years.

"One of the hands said I'm supposed to tell you that a longhorn broke fence," Abe said without sitting up. Or even opening his eyes. "It made it to your truck, and its horn hooked your radiator. Busted it. The radiator, not the horn. The horn's all right, I reckon. You'll have to take one of the other trucks if you're going anywhere."

There went the old wives' tale of three. Maybe old husbands' tales had four bad things going wrong. If so, then he'd fulfilled that quota, too.

Downing some more coffee, Dylan headed off the porch and toward the large detached garage for another vehicle. However, before he could even make it there, he saw something sparkly on the stone path. A silver purse that was smaller and flatter than the palm of his hand. It had some chew marks on it and was wet, possibly from dog slobber.

Since this likely belonged to the naked woman, he opened it to see if he could find her ID. And there it was—her driver's license along with a credit card and some lipstick. There was also one of those stupid Dylan Granger Sex Bingo cards folded up inside.

Thankfully, it was blank.

He pulled out the license and looked at her birth date first. She was twenty-six. Way too young for him but at least she was legal. Then he read the name, and his stomach went to his ankles. Because it was Misty Turley, the same last name as the judge who was pissed at him. And with the way his morning was going, Dylan seriously doubted that was a coincidence. No, this was likely another of his daughters. One younger than Melanie.

Maybe he could send Walter Ray a whole case of scotch.

Dylan didn't know exactly how many daughters the judge actually had. Walter Ray had gotten divorced years ago, and when his ex-wife had moved away, the girls only visited Wrangler's Creek every now and then. Or at least that had been the case until Melanie had moved back after she'd finished college.

He picked up the purse so he could take it back inside and add it to the pile of clothes. Since the identity of the naked woman was bad news number five, that had to mean he was good to go at least for the rest of the day.

Or not.

Dylan heard the sound of an engine right before he saw the cop car pull up in front of the house. It wasn't the local cops, either. The cruiser had San Antonio Police on the door.

A tall, lanky man in uniform stepped out. "I'm looking for Dylan Granger," he said, and he flashed his badge.

Hell. What now? Had Walter Ray sent someone to look for his daughter?

"I'm Dylan Granger." He tucked the purse in his back pocket and walked toward the cop. "Is there a problem?"

The cop didn't answer. He just motioned to someone inside the cruiser, and a moment later, a gray-haired woman stepped out. She wasn't alone. She was gripping the hand of a little boy who couldn't have been more than two or three years old.

Dylan silently repeated that—*hell, what now?*

"You need to sign for him," the woman said. She had some papers in her left hand, and she started toward Dylan, pulling the little boy with her.

Dylan shook his head. "Why do I need to sign? And who is he?"

The woman smiled as if there was something to smile about. "Well, Mr. Granger, according to this paper, this precious little boy is your son."

CHAPTER TWO

MAJOR JORDAN RIVERA caught a reflection of herself in the airport window and realized something.

She totally sucked at disguises.

The floppy white crocheted hat with its drooping sides, the fuzzy mauve hoodie and bulging sunglasses made her look like a perverted Easter bunny.

She was drawing attention to herself. The exact opposite of what she wanted to do. It wasn't good attention, either. People snickered. There were elbow nudges and behind-the-hand whispers.

The next time she needed a disguise, she really had to put more thought into it. And not get her traveling clothes from the Lost and Found at the base hospital. In hindsight, she wasn't convinced the items had actually been lost but purposely abandoned because no one wanted to be seen in them.

She kept walking from the gate where her flight had just landed, and she took out her phone. One look at it, and that got her attention off her inadequate disguise skills. The phone screen was filled with missed calls that she'd received while on her flight from Germany to Atlanta. The most recent one, though, caused her to frown and silently curse, and it had come in just five minutes ago.

Why the heck was her ex, Dylan Granger, calling her?

Maybe he'd heard that she was going to be stationed at the base in San Antonio and wanted to welcome her "home." Or tell her how sorry he was for what'd happened to her. The latter would be far worse than the former so Jordan deleted that one without even listening to the voice mail Dylan had left. She didn't have time for a blast from the past, especially when it would mean talking about wounds—both old and new ones.

She quickly went through the rest of the list. There was a call from her good friend and occasional boyfriend, Lieutenant Colonel Theo Shaw, but it could wait because Theo was no doubt just checking on her. Too bad that she needed to be checked on.

And Theo knew that firsthand.

Jordan knew it, as well, but he'd have to wait. She didn't delete his voice mail, though, the way she had Dylan's, and she kept scrolling. Crap. There were seven calls from her cousin, Adele, and two from an unknown number.

Obviously, something had gone wrong.

But then, there was often something wrong when it came to Adele. She was Jordan's first cousin, but they'd been raised together after Jordan's aunt died from breast cancer when Adele was just a baby.

Since Jordan was six years older, she'd become the big sister. The kind of big sister that Adele thought should bail her out, *repeatedly*, when she got into tight spots. Which happened way too often. Adele considered herself an activist, always chasing some cause or another, but that chasing had often gotten her into trouble with the law.

"Welcome home, Major," an elderly man said as he walked past Jordan.

It wasn't unusual for strangers to greet her when she was in uniform. They often would thank her for her service, but even with the shady-bunny clothes, this man had obviously recognized her. That meant he'd likely seen the news stories about her. About the helicopter crash and her being taken captive.

Jordan still wasn't able to say POW, but she suspected the news outlets here in the US had plastered those initials in their headlines. Ditto for her rescue, too.

"You're a hero," the man added.

No. She wasn't. Far from it. Her rescuers were the real heroes. And Theo was part of that hero team that'd gone in and extracted Jordan and six others from what could have become a deadly situation.

Yes, Theo knew firsthand what it was to be a hero. He also knew that what had happened five weeks ago was still eating away at her.

Despite that eating away, Jordan managed a smile and a polite nod to the man who'd welcomed her home. Then, she pulled the floppy hat even lower over her face so that no one else would recognize her.

Thankfully, there didn't appear to be any reporters, but then maybe enough time had passed since the helicopter crash and rescue. And during those five long weeks, she'd been tucked away at the hospital in Ramstein, Germany. When Jordan had finally gotten her medical clearance, she'd kept her travel plans a secret from everyone but Adele, Theo and the handful of people in her immediate chain of command.

The fewer "welcome home/you're a hero" greetings she got, the better.

Jordan kept weaving her way through the stream of passengers who were moving to and from the other gates. She'd gone nearly four months on this deployment without the smells of fast food and the thick crowds, a reminder that she hadn't missed either. But that could be the headache and nerves talking.

Once she'd dealt with whatever family emergency was going on, had downed some ibuprofen and spruced up the disguise a little, then she'd buy herself a burger and chocolate shake. There'd be plenty of time for that because she had a three-hour layover before her flight to San Antonio.

Moving as fast as she could with her carry-on luggage and laptop bag, she finally saw the sign for the women's restroom and threaded her way out of the crowd to duck inside. Jordan located an empty stall that was at the far end of the room, and the moment she was inside, she shut the door and took out her phone. She'd learned from experience that it was often best to deal with family matters in private.

Sometimes, yelling was involved.

And even though this bathroom stall wasn't exactly private, it would have to do.

While Adele might not have remembered that Jordan had been on an international flight and couldn't answer her phone, something had obviously happened.

Something urgent.

Of course, there was usually something urgent in Adele's life—most of it from her own not-fully-thought-out actions. But whatever was wrong, maybe it was something that Adele had already managed to fix in the past seven hours since she'd made the first call. If not, then Jordan would figure out a way to take care of it for her. That was the one good thing about her being assigned to San Antonio. She'd be nearby when Adele needed her.

That was also the bad thing about being assigned there.

Sometimes, like now, Jordan wondered if she was actually helping or if she'd just become an enabler to Adele's insane life choices.

Jordan hit the call-back button on Adele's number. No answer. So, she played the first of several voice mails, and she immediately heard Adele's frantic voice.

"Jordan, I'm in big trouble. I need to talk to you. Call me ASAP."

Even though Jordan had gotten many, many messages like that from Adele over the years, it still twisted her stomach. Still made her angry, as well. Adele was twenty-eight now, too old to be getting into trouble and calling her big *sister* for help. But then, Adele didn't have anyone else.

Neither did Jordan.

And that's why the knot twisted even harder.

The next two voice mails had the repeated gist of the first message so Jordan kept going through them, hoping for some explanation.

"Where are you?" Adele had shouted in the fourth one. "I need you. Corbin needs you. Why aren't you answering your bleeping phone?"

"Because I was on an international flight that I told you about—twice," Jordan grumbled. Behind her, the automatic toilet flushed. “And why are you using words like *bleeping*?” But she was obviously talking to herself.

Jordan didn’t know who Corbin was, but since it had been over a year since she’d seen Adele, it was possible that was the name of her current boyfriend. Also possible that this Corbin was the reason Adele was in some kind of trouble. Adele didn’t usually make good choices when it came to men or her social/political causes—a reminder that only twisted Jordan’s stomach even more.

Before she went to voice mail number five, Jordan tried to call Adele again. Still no answer, and she hoped this was a case of Adele’s crisis already being fixed. Maybe Adele and Corbin were in the kiss-and-make-up stage and had turned off their phones so as to not be disturbed. If so, then Jordan was definitely going to have that burger and shake. Maybe a margarita, too.

After Jordan left a message for Adele to call her back, she played the next voice mail. This one didn’t start with a shout but rather a sob. “Oh God. Jordan, I really screwed up. I’m so sorry. Please don’t hate me. *Please.*”

That hit Jordan far harder than the shout had. Adele apologized a lot, but an apology mixed with tears was never a good sign. With her hands a little unsteady now, Jordan quickly scrolled down to the next voice mail.

But this one wasn’t from Adele.

It was a number that wasn’t in Jordan’s contacts, and when she hit Play, the voice was unfamiliar, too. “Major Rivera, I’m Ruth Gonzales, a social worker from the Department of Human Services in San Antonio. Could you call me immediately?"

Jordan's stomach did more than merely tighten. It went to her knees. She doubted it was a coincidence that DHS and Adele had left her messages within the same hour. But what the heck was going on? There was only one more voice mail, and it had also come from the social worker's number.

Her hands were more than just a little unsteady when she hit Play, and her heart was beating hard enough that it might be difficult for her to hear. "Major Rivera," the message said. "This is Ruth Gonzales again from the DHS, and I just wanted you to know that it's all been worked out. Corbin is on his way to be with his father."

All right. That calmed Jordan's nerves and heartbeat some. Or at least it did until she thought about why a social worker would have contacted her to tell her that Adele's boyfriend was with his father.

A social worker wouldn't have done that.

Mercy. Yeah, this was bad.

Jordan hit the button to call Ms. Gonzales to find out what the heck was going on, but she had to wait through five long rings before the woman finally answered.

"This is Major Jordan Rivera—"

"Oh yes," the woman interrupted. It was the same person on the two voice mails. "Didn't you get my message? It's all taken care of."

"Yes, I got your message, but I don't understand. Who's Corbin?"

Silence. And it lasted even longer than the telephone rings. "He's your cousin's two-and-a-half-year-old son."

The relief came just as the toilet flushed again. This time, though, the plastic seat cover decided to switch itself out, as well. The whirling-grinding sound was so loud that Jordan had to raise her voice to make sure the social worker heard her.

"There's been some mistake. Adele doesn't have a child."

"But she does." Ms. Gonzales sounded pretty adamant about that.

However, Jordan was equally adamant. "If Adele had had a baby, she would have told me."

Though the moment the words left her mouth, Jordan got another of those bad thoughts. *Maybe* Adele would have told her. Unless she'd thought it would upset Jordan.

Which it would have.

Adele had no business having a child when she could barely take care of herself.

"It was your cousin's name on the boy's birth certificate," Ms. Gonzales went on. "And she had his social security card. The child even called her Mama." The woman paused. "Major Rivera, I watch the news so I know who you are. I'm also aware of what you've been through."

Jordan heard something in the woman's voice that she'd been hearing way too much of lately—sympathy. Not just a little dose of it, either. It was the *poor, pitiful you* tone. Since she was a woman, everyone thought the worst. That she'd been sexually assaulted. She hadn't been. But during those two days she'd been held captive, Jordan had imagined in crystal clear detail all the bad things that could have happened to her.

She'd broken down and cried.

Some *hero* she turned out to be.

"Major Rivera," the social worker said, getting Jordan's attention. "Adele explained that you've been out of the country for months and that you were coming here on leave in between assignments, but do you have any idea what's going on?"

Apparently not. "Why don't you fill me in?" Jordan suggested.

It sounded as if Ms. Gonzales dragged in a deep breath. "Well, before your cousin was arrested, she brought her son to me, hoping that he wouldn't be put in foster care while she was in jail. She said she didn't have time to take him anywhere else because the cops followed her here."

There was only one word that Jordan managed to hear in that explanation. "Arrested?" she howled. "For what?"

"Uh, I'm not at liberty to discuss that, but maybe you can talk to Dylan Granger about it? If you're comfortable talking to him, that is. Your cousin said something about things being strained between you two. Because he's your ex-husband."

Even though the toilet was flushing nonstop as if it were possessed by a demon, Jordan had no choice but to sit down on it. The automatic plastic cover seat slithered like a snake beneath her butt.

"Dylan Granger?" Jordan managed to repeat.

"That's right." Ms. Gonzales sounded downright perky that Jordan had managed to make the connection. "Your cousin gave him temporary custody of Corbin because Dylan Granger is the boy's father."

DYLAN NOW KNEW firsthand what it was like to be a Ping-Pong ball. He was volleying stunned glances between the paperwork the social worker had handed him and the little boy who was standing just a few feet away from him.

He was a cute kid. Dark hair and big blue eyes. And he was eyeing Dylan with as much concern as Dylan was eyeing him.

According to the paperwork, the boy's name was Corbin Dylan Rivera, and his mom was none other than his ex-wife's cousin, Adele. Dylan hadn't had Adele's number, and that's why he'd gotten Karlee to locate Jordan's, but his ex-wife hadn't answered when he'd tried to call her.

Of course she hadn't.

She was Adele's gatekeeper, and if Jordan knew there was any possibility that he'd fathered a child with Adele, then his ex might be on her way to issue some of the same kinds of threats as Judge Walter Ray had the night before. And Jordan just might have the right to carry out those threats, too.

Because this wasn't just unforgivable. It was also a really shitty thing to do. It didn't matter that Jordan and he were divorced. Adele was Jordan's family, and this was like dicking around with someone she thought of as a kid sister.

"Are you okay?" Karlee asked him.

Dylan didn't even try to lie. "No."

Shortly after he'd gotten hit with the *he's-your-kid*

bombshell, the bones in Dylan's feet and hands had vanished. That's why he'd sunk down onto the porch steps. That was also about the same time that Karlee had come outside. Why, he didn't know exactly, but it was possible that she'd heard the police car. Or his stunned groans. Once she'd alerted his brother that something was wrong, Lucian had come out, too. So had the two housekeepers and Booger.

Lucian was now reading through the papers—a good thing because Dylan was worried he might no longer be capable of seeing words much less understanding them. Karlee was next to Dylan, her hand making slow, circular motions on his back. She was also doing some volleying glances of her own. No doubt trying to figure out if the kid looked like him.

Booger was gnawing through the heel on Dylan's right boot.

Dylan wasn't anywhere near that stage yet of picking through the boy's features. He was still trying to wrap his mind around the basics of me, father/you, son. Still trying to rein in his emotions, as well.

Still trying to stop all those wussy groans that he was making.

It was time to man up and get some answers as to what was going on. Or read something. Or stand up. He could groan later, in private.

"How old is he?" Dylan pressed, but it was a question that caused both the cop and the social worker to huff. That was probably because he'd already asked them that or had already been told. At the moment, his mind felt a little like a sieve.

"Corbin's two and a half," the social worker answered. She'd told Dylan her name, Susan something-or-other. So had the cop, Officer something-or-other. But that information wasn't sticking in his head, either. "And you need to sign for him, remember?" she reminded him.

Yeah, the social worker had made the signing thing pretty clear, but Dylan wasn't sure he could hold the pen she kept thrusting at him much less sign his name. Hell, he still had trouble standing when he finally managed to get to his feet.

"Here are Corbin's meds." Susan handed Dylan a bag. "He has asthma, and the directions are on the inhaler. It's important that he not miss a dose because it could be dangerous."

Shit. That sent Dylan's heart into another tailspin. Not only did he have a kid, but he had one with a medical problem. One that could be *dangerous*.

Lucian didn't seem to hear any of that. He huffed when he handed the papers back to Dylan, but he aimed his attention at the social worker. "Why was Adele arrested?"

Susan looked at Officer something-or-other, and both ended up shaking their heads. "Look, I don't know the charges against her," the cop explained. "I'm only trying to do my job. Just have your brother sign the papers so I can be on my way and get to my kid's ballet recital."

"Dylan's not signing anything until our lawyer gets here," Lucian snapped. "And until I'm convinced this child is actually his. What proof do you have other than Adele's claim?"

It was a good question, and everyone seemed to

think Dylan had the answer. The cop, social worker, Karlee and even Booger looked at him. No doubt waiting to hear him say the magic word.

Yes. Or no.

But at best Dylan could only offer a *maybe*.

He didn't remember ever having sex with Adele. Even if she hadn't been Jordan's cousin, she was so not his type. He didn't have a thing for women with *trouble* written on them—literally. Jordan had told him that when Adele had been just fifteen, she'd convinced some tattoo guy to ink *TROUBLE* across her chest. There was no way Dylan would have willingly gotten involved with her.

That said, just this very morning, he'd woken up from a hangover with a naked woman in his bedroom. The last time he'd had a memoryless hangover like that was more than three years ago.

Right around the time Corbin *Dylan* Rivera could have been conceived. Why would Adele have named the boy after him if he wasn't Corbin's father?

"There's no other proof—" Susan said at the same time Corbin interrupted her and said, "What de doggy's name?"

The sound of his voice seemed to freeze everybody for a couple of seconds. For Dylan, it was because that little voice stirred something inside him. It was a reminder that this was a living, breathing, speaking child and not just some signature required on a paper.

"Booger," Dylan told him.

The right side of Corbin's mouth lifted in a smile, and the Yorkie must have taken that as a "Come here, boy" because the dog quit chewing on Dylan's boot and trotted toward the child. What was even more surprising was that he didn't immediately start chewing on any part of Corbin or his clothing. Booger just sat there, calmly looking up at Corbin.

The boy bent down and ran his hand over the dog's head, a soothing gesture, much like what Karlee was doing to Dylan. The hand running soon turned to a full pat before Corbin sat down on the ground with the dog. Booger jumped straight into his lap and started licking his face.

Corbin laughed.

That stirred yet something else in Dylan. He didn't know much about kids, but Corbin wasn't asking about his mom. Nor was he asking who these strangers were who were staring at him. He must have heard the social worker say that Dylan was his father, but he hadn't brought that up, either. Maybe it was simply because he was too young to express himself that way, but Dylan thought of another possibility.

A bad one.

Maybe Corbin's life with Adele had been filled with stuff just like this. Maybe he'd been shuffled around until Adele had no other place to shuffle him.

And that felt like a kick in the teeth to Dylan.

It had been bad enough that he might have a son that he didn't know about, but it was a whole new level of hell to think this child might have been neglected or mistreated.

Dylan snatched the papers from Lucian and glanced through them. Now that he was seeing things a little clearer, he noticed what was in the document. It wasn't an acknowledgment of paternity but rather a temporary custody agreement that would expire in just thirty days. One that Adele had already signed.

"Don't do that," Lucian warned him when he took the pen from the social worker. "Wait until the lawyer gets here. Wait until we can do a paternity test."

But Dylan ignored him and signed it. The moment the woman had the papers, Dylan held out his hand to Corbin. "Are you hungry?"

Corbin nodded so fast that it tugged away at Dylan again. It had no such effect on Lucian, though. He was trying to get the signed paper back from Susan, but Dylan ignored that, too, and he led Corbin onto the porch.

The housekeepers parted like the Red Sea to let them through the front door, but the moment Dylan was in the foyer, he spotted a problem.

The naked woman. Misty Turley.

Thankfully, she was dressed now. For the most part anyway. One of the heels was broken so she was hobbling down the steps, and the right strap on her barely there dress had slipped off her shoulders, pulling down the dress so that her nipple was practically showing.

She opened her mouth, but then her attention fell on Corbin. "Oh," Misty said. "Sorry." She fixed the dress, swiping at it. "Is this one of your cousins?"

Dylan looked at Corbin. Corbin looked at him. And Dylan just shook his head. No way would any of this stay a secret for long. The housekeepers had already disappeared, which meant they were likely off somewhere phoning and texting every person they knew. It was possible it'd be on the news before Corbin and he made it to the kitchen.

"He's my son," Dylan answered, and he was more than a little surprised at how easily those words rolled off his tongue.

Misty's eyes widened, and her face flushed. "Oh," she repeated. "I'm so sorry." She repeated that again, too, and with her forehead bunching up with every step, she went to him, the sound of her broken shoe slapping on the marble floor of the foyer. "I didn't know."

Welcome to the club.

Misty looked around as if trying to figure this all out. Dylan suspected that he had the same kind of look in his own eyes.

"I had the limo you hired drop me off here last night," Misty whispered. "It was all because of that bingo card. I got the one that said *surprise s-e-x with Dylan Granger*. But I fell asleep while I waited for you to come home."

Dylan really didn't want to get into this right now, but he had to ask. "How'd you know where my bedroom was?"

"My sister, Melanie, mentioned it in conversation. But don't worry," Misty quickly added, "I'll put a stop to that stupid game. Little pitchers have big ears, and you wouldn't want your son hearing about it."

Dylan couldn't agree more. The game had been an embarrassment right from the start, but nothing he'd said in protest had stopped it. Who knew that instant fatherhood would do the trick?

"You need a ride home?" Dylan asked when Misty started for the door.

Misty shook her head. "I'll ask one of your hands. You've got more important things to do." She mumbled another apology and headed out, past Lucian and Karlee who were still talking to Susan and the cop.

Yeah, he did have plenty to do, and Dylan started with looking in the bag. There was indeed an inhaler, and just as the social worker had said, the directions were on it. He'd need to make sure Corbin took it in the morning.

"Morning," Dylan mumbled. It hit him then that for Corbin to be there in the morning, he would also be spending the night.

Thirty of them.

There went Dylan's heart racing again.

"I gotta pee-pee," Corbin said.

The kid might as well have announced he needed a rare form of uranium to save the world. Like just about everything else that'd happened this morning, Dylan didn't know how to handle it. Was Corbin wearing a diaper? If so, Dylan was positive he didn't know how to deal with that, but maybe Susan or the cop did.

He went to the powder room that was just off the foyer, and Dylan threw open the door. "Wait here," he told Corbin, and he hurried back to the porch to get help from the social worker. Since she was still in an argument with Lucian, Dylan took hold of Karlee instead.

"Corbin has to go pee-pee," Dylan said, and he wished he hadn't repeated the boy's words.

Apparently, being superefficient didn't just apply to Karlee's business skill set because without hesitating, she nodded and went to the powder room as if this, too, was part of her job description. But by the time they got there Corbin already had his elastic-waist jeans down to his knees. His superhero underpants, too, and he was peeing. The stream wasn't going in the toilet because he wasn't tall enough, but it was landing in the general vicinity of where it was supposed to go.

"Flush," Corbin said. Or rather he said an approximation of that as he flushed. "Pull up." Another approximation that he said, though Dylan did have to help a little when his jeans got caught on his butt cheek. "Osh hands."

Dylan helped with that, too, by lifting him up to the sink, but Corbin managed the soap and water all on his own. He dried his hands on the sides of his jeans. There was a towel by the sink, but the jeans worked, too.

Dylan glanced out the front door. It was still wide-open, and he could see that the cop and Susan were now gone. Lucian was there, though, pacing and talking to someone on the phone. Their lawyer, probably. Lucian wouldn't give up on finding a way to undo this.

"Lunch now?" Corbin asked. Or rather, "'unch now." He tugged at Dylan's hand.

Dylan's next moment of panic wasn't as strong as the pee-pee reaction. Food, he could handle. Or at least semihandle.

"Sure. This way," Dylan said, and he was about to lead the boy to the kitchen, but Lucian came toward them.

"Have you lost your mind?" Lucian growled. "Why the hell—"

"Uh, I'll see what Corbin and I can find to eat," Karlee interrupted. Probably so that the boy wouldn't have to hear this, she whisked Corbin away with Booger scampering after them.

"Why in the blazing hell did you sign that paper?" Lucian demanded.

"Because it was the right thing to do. Even if he's not mine, he needs a place to stay until all of this is sorted out. And besides, it's only for thirty days."

Lucian gave him a look that could have melted a glacier at the peak of the Ice Age. "The temporary custody arrangement is for thirty days, and then there'll be a hearing."

Dylan shrugged. "By then Adele should be out of jail, and we'll get this all worked out."

"No." And because Lucian didn't immediately add anything to that, Dylan didn't have a clue which of those two things got the no-vote. "Adele won't be getting out in thirty days," Lucian snapped. "With her criminal record combined with the current charges, she'll be lucky if she gets out in five years."

Shit on a stick. There came another of those funny feelings. A sick one in the pit of his stomach.

"And as we speak," Lucian went on, "Adele's lawyer isn't working on getting her released from jail. Instead, he's filing the paperwork to give Corbin to you *permanently*."

CHAPTER THREE

"DO YOU REMEMBER when you got that tat in Singapore?" Theo asked her.

With a question like that, Jordan knew where this phone conversation was heading. It was going to be a mini life lesson. One that she wouldn't want to hear but Theo would tell her about anyway.

The tat had indeed been a huge mistake. It'd not only gotten infected and ruined the rest of their vacation, but the inker had also botched it big-time. The Chinese symbol was supposed to be for "military" but instead looked like a stick figure with an enormous engorged penis. Worse, the penis pointed in the direction of her butt, making it look like a sordid sexual invitation to anyone who got a glimpse of it.

"Well, I think this is an even worse mistake than the tat," Theo concluded. "It's not a good idea for you to make this trip."

And therein was the mini life lesson Jordan had been expecting while she drove from the San Antonio Airport to Wrangler's Creek. Theo was right, though. It wasn't a good idea. But it wasn't as if she had options. No. Dylan and Adele had seen to that.

"I can be there in Wrangler's Ridge in a day or two. I'm sure I can get leave, and I can help you deal with this situation," Theo added. He'd already made that particular offer twice. It had preceded the tat reminder.

"Wrangler's *Creek*," she automatically corrected. "And really, there's no reason for you to fly all this way." Especially since Theo was stationed in Germany. Also, he'd eaten up a lot of his leave to be with her during her so-called recovery.

"Yes, there's a reason for me to be there. A damn good one. *You*," he argued. "You don't know what you'll be facing there. Adele can be so…unpredictable."

Theo knew that firsthand, as well. He'd met Adele a few years back when they'd all ended up in San Antonio while Jordan was on leave. Adele had gotten mixed up with a group protesting a cause that Jordan couldn't even recall. Things had gotten out of hand, rocks had been thrown, windows of an office building had been damaged. The only reason her cousin hadn't been arrested then was because Theo had stepped in to talk the cops out of hauling her off to jail.

Theo had this whole rescue/hero thing down pat.

"Do the people there in Wrangler's Creek even know you're coming?" Theo asked a moment later.

Once she'd arrived at the San Antonio Airport, Jordan had texted Dylan to inform him that she was on the way, but she hadn't checked her messages since then. She didn't want to give him the chance to tell her not to come.

"It'll all be fine," Jordan assured her, though at best that was wishful thinking. Or possibly a whopping big lie.

Theo must have picked up on her doubt because he

made a sound that he wasn't quite buying it, either. "I hate that you have to go through this alone."

Jordan knew Theo had her best interest at heart, but there was nothing that would stop her from making the drive so she could see Adele's son and confront Dylan. She certainly wasn't going to wait a day or two, either. She had waited long enough with the layover in Atlanta and the flight itself to San Antonio. And she'd seethed every minute of the delay. First for Adele not telling her that she'd had a child and second for Dylan screwing around with someone in her own family.

The man had no boundaries.

Of course, Jordan could say the same thing about Adele, but Dylan was six years older than Adele. He should have known better and kept his jeans zipped when she was around. Of course, from the bits and pieces she'd heard over the years, Dylan frequently unzipped.

But Dylan and Adele's son wasn't the only concern. There was the issue of Adele's arrest.

Jordan had yet to find out the charges because she hadn't wanted to call Dylan to ask him the specifics. A conversation like that was best face-to-face, but whatever Adele had done, Jordan needed to start working on getting her out of jail. That meant hiring a lawyer if she didn't already have one.

"Are you still there?" Theo asked.

That's when Jordan realized she hadn't responded to the last thing that Theo had said. She was too busy bashing Dylan and Adele in her head.

"Yes, I'm here," Jordan answered. "I just have a lot on my mind. And I'm trying to focus on the traffic."

That last part for sure was a big fat whopper. Because there was no traffic to speak of. However, she wanted to get this call finished so she could gear up for the battle ahead.

"I won't keep you on the line then because I don't want you to get in an accident," Theo said, and he paused again. "Look, I know the timing for this is all wrong, but have you given any more thought to what we talked about last week?"

Obviously, he was keeping her on the line despite his worry about an accident. But yes, she had thought about it, along with the swarm of information and memories. The swarm moved so fast sometimes that it was hard to catch onto only one piece. Well, except for the bad stuff. The bad memories had a way of lingering longer than the rest.

"You know how I feel about you," Theo went on, "and after what happened, it's made me realize that life's too short not to hold on to the things we have. God, Jordan, I could have lost you."

By *things*, he meant love. Theo loved her. Jordan had no doubts about that. He'd risked his life to rescue her, and he would do it again if necessary. Since her rescue, he'd made it clear that he wanted marriage. Jordan wanted that, too.

But she didn't love him.

"I'm still thinking about it," she settled for saying. She hated blowing him off like that. He deserved better. But right now, her emotional energy was spent. Any energy she could muster would be to work out this mess with Adele and Dylan.

Now it was Theo who hesitated. “Just promise me that while you’re there, you’ll keep taking your meds.”

Yes, *that*. Jordan was sorry she’d told Theo that the doctors at the base in Ramstein had prescribed her anxiety meds. And she’d taken them, too, while she was there for medical evaluation and debriefing. She’d also taken some on the flight because being in closed-in places made her feel on the verge of a panic attack.

But Jordan wasn’t sure about continuing the drugs. They made her feel out of it, as if she weren’t quite herself. No need to have pills do that since she already felt that way.

“I brought my meds with me,” she said, and hoped that Theo wouldn’t say anything more about it.

He did.

“I just don’t want the flashbacks to hit out of the blue and pull you down,” he went on. “The meds will help you stay ahead of things.”

In this case, *things* meant the fear that kept coming back. It washed over her in waves, and yes, it did hit out of the blue.

Often.

And sometimes, it was so bad that she thought the panic might finally win and that she would have a full-blown attack. However, she doubted any dose of meds was going to make her forget that she’d been at the mercy of men, soldiers, who at any moment could have killed her and the rest of the crew.

“I need to go,” Jordan told him. “I’m in Wrangler’s Creek, and I’ll be at the Granger ranch soon. I’ll call you when I know more about Adele and Corbin.”

Just saying the boy’s name brought on a new kind

of wave. A jumble of emotions. More anger at Adele for keeping him a secret. Concern for what would happen to him now that Adele was in jail. But there was also love. Despite the circumstances, Corbin was her flesh and blood, and even though she'd yet to lay eyes on him, she loved the little boy.

Jordan ended the call with Theo and took the turn down Main Street. A definite blast from the past. She'd been raised in Wrangler's Creek, but it'd never especially felt like a place she wanted to be. The only times she'd been at peace here had been while she was with Dylan.

And that hadn't lasted, either.

The restlessness had come. The feeling of inadequacy that most people from the other side of the tracks probably felt. She hadn't been grounded here like Dylan. She still wasn't.

After their marriage had ended, she'd had no trouble going. She had moved, leaving Adele and her mother behind. By then, her dad had been long gone. After Adele had finished high school, she'd also left—that'd been only a couple of months before Jordan's mom had been killed in a car accident. After she'd died, there had been no reason for Jordan to come back.

Not until now.

Her chest tightened when she reached the gate to the Heavenly Acres, Dylan's family's ranch. The name was one of those ironies of life because so few heavenly things had actually happened there. Dylan's family wasn't exactly the heaven-inducing sort. For that matter, neither was Dylan unless it was a veiled reference to his sexual abilities. Those *abilities* were one of the big reasons he'd convinced her to marry him. They had temporarily glossed over problems that couldn't have stayed glossed over for long.

The gate was open, no doubt left that way for her since it was normally closed, but that didn't mean the Grangers were welcoming her. Not a chance. Jordan figured she'd managed to rile every single one of them when she'd ended things with Dylan. She would no doubt rile them further today when she confronted Dylan.

Other than a new house by the creek, the ranch looked pretty much as it had way back when. There were acres of pastures and pristine white fences. Plenty of livestock, too. All the things to let her know that the Grangers were still as wealthy as they always had been.

The tightness in her chest went up a huge notch when she pulled into the driveway of the massive house—yet another sign of wealth.

Despite having been married to Dylan, Jordan had never spent a single night in the place. Dylan and she had lived in the little guesthouse at the back of the property. It hadn't been nearly as grand as the family "estate," but it had given them the privacy that they'd thought would somehow help them succeed at something that had been doomed right from the very start.

Jordan pushed that all aside now. Pushed away her tat/mistake conversation with Theo, too, as she pulled to a stop in the driveway. She glanced in the mirror to see if she looked as nervous and worried as she felt.

She did.

If she'd been in a police lineup, she would have been an immediate suspect for multiple felonies because the nerves were showing all over her face. Her eyes were even a little twitchy. She'd ditched the perverted Easter bunny hoodie and hat. Now she did the same to the sunglasses, and she felt instantly naked.

Exposed.

Which really wasn't a good thing to feel around Dylan. He had a way of undressing her with that bedroom smile. Or at least once it'd been bedroom-y. As upset as she was about all of this, it was highly likely she was immune to Dylan and anything he dished out.

When she stepped out of her rental car, she got another reminder. Of the scalding Texas heat. It was May, not yet summer, but even though the sun was about to set, the temps were still in the midnineties. Of course, it'd been hot on the deployment, but there'd been no thick humidity or pollen.

Before Jordan had even made it a step, the front door opened, and she tried to steel herself up to see Dylan. But what she saw was actually a friendly face.

Her old high school pal, Karlee O'Malley.

With a big smile and her arms outstretched, Karlee ran to her and pulled Jordan into a hug. "It's so good to see you. Wish it were under better circumstances," she added in a whisper.

Yes, Jordan wished that as well, but the truth was she wouldn't be here at the Granger ranch if it hadn't been for those circumstances.

Karlee eased back from the hug, sliding her hand around Jordan's waist to get her moving toward the house. "I hope we'll have time to catch up…after you've chatted with Dylan and met Corbin, that is." She paused a heartbeat. "How are you?"

Jordan knew that question encompassed more than just Adele's bombshell. Karlee had no doubt heard about the other thing. "I'm okay."

Karlee lifted her eyebrow.

"Not okay with Dylan," Jordan corrected. "I guess he doesn't have the same man-rules as most guys about having sex with someone in your ex's family."

Karlee didn't argue with that or jump into some Dylan bashing. She just led Jordan into the house. Still no sign of Dylan, but Lucian was there, talking to someone on the phone. However, when he spotted Jordan, he stopped and issued a terse "I'll have to call you back" before he ended the call and stared at her.

"Jordan," Lucian greeted. It wasn't anywhere on the friendly scale, but unless Lucian had changed a lot, it was downright warm and fuzzy for him. "It's been a while." Again, warm and fuzzy.

And that made Jordan silently curse.

He was treating her with kid gloves, and while she didn't especially want a confrontation with the head of the Granger empire, she didn't want him to look at her in that "poor, pitiful you" kind of way.

"Where are Dylan and Corbin?" she asked, and she didn't bother to make her tone polite. Even with her bark, it didn't cause Lucian's "soft" expression to change.

Lucian hiked his thumb toward the back of the house. "They're in the sunroom. This way." Apparently, he thought her captivity had robbed her of memories about the layout of the house because he started ahead of her, showing her the way.

"Are things about to get ugly?" Karlee asked, following them. "Because if they are, I can take Corbin outside to play."

It was a kind offer, and Jordan hoped she didn't have to take Karlee up on it. Still, Jordan wasn't sure if she'd be able to keep her temper in check when she confronted Dylan. She didn't want to yell in front of Corbin because it might frighten the little boy. It turned out, though, that her first response wasn't to rant and rave. It was to try to hang on to her breath.

Because the air vanished when she saw Dylan.

Crap. She wasn't immune to him after all.

He was indeed in the sunroom, and when Jordan stepped in, he looked at her, their eyes automatically connecting. For just a split second, the past fourteen years vanished. So did much of her dignity and common sense, and Jordan felt like a teenager again.

One who was kicked in the butt by the old lust.

And she silently cursed it. *Really?* After what he'd done, her body still wanted him?

Apparently so.

That probably had a lot to do with the fact that Dylan was still a lust-inducing cowboy with his rumpled dark brown hair and lazy smile. A smile he gave her until he remembered there wasn't anything to smile about. Or at least there wasn't until the little boy peeked out from behind Dylan's leg.

Mercy, that face. Pure cuteness framed by curly hair. She had already known that she loved this child, but she had way underestimated the intensity of that love. All the anger inside her just vanished.

Corbin had a toy horse clutched in each hand, and judging from the other toys scattered around the sunroom, Dylan had managed to bring in plenty of stuff to keep a toddler entertained.

"It's okay," Dylan said to the boy. It was a tone that Jordan had thought she would never hear him use.

Because he sounded like a father.

That was a pretty fast transition, considering that Dylan had only known about Corbin for less than eight hours. And Corbin seemed to have adjusted, as well. At least he wasn't crying. Unlike her. Jordan felt the tears in her eyes and quickly blinked them back.

Dylan scooped up Corbin and walked toward her, his attention not on her, thank goodness. Jordan didn't want him to see the hint of those tears. Lucian was already looking at her as if she were a damaged box of goods, and Jordan didn't want to see that in Dylan's eyes, too.

"How is he?" Jordan managed to ask after she cleared her throat.

"He's doing great," Dylan answered, smiled, and Corbin gave him a smile right back.

On the surface, that was a good thing, Jordan reminded herself, but there were plenty of things not so good about this situation. "Any health problems?" She groaned because she sounded like a nurse and not the concerned relative that she was.

"Corbin has asthma," Dylan explained. "But we have his meds."

Asthma. She tried not to react to that, but it was hard. "Adele had that when she was a kid." And she'd had a couple of attacks that were so bad that she'd landed in the hospital. Hopefully Corbin wouldn't have to go through that.

Even though Dylan and she needed to talk, Jordan went closer, touching Corbin's arm with just her fingertip. "Who dat?" he asked Dylan.

"Jordan," she answered. And she wished she could put the aunt label in front of that. It sounded better than mere *cousin*, and it certainly didn't stand up to the label that Dylan had.

Daddy.

But that didn't erase the history that Jordan had with Adele. They'd been together for years, but she was betting Adele's relationship with Dylan hadn't lasted long at all. Probably a single night.

"Should I take Corbin so you two can talk?" Karlee offered.

Neither Jordan nor Dylan jumped to say yes, but Jordan finally had to nod. Dylan nodded, too, but he hesitated even longer than she did.

"Maybe you can go ahead and give him some dinner?" Dylan asked Karlee.

"Ice tream?" Corbin said, his whole face lighting up.

"For dessert," Dylan assured him, jostling his hand through Corbin's hair. "But you got to eat the real food first. Sorry."

Corbin gave a little shrug that was almost identical to the one that Dylan gave him. It was a cute moment. One that made Jordan feel as if she'd just got caught in a downpour while wearing her Sunday best. She didn't want it to pop into her head, but the thought came anyway. Fifteen years ago, this was the life she'd planned.

Dylan and a baby.

Now, here she was, thirty-four years old, and she didn't have either of those things. Not that she wanted

Dylan. Not as a husband and father anyway. She couldn't stop the involuntary lust reaction, but her head knew that she was a lot better off without him.

Jordan had to keep repeating that to herself.

Corbin gave them a wave as Karlee ushered him out of the room, and Jordan waited until he was out of earshot before she snapped toward Dylan. "What happened to Adele?" she demanded. "And why are you Corbin's father?"

Jordan really wished she'd figured out a better way to phrase that second question, and she hoped Dylan didn't give her a smart-mouthed lesson about the birds and bees. But no lesson. He looked, well, uncomfortable. That was a good start, but Jordan wanted a lot more than a squirming look from him.

"Adele's been charged with being in possession of stolen goods," Dylan explained. "*Lots* of stolen goods. Specifically, forty-eight cases of SpaghettiOs and another thirty crates of Ding Dongs."

Jordan was sure that she blinked. "Excuse me?"

"You heard me right," Dylan assured her, his expression flat now. "Adele arranged to receive stolen food. Apparently, she did it for a homeless shelter that'd lost its funding."

She stood there, stunned, for several moments. All right. Stolen goods—even those taken for a noble cause—would definitely lead to an arrest. But the charge didn't sound serious enough to force Adele to hand over custody of her son.

"Adele can get probation—" Jordan started, but Dylan interrupted.

"No. She won't. I haven't personally spoken with

Adele," Dylan went on, "but from what I've been able to find out from her lawyer, she's getting some kind of plea deal to give the cops the names of others involved in the theft ring."

"A *theft ring*?" Jordan howled. "She talked other people into helping her with this lunacy?"

"It looks that way. Some of them stole cases of flip-flops and raincoats." He paused. "I can't make sense of it, either. I mean, if you're going to steal stuff for a homeless shelter, why take these things?"

Jordan didn't have to think about it for long. "The food items are Adele's favorites. Along with tacos."

"Those were stolen, too," Dylan added. "The boxed makings for them anyway." He huffed. "And the flip-flops and raincoats?"

Jordan had to shake her head. Even she couldn't fit that into Adele's crazy logic. "So, we're talking a lot of goods worth...what...hundreds of dollars?"

"Thousands," he corrected. "Even with the plea deal, though, it'll be a longer than average jail sentence because this isn't her first offense."

Oh God. When this conversation had started, Jordan thought the worst she would hear was that Adele was a misguided activist who was going to end up with hours of community service—something Adele would have probably enjoyed doing. Apparently not, though.

Jordan located the nearest chair and sank down onto it.

"Are you okay?" Dylan asked at the same moment that Lucian said, "I'll get you some water."

Jordan waved Lucian off. Water wasn't going to help this. Heck, straight shots of liquor wouldn't, either.

"You didn't know about Adele's prior arrests?" Dylan threw out there, but he didn't wait for her to answer. "And yes, that's plural. Four years ago she was arrested for trying to break into a jail and then for assaulting a guard when she kicked him in the nuts."

Jordan had given more blank stares during this conversation than she had in years. "Adele tried to break *into* a jail? Why?"

Dylan shrugged. "One of her activist friends had been arrested, but Adele thought he'd been wrongfully accused. Anyway, she's still on probation for that and for some other things, and that's why she won't get parole for this latest stunt."

God, she'd been living under a massive rock when it came to Adele. Jordan had thought that because she hadn't heard from her cousin that all was well. Or rather, well-ish. Things were never truly right when it came to Adele. But she hadn't expected something this big. This wrong.

Dylan sat in the chair across from her though she didn't think it was because he was unsteady on his feet. Like her. No. But he was giving her the same kind of "you're broken" look that Lucian was.

Since Jordan didn't want to admit there was apparently so much about Adele that she was clueless about, she just moved on to the next question. "You didn't know Corbin was your son?"

Dylan immediately shook his head. "I haven't seen Adele in over three years."

You didn't need any math skills to work that out. He'd last seen her when Corbin was conceived. Which made Jordan wonder—why hadn't Adele told him? Heck, why hadn't Adele told *her*?

Lucian walked closer and stood behind his brother. "Dylan doesn't recall being with Adele."

Jordan knew where this was going. "You were drunk."

Heck, Adele likely had been, too. That didn't make things easier though for Jordan to swallow, but she was well aware that Dylan had trouble remembering things when he drank.

Because it had happened the night they'd eloped.

After an incredible night of newlywed sex, Dylan had woken up, not remembering that he'd married her. Things had gone downhill from there. Unfortunately, even "downhill" had involved more incredible sex.

"I would have thought you'd learned your lesson," Jordan mumbled.

"You'd think, especially since I've blacked out three times now," Dylan mumbled back. "But in Adele's case, it wasn't booze. I had a bad reaction to some prescription cold meds. I remember seeing Adele that night, but that's about it."

So, once with her and another time with Adele, but Jordan didn't want to know about the third.

"Because Dylan can't remember—that's why I want him and Corbin to take a DNA test," Lucian said.

Dylan huffed. The kind of huff that came when an argument happened that the person already thought had been settled. "I don't think Adele would lie about something like this."

Yep, they'd already argued, and as much as Jordan hated to admit it, she could see Lucian's side of this.

Plenty of Granger money was at stake, maybe millions, and all because of drunken sex. Or in this case, medicated sex.

Lucian looked at Jordan as if she might take his side. She wouldn't. That's because she was about to bring up her own argument, and judging from what she'd witnessed between Dylan and Corbin, Dylan wasn't going to like it.

She stood, dragging in a deep breath so she could start. But before she could get a word out, a little dog came trotting into the room. It had a piece of paper in its mouth. The dog went straight to Dylan and deposited it at his feet.

"Shit," Dylan said.

"Hell," Lucian said.

And both of them grabbed at it. The dog was quicker, though. As if this were a fine game the Yorkie was enjoying, he snapped up the paper and scurried to the other side of the room.

"Don't let him eat it," Dylan warned his brother. "He's been shitting elastic all day from those red panties. I don't want him shitting paper, too."

Since that seemed unhealthy for the dog, Jordan went to help. Dylan, Lucian and she cornered the critter by a pair of wicker chairs, but just as Dylan was reaching for him, the dog ran through Dylan's legs. That brought on more cursing, and they hurried after him.

"Booger!" Dylan snapped. "Drop that."

With a name like Booger, Jordan doubted this was Dylan's dog. No, this looked more like something his mother, Regina, would have.

Booger jetted around the room, somehow managing to keep hold of the tattered paper he was carrying. Jordan got lucky when he charged in her direction, and she managed to latch onto the paper. And that's when Jordan saw what it was.

The Dylan Granger Sex Bingo Game.

She got only a glimpse of one of the boxes—get a stomach licking from Dylan—before Dylan snatched it away from her. He didn't even look at it before he mumbled some profanity, crumbled it up and stuck it in his back pocket. Jordan hadn't needed proof that her ex had gotten on with his life, but that was it.

"Any winners?" she asked, but Jordan waved that off.

Of course there were winners. Dylan was a hot, rich, charming cowboy. The red panties that the dog had partially eaten had likely belonged to one of the players of the game. However, there was something that Dylan couldn't charm his way through.

Fatherhood.

Corbin needed stability. Someone who could help him manage his asthma in case Adele ended up in jail for a while. She figured after Dylan gave this some thought, that he'd actually be relieved by what she was about to say.

"I know that Adele signed over temporary custody to you." Jordan looked Dylan straight in the eyes. "But she only did it because she thought I wouldn't be in the picture. Well, I can be. And that's why I'm here. Because I should be the one to have custody of Corbin."

CHAPTER FOUR

HELL IN A turd-filled handbasket. Dylan's head was no longer throbbing so he didn't have any trouble hearing what Jordan had said.

I should be the one to have custody of Corbin.

No trouble feeling the kick-to-the-gut reaction that he had, either. Or the anger. Really bad, pissed-off anger.

That particular emotion wasn't exactly a new feeling when it came to Jordan. They'd had way too many arguments before they'd split, but "out of sight" had cooled down some of that old ire. However, it hadn't done squat for the way his eyeballs kept looking at her.

Specifically, at her mouth.

It had been Jordan's mouth that'd first attracted him, and it was apparently still a lust magnet. Thankfully, though, he could push the lure of that mouth aside since it'd been the very part of her body to utter those words that'd riled him.

"I'm Corbin's father," Dylan reminded her.

"Biologically," Jordan countered.

"Maybe," Lucian reminded both of them.

Both Jordan and Dylan shot him glares. Dylan's was meant to stop any future reminders like that from anyone, not just Lucian. Yeah, there were a lot of things in question, but Dylan was going to believe Adele on this. He also wouldn't just hand over his son to Jordan. Or anybody else for that matter.

"Is this about that bingo card?" Dylan asked her. "Because if it is, I didn't start that dumb game."

Jordan took a deep breath. "It's not just the game. It's your, well, lifestyle. Red panties and sex cards. That can't be good for Corbin."

It wasn't. But Dylan had planned on making some big changes in his life. Not that Jordan, Lucian or anybody else would believe it, but he would. He'd do whatever it took to make sure Corbin had a good life.

A good life that Jordan might not be able to give him.

"You're still in the Air Force?" he asked.

Dylan knew it wasn't just a simple question. There were other questions that went along with that, including the "right back in her face" reminder that deployments and overseas assignments might be good for a military officer but not necessarily for a toddler.

Jordan nodded. "I'm still in. For now. I'm being assigned to Lackland Air Force Base in San Antonio. But I've been…rethinking things."

He saw it then, the slight shift of her posture, and she glanced away. Not exactly any in-your-face gestures, but Dylan could see something simmering just beneath the surface. And he wanted to kick himself. She was rethinking things because she'd been held captive by those insurgents.

Now he was the one who had to glance away from her. Even though Jordan and he hadn't seen each other in years, she'd once been his wife. He still cared for her.

Or at least he had cared before she'd done that custody-challenge throwdown about a minute ago. Now he was riled, along with wishing that something that bad hadn't happened to her. But it had happened, and Dylan had to take it into account.

"Are you okay?" he asked her. And, yes, he probably should have figured out a different way to ask if she'd gone bat-crap crazy because of being held captive when she was on deployment.

Jordan's eyes narrowed a little. Her mouth tightened, too, a reminder that yes, that mouth still had a way of getting his attention. That's why Dylan looked away again.

"I'm fine." Her tone was snappish, but it was like a person gushing blood saying that it was just a flesh wound. No way could she be fine after something like that, especially since it'd only happened weeks ago. Some folks didn't get over trauma like that—ever.

"I can get out of the Air Force if I want," she added a moment later, and her voice was a lot more even-keeled now. "While I'm on leave, I'm considering my options."

Well, Dylan wanted her to consider those options elsewhere. But he immediately frowned at that thought. Feeling that way wasn't right. Jordan was Corbin's family, too, and the kid would need all the support that he could get.

"If you're at Lackland Air Force Base, does that mean you won't be deployed or have to go do temporary duty somewhere?" he pressed.

Jordan shook her head. Hesitantly shook it, though. "There's still a chance something like that would happen." Her tone was hesitant, too.

That was his winning argument, all wrapped in her own words. Well, it was a winner if she stayed on active duty and took that assignment.

"So, you're saying you'll get out of the military, move back here and sue Dylan for custody," Lucian clarified. His brother didn't say it as mean-spirited and grouchy as he could have. He did it more the way he would while negotiating a business deal that he wasn't especially sold on. However, Dylan knew how Lucian wanted this particular deal to go down.

With Jordan getting custody.

And preferably, having the DNA results to prove that Corbin wasn't even a Granger. That would tie everything up in a neat little package for Lucian.

Dylan didn't want either of those things, and the only reason Lucian did was he thought this would interfere with business as usual. And all because he thought Dylan was too much of a screwup to handle raising a kid. Of course, Jordan felt the same way. He could see that in her eyes.

"Don't look at me like that," Dylan grumbled at the exact moment that Jordan said, "Don't look at me like that."

Obviously, they quit giving each other the *looks* that'd caused their comments, but that's because they were both surprised now. And frowning. Even after all these years, they were on the same wavelength.

"I'm not broken," Jordan snapped. "I was doing my job when I was taken—a job I was trained well to do—and then I was rescued. End of story."

Since she'd gotten a little louder and a little crisper with each word of that explanation, Dylan doubted it was anywhere near the end. Nope. His sex bingo past didn't hold a candle to possible PTSD, though Dylan wasn't especially pleased that he'd won this particular contest.

Dylan was about to tell her how terrible he felt about this god-awful thing that'd happened to her, once he figured out how to say it, that is, but her phone buzzed before he had a chance to work that out.

Jordan yanked the cell from her jeans pocket, and when she saw the name on the screen, she glanced up at the ceiling as if asking for some divine intervention. Obviously, this wasn't a call she especially wanted to take. Probably because she was more interested in continuing her debate with Dylan, but she hit the answer button anyway.

"Theo," she greeted the caller.

Theo. She hadn't exactly said that with love and affection, but judging from the way the name just rolled off her tongue, it was a name she said often.

"I'm sorry, but I can't talk now," she added, dodging Dylan's gaze.

Yeah, definitely a rolling off the tongue kind of name. Which meant this guy was probably her boyfriend. Or maybe even her fiancé. She wasn't wearing an engagement ring, though. But then, the only jewelry she had on was a thin gold chain around her neck.

"No, we're working that out now. I'll call you later," Jordan told him. She hit the end call button, put her phone away and faced Dylan again. She looked a lot more steeled up than she had earlier so Theo must have worked some good mojo with whatever he'd said to her.

However, the "working out" didn't get to happen

because the doorbell rang. Dylan really didn't want to deal with anything else today, but apparently someone answered it because it wasn't long before Dylan heard the footsteps. And the voice that went with them.

"I need to see Dylan right now."

Great. More complications.

Maybe he should look to the ceiling for some divine assistance, too. Because that voice belonged to none other than Judge Walter Ray Turley.

Several moments later, the hulking man appeared in the doorway of the sunroom. It would have been impossible to miss him since the judge was built like a sumo wrestler, and his facial expressions were just as intimidating. Thankfully, he wore more clothes, though. Walter Ray didn't seem to make good use of his champagne budget. He was wearing jeans and a yellow plaid jacket that clashed with his dark red cowboy hat.

There was also that nose.

Walter Ray probably didn't know that most folks called him dick-nose, and it was a well-earned moniker. It was one of those noses that made you stare and wonder why the heck he hadn't run to a plastic surgeon.

Dylan's first reaction was to tell the judge to get lost. Lucian must have known that, too, because he shook his head. Definitely a silent warning. Without saying a word, Lucian lectured him about the fact that Walter Ray was a powerful man in these parts. A powerful man with multiple daughters, two of whom Dylan had seen naked. And one of the daughters had won the sex bingo game. For the sake of business, Dylan decided to hold his tongue.

For as long as he could.

But his fun meter was at zero right now, and the judge had better not do anything to send that meter into the minus setting.

Karlee was right behind the judge, and she was communicating without words, as well. Dylan recognized the silent apology she was giving him. "Corbin and I were waiting for the pizza I ordered," Karlee said.

In other words, she'd opened the door without realizing it was the judge. That was okay. If Karlee hadn't answered the door, it was very possible that one of the housekeepers would have. Plus, as riled looking as the judge was, he probably wouldn't have just left without seeing Dylan.

Karlee had Corbin by the hand, and the boy was munching on an apple slice. Despite the frustration over this visit and Jordan's demand, Dylan found himself smiling at Corbin.

And Walter Ray noticed, too.

"So, this is your son," Walter Ray grumbled as he slid glances between Dylan and the boy. Jordan got in on that glance sliding, too.

Karlee must have decided that all the glancing might lead to some things being said that she didn't want Corbin to overhear so she led the boy out of the sunroom and back toward the kitchen.

"Yes, he's mine," Dylan verified.

Dylan didn't have to guess how the judge had found out about Corbin. Misty had likely told him. He hoped Misty hadn't told him about stripping naked and sneaking into Dylan's room. If so, this conversation might go in an R-rated direction.

Walter Ray stared at him a long time as if waiting

for Dylan to launch into some kind of lengthy explanation. Maybe about Corbin. Maybe about what'd gone on at the party the night before. Maybe about Misty and her missing panties. Since Dylan knew a couple of those discussions could get him in hot water, he just stared back at the man and stalled to see where this would go.

The return stare didn't help ease Walter Ray's intensity, but he did shift the direction of it. He turned back to Jordan. "The boy is your son?" he asked her.

Even though it was a pretty straightforward question, Jordan hesitated. Maybe because she didn't think it was any of the judge's business. It wasn't. But the long pause might also be because she hadn't finished her conversation with Dylan and the judge was interrupting that.

"Corbin's mother is Adele," Dylan provided. "She gave me custody because of some personal issues she's having."

Of course, it wouldn't take the judge long to figure out that *personal issues* was code for Adele getting arrested. It also didn't take long for Jordan's eyes to narrow again, no doubt because Dylan had spelled out that part about him having custody.

"So, Jordan and you aren't back together," Walter Ray concluded. His expression lightened up a little so he must have taken it as good news. Sort of. "FYI," he added to Dylan, "it's not a good idea for a man to bed his ex-wife's kin."

"Hmmp," Jordan said, and it was a sound of agreement.

Dylan added his own grunt to agree to that. Maybe

though, the judge had meant that advice for Jordan and Adele and not his own two daughters. Though Dylan had only bedded one of the Turley sisters, Melanie, if Walter Ray found out about Misty staying the night—naked, no less—then things might take an even-uglier turn than they already had.

"I got your text with your vow of celibacy," Walter Ray threw out there. Dylan groaned, but the judge just kept on yapping. "It seemed like a good start, but I'm not thinking that so much right now."

Neither was Dylan. There was nothing *good* about a drunken vow of celibacy.

Walter Ray turned to Jordan. "Maybe you should step out of the room so Dylan and me can talk. Man-to-man. I know you've been through a bunch of bad stuff, and I don't want you to hear anything that'll upset you."

Jordan's *hmmp* turned to a groan. She probably didn't like that bad stuff/man-to-man remark, and she likely didn't want to leave, either. After all, in her mind she thought they still had to discuss Corbin's custody, but as far as Dylan was concerned, there was nothing to discuss. It was a done deal.

"Our conversation isn't over," she warned Dylan, but at least she headed out of the room.

Dylan heard the front door again, but he seriously doubted that Jordan had just left. No. This was probably the pizza delivery that Karlee and Corbin had been waiting for.

"Did you get the scotch Dylan sent you?" Lucian asked the judge as soon as Jordan was gone.

"Sure did. I'm guessing that's your way of apologizing?" Walter Ray added, not to Lucian but to Dylan.

Since Dylan didn't know the scotch had been sent, probably either by Karlee or Lucian, Dylan just nodded.

"Well, I wasn't gonna accept your apology." Walter Ray gave his huge belt buckle an adjustment. "But Melanie said you've been under a lot of stress. She's the one who talked me into coming here and patching things up between us."

That would be good, but no doubt came with strings.

"I'm guessing you'll be calling Melanie soon to chat to her about the boy you had with Adele," the judge went on. It wasn't a question.

Dylan huffed. He didn't mind smoothing things over for the sake of business, but he wasn't a doormat. And he wasn't going to stand here and kowtow to this man.

"I'm not marrying your daughter," Dylan spelled out to Walter Ray.

Lucian shot him a glare that could have withered a cactus on the spot. It was similar to the glare he'd given Dylan the night before when he'd gotten into it with the judge at the party. Dylan remembered all of that now, but apparently, he hadn't gotten into it deep enough since it still hadn't sunk into Walter Ray's head.

"I'm not going to be roped into marrying someone simply because she chose to go to bed with me," Dylan explained. "Hell, if I did that, I'd be married to…too many women."

Best not to even attempt a number on that.

Lucian stepped forward, obviously ready to intervene, but Dylan held up his hand to silence him so he could finish having this out with Walter Ray. "I made it clear to Melanie that being with her wasn't a commitment. She knows that, and now I'm making sure you know it, too."

Walter Ray's glare topped Lucian's, something that Dylan hadn't thought possible. "You toyed with my girl's feelings. She's in love with you."

Dylan had indeed done some toying, but he doubted she was in love with him. Melanie was more sensible than her dad and had likely mentioned the *l*-word when Walter Ray had discovered the bingo card. Still, he needed to have an air clearing and smoothing over with Melanie in case there was an outside chance that she had indeed been hurt.

But all of this was a "big can of whip-ass" revelation for Dylan.

He'd made that celibacy vow when he was drunk, but it was a stellar idea, and it could be the first step toward moving on to the next stage of his life. Too bad it'd come so soon after seeing Jordan. Or rather, *remembering* Jordan.

There was hardly a day that'd gone by over the past fourteen years that he hadn't thought about her, but he'd always been able to push those old flames aside. It was hard to do that now with her just a few rooms away. Maybe though, he could regain his footing and rein in his bedtime memories once she was on her way. Then, he could get on with his new path to celibacy without any temptations from the past.

Walter Ray leaned in closer, and the man violated a whole bunch of Dylan's personal space. "You don't want me on your bad side."

"No, I don't," Dylan assured him. "But I'm not marrying your daughter for the sake of keeping peace between us. I'm a father now, and I need to focus on my son."

Even though it was logic that Dylan thought a father could understand, that argument didn't seem to appease Walter Ray one little bit. The man looked at Lucian as if he expected him to scold Dylan. Thankfully, Lucian didn't do that. Not with words anyway, but Dylan suspected they'd have it out later. Because this could indeed affect business. Even if it did, though, Dylan wouldn't be Lucian's doormat, either.

"You better hope you don't need any favors from me," Walter Ray warned Dylan. He extended his glare to Lucian, too.

Lucian moved to Dylan's side. "And you'd better hope you don't need any favors from us." That was the tone that had earned Lucian the nickname of Lucifer.

The staring match started—a game of eyeball chicken—and it didn't surprise Dylan when Walter Ray was the first one to look away. Lucian's venom wasn't something that anybody wanted to dick around with because Lucian could be, well, a dick, and his bad side could be a whole lot worse than all the collective bad sides in town.

"My beef's not with you," Walter Ray grumbled to Lucian after he'd lost the eyeball-chicken match.

"If it's with my brother, then it's with me," Lucian assured him. "You can show yourself out."

Dylan didn't know who was more surprised—him or Walter Ray. His guess was Walter Ray, because the man's face turned red. He looked like an inflamed testicle, and it didn't go well with the dick-shaped nose.

Walter Ray stood there several more long moments,

volleying his glare, getting redder and sputtering out some ripe profanity until he finally turned and left. He made his size known with his clomping footsteps. And then he slammed the front door.

"You fuck this up, and I'll smother you in your sleep," Lucian snarled to Dylan as he walked out.

Ah, there was Lucifer again, who'd stepped up to dissolve the caring brother. And Dylan didn't get a chance to ask him what would cause that potential smothering. Hurting the family business or messing up things with Corbin. The first was a huge possibility now that they were on the outs with Walter Ray, but Dylan thought he could still do all right by Corbin.

Of course, that started with laying down some ground rules to Jordan. No custody for her, but he would be generous with visitation when she wasn't off doing her duty for the military. Once he had made that clear, then she could be on her way to work out those changes she'd talked about.

Changes she would be making with *Theo*, no doubt.

Dylan could smell the pizza once he stepped out of the sunroom, and he crossed the foyer and went into the kitchen. Corbin was at the table, chowing down on a slice with a small plastic cup of milk next to his plate.

"Pep-ronni," Corbin announced.

It was indeed pepperoni with extra cheese. Dylan's favorite. Apparently, it was Corbin's favorite, too.

Karlee was sitting across from the boy. She smiled at Dylan when he came in, but the smile didn't quite make it to her eyes. He had no idea why, but maybe she'd overheard the argument that Lucian and he had had with the judge.

He glanced around the large eat-in kitchen, but there was no sign of Jordan. “Did she leave?” he asked Karlee.

She shook her head and motioned to the side porch. “Jordan got a call and stepped out there to talk.”

Probably Theo again.

It really wasn’t an adult thing to hate a person sight unseen and when he knew little about him, but Dylan did know one important thing. That he was green-eyed-monster jealous.

Yep.

It made no sense. He hadn’t been married to Jordan in a long time, and they’d obviously both gotten on with their lives. Still, it stung, and Dylan wasn’t sure he wanted to think long enough about it to figure out why.

Dylan gave Corbin a thumbs-up when the boy finished his pizza and went into the box for another slice. Corbin grinned around the next bite he took. Dylan intended to do some eating and grinning, too, but then he looked out the side French doors and saw Jordan. Her back was to him, and she wasn’t talking on the phone, which meant she’d finished the chat that had required some privacy.

“Whatever you do, don’t show any hints that you feel sorry for her,” Karlee said when she followed Dylan’s gaze. “Jordan’s upset that folks treat her like she’s damaged goods because she’s not. She says she’s fine.”

That worked for him. He didn’t want her to be damaged or feel as if she was. He wanted her tough and strong, like the old Jordan. His Jordan.

Well, when she had been *his*, that is.

But that was a lot of water under an old bridge. She

had a new life, and so did he, and it started with those ground rules.

His phone buzzed, and when he saw his mom's name on the screen, he let it go to voice mail.

"I'll be right back," he told Corbin and Karlee, and he headed to the French doors. Dylan took a deep breath. Several of them. And he planned out exactly what he was going to say to get Jordan to leave and forget all about trying to get custody of Corbin.

The moment he opened the doors, Jordan whirled around to face him, and those ground rules floated off like dandelion fluff. That's because the unguarded look she gave him sent him spinning back to when they were nineteen and crazy in love.

But now he was obviously just "ordinary/not in love" crazy.

Because there was no way his body should feel that need slide through him. No way he should be staring at her mouth as if he wanted that instead of a slice of pizza. Thankfully, Jordan put a quick stop to it by saying just a handful of words.

"Your mom just called me."

Dylan hadn't seen that coming, and he wondered if it had something to do with the call that she'd just made to him. He got the feeling that it did when his phone buzzed with yet another call from her.

"You should answer that," Jordan insisted. "Because your mom knows about Corbin. She knows that I'm here, too, and she just told me that she wants me to stay at the ranch until we've all had a chance to talk. She's hoping to be back here by tomorrow night."

Crap. That wasn't good. Yes, his mom, Regina, co-owned the house, but it wasn't her place to do this. Not when it would put Jordan, Regina and him under the same roof.

Dylan was about to hit the answer button to take the call, but then Jordan said something else that had him saying something much stronger than *crap*.

Jordan looked him straight in the eyes. "And Regina's talking to her lawyer now so that *she* can petition to get custody of Corbin."

CHAPTER FIVE

JORDAN GLANCED AT the clock on the nightstand and groaned. Five thirty in the morning. It was a full hour earlier than her normal time to get up, but the cold sweat had woken her. Sweat that had wet her camisole to the point where it was uncomfortable. She got up, shucked it off and went to the shower.

Maybe it wouldn't be too long before Dylan and Corbin got up, too, and then she could resume the *chat* that Dylan and she had had on and off the night before. The chat where he'd let her know that he was pissed off at what was happening.

And Jordan couldn't blame him.

She'd thought Regina's out-of-the-blue custody demand was a bad idea from the very moment the woman had made it. She believed it was an even worse idea when Dylan and his mom had gotten into an argument that ended with Regina standing her ground. And now that it was morning, Jordan still believed it was bad. That's why she was here, at the ranch, in one of the many guest rooms so that eventually Dylan and she could work out what they were going to do.

Jordan hadn't gone to the inn in town as she'd planned because there hadn't been a room available. Plus, she hadn't wanted to be that far away from

Corbin. She was worried that once he realized his mom wasn't around, he might feel abandoned, and Jordan wanted to be there for him.

Of course, Dylan wanted to be there for the boy, too. And he was. Dylan had stayed right there through the pizza dinner, Corbin's bath and putting him to bed in the room next to Dylan's. Dylan had insisted on that, and then had also insisted that he would sleep on the floor next to Corbin's bed in case the little boy got scared about being in unfamiliar surroundings.

Jordan had also wanted to stay with Corbin, but she hadn't intended to compound Regina's bad idea with one of her own. It just wouldn't have been good for her to be that close to Dylan. Because despite their dispute, and now their joint dispute with Regina, there was still lust in the air.

For some stupid reason, she kept thinking about kissing Dylan. Probably because kissing had been one of his best talents. She wasn't sure how a man became good at something like that. Plenty of practice, probably, but he'd been a downright pro even back in the days when she'd been the recipient of some of Dylan's first kisses. Maybe it was the shape of his mouth. Or the gentle but coaxing pressure. Or that taste.

Mercy, that taste.

She'd never been able to label it, but it was some sort of version of cowboy sin.

Which was exactly why she should stop thinking about it.

Jordan finished her shower and dressed as quickly as she could. And the *quickly* included not looking in the mirror any longer than necessary. She was having trouble with mirrors these days because she didn't want to see her own face. After she'd been rescued, she had seen her reflection in the helmet-visor of one of her rescuers. That image of her stark fear was what she saw now whenever she caught a glimpse of herself. No need for her to relive that. Instead, she focused on the shimmer of gold from a navel ring as she pulled on her jeans and top.

In hindsight, getting the ring seemed silly. Like a mistake that she should fix by just taking out the little circle and letting the piercing heal. But she'd wanted to do something, well, different. Something that got her mind off what'd happened, so the day she'd gotten out of the hospital, Jordan had found a place to do it. The piece of jewelry had gotten her through some tough mornings while she'd dressed.

And it was large enough that it sort of looked like a much-thinner version of her old wedding ring.

A reminder that kept troubling her a little.

Since she didn't want to deal with her inability to remove unwanted body jewelry, she switched her attention to Dylan's mom. Instead of labeling the taste of his kiss, she should be figuring out Regina's angle. Or if there even was an angle. The woman had said a boy needed a mom, and that since Adele was locked up and Jordan was in the military, that she—as Corbin's grandmother—should get custody.

It was an old-fashioned idea that a woman/mother would be a better parenting choice, but then Regina could be set in her ways. Ironic though, that after her own divorce, Regina hadn't been around much afterward to actually raise her own kids. Neither had her ex-husband. Child-rearing responsibility had been pretty much left to Lucian. But according to what Karlee had said, in recent months Regina had seemingly wanted to make up for lost time with her kids. Karlee's theory was since Regina's brush with death from breast cancer, she was now trying to be the mom she probably should have been all those years ago.

And Regina was extending that mom-hood to being a hands-on grandmother.

During the arguments that Dylan had had with his mom the night before, he'd accused Regina of matchmaking. Jordan also agreed that could be a possibility. And trying to interfere in her son's love life was a lot easier to swallow than believing the woman wanted to keep Dylan from getting custody of his son. That meant Regina likely thought the same thing as everyone else.

That Dylan wasn't responsible enough for fatherhood.

Jordan was sure that stung for him. The same way it stung for her when people gave her that *poor, pitiful you* look. But in Dylan's case, folks might be right.

Might.

She didn't really know the man that Dylan had become, but the preliminary signs weren't good with the sex bingo card that the dog had brought in. Of course, maybe the card was a prank and there weren't others floating around out there, waiting to have enough sex boxes ticked off.

Jordan put on some makeup and a dress since she'd have to see both Adele and a lawyer today. She also wanted to spend as much time with Corbin as possible. Dylan had had extra hours with the boy, and while this wasn't a competition, Jordan wanted Corbin to know her as well as he did Dylan. Besides, it probably wouldn't be long before Regina arrived and threw things into even more chaos.

Before she headed downstairs in search of the coffeepot, Jordan gave herself a final but fast check in the mirror, and she wanted to curse when she saw what was dangling out from the neck of her dress.

The wedding band and engagement ring.

The very ones that Dylan had given her over fourteen years ago.

They weren't something she usually wore. In fact, she normally opted for no jewelry at all, but when she'd decided to fly from Germany to San Antonio, she'd put them on the gold chain with the intention of somehow getting them back to Dylan. After all, the diamond was huge, probably two carats, and since she had been the one to end things, it'd never seemed right to keep them. Now that she had finally seen him, she would be able to return them to him.

For now though, she shoved the rings back beneath the dress and tiptoed out of the guest room and into the hall. Since everyone was probably still asleep, she kept tiptoeing past Corbin's room, but when she saw the door was open, she peeked inside.

And her heart went to her toenails.

Because he wasn't there. Neither was Dylan. The room was empty. So was the adjoining bathroom because Jordan had a quick, frantic search in there before she went running down the stairs. My God. She hoped Dylan hadn't run off with the boy as a way of avoiding custody showdowns with her and his mother.

Jordan definitely wasn't tiptoeing now. She was taking the steps two at a time and trying to stave off the thoughts that something bad had happened when she spotted Karlee.

Karlee was wearing pj's and looked as if she'd just gotten out of bed. She immediately put her index finger to her mouth in a "stay quiet" gesture. Then, she motioned for Jordan to follow her. Since Karlee wasn't alarmed, Jordan tried to tamp down the panic bubbling up inside her. She didn't succeed in doing that until they got into the kitchen and she saw Corbin.

And Dylan.

The two were asleep. Dylan's head was resting on the kitchen table while Corbin was sacked out in the booster seat that one of the housekeepers had located in the attic. His head was on the plastic tray. There were cereal bowls next to each of them, and Booger was napping underneath Corbin's chair.

"Corbin got up at four," Karlee whispered. "I heard Dylan bring him down here so I came to check on them and make some coffee."

Instant guilt. Jordan felt a boatload of it because she hadn't heard a peep from either of them. Though Karlee obviously had.

"Dylan should have woken me," Jordan muttered.

Karlee lifted her eyebrow. "You really think it'd be wise for Dylan to come to your bedroom? If I recall our teenage years, you used to sleep practically commando."

Jordan still did. Usually she just wore panties and maybe a camisole. So, Karlee was right—it probably wouldn't have been a good idea for Dylan to knock on the guest room door since he would have been looking all sleepy and hot.

As opposed to his usual hot and awake.

"When I came back down a couple of minutes ago," Karlee went on, still keeping her voice low, "I found them like this." She quietly went to the coffeepot, poured Jordan a cup, and then topped hers off. "You think I should wake them?"

Jordan shook her head. Though it was tempting. She would have liked to talk with Corbin. Even have cereal with him. But he was sleeping, well, like a baby. So was Dylan, for that matter. And yes, he was in the hot and sleepy mode.

Karlee and she took their coffee into the foyer. That way, Jordan could still be close enough to Corbin if he woke up, but she could also talk to Karlee without the risk of the boy hearing.

"I didn't think you'd be here," Jordan said. "I thought Lucian and you were going back to San Antonio."

"Lucian wisely delayed the trip." She stared at Jordan from over the top of her coffee cup. "So, just how riled is Dylan about Regina? How pissed off are *you*?"

It didn't surprise her that Karlee knew about Regina making her own bid for custody of Corbin. Karlee probably had heard Dylan talking to his mom on the phone. In fact, it was possible that people in Kansas had heard it. Jordan hadn't yelled, but that's exactly what she'd felt like doing.

"How pissed off am I?" Jordan repeated. "Remember that time when we were in middle school and Dylan put a frog in my backpack as a joke to scare me?"

Karlee quickly nodded. "And it peed and crapped all

over your homework and ruined it. Ruined your backpack, too, and then you got detention for yelling and cursing when you saw what'd happened."

Yep, that was the incident all right. What Karlee had left out was that the detention had in turn gotten her grounded. "Well, that anger was a drop in the bucket to how I feel about what Regina's trying to do."

Karlee fought a smile. "At least Dylan did the frog thing to show how much he liked you."

Dylan had indeed claimed that several years later after they'd started dating. But Jordan had always suspected it'd been more of a dare or bet.

"I think Regina might have a different motive," Karlee continued. "She's up to something." Jordan made an immediate sound of agreement. "Last year she tried to fix Eve Cooper up with Dylan," Karlee added.

Jordan nearly choked on her coffee. Eve and Dylan's brother Lawson had not only been lovers, they'd been in love. Or at least they had before they'd broken up when Eve had moved to Hollywood to be a TV star.

"And now Lawson and Eve are getting married in two weeks," Karlee went on. "I'm positive Regina tried to throw Dylan at Eve just to make Lawson realize that he couldn't live without her." Karlee lifted her eyebrow as some kind of warning.

A warning that Jordan thought she had figured out after a long sip of coffee. "She wants Dylan and me to team up and fight her. That'll put us on the same side."

Now it was Karlee who agreed. "Don't be surprised if Regina doesn't bring up that Dylan and you should remarry for the sake of the child."

That wasn't going to happen. Dylan and she had had

their shot—at a time when she didn't have the baggage she had now. Besides, she didn't need to be married to be good at raising her cousin.

"Be honest. Does Regina actually stand a shot at getting custody?" Jordan asked.

Karlee lifted her shoulder. "She's got money to fight this if it comes down to it. Of course, Dylan's got money, too, but Regina's probably better connected with the right people if this actually turns into a court battle."

Well, Jordan didn't have money or the right connections, but she had something else. Adele. They'd been close, once, and while Jordan definitely didn't care for Adele sleeping with her ex, she would put that aside. Somehow, Jordan had to convince Adele to give her custody. That would shut down any fight that Regina tried to start.

"I need to go into town," Jordan said. "I don't have a lawyer, but I have to find one. Got any recommendations?"

"Anna McCord-Moore," Karlee quickly provided. "She has a new practice, is new in town, too, but she's the only one in a hundred-mile radius who doesn't have ties to the Grangers."

Then Jordan would definitely be seeing the newcomer. "I also need to check if there's a room available at the Red Rooster Inn. Best if I don't stay here—" Jordan stopped when Karlee kept shaking her head.

"Don't stay at the inn. A group of kids from a rival basketball team released a dozen green garden snakes into the inn as a prank, and they've only found eight of them. The snakes, I mean. They rounded up all the pranking kids."

Jordan shuddered, cringed. She'd been in combat zones and could handle the bloodiest field injuries, but there was no chance she'd walk into the inn knowing there could be snakes.

"You could stay in the guesthouse," Karlee reminded her. "I set up my office in there, and I sleep there sometimes when Lucian's in town, but you can just shove my stuff to the side to make room for your things."

Great. The guesthouse. The very place where Dylan and she had been newlyweds, and it was only a stone's throw from the main house.

No chance of escaping old memories there.

Still, she'd be close to Corbin so she had to keep it on her list of possibilities. While she was in town, though, she would look for something else, maybe a short-term rental. If she had time, that is. She didn't want to be away from Corbin for too long, but there were still things she had to do.

"I need to go into San Antonio to drop off some paperwork at the base, and then visit Adele at the jail." Jordan added.

Karlee sighed, patted her arm. "I can go with you."

"No. That's a kind offer, but I'd rather you stay here with Corbin. I feel like you're the only person on my side."

Karlee didn't jump to agree to that.

Oh no. "You'll take Dylan's side because of Lucian," Jordan said.

Karlee frowned. "I'm taking Corbin's side because of Corbin. Maybe you'll get good news at the jail.

Here's hoping the charges against Adele aren't as serious as we've heard."

Maybe. But even if they weren't, Jordan had to look at the big picture here. This was Adele's third arrest, and even if she did get out of jail soon, the courts might not grant her custody. Heck, Jordan might not want her to have it, either. Like Karlee, Jordan really did want what was best for Corbin, and Adele might not be in that "best" category. Neither was Regina. Or Dylan.

Heck, she might not be in it, either.

With that dismal thought now firmly planted in her head, Jordan took out her phone to make the call to the jail, but the sound of little hurried footsteps stopped her. It was Corbin coming into the foyer, and Booger was right on his heels.

Just seeing the little boy instantly improved her mood. A mood that got slightly dampened, though, when there was the sound of big hurried footsteps and Dylan came in right behind Corbin and Booger.

Corbin didn't stop. He only spared Karlee and her a glance before he ducked into the powder room. Dylan did more than glance at Jordan, though. He didn't give her a glare. It was more of a mix of fatigue and frustration.

Jordan was right there on the same emotional page with him.

Which caused her to silently groan. If Regina's plan was indeed to get them together, then this was probably the first step.

Dylan went to the bathroom to look in on Corbin, a reminder for Jordan that she didn't know much about the toileting habits of a toddler. Dylan seemed to be comfortable with it, though, and when Corbin came out, drying his hands on his pj's, she finally got a smile that warmed her from head to toe.

How was it possible to love someone this much?

Jordan didn't know, but she thought Dylan might be asking himself the same question.

She stooped down to get on his eye level, but despite the smile, Corbin didn't come to her. He stayed close to Dylan, hooking his arm around Dylan's leg.

"You look so much like your mom," Jordan told him, touching her fingers to his hair. But she immediately regretted saying that.

Corbin looked up at Dylan. Definitely no smile now. "Where's Mommy?"

Good grief. Now she'd upset him. Dylan scooped him up and brushed a kiss on his forehead. "Mommy's on a trip. You'll get to stay here for a while, and it'll be fun. Booger will be here with you."

Until Dylan added that last part, Corbin still had that sad look on his face, but one mention of the dog perked him up. Corbin reached for Booger, and Dylan placed the child on the floor so the playing could commence. It was the same kind of play that had gone on the night before with Corbin running around in the foyer while Booger chased him. It was loud, and giggles and some barking were involved. If Lucian was still sleeping, he soon wouldn't be.

Dylan smiled at them, but then he took a deep breath and turned his attention to Jordan. "Mom texted me earlier this morning. She's at the airport in Costa Rica, waiting on standby for a flight out."

Karlee apparently thought that was her cue to give

Dylan and her time for a private conversation. "Corbin, why don't we see if there are any cartoons on TV?"

That made the boy smile and nod, and he waved at Dylan before Karlee, Booger and he headed for the sunroom. There was a TV just steps away in the family room, but Karlee probably thought it was wise to move out of earshot in case Dylan and she got into an argument.

"I hope you're as pissed off at Regina as I am," Dylan threw out there.

Jordan smiled before she could stop herself. "Karlee and I just had this conversation. I'm poopy-frog-in-the-backpack mad times infinity."

He winced, then smiled. Great. It was the full thousand-watt Dylan smile. Subtle but somehow dazzling at the same time. It accompanied a full dose of the Dylan charm. The little dip of his head. A slight lowering of his eyelids. All blended together with the sexy stubble and tousled hair.

Damn him. She still wasn't immune to it after all this time. It helped, though, when she remembered the arguments.

"If my mom doesn't back down," he said, his smile disappearing, "I'll fight her. But I don't want to have to fight you at the same time."

If she'd still been in middle school, Jordan would have gotten detention for the curse word that left her mouth. "This could be exactly what your mother wants—me and you working together."

Dylan didn't hesitate. He nodded. "Could be. The woman can be sneaky. And that's why we might be able to stop her in her tracks."

It didn't take Jordan long to see where this could possibly be going. "Oh God. You're not suggesting we pretend to be a couple so she'll back off?"

"No. But that was one of the ideas I came up with. Don't worry, I nixed it. That and several other ones that were even worse. Like us remarrying."

She choked on the breath that she sucked in too fast, and it caused Dylan to smile again and give her a fake pat on the back. "Then I remembered why that couldn't happen." He paused. "Wanderlust and roots as deep as Texas don't make for a peaceful home."

It wasn't the first time she'd heard him say that. Of course, she was the wanderlust part of that. "I'm the reason things fell apart." And she added a little snark to that.

He hiked his thumb to his chest. "Roots as deep as Texas," he repeated. "I'm the reason things fell apart. That, and I kept letting my family interfere."

That cooled down some of the snark that would have almost certainly found its way to her mouth. But Jordan quickly realized that a cool-down snark wasn't much of a wall, and she needed a wall between Dylan and her because of her lacking immunity to his smile.

And the rest of him.

For a moment, she didn't keep the memories at bay. It was a whopper of a mistake. Because whenever Dylan was this close to her, it was always easier to remember the way he kissed her way back when. The way it felt to be in his arms. Easier to remember the sex, too.

Jordan was still trying to pull herself out of the memory mess she'd created when she heard a tap on the front door. She stepped way back from Dylan even though there'd already been three or four feet of space between them. Despite that space, though, it felt as if they'd been caught doing something wrong.

"That can't be my mother," Dylan said, checking the time. "Unless she got a quick flight out."

Jordan hoped that wasn't true, but it was too early for a mere visitor. Too bad because she'd wanted to have a chat with Adele and a lawyer before Regina got there. She also wanted to steel herself up.

Dylan was on the way to the door when there was another tap. Maybe Regina had forgotten her key. But it wasn't Regina.

It was a tall, curvy blonde that Jordan didn't recognize. Not at first anyway. She picked through the features, did a mental age progression and realized this was Melanie Turley. She'd been four grades behind Dylan and her in school so Jordan didn't really know her.

Obviously Dylan did, though.

The moment he had the door fully open, Melanie practically flew into his arms. Or rather she would have if his arms had been open. They weren't. Melanie's breasts ended up smacking against his chest, and Dylan staggered back. Melanie caught onto him. He caught onto her. And the woman ended up in his arms after all.

"I didn't want to ring the doorbell because I didn't want to wake everyone," Melanie said. "Dylan, we have to talk." She was still on the last syllable of the final word when her attention landed on Jordan, and Melanie sort of froze.

Jordan felt herself freeze some, too, and she felt other things, as well. The punch of jealousy that was no doubt left over because of the lust.

Dylan moved back from the woman, much as he'd done to Jordan just seconds earlier, and he followed Melanie's gaze to Jordan.

"Jordan," Melanie said on a rise of breath. "Dad told me you were back for a visit, but I thought you'd be staying at the inn."

Jordan shook her head. "There were no rooms available for last night. And then there were the snakes." Of course, that sounded like lies. Jordan wasn't concerned about that, though.

Apparently, Melanie wasn't concerned about it, either, because she only glanced at Jordan before turning back to Dylan. "Your mother called my dad, and she wants him to try to help her get custody of your son."

Jordan had been about to head to the sunroom, but that stopped her. Walter Ray was a judge, and he'd visited Dylan just the day before.

Dylan cursed and scrubbed his hand over his face. "What'd your dad say?" he asked.

"That he'd think about it." Melanie's forehead bunched up. "Dylan, I think he'll do it. Not because Regina would make a better parent but because he's upset with you."

Now it was Jordan who cursed. "Would Walter Ray have any kind of influence in something like this?"

But she already suspected the answer was yes before Melanie gave her a flat look. After all, the man was a judge, which meant he probably knew plenty of lawyers and other judges.

"My dad can be an asshole," Melanie spelled out for her. "And Dylan's not exactly in his good favor right now."

Jordan wished now that she'd stayed to hear what the trouble was between Dylan and Walter Ray. But she suspected it had to do with Melanie.

Melanie turned back to Dylan. "I think I know a way to fix this. A way that'll make my dad happy and will get both him and your mom to back off." Melanie took a deep breath. "Dylan, let's get married."

CHAPTER SIX

FROM THE MOMENT that Dylan had seen Melanie in the doorway, he'd figured something was up that he wouldn't like. And he'd been right.

"Married?" he repeated just to make sure he'd heard Melanie correctly. After all, he was functioning on only an hour or two of sleep and no caffeine. He was surprised he could stand upright.

"I'll just be going," Jordan said, fluttering her fingers toward the sunroom. "I'll check on Corbin, and then I need to drive into San Antonio to see Adele."

Dylan wanted to see Adele, too, but obviously Jordan had coffeed up because she jetted out of the foyer so fast that he didn't get a chance to say anything else to her. She might have thought he needed time to mull over Melanie's proposal. He didn't.

The answer was no.

But Jordan didn't wait around to hear that, and Dylan was betting as soon as she looked in on Corbin that she'd be heading out through the back door so she could avoid Melanie. And him. That was too bad because before Melanie's interruption, he'd thought Jordan and he were making some progress. They hadn't glared at each other anyway, but he was betting that would change if Jordan thought he was teaming up with Melanie to shut her out of the custody battle.

Of course, Jordan might be plotting her own shut out. Since she was going to see Adele, it was possible she could talk her cousin into changing her mind about who would raise Corbin. And Adele just might do it, too.

That put a big knot in his stomach.

"Well?" Melanie prompted. Obviously, the woman couldn't tell from his uncaffeinated, bleary-eyed expression that he was so not in a marriage proposal kind of mood and might not be for the next decade.

Because Melanie was a nice person, he tried to say this as gently as he could. "I can't marry you. No, not even for the sake of custody," he quickly added when she opened her mouth, no doubt to argue her case. "If Walter Ray casts his lot with my mom, then so be it."

Though he hoped like hell that didn't happen. Especially since he was sure both Walter Ray and his mom were doing this for all the wrong reasons. Walter Ray, so he could get Dylan to marry his daughter. And his mom, so she could get him to marry his ex.

"But I don't want you to lose custody of your son," Melanie pointed out.

Neither did Dylan, and he did think it was mighty big of Melanie to have that much concern about a child he'd had with another woman. Or maybe she just figured this was her best shot at becoming Mrs. Dylan Granger.

"Look, Melanie, I'm no prize," he said. "You don't want to marry me. I suck at marriage and relationships."

Her sigh and the look in her eyes disagreed with that. “That was a lifetime ago,” Melanie interrupted. “You’re not the same man you were then.”

Yeah, he was afraid he was. He’d cut down on the partying some, but he was still anchored to this house, to this life and to the family that he sometimes wanted to fling into an alternate universe. And the real butt-kicker, he was the same person who’d failed at the biggest and most important thing he’d ever done—promising Jordan that he’d be with her until death us do part.

Of course, plenty of people went through a divorce and were just fine. Those same people probably hadn’t gone from one screwup to another in their lives, either. Most people got past it.

Dylan hadn’t.

Because every time he looked at his wedding band in his nightstand drawer, he knew that the screwup label would stay with him forever. And that’s why he had to try to stop the cycle now. He had to do better by Corbin than he had with Jordan and himself.

“Just think about what I said,” Melanie pressed. She would have also pressed a big kiss on his mouth, but Dylan turned at the last second. Her lips landed on his cheek.

Melanie looked disappointed when she pulled back. Dylan figured he just looked as if he’d dodged a bullet. A kiss, a real one, could give Melanie hope that he didn’t want to give her. Then again, sometimes his breathing seemed to give her hope, too.

When Dylan finally managed to get Melanie out the door, he immediately headed to the sunroom, not only to check on Corbin but also to see Jordan. He wanted her to know that he hadn't teamed up with Melanie in this custody mess. But Jordan wasn't in the sunroom.

However, Lucian was.

And judging from his expression, he wasn't a happy camper. His brother was pacing and talking on his phone while Karlee and Corbin sat on the floor in front of the TV. Karlee had managed to find a cartoon, and both Corbin and Booger were glued to the set.

Karlee immediately got up and went to him when he glanced around the room, looking for Jordan. "She went to see Adele," she said when she reached him.

Since he'd been expecting that, it wasn't a surprise. What was a surprise, though, was that he actually felt disappointed. Obviously, certain parts of his body had wanted to see her, a reminder that he needed to have a long talk with those parts. It really wasn't a good idea to be lusting after his ex this way, especially since he'd just had that "I suck at relationships" chat with Melanie.

"The visit with Adele will be hard for her," Karlee went on, whispering now. "Hard on Adele, too, I'm sure."

Yeah, and Dylan needed to keep that in mind when he paid his own visit to Adele. The woman wasn't just in jail, she'd also had to give up her little boy. Even if Adele wasn't up for mother of the year award, that had to cut her to the core.

"Lucian's on the phone with your mom," Karlee added.

Yet another woman out of the mother of the year competition. And it explained the intense scowl on his brother's face. Dylan was doing some scowling, too, but that ended when Corbin burst out laughing at something that happened on TV. It made Dylan smile and remember that he, too, had been a burst out laughing kind of kid.

"Thanks for watching him," Dylan told Karlee.

She nodded. "I'll do what I can to make this easier for all of you."

That applied to pretty much everything Karlee did. She was devoted to Lucian, which meant all the Grangers, including him, reaped the benefits of that.

Dylan slipped his arm around Karlee and hugged her. "Maybe one day Lucian will wake up and see that you're a keeper."

Her eyebrow came up. "Who says I want him to wake up? I'm fine with the way things are now." Dylan might have argued that, but Karlee continued. "Besides, the Granger men don't have good track records when it comes to commitments."

They didn't. Lots of divorces and broken hearts. His included. It was the reminder he needed to quit thinking about Jordan and the tug she had on his body.

"I'm worried about Jordan," Karlee threw out there.

Well, hell. That wasn't a good start to his *quit thinking about her* reminder.

"You saw on the news what she went through," Karlee went on. "That only happened a little over a month ago, and Jordan still has to be dealing with it."

Yeah, she did. And he'd seen the news. Hadn't been able to turn away from it despite it giving him a sickening helpless feeling. During those hours that she was held captive, there was all kinds of speculation about what might be happening to her. Torture, rape. Execution. That's why Dylan had been beyond thankful when she'd been rescued and a picture of her showed no signs of injury.

That didn't mean Jordan came out unscathed, though.

Dylan was more than a little bothered by that. Bothered that he might be contributing to her stress. It was a loop of guilt and frustration added to the other loops of lust and being pissed off.

"You're not suggesting I give her custody because she's a military hero," Dylan said to Karlee.

"No." Karlee didn't hesitate. "In fact, that might not be the best thing for her. I know she loves Corbin, and he's family, but..." She waved the rest of that off.

Dylan filled in the blanks. Either way, this could break Jordan. Or at least it could do that to a weaker woman. But Jordan wasn't weak. She'd known right from the get-go that she wouldn't be happy in Wrangler's Creek. Too much had gone on in her childhood. Too much pain. Yet, she'd tried to set that aside when she'd married him.

And she'd failed.

That didn't make her weak, though. Because as soon as she realized that they couldn't make a go of it, she'd cut her losses and gotten on with her life. She'd do the same now if she didn't get custody of Corbin.

He hoped.

But Dylan would try to keep an eye on her just in case.

"Lucian wants to talk to you," Karlee said, patting his arm. She went back to the TV area and Corbin.

Lucian had indeed finished his call and was motioning for Dylan to move to the other side of the room with him. Great. More bad news was coming, and it was bad enough that Lucian didn't want a toddler to overhear.

"That was Mom," Lucian started—after he groaned and muttered some profanity. "She's already had a chat with one of our lawyers about Corbin's custody."

He didn't even bother groaning since this was just the tip of the iceberg. Dylan would save up his groans and give a big, collective one when the crap news stopped pouring in.

"Mom talked to Walter Ray about it, too," Dylan explained. "Melanie was just here to try to coax me into marrying her with the notion that it would stop Walter Ray and Regina from teaming up against me."

"She's gone batshit crazy," Lucian grumbled.

Dylan didn't know if Lucian meant their mother or Melanie. He could see an argument for both. "Even if Mom and Walter Ray do try this, it shouldn't matter. I'm the one with the strongest claim to raise him because I'm Corbin's father."

Lucian stared at him. "Are you? And before you get mad at me pointing that out, let me have a DNA test done. He doesn't look like you—"

"Because he looks like Adele. And until I have a reason to doubt her, there'll be no DNA test."

Dylan said that a little louder than planned, and it got Karlee's attention. She started walking their way.

"Adele's a criminal," Lucian pointed out. "That and that alone should be grounds to doubt her."

It wasn't. And Dylan hoped his glare not only let Lucian know it but that it would also get his brother to back off. For once he was not going to let Lucian browbeat him into doing something. He was just going to accept Corbin as the incredible "gift" that he was. He wasn't ready to deal with DNA tests and any other legalities that Lucian wanted to ram down his throat.

Dylan had to continue the glare when the doorbell rang. Hell. Had Melanie returned for round two of an argument she stood no chance of winning?

"I'll get it," Dylan grumbled.

The bell rang again, followed by a heavy-handed knock. If it was Melanie, she was either impatient or madder than a hornet, and Dylan was quickly reaching that "hornet mad" threshold, as well. That's why he threw open the door, ready to tell Melanie to back off.

But it wasn't Melanie.

It was a tall guy in a military uniform. And he was smiling, though Dylan couldn't see diddly to smile about. It was still way too early for visitors.

"Lieutenant Colonel Theo Shaw," he said, thrusting out his beefy hand for Dylan to shake. "I'm here to see Jordan."

Of course he was. This was the *Theo* who'd called her the night before, the one whose name had rolled off her tongue too easily for them to be just casual acquaintances. This guy was probably her boyfriend. Or maybe her boss. Dylan thought the rank he was wearing was higher than a major, and Theo sure had a lot of ribbons and such on his uniform. He looked like someone who could have been on a recruitment poster.

Dylan was pretty sure he was going to hate him.

"Jordan's not here," Dylan said, and he managed

to keep his tone just a slight notch away from a hostile growl.

"Oh." Theo's eyes widened a second, and he slid those widening eyeballs over Dylan, sizing him up—much the way Dylan was doing to him. "And you are?"

There really was no good reason not to tell Theo his name, but Dylan paused anyway. "Dylan Granger."

Dylan expected to see some kind of recognition on Theo's face, maybe an "Oh, you're Jordan's ex." But he said nothing like that. Theo went in a different direction. "The sex bingo card guy."

All right. Dylan hadn't expected that to come up. Nor did he like Theo's laugh that followed.

"I stopped by the gas station on the edge of town, and the clerk was a blonde about yay high." He put out his hand, palm down, even with his shoulder. "She had a card, and she was talking to her friend about it." Another laugh. "Man, oh man, there were some funny squares on that card."

"Yeah, real funny," Dylan grumbled.

He thought the yay-high blonde was one of the Busby sisters. One of them did indeed work at Arlo's gas station and on occasion, she was a blonde. But Dylan had never been with any of the women in that family. He doubted Theo would believe that, though.

"You're a local celebrity," Theo went on. "Or should I say local sex god." But the laughing stopped, and his face tightened up as if he'd just caught the smell of fresh cow shit. "You're also Corbin's biological father."

Normally, Dylan didn't hate those two words paired together. Biological father. But he hated them now.

Then again, he probably wasn't going to like anything that came out of this joker's mouth.

"Father," Dylan corrected. "Corbin's my son, and his mother gave me custody of him."

That silenced Theo for a couple of seconds while he kept staring at Dylan. Maybe because Jordan had led Colonel Thunderstruck to believe that she would be getting custody of the boy.

"Uh, Jordan said she was staying here," Theo continued once he got his mouth working again.

That meant Jordan had called him last night, probably after she'd gone to the guest room. "She's not here at the moment."

Theo's eyes didn't widen that time, but he did seem suspicious, and he took out his phone. "Oh well. I guess I'll have to ruin my surprise visit by calling her."

"Guess so," Dylan mumbled, still managing not to growl though he figured he looked hostile.

Theo pressed Jordan's number, and Dylan was close enough to him to hear it ring and ring and ring before it went to voice mail. "Well, this is inconvenient," Theo griped, slipping his phone back into his pocket. "Any idea where she is or when she'll be back?"

Dylan had an idea. According to Kaylee, she was probably at the jail, but Jordan could have also made a side trip to the base or was talking to a lawyer. However, Dylan wasn't sure if Jordan wanted Theo to know that. If she did, she would have called and told him herself. That's why Dylan shook his head.

Definitely no laugh that time. Theo huffed and fired some glances around, not just inside the foyer but also the yard. "Jordan's talked about this town. This *place*," he amended. "It's filled with bad memories for her."

Dylan knew he was a big part of that memory pool, and that's probably why he took exception to the comment. "It wasn't all bad," Dylan corrected. "Jordan lived here when she and I were married."

There was eye widening, the kind that came with mild surprise. And then there was eye widening, the kind that came with WTF are you talking about? Theo was doing the latter.

"I'm her ex-husband," Dylan added, just in case Theo hadn't gotten that.

Muscles flickered and tightened all over Theo's face. His mouth flatlined, and his nose did that twitch thing as if he'd smelled something bad. "Funny that Jordan never mentioned ever being married." He pulled back his shoulders. "But then she probably never told you that I'm her boyfriend."

"I heard her say your name a time or two," Dylan settled for answering.

It was petty to be playing games like this, but sadly, he was enjoying it a little too much. Which made him feel stupid, of course. Jordan had a right to have boyfriends. She had a right to be happy.

The muscles in Theo's face relaxed some, and he smiled. "Oh well. I guess we all got our little secrets, and you're Jordan's." He paused and snapped his fingers as if figuring out something. "So, you're Jordan's ex, but you slept with Adele." More laughter. "Yep, I can see why you got a bingo card named after you."

Dylan wished he had superpowers so he could vaporize every single one of those damn cards. Along with vaporizing Theo.

"When Jordan comes back, I'll tell her you stopped by," Dylan said, and this time he couldn't help himself. It was a hostile growl, and he would have shut the door if the guy hadn't caught onto it with his beefy hand.

"I'd like to wait for her if you don't mind." That was kind of a growl, too.

Dylan huffed and scrubbed his hand over his face. "Look, it's been a bad morning, and I want to get some coffee and spend some time with my son."

Just as soon as he said that, Dylan's future sort of flashed before his eyes. Jordan wasn't going to care for it if he'd turned away her boyfriend, especially since he was doing it because he didn't like the guy. Jordan and he were already at enough odds without him dissing Lieutenant Colonel Wonderful.

"You can wait for Jordan in the living room." Dylan hiked his thumb in that direction. "If you need something, just ask one of the housekeepers." If he could find one, that is. They only seemed to turn up when you didn't need them.

"Thanks, man. I appreciate it." Theo used his keys to lock the door on the car parked out front. A rental, no doubt. "I really need to see Jordan ASAP. By the way, how is she?" he asked, coming into the foyer.

Most people looked around the sprawling place their first time inside, but Theo didn't even spare it a glance.

"She's worried about Adele and Corbin," Dylan answered. Not a lie, but not the total truth, either. Karlee had said she was concerned about Jordan and so was Dylan. Apparently, so was Theo since he was here.

"Are Jordan and you stationed together?" Dylan asked as he led him toward the living room.

Theo shook his head. "No, I'm in Germany, and she'll be reporting for duty at Lackland, where she'll be for three years."

Jordan had made that sound as if it were up in the air as to whether or not she'd be assigned to the base. And maybe it was. But there was a bottom line here—Jordan hadn't been able to stay in Wrangler's Creek, and he doubted she'd gotten enough blood transfusions to rid her of her wanderlust.

"I won't tell you how many strings I had to pull to get the flights back here," Theo went on. "But I needed to see Jordan. She wasn't sleeping all that well when she was in the hospital."

Dylan doubted she was sleeping well now, either. In addition to the nightmares she was likely having thanks to being held captive, now she had to worry about Corbin and Adele.

When Theo made it to the living room, he sank down onto the sofa, letting out a sigh of relief. Obviously, he was glad to get off his feet. Too bad those feet were under the same roof as Dylan.

Theo lay back against the cushions, and while he looked as if he might be ready for a nap, he kept his stare on Dylan. "I was head of the team that got her out of there. Did you know that?"

This time it was Dylan who had to shake his head. So, Theo had rescued her. He was, well, a real hero. No wonder Jordan had been calling him.

"She'll try to blow it off," Theo went on, "but she

had a tough go of it." Before Dylan could even react to that, Theo smiled. "I'm hoping I can fix that."

On the surface, that sounded, well, good, but it gave Dylan a bad feeling. "Fix it, how?"

Theo blinked. "Well, fix it for Jordan. You might not think it's the best for you, but maybe it is. I mean, after seeing that bingo card."

Dylan cursed. What the hell did that have to do with anything?

Theo reached in his pocket. "Since I can't talk Jordan out of wanting to raise her cousin's son, then I think this will make things easier for her."

Dylan thought the guy was taking out his phone. But no. It was a small jewelry box. When Theo flipped it open with his thumb, Dylan saw the ring. Not just any ordinary one, though.

A diamond engagement ring.

"I'm here to ask Jordan to marry me," Theo announced. "And I think she'll agree, since that way I can help her get custody of Corbin."

CHAPTER SEVEN

THIS WAS NOT Jordan's first time visiting a jail. Not even close. Her folks had been picked up several times on DUIs and disorderly conduct. As a minor, Adele had been hauled in for unlawful assembly at a protest. But each of those other jail visits had resulted in Jordan getting her assorted family members out, once she'd made arrangements with their bail bondsman, that is.

That wasn't going to happen today.

Jordan had learned from San Antonio PD that Adele had indeed been arrested for possession of ridiculous quantities of SpaghettiOs and Ding Dongs. And Twizzlers. Dylan had forgotten to mention those, but apparently the sugar content in the Ding Dongs hadn't been sufficient for Adele so she'd gone after the Twizzlers, too.

Along with the food items, there'd also been the raincoats and flip-flops. Case after case of them. And environmentally friendly, spring-fresh deodorant. Jordan didn't know the logic behind Adele and her cronies stealing those items, but all of it had been in Adele's garage and in a storage facility that she'd rented—in Adele's own name.

The cop at the jail had fought back a smile while going over some of the charges with Jordan. He hadn't smiled, however, when he'd explained the second part. That the arrest had come while she was still on probation.

There was no chance of the new charges being dropped because Dylan had been right about the plea deal. Adele had accepted an agreement with the district attorney to plead guilty in exchange for a maximum sentence of five years.

Five years!

It was too much to hope that Adele could go that entire time without getting into even more trouble so she'd likely serve the full term. That would mean Corbin would be nearly eight before she got out. By then, her son wouldn't even know who she was.

With that depressing thought taking hold of her, Jordan sat at the table in the visiting area and waited for the guards to bring in Adele. It was a big room with lots of tables, and there were guards and other visitors milling around. Still, it felt claustrophobic. Probably because there were no windows and no easy way out. If she felt the panic building inside her, she couldn't just run outside. She'd have to go back through security which could take minutes or longer.

It was the *longer* that was causing her breath to go thin. Causing the tightness in her chest, too. In hindsight, she probably should have dosed up on her anxiety meds before coming here, but she hadn't wanted to be in a fog.

Since Jordan hadn't been able to bring anything into the visiting room with her, she couldn't look at her phone for a distraction. So she focused on the images that popped into her head.

Corbin.

He was definitely her top concern right now. More than Adele. More than Dylan. Of course, thinking about Dylan caused the image of him to appear. A much-too-clear image. Of him naked, and participating in that stupid bingo game.

A stomach licking from Dylan.

When they'd been lovers and married, Jordan hadn't remembered him having a preference for licking that particular body part, but maybe he'd developed a taste for it over the years.

A taste of it with other women.

She silently cursed that thought and tried to shove it aside. It shoved all right, but new ones came. Of what other licking deeds might be on that card. And how many of them Dylan had actually done. Jordan was betting if she had one of those cards, she could win hands down with just the things Dylan and she'd done. Heck, the whole card would be x-ed out.

Which wasn't necessarily a good image to have in her head. No. Best not to remember all the things that they'd done together. Thankfully, she had a little help with that because a guard led Adele into the room. Adele's face lit up when she saw Jordan. But Jordan was certain she did the opposite of lighting up.

"No physical contact with the prisoner," the guard warned Jordan when she stood.

Adele was obviously aware of the rule because she didn't even move in for a hug. Still smiling though, Adele sat in the chair across from Jordan. "You came," she said. "I wasn't sure you would."

"I always come when you're in trouble," Jordan grumbled. "And right now, you're in huge trouble."

Jordan had to admit, though, that despite the huge trouble, Adele looked amazing. She still had that hippie/Bohemian vibe even while wearing an orange jumpsuit. It was probably because of her long flowing black hair, makeup-free face and the daisy/peace symbol tats on the backs of her hands.

"All the panties in this place are polyester, not cotton," Adele whispered when she leaned closer to Jordan. "The women complain about it, and nothing happens. Do you know how unbreathable poly panties are?"

No amount of reining in her anger would have worked for Jordan. She felt a glare coming on. "I didn't come here to talk about panties."

"I know," Adele admitted. "Go ahead. Start telling me how stupid I was, not just for the stolen stuff but also for what happened between Dylan and me. But I swear the stolen stuff was for a good cause. Think of all those homeless people who would have been fed and clothed. The shoes they usually have are closed-toed and hot, and they get rashes on their feet in this Texas heat. And who doesn't need a raincoat in spring?"

"I didn't come here to talk about foot rashes, either." Though Jordan would like an explanation of how Adele had ended up in Dylan's bed. "Were you drunk when you did this?" Jordan snapped. Actually, that question applied to both Dylan and the stolen goods.

Adele looked totally insulted by that. "Of course not. I haven't gotten drunk since I got pregnant with Corbie."

Jordan guessed that was her pet name for the boy. It was cute but not cute enough to overcome the anger. Especially since the drunken episode had been with Dylan. And Adele hadn't bothered to mention any of it to her. Jordan had had to learn about it from the social worker.

"You didn't tell me about *Corbie*," Jordan pointed out. "I saw you a year ago, and you didn't even hint that you'd had a child. You certainly never mentioned being with Dylan."

Adele made a "duh" sound. "Because I knew you wouldn't be happy about me being a mom, or that I'd been with your ex-husband, and I didn't want to have to argue with you. Especially since I knew you'd only be around a day or two before you took off again."

That was true about the day or two part, but Jordan refused to feel guilty. Or at least she didn't want to feel it. But she did.

"How is Corbie?" Adele asked.

Jordan frowned because that should have been the first thing out of Adele's mouth instead of a complaint about panties. "He's at the Granger Ranch. With Dylan." And she decided to backtrack a little. "Where was Corbin when you were stealing food and flip-flops?"

Adele gave her another totally insulted look. "With a sitter. I wouldn't have taken him with me for something like that. It was well past his bedtime."

Well, that was something at least. Adele hadn't involved her toddler in her felony-related activities.

"I'd like to see Corbin," Adele continued a moment

later. "I know this isn't the best place to bring a little boy, but I'd like to see him so I can say goodbye."

Until Adele had added that last part, Jordan had been about to agree with her, that this wasn't a good place for Corbin. "Goodbye?"

Adele nodded. "Just one visit, and I won't see him again until I get out. I don't want him back here. As he grows up, I don't want all his memories to be of me like this." She waved her hands over the orange jumpsuit.

"Corbin will have memories of that whether he sees you or not. Eventually, he'll ask about you, and he'll be able to find out the truth with an internet search."

Again, Adele nodded. "But it's different seeing it on a computer screen than in real life." She blinked hard when the tears shimmered in her eyes.

Jordan was actually thankful for the tears. Sometimes, Adele got so caught up in her social causes that she didn't make the connection to how it was affecting her life. And the people around her.

"What's best for Corbie," Adele went on, "will break my heart. He's my precious little man, and I love him. But it's best if I say goodbye and step away."

Jordan could partially agree with that, though there was another side to this. "You'll be out of jail in five years, maybe less. Do you really want to come back into Corbin's life as a stranger?"

"No," Adele quickly answered. Then, she paused. "I'm not sure it's a good idea to come back in his life at all. I mean, by then he'll be a big boy. He'll be so much better off than he would be with me."

Probably. But Jordan couldn't bring herself to say that aloud. Dylan would certainly give Adele any amount of money for child support so that would help. However, Adele would always be Adele.

Focused but flighty.

Not a good combination when it came to raising a child. Adele and she had both had bad childhoods, and Jordan hated that Corbin might have to go through anything even remotely like that.

"Regina wants custody of Corbin," Jordan told her.

Adele didn't seem surprised by that, and she nodded right away. "Yes, her lawyer's already called here, asking to see me. We've got an appointment this afternoon."

Regina wasn't wasting any time. "I hope you'll tell the lawyer to take a hike."

Adele shrugged. "I'll listen to what he has to say."

Jordan groaned. There were already enough complications without Regina doing a full court press.

Adele's expression changed when she looked at Jordan again. Not a smile exactly, but it was a good attempt at one. "How are you?" Adele asked. "I saw the reports on the news and organized a candlelight vigil for you. Nearly a hundred people showed up. We chanted and did yoga."

"Thank you." Jordan meant it. She was grateful to anyone and everyone who'd tried to give her spiritual support during her captivity. But it wasn't what she wanted to discuss now. "You knew I'd been rescued and that I was coming here on leave. I told you my flight number and the time I'd arrive. Why didn't you just wait and hand Corbin over to me? I'm your family, Adele."

Adele dragged in a long breath, and the teary eyes returned. "I love you. You know that."

"But?" Jordan questioned when Adele didn't continue.

"But I want Dylan to be the one to raise Corbie. I know he's not perfect," Adele quickly went on before Jordan could say anything. Especially say anything about how hearing that crushed her heart. "But he can give Corbie a home. And I believe Dylan can love him."

There it was. All spelled out for her. And the problem was that it was all true. The Granger money wouldn't hurt, either, and while Jordan would have liked to blow that off, she couldn't. She'd grown up poor and knew that it sucked. Of course, money alone wouldn't fix things, but Dylan did indeed seem to care for the little boy.

Jordan wasn't ready to give up on this just yet, though. "I love Corbin, too."

"I knew you would. Corbie's a real sweetheart." Adele paused again. "He deserves the best."

"And I'm not the *best*," Jordan said in a mumble. That stung, bad, and in the heat of the moment, she nearly started to point out all of Dylan's flaws.

But in Adele's mind, Jordan's flaws outnumbered his.

"This way, you don't have to give up the life you love," Adele went on. "You know you'd never be happy in just one place. You never have been. And Corbie needs stability."

"I don't have to live in Wrangler's Creek to give Corbin stability," Jordan pointed out. "That can happen anywhere he and I happen to live."

Adele looked her straight in the eyes. “But it’s what I want for my son. Honestly, it was the only home I ever had, and despite how bad things got with your mom, it was a home I loved. I want that for Corbie. I certainly don’t want him being moved all over the world with you on assignments.”

Jordan opened her mouth to say that military kids were usually well-adjusted, but Adele continued before she could say anything.

“There’s only one way I’d change my mind about custody,” Adele insisted. “You get out of the military and move back to Wrangler’s Creek to be with him.”

Stunned, Jordan stared at her. “Is that all?” she asked with just a touch of sarcasm.

“No.” Still staring into Jordan’s eyes, Adele leaned in closer again. “You’d have to promise me to raise Corbie with Dylan. Not as his ex but as a family. The three of you together. Until I’m sure it’ll actually work, Dylan will keep full custody of him.”

That certainly didn’t sound flighty. It sounded like a decree. And Adele must have thought she’d made that decree crystal clear because she got up and walked out with the guard.

Jordan waited a few seconds to see if Adele would return, but when she didn’t, she headed back through the security checkpoint so she could gather her purse and phone.

“Done already?” the guard asked. He was the same one who’d searched her when she’d first come in, and like before he gave her that look of sympathy that she got from anyone who recognized her.

"Yes." Jordan checked the times. She'd only used half of her allotted thirty minutes with Adele.

"I hope it wasn't too hard on you," he went on. Yes, definitely sympathy.

"It was okay," she lied.

"Good," the guard said, handing Jordan her things. "Now I'll be able to get your cousin's other visitors in as soon as they're done with the paperwork."

Jordan had already taken a step, but that stopped her. "Other visitors?"

The guard nodded, and even though he didn't tell her the visitors' names, Jordan got a glimpse of them on the screen.

Heck.

What were they doing here?

CHAPTER EIGHT

JUDGE WALTER RAY TURLEY and Regina Granger.

Jordan doubted there was a good reason for the duo to be visiting Adele unless they were actually pairing up now to bark up this custody tree. She'd considered waiting around to confront them, but Jordan had left, figuring it wasn't a good idea for her to get in a shouting match in a jail. Especially when that guard had already thought she was fragile and maybe unstable.

Unfortunately, Adele thought that, too.

Family.

That word sure took on a different meaning than it had before Jordan's visit with Adele. Her cousin had used family as strings to tie around Jordan's possible custody request. Strings that involved Dylan and Jordan playing house. And if Jordan didn't play, then she wouldn't get the chance to raise Corbin.

Twenty-four hours ago, Corbin hadn't even been on Jordan's radar, but now that he was, it hurt to think she could lose him. But what hurt even more was that Adele didn't have enough faith in her to believe that she would be the right choice as a parent. Instead, Adele had chosen Dylan.

Jordan heard the dinging sound on the dash of her rental car and saw the low gas gauge. Good thing she'd gotten the warning, or as distracted as she was, she might not have noticed. That definitely wasn't good. She needed to get her mind back on not only her driving but also what she was going to say to Dylan about the visit with Adele. She'd have to tell him the truth.

Wouldn't she?

Of course, she would. And Jordan silently cursed herself for even that blip of a thought to keep it from him. But maybe once Dylan heard Adele's decree, he would still be able to see Jordan's side of this. And that side was she thought she could be the better parent.

While she thought about the argument she could give him, Jordan pulled into the Pump and Ride, Wrangler's Creek's only gas station. Like everything else in town, there'd been no changes here. In fact, there were the familiar cobwebs. When she'd been a teenager, they'd made fun of the spidery blobs in the corners of the windows, and they were still there.

Even the sign on the pump hadn't changed. It still said "pay inside before you pump" so Jordan went in to see another familiar fixture. Arlo Betterton, the owner. Same white hair and beard, same round belly stuffed like a sausage into his too-tight overalls. The overalls might even have been the same ones he'd worn fourteen years ago.

"Well, looky here," Arlo said. "I got a war hero in my place of business."

"I'm not a hero," Jordan automatically grumbled, but she didn't say it loud enough for him to hear. She'd learned from the looks she'd gotten that people didn't want her to be bitchy about the hero label. Maybe because it made her seem ungrateful for being alive.

"I need some gas." And she did say that aloud. Jordan took out her credit card and handed it to Arlo to swipe on the antique-looking machine.

"You home for good because of Adele's boy?" Arlo asked. He didn't swipe the card. He stood behind the counter grinning at her.

"Right now, I'm just on leave. And I need to get back to the Granger Ranch," she added.

That addition did no good whatsoever in getting him to hurry. "Well, I'm sure that mess with Adele will all work itself out. That girl always was spirited."

That was one way of putting it. If spirited was code for pain in the butt. But even now, Jordan felt guilty about thinking of Adele like that. After all, Adele was behind bars and could be there for a long time, and she didn't want to kick her when she was down.

"So, your fella came to town with you," Arlo said a moment later.

Jordan shook her head.

"The Air Force fella," Arlo added. "He was by here this morning getting gas."

It was possible that her heart skipped a couple of very necessary beats. Jordan whipped out her phone to call Theo to make sure he was anywhere but here, but then she remembered she'd turned off her phone when she was at the jail. She had three missed calls from Theo and one from Dylan.

Oh mercy.

Had Theo actually gone to the Granger Ranch? Probably. Because the way her luck was running, he wouldn't have gone anywhere else.

"Uh, I'm in a hurry," she spelled out to Arlo. "Just swipe my credit card so I can get the gas and go."

"Will do." But Arlo still moved at a snail's pace. "I'm guessing Wrangler's Creek's looking pretty small to you now that you've been all over."

She made a noncommittal sound and tapped her fingers on the counter. Or rather she tapped them on the paper that was there. Not just mere paper though, Jordan realized. It was one of the Dylan Granger Sex Bingo cards.

Jordan hadn't expected to make the small gasp that escaped from her throat, and Arlo quickly saw what had gotten her attention. He cursed. "Genie Busby musta left that here. That girl's always up to something. Of course, most girls are up to something when it comes to Dylan."

He laughed.

Jordan didn't.

Since Arlo still hadn't processed the credit card, she took it from him and handed him a twenty-dollar bill. That wouldn't fill up her tank, but it was plenty enough to get her to the ranch.

"You can take the bingo card if you want," Arlo said. "Of course, you wouldn't have any trouble winning. Not that you've done any of those things in recent years, mind you, but from what I've heard, there's no expiration date."

Like the gasp, Jordan hadn't intended to take the card, but she changed her mind at the last second. Seeing it would be a reminder that she should think hard before just giving up on her bid for custody.

As soon as Jordan got the gas, she drove away from

Arlo's, heading for the ranch. She'd intended on stopping in town to see the lawyer Karlee had recommended, but that could wait. First, she'd need a private word with Theo to tell him that this was not a good time for him to be there. And then she'd need a private word with Dylan.

But privacy wasn't going to happen.

Jordan realized that as soon as she got to the ranch and the main house came into view. There were people all over the front yard. And a horse. Dylan was on that horse, and he had Corbin in the saddle with him. There were smiles and some picture taking going on.

Since she couldn't actually pull into the driveway because of all the people and vehicles, Jordan parked on the road and walked up. As she got closer, she had no trouble recognizing the others. Karlee and Lucian were there. Then, beside them were Dylan's other brother, Lawson, and Lawson's soon-to-be wife, Eve Cooper. Lawson was holding a baby who looked to be about a year old, and there was a teenage girl standing on the other side of him. Dylan's sister, Lily Rose, was also there and her husband, Jake Monroe. Lily Rose was also holding a child.

Apparently, this was some kind of family reunion, no doubt so that Dylan could show off his cowboy son. There was no sign of Theo, though.

Jordan got smiles from Karlee and Eve. The others were a little frosty, though, probably because they still saw her as the woman who'd broken Dylan's heart. It didn't help that they likely knew she had returned to try to take the smiling little boy, which would only hurt Dylan even more.

“Horsey,” Corbin proudly announced.

“Yes, I can see that.” Jordan managed a smile, too, and it extended to Eve when the woman hurried over and pulled her into a hug.

“I’m glad you’re home.” Eve didn’t ask if she was okay, but Jordan could see the question in her eyes.

“I’m fine,” Jordan lied. “Congrats on getting married. You and Lawson are finally saying ‘I do,’ huh?”

“Long past due.” She tipped her head to the teenager. “That’s our daughter, Tessie, but I suspect you’ve read about her in the tabloids.”

She had indeed. Eve had been the star of a TV show that had long since ended, but she was still apparently fodder for the tabloids, especially when it’d come out that Lawson and she had had a love child together when they were just teenagers. The girl was the spitting image of him.

“Please come to the wedding, a week from Saturday at two o’clock,” Eve went on. “It’s nothing formal, just friends and family. It’ll be in the rose garden at my house. And Corbin’s going to be the ring bearer.”

Until Eve had added the last part, Jordan had already geared up to decline. No way would most of Dylan’s family want her there. But since Corbin was going, that changed things. “I’d love to come. Thank you.”

Eve hooked her arm through Jordan’s and led her into the lions’ den, aka the wall of Grangers and Grangers-in-laws. Jordan looked up at Dylan, and though he almost certainly wanted to know how her meeting with Adele had gone, he, too, managed a smile, and he tipped his hat.

Damn him.

He was too charming, considering they were at odds. Of course, he was probably hoping to beat those odds by showing her the best side of him. In this case, the best side was his butt in those jeans, and she got a nice view of it when he handed Corbin to Karlee and then climbed out of the saddle.

Jordan went to him, hoping now that Corbin's debut ride was over that the others would start to leave. They didn't. They stayed, chatting, taking pictures and occasionally giving her a wary glance.

No wariness for Corbin, though. "I ride de horsey," he gushed. And clearly, he'd loved it because he would have gone right back to the mare if Karlee had let go of him.

Even though talking to Dylan was important, Jordan took a moment to kiss Corbin's cheek and listen to the boy go on about the ride. She only understood half of what he said, but that didn't matter. He was happy, and that both helped and hurt her. It helped because he wasn't fussing and fretting about missing his mom. Dylan had obviously seen to that. But it hurt, too, because if she got custody, she'd be taking him away from all this.

Dylan walked toward her, and with each step he got to listen to his family praise him about Corbin. Of course, the praise was for Dylan, too, and she didn't think it was her imagination that his siblings were seeing him in a different light.

Again, that was both good and bad for her.

Good because she wanted Dylan to see his worth, that while Lucian might be in charge of running things, it was only because of Dylan that those things ran smoothly. She just wished he wasn't seeing it now because it would make him a more formidable foe. He was already too formidable as it was.

Jordan opened her mouth to tell Dylan that they needed to talk, in private, but before she could get a word out, she heard someone call her name.

Theo.

He came out of the front door, and the moment he reached her, he picked her up and twirled her around. "That's a Texas-size hello," he joked.

And perhaps the start of a Texas-size puking. Jordan hadn't managed to eat anything yet, and her stomach was churning from all the acidy black coffee she'd had to fight off a headache. The twirling didn't help. Actually, Theo being here didn't help, either.

Jordan maneuvered herself out of his arms so that he could get her feet back on the ground. She glanced around to see everyone's reaction. They were all staring at her. Even Corbin and Dylan.

"I was about to mention that your *boyfriend* was here." Dylan didn't just say it, though. He drawled it. But she thought there was an edge to that charming speech pattern. And the look he gave her dared her to deny that *boyfriend* was the right label.

Even though it wasn't.

Theo seemed to be giving her the same dare. Maybe because he was going on past history here. Theo and she had indeed been lovers, but that'd been nearly two years ago, and before her rescue, it'd been months since Jordan had seen him.

"Why did you come after I told you not to?" she asked Theo. "How did you get here so fast?" Jordan had another question that she didn't add—how soon will you be leaving?

"I'm here because of you, of course. I called in plenty of favors to make this trip. Did you know that Wrangler's Creek isn't even on the GPS?" But he didn't wait for her to respond to that trivial comment. Theo took her by the hand, leading her inside. "Come on. I've got something to ask you. Something that will solve your problems."

Oh God. She didn't like the sound of that, and that's why Jordan held her ground. She turned back to Dylan to see if he knew what was going on.

She would bet her eyelashes that he did.

"Did you have anything to do with this?" she asked him.

Dylan held up his hands. "Hey, I got my own troubles. Melanie wants me to marry her so that Corbin can have a two-parent family."

Jordan mentally repeated that *Oh God*. She repeated it again when she realized why Dylan was telling her that.

Crap. Crap. Crap.

Theo had come here to propose.

She glanced at both Dylan and Theo, and decided she would wait to turn down Theo's offer since it was also going to involve convincing him to leave ASAP. That might take a lot longer to do than an ASAP. Her conversation with Dylan about Adele should be much shorter. Or at least it would be unless he told her that he was taking Melanie up on her offer to "team up" with him.

Dylan seemed to know her decision before she even

said a word. "Why don't you come with me to put up the mare?" he suggested.

"Ride da horsey 'gin?" Corbin asked.

"After lunch." Dylan goosed him in the stomach, causing Corbin to laugh, and Dylan followed it with a kiss to the top of the boy's head.

Jordan kissed Corbin, too, but it probably looked as if she'd done it only to prove that she loved Corbin as much as Dylan did. Which she did.

"I can go with you to put up the horse," Theo said, following her.

"No. That's okay," Jordan assured him. "Dylan and I need to talk."

"Yeah. He's already told me everything. I'd like to hear your side of it, too." And Theo kept coming. He wasn't usually this pushy, but Jordan suspected he was more than a little jealous, especially if one of the things Dylan had told him was that he was her ex-husband.

When Dylan reached the horse, he got back on, and in the same motion, he took Jordan by the arm. With some jostling around, he pulled Jordan into the front of the saddle with him.

"Really?" Jordan protested, and she would have gotten right down if she hadn't seen Corbin's reaction.

Corbin giggled and clapped his hands when he wriggled free of Karlee for a moment. Karlee quickly took hold of him again. "Jordy and Daddy ridin' horsey."

"Karlee and I've been working on him saying your name," Dylan added to her. "He's just about got it down pat."

That touched Jordan far more than she wanted to admit. Because it seemed to mean that Dylan wasn't going to try to shut her out of Corbin's life. So, instead of her demanding that Dylan put her down, she stayed in the saddle.

"Don't worry. I'll bring her right back," Dylan said to Theo, and even though Jordan couldn't see Dylan's face, she'd bet that he was smiling.

Theo sure wasn't.

He was looking at her as if she'd betrayed him. She hadn't. Not really. But this might be the fastest way for her to have a private conversation with Dylan. Of course, there was no way she could justify why Dylan and she both needed to be on horseback to do that.

Since it was only a short trip from the front of the house to the barn, Jordan decided it was best to get the talk started. That way, it would maybe keep her mind off the fact that their bodies were squished against each other. Specifically, her butt against the front of those great-fitting jeans.

"Your mother and Judge Turley came to the jail to visit Adele," she threw out there. "They were there when I left."

It got the exact reaction she expected. Dylan cursed. "I'm betting nothing good will come of that."

That was a bet she wouldn't take because it was a sure thing. "Adele also wants to see Corbin so she can say goodbye," she added, and Jordan risked glancing over her shoulder to see his expression.

She shouldn't have.

Because the motion caused his mouth to brush across her cheek. It felt like a kiss. Damn it. Lust and empathy were not a good combination.

"Okay. I can arrange to take Corbin there." Though he sounded as hesitant about it as Jordan was.

She had to take a deep breath to continue with the rest. "Adele gave you custody because she thought you could give Corbin a more stable family life." Another pause, another breath. "After seeing him with you and your family today, I can understand where she's coming from. But I'm still not sure it's the right thing."

He made a sound of agreement. Did that mean he agreed? Or was Dylan just having doubts about all the time and work it would take to be a good father?

"Did Adele mention if it was okay for *me* to visit her?" he asked.

"No." And Jordan felt guilty for not broaching the subject with her. Of course, that whole conversation with Adele had been stressful enough without adding more talk of Dylan to it. "It didn't come up."

He reined in the mare once they were inside the barn, slid out of the saddle, and then helped her down. He didn't say anything, though, until she was facing him. "I turned Melanie down, of course, but I suspect it'll take me repeating it a couple more times before it sinks in. When it does, she'll probably be pissed off enough to throw her support to my mother and the judge."

That's the way she figured it would go, too. Still... "Adele was adamant about you having custody."

"And my mom and Walter Ray might persuade her to change her mind," Dylan quickly pointed out.

Jordan wished she could say that wouldn't happen, but if Adele's flighty response kicked in, anything was possible.

"I don't want to lose him," Dylan added. He cursed and shook his head as if he'd admitted too much to her.

Since Dylan had dived right into those emotion-filled waters, so did she. "Neither do I."

And there it was, the standoff that pitted them against each other.

Of course, it wasn't the first time they'd been at odds. They'd had plenty of arguments when they were married, and the biggest argument of all had come when she'd asked for a divorce and Dylan had wanted her to stay and make a go of it. She still wasn't sure about staying, and it might not even be necessary if she did indeed raise Corbin.

Dylan shook his head again, this time as if pulling himself out of a trance, and he glanced around at the inside of the barn. "We've had a lot of meaningful discussions here over the years."

Yes, they had, and this was one of them. Perhaps one of the most important. But other things had happened here, too. Specifically, sex.

On several occasions.

No way did she want to be thinking about that now so Jordan turned to walk out. Best if they finished this talk outside. She started in that direction but made another mistake. Of course, everything about this little adventure had been a big error in judgment. This time, though, the error came from looking at Dylan again. It was a glance, but he was glancing at her at the same time.

Jordan could have sworn it caught her panties on fire.

Something was on fire, anyway. And they'd both obviously gone stark raving bananas because Dylan cursed, hooked his hand around the back of her neck and hauled her to him.

And he kissed her.

Jordan didn't put up a fight. None whatsoever. She just moved right into that kiss as if it were amazing and wouldn't complicate the devil out of her life. Well, it was amazing, but there were complications right from the start.

For one thing, Dylan never merely just kissed. It was always a couple of steps beyond that. Bodies touching—this time their fronts. She felt the slight stubble on his jaw. Drew in his scent and tasted the daylights out of him.

If you bottled really strong guilty pleasures, that's how it would taste.

Like premium chocolate, ice cream, birthday cake and other edible things.

Jordan slipped right into that taste, which meant moving even closer and slipping right into his arms. He used all those maneuvers to turn her, and Jordan felt her back land against a stall door. The mare snorted, a sound that should have brought her back to reality since Dylan and she were kissing in a barn.

It didn't.

The only reality she seemed to want right now was a four-letter word. And that word was *more.*

Oh yeah. Her on-fire panties snapped right in that "more" direction, and that's exactly what Dylan gave her. All the years just melted away, and the melting didn't take the lust with it. It stayed, burning hot and making her tug him closer and closer. Until she could feel every wonderful inch of him.

Some inches were more wonderful than others, of course.

"Someone's coming," Dylan said.

Jordan was so caught up in the heat, it took her a moment to realize that wasn't a sexual reference. Someone literally was coming into the barn because even over the drumming in her ears, she could hear the footsteps. She pulled away from him just as Theo arrived.

Theo looked at her. Then, at Dylan. Before he cursed. "You've been crying," Theo said, going to her.

Jordan had no idea what had caused him to think that. She was nowhere near tears, but a possible orgasm had been imminent. Theo pulled her into his arms, hugging her the way someone would a child. He even patted her on the back.

"I'm so sorry," Theo added. "I knew this would upset you."

Dylan wisely stepped back, pulling off his Stetson and holding it in front of those wonderful inches of him that were somewhat prominent behind the zipper of his jeans. He also lifted his eyebrow, and for something that wasn't even a word, it managed to say a lot. For instance, are you really going to stand there and let your *boyfriend* think you've been crying?

Yes, she was, but that was only because she didn't want to have to explain the kiss. Not only to Theo but to herself. Later, when she was alone, she could give herself a good mental kick for letting it happen. It didn't matter that she'd been thinking about kissing Dylan since she'd come back to Wrangler's Creek. It didn't matter that it had been a good stress reliever. She still needed that kick to knock some sense into her.

"Could you give Jordan and me some privacy?" Theo asked Dylan.

Dylan's mumbled "okay" was hesitant, but that was perhaps because he was going to have trouble walking. Also maybe because he wasn't sure Jordan actually wanted privacy with Theo. She didn't especially, but there were some things she needed to say to him so she nodded. Dylan returned the nod and got moving.

She'd been right about him not being able to walk well. But as soon as he made it out of the barn, Jordan turned to Theo.

"I appreciate you worrying about me. I do, but I won't marry you," she said right off.

Theo's mouth tightened. "Dylan told you. I'd wanted that to be a surprise."

"Oh, it was," she assured him. "But it wouldn't have mattered if the surprise had come from you or him—my answer would still be the same. I'm not marrying you."

"You married Dylan," he pointed out.

Dylan had obviously been chatty today. "I did, a long time ago. It was a mistake then, and it'd be a mistake now for me to repeat it." Now she was babbling.

Theo stared at her and slowly released the breath he'd been holding. "I just don't want you to have to go through this alone. And I know you want him because I saw the way you kissed him."

Jordan was certain her own face did some tightening.

"Corbin," Theo clarified. "I saw the way you kissed him."

Oh yes. She certainly hadn't forgotten about that, but Dylan's kiss was much fresher in her mind.

"I love Corbin," she admitted. "And I haven't decided if I'm going to quit fighting for custody. But even if I do quit and Dylan keeps him, I'll still want to see Corbin. I'll want to be part of his life."

Theo kept staring at her. "What are you saying, exactly?" But he didn't let her answer. "You've been in the Air Force for thirteen years, three enlisted and ten as an officer. You could get retirement pay in only seven more years."

All of that was true, but it had nothing to do with Corbin. Not really. If she spent seven more years in the military and stayed on her current career track, Corbin would be nearly ten before she could come back permanently to Wrangler's Creek.

If she wanted permanent, that is.

And that was the problem. She needed to figure out if she could keep the past in check and be part of Corbin's life here, with his father.

"Does this mean you're staying here?" Theo asked.

"For now. I don't have to report into the base for a couple more weeks, and I'll delay that by using my personal leave." No one at the base was going to question her need to take more time. "I want to spend that with Corbin."

He stared at her as if waiting for something. Maybe for her to change her mind or have this make sense to him. That wasn't going to happen.

"You're under a lot of stress," Theo finally said. "Do you remember that time you went to that spa in Trinidad? You thought your Spanish was good enough to request a bikini wax, but it wasn't."

Jordan huffed. Another life lesson. But Theo seemed

to want to tie those lessons to some of her worst moments. The penis tat and now a reminder of a massage appointment that had turned into a Brazilian followed by some bleaching of her lady parts and other areas near her lady parts. She'd gotten a bad rash and had then had to muddle her way through an ER visit.

"What I'm trying to say," he went on, "is you could be making a mistake even bigger than the waxing and bleaching. Do you really think it's a wise idea to be here under the same roof as your ex-husband?"

Finally, there was an easy question to answer. No. It wasn't wise. In fact, it was perhaps one of the most unwise things she'd ever done. But she was staying. And, no, it didn't have anything to do with that scorcher of a kiss.

Jordan didn't repeat her refusal of the proposal he hadn't actually asked. She didn't spell out that he should leave and go back to work, that she would be fine. But thankfully, Theo seemed to get all of that. He leaned in and brushed a kiss on her forehead. It was much like the chaste but loving kiss she'd given Corbin.

"Just promise that you'll call me if things get bad," he added in a whisper.

She nodded, though it was a promise she probably wouldn't keep. Her go-to response when stressed wasn't to reach out for help. It was to retreat within and have a panic attack—in private.

Best not to spell that out to Theo, though, since his forehead was already bunched up with worry.

"I'll be fine," she added, and she hooked her arm through his to get him moving toward the house.

There was no sign of Dylan, but it didn't take too

many steps before Jordan heard the chatter coming from the front of the house. Obviously, Dylan's family was still there, but there was a voice that hadn't been there when she'd made the trip to the barn.

Regina.

"There he is," Regina said. Judging from her gushy tone, she was talking about Corbin.

That got Jordan moving faster, and she let go of Theo's arm so that she could run the rest of the way. Yes, it was Regina all right, and she had indeed been talking about Corbin. Dylan was holding the little boy, but Regina had out her hands, trying to coax Corbin to come to her. He wasn't having any part of that, though, and had his face buried against Dylan's neck.

"Is there a problem?" Jordan immediately asked.

That got Regina to stop her coaxing attempts, and she turned and looked at Jordan. She wasn't sure what to expect from the woman since Regina had disapproved of her and Dylan's marriage.

Though Regina had disapproved of the divorce even more.

Jordan had never been able to figure the woman out, and she didn't have her figured out now. That's because Regina smiled, and stretching out her arms again, Regina went to her, pulling her into a hug.

"I'm so glad you're here," Regina said, and she pulled back, their eyes connecting. "I was just about to tell Dylan about my visit with Adele, but now you can hear it, too." Regina's smile widened. "Adele and I had a wonderful visit. Just wonderful."

That didn't sound good at all, and Jordan moved to Dylan's side. "What did Adele say?" Jordan pressed.

More smiling. “Adele’s rethought this whole custody thing, and we’ve worked out a solution that should make all of us happy. The three of us will raise Corbin. Together.”

CHAPTER NINE

The three of us will raise Corbin. Together.

To Dylan, that sounded about as appealing as having every strand of his body hair plucked out with rusty tweezers.

It wasn't that he didn't love his mom. He did. But he loved her much better when they weren't around each other. Like now. Regina was *coochie-coochie-cooing* Corbin and smiling like a crazy person. Crazy because there was no one else joining in on that smilefest.

Including Jordan.

Apparently, she'd had enough of Regina's baby talk because she huffed and moved in front of the woman. "What do you mean about us raising Corbin together? Adele told me that she wanted Dylan to have custody."

As if stepping away from a coiled rattlesnake, Lawson, Lily Rose and their families all started to move, heading back to their vehicles. Even Karlee and Lucian went inside. Not Theo, though. The man must have thought his presence was somehow going to help this situation. It wouldn't. Jordan realized that, too, because she glanced at him.

"Theo, I need to stay here and work out some things," Jordan said. "I'll call you later."

It had a distinctive *don't let the door hit you in the*

ass tone to it, and lover boy finally seemed to get it. First though, he went to Jordan and hugged her. Then, Theo kissed her. Though it was just a peck on the mouth.

Dylan could do a whole lot better. Heck, that whole lot better had happened just minutes earlier in the barn, and he was still feeling the effects of it, too. Later, Jordan would likely want to talk to him about it, if only to tell him it was a mistake that shouldn't happen again. He'd agree.

And then probably kiss her again.

When it came to Jordan he pretty much had no willpower. Dylan wasn't proud of that, but sometimes that idiot behind the zipper of his jeans didn't give him a choice about such things.

At least what he felt for her was just physical. It would have been worse if his heart had gotten in on this. He was no longer in love with Jordan—and he had to make sure it stayed that way. He definitely didn't want old emotion and baggage to interfere if Jordan and he had to team up against the *coochie-coochie* woman who'd given birth to him.

"Remember that time we took a trip to Mexico?" Theo asked her. Apparently, he'd decided to linger around a bit after all.

Jordan groaned loud enough that Dylan was guessing that wasn't a pleasant event. "Theo, I don't want to talk about rashes, bleaching or tats."

Yeah, definitely unpleasant, and Dylan hoped all of those things hadn't actually happened on that one trip.

"Neither do I," Theo assured her. "I want you to remember that I had the right idea about hiking out to those ruins. Remember? A hurricane washed them away just a month later, and if you hadn't seen them when you did, you would have missed the chance of a lifetime."

Her next huff wasn't as loud as the first one, but it still smacked of frustration. "Just go ahead and say what you're trying to say and quit trying to tie it to a lesson."

So that's what Theo was trying to do. Dylan wondered if Theo knew that he sucked at it.

"I'm well aware that the timing is bad for this," Theo continued. He took the ring box from his pocket and handed it to Jordan, obviously ignoring all the mood signals she was giving him. Even Corbin could have picked up on her body language, and the language was yelling that this was the worst possible time to give her an engagement ring. "But I want you to hold on to this for a while and think about it."

She was shaking her head the whole time he was talking, but that didn't stop Theo from pushing the box into her shirt pocket. Jordan looked ready to push it right back at him, maybe into his face, but Theo took off, practically running to get into his car. He didn't drive away, though. He sat there and made a call. Maybe to the airlines to work out a return flight.

Now that he had some semiprivacy with his mom, Dylan went with the most obvious question. Well, the most obvious other than why she had taken up baby babbling. "Why are you doing this?" Dylan came out and asked her.

"Because I love this little snookum." Regina just kept up the attempts to goose, patty-cake and do other things that only seemed to make Corbin hide his face even more. At this rate, the kid was going to smother himself.

"Please stop," Dylan warned her, but he tried to keep his tone pleasant so he wouldn't upset Corbin. "And talk to me. Use adult words and your inside voice. Why?"

Finally, his mother's expression got serious, and Jordan must have known the next part of this conversation wasn't going to involve any patty-cakes. "Corbin, would you like lunch now?"

That got the boy's head lifting off Dylan's shoulder. "Pep-ronni?" Corbin asked.

"Maybe. If there's any leftover. If not, I'll fix you something." Jordan took him from Dylan, easing Corbin into her arms.

Dylan had to hand it to Jordan. She didn't glare at his mom as she took Corbin inside. But Dylan doubted he was able to hold back in the glare department. He didn't like that he was going to have to say some unpleasant things to her.

In his mind, Dylan said: *Remember when Dad and you got a divorce, and you stepped up to become this wonderful mom who made sure her kids weren't hurt from the flak of a nasty divorce?*

And his mom probably would answer: *There's no need for sarcasm. I was an emotional mess, and it wouldn't have helped any of you had I stayed.*

Then, he would snap: *An emotional mess would have been better than no mess at all, and I can't forget that you left Lucian to finish raising us. FYI, Lucian hasn't forgotten it, either.*

That was the past, his mom would argue.

And then she would probably start to cry.

Dylan silently cursed. It was impossible to argue—even mentally—with a crying woman, especially when these tears wouldn't be fake. Words, even truthful ones, would hurt her, and as mad as he was, he couldn't do that. Well, not unless she kept pressing about this custody and doing that annoying baby talk. So he tried a different angle.

"You'rc rccovcring from brcast canccr." And Dylan said that out loud.

"I'm in remission." But yes, even that caused her eyes to water. "I think Corbin needs all of us," Regina went on. "I certainly need him. I lost all those years with Lawson and Eve's daughter, because I didn't know about her. Well, I don't want to lose another minute with my grandson."

"You already have a grandson. Two of them." His sister's son and Lawson's stepson.

Regina nodded. "I could have a dozen, and I'd still want this time with Corbin. All of my grandbabies are precious to me. And I know I wasn't the best mom, but I want to change all of that. I want to be there for Corbin."

"That doesn't mean you should push for custody," Dylan countered.

If she heard him, she didn't acknowledge it. She just kept on talking. "And you haven't been the most reliable with the steady flow of women in and out of your bed. Did you know there's a bingo game about you and that one of the squares is have sex with Dylan during a thunderstorm?"

Well, that explained why he kept getting calls from women when there was rain in the forecast.

He needed to gather up those cards, and he couldn't be the one to do it since most were in the hands of women who wanted to play the game. He'd need to pay one of the hands to collect them. Or maybe he could offer a reward for anyone who turned them in. A reward that didn't involve any kind of sexual favors.

"I didn't start the game," he assured her. "Hell, I'm not even playing it, and there have been no squares filled recently."

Unless there was one about kissing his ex-wife in a barn. That one would have gotten a box ticked off for sure.

"But you have to admit that you've been pretty liberal with your…square filling," his mother added.

He would eat a field of cactus before admitting that to her. That definitely wouldn't help him with this argument he was trying to win.

"I'm not doing this to be mean," Regina went on. "But I'm worried that Jordan and you aren't going to be able to do right by that boy."

Dylan was worried about it, too, but there'd be more cacti on the menu before he let his mom know that.

"Adele wanted me to raise Corbin," he reminded her. And since Jordan had already told her that, it wasn't the first time his mom had heard it.

Regina nodded. "She did until we had a chat. Did you know that she was drunk the night Corbin was conceived?"

Hell, that must have been some conversation. A reminder that he was going on the wagon. And trying out celibacy for a while. Ironic since the no-sex vow had come from drinking too much.

Because a discussion about Corbin's conception wasn't going to win him any arguments, either, Dylan went with a different approach. "What did you and Walter Ray say to Adele? And why did you even take the judge with you to the jail?"

For just a second his mom's eyes widened, so maybe she didn't know that he was well aware of Walter Ray tailing along on the visit. The eye widening soon turned to some gaze dodging, though.

"Walter Ray is a friend, and he's been, well, giving me some legal advice. Believe me when I tell you that I think this is for the best," his mom said. "For now, just sleep on what I'm about to tell you and see how you feel about it in the morning. I'm betting you'll feel a whole lot better about it."

That was code for this was going to piss him off even more than he already was.

"Jordan is probably going to fight to get custody of Corbin," Regina announced as if that was some big surprise. It wasn't. "And that wouldn't be a good idea."

Again, not a revelation. Dylan was still working with the wacky notion that a father had more say in something like this than a second cousin.

"Walter Ray found out some things," Regina added a moment later. "Things about Jordan." She paused. "Jordan's on meds, Dylan."

Okay, finally they were at the revelation stage. Well, sort of. "After what she went through, it's not surprising that she'd need something to take the edge off the anxiety."

"It's more than just to soothe the edge." With all the other pausing and ho-humming she'd been doing, he hadn't expected his mother to answer that quickly. "Walter Ray talked to some friends at the base, and even though what he heard isn't anything official, it's possible that Jordan's not mentally stable. And that she never will be."

Dylan opened his mouth to defend Jordan but then realized he couldn't.

His mother looked him right in the eyes. "That's why you and I need to work together to make sure that Adele doesn't hand Corbin over to Jordan."

JORDAN WAS BACK *THERE*. In the dark hole in the ground where the men had put her. She could smell the hot sand, feel the grit of it on her skin and the itchy sweat snaking its way down her back.

She grabbed onto the sides of the hole. Trying to use anything for leverage, but she couldn't get her footing, and that only caused the panic to rise in her even more.

She was dreaming. Jordan knew that but couldn't stop the images from coming. Her nerves were firing just beneath her skin, and her breathing was way too fast. She would soon hyperventilate, maybe even pass out.

God, she wanted to pass out.

Even if it was for a couple of moments, she didn't want to know she was there. There, where she had no control and was at the mercy of these men.

She was a coward.

Despite all her training and experience, she hadn't felt brave. Only afraid. And she was still afraid. Even though Theo and the others had pulled her out of that hole, it didn't stop. She still didn't have that same sense of who she'd once been…

"Uh, could you let go of my balls?" someone gritted out.

The words were so clear. So jarring. And they immediately snapped Jordan out of the dream. Her eyes flew open, and that's when she realized those words weren't part of those other images of that place. Someone had actually spoken them.

Dylan.

Thanks to the moonlight streaming through the window, Jordan had no trouble seeing him. He was on her bed, looming over her, and she did indeed have her hand clamped around his man parts. And he had a severely pained look on his face.

The pained look lessened some when she let go of him.

"Sorry," she mumbled.

Grunting and groaning, he rolled away from her, landing in a flop on his back next to her. "Nothing wrong with your grip," he said, though the pained look extended to his voice.

Jordan glanced around, trying to figure out what was happening. The dream was gone, chased away by Dylan's voice, but the rest of this wasn't making sense. Dylan was in her bed, and he was wearing only his boxers.

"What are you doing here?" she asked.

He didn't look at her. Dylan just lay there on his back while clutching his groin and doing battle with his sputtering breath. "You were talking really loud in your sleep, and I thought something was wrong."

Oh mercy. Talking? Worse, it'd been enough to wake Dylan in the other room. Jordan hoped she hadn't said anything that she didn't want Dylan to hear. And since she'd been dreaming about the hole, everything about it fell into the category of something she hadn't wanted him to hear.

"Are you okay?" she pressed. "Did I hurt you?"

"Yes to both. Or at least I will be okay when the breath-robbing agony goes away."

And speaking of *breath-robbing*, that's what happened when Dylan turned his head and looked at her. That's because, despite the pain, he gave her one of his smiles. The kind of smile that usually rid her and other women of their common sense. Common sense would have turned down the burner on the simmering heat and sent him back to his own room.

That didn't happen.

Jordan just stayed put. Eyes locked. And she froze when he reached up and pushed her hair from her face. Jordan tried to steel herself up for whatever he was about to do. A scalding kiss, maybe.

Maybe sex.

Sex that couldn't happen despite the fact that he was in bed with her. At least they weren't naked.

"My balls are better," he said, and he rolled off the bed and to his feet.

Well, that was good, and thankfully it wasn't one of Dylan's sweet-talk lines to go with that common-sense-stealing smile.

"Next time I hear you talking and thrashing around in here, I'll wear protective gear," he added. Then the smile faded. “My guess is that you’d dread just about anything I say right now?”

That was true. Jordan didn’t want to talk about the hole, the dream, the thrashing around or talking in her sleep. Ditto for the condition of his balls. And she definitely didn’t want to talk about that kiss in the barn. Or the fact that he’d slept with the person she thought of as a kid sister.

Though, one day, she did want to have it out with him about that if he ever remembered sleeping with Adele, that is.

She nodded in answer to his question.

He nodded as an acceptance of that.

Good. They were on the same page. There was nothing to discuss. No reason for Dylan to stay. And that’s why Jordan was surprised at what she felt when he walked out of the room.

Disappointment.

Dylan made it all the way to the door before he stopped. He didn’t turn around. He kept his back to her. “The ball squeezing at least stopped me from getting a hard-on.”

Jordan looked down at herself. No gown—she hadn’t gotten around to washing it. No bra. No panties. Hell’s Bells. She was naked.

“Love the navel ring, though,” Dylan drawled as he strolled away.

CHAPTER TEN

DYLAN HAD TAKEN one part of his mom's advice and had slept on it.

Well, he'd tossed and turned while in bed all the while thinking about the roller-coaster ride that Adele was taking them on with her stupid demands. Walter Ray was taking them for a ride, too, by putting doubts in his mind about Jordan's mental state.

Seeing Jordan in her birthday suit had also caused Dylan some sleepless moments. And it had also required him to take a cold shower. If she'd grabbed his dick instead of his balls when they'd been in that bed, he might have had some tossing and turning about having sex with his ex. Something he would have regretted, afterward anyway.

Jordan had been the first woman he'd ever seen fully naked. Of course, she'd still been a teenager then. Just sixteen. Despite that tender age, he'd set all standards by Jordan's body, and she was still hands down the winner. That reminder definitely hadn't helped things, and it'd gotten mixed and mulled around when he'd been trying to sort out how he was going to handle this mess with his mother and Walter Ray.

Now that it was morning, one thing that Dylan knew for a fact was that his mother had been wrong. Not just about her custody bid but also the sleeping on it. He didn't feel one bit better about sharing custody or the house with her or Jordan.

He figured Jordan and he were on the same page, too. Because all these hours later, she was just as riled at Adele as he was. Too bad that neither of them could actually tell Adele that to her face, but so far the woman had turned down their requests for visits.

At least Regina, Jordan and he had worked out a schedule so they didn't step on each other's toes while his mom and he would also keep an eye on Jordan. They would get Corbin in two-hour increments, and there was a no interference rule. When it was Dylan's two hours, then Jordan/Regina couldn't interfere. The same applied when it was their time.

During Dylan's two-hour shifts, he had learned that being a dad was the best thing in the world. Hell, no wonder people did this. But the goal was for him to be a full-time dad. No splitting time. No one, aka Regina, looking over his shoulder to make sure he wasn't screwing things up. He might be able to reach that goal when and if Adele would see him.

Pushing that aside for now, Dylan signed the latest invoices for the ranch and moved on to the rest of the paperwork that was on his desk in his home office. Normally, he didn't mind doing ranching stuff, but he had a distraction today.

Jordan and Corbin.

It was her two hours with the boy, and they were playing in the yard in direct line of sight from his window. Well, it was direct if he moved to the side a little, which he'd done. He wasn't sure exactly what game they were playing, but it involved tossing a ball that neither Jordan nor Corbin managed to catch, followed by chasing, then followed by falling to the ground and laughing.

Booger was in on the playtime, but his participation was limited to sprinting around them in circles while stopping occasionally to try to piss on something. Once, it'd been Jordan's leg, but she'd managed to get out of the way in the nick of time.

He signed another invoice and read a supply report, but every few seconds, he glanced at the timer. His shift was coming up in only fifteen minutes, and he was going to take Corbin to the barn to show him a new horse they'd gotten in. It wasn't one that Corbin could ride since Lucian was going to use it to help him train for the bronc riding event in the charity rodeo, but Corbin enjoyed just looking at the horses and tossing hay around. The kid could make a game out of anything.

There was a knock at the door. A lazy-sounding tap. And a moment later, the cook, Abe Weiser came in. The man moved with as little effort as his knock so it took him a few seconds to make it to Dylan.

"That'll be six hundred and thirty dollars," Abe announced, and he dropped a stack of papers on the desk.

But these weren't business invoices. They were the sex bingo cards.

"There's sixty-three of them at ten dollars apiece," Abe reminded him.

That had indeed been the deal. A deal that all the hands and the two housekeepers had turned down. Only Abe had agreed to go around collecting them, and that was after he'd negotiated for paid time off to do it. While Dylan would gladly pay every penny to get the cards, it was disturbing that there were so many of them.

And not all of them were blank.

In the couple that Dylan looked at, some of the boxes had been filled in, including one that claimed he'd given someone a belly hickey. Since there were no names or dates on the card, he didn't have a clue who'd marked it. Or if it was even true because he was certain he'd given a belly hickey or two over the years.

Yeah, celibacy was looking pretty darn appealing.

"Where and how did you get these cards?" Dylan asked, and he hoped the cook hadn't resorted to thievery.

"I stole some of them," Abe readily admitted, causing Dylan to wince. "And in a couple of cases, I bribed a sibling to get them." He paused. "I figured you'd pay me back for the bribes. That's another eighty-one dollars and sixteen cents."

Dylan nearly asked why the odd number, but he really didn't want to know. He just wanted the damn cards. He'd already called Tiffany Kelly and demanded that she not print any more. Tiffany had blown it off with a flirtatious giggle and a request for thunderstorm sex, but she'd finally understood when Dylan had told her that something like this could jeopardize custody of Corbin.

"I'll keep looking for more," Abe went on. "Should I search outside of Wrangler's Creek?"

"Not for now. Keep it local." But if the cards continued to show up, he might have to hire a team of gatherers like Abe to scour the state.

Dylan wrote Abe a check from his personal account. Money well spent. Plus, it was the most work he'd ever known Abe to do. For a cook, Abe didn't spend much time in the kitchen. Actually, the bulk of his day was devoted to napping.

After Abe left his office, Dylan started shredding the cards, and since the paper was thin, he was able to triple them up to make the process go faster. Each grind of the blades felt like a victory. What didn't feel like a victory was the call he got while he was still shredding.

Melanie.

Since it was so close to his time with Corbin, Dylan let it go to voice mail. But eventually he was going to have to talk to her and repeat his refusal of her marriage offer. He had to believe that eventually it'd sink in.

Once he'd finished with the shredding, he stood and looked out the window, expecting to see Jordan and Corbin playing. They weren't there. Even Booger was no longer doing his pee-markings.

Dylan felt a quick tug of panic that caused him to frown. He'd known about his son for only two days, and yet his go-to response was that something godawful had happened. That he'd gotten hurt while playing and Jordan had had to rush him inside. And in the next couple of seconds, Dylan realized how parents got from worrying about a child to that whole "in a ditch" thing they were always coming up with.

Great. At this rate, he'd be a celibate teetotaler with an ulcer.

Running now, he made his way through the house,

in search of them, and the relief came when he heard Jordan's voice. Or at least it came until he actually heard her words.

"I just need to put a bandage on it," she said. "Don't cry, Corbin. It'll be okay."

That put his worrying into overdrive, and he raced toward the sound of her voice. She was in the bathroom near the back porch. The door was open, and when Dylan went bursting in, he saw something he darn sure didn't want to see.

Blood. It was on a tissue next to the sink. Next to it was a first aid kit.

Corbin was sitting on the counter with Jordan right in front of him, and the boy did look on the verge of crying. Dylan immediately searched him for signs of injury. None. But then Jordan turned, and he saw the blood on her arm.

There was no alarm in her eyes until she saw the alarm in his. "Is something wrong?" Jordan blurted out. But then she followed his gaze to her arm. "There was a rock in the yard, and I fell on it. It's just a scratch."

The relief came. Then, more panic. He needed to check the yard for rocks and such, so that this didn't happen again. It was indeed just a scratch, but it could have been much worse if Corbin had fallen on it.

"Jordy got boo-boo," Corbin said, and he still looked as if he might cry.

"It's okay, really," Jordan assured him, and as soon as she had the bandage in place, she brushed a kiss on Corbin's head. Corbin sort of melted against her, going right into Jordan's arms.

"He asked about his mommy," Jordan mouthed to Dylan.

Hell, that caused panic, too, even though he'd expected that to happen. Despite everything, Adele was still Corbin's mom, and he had to be missing her.

Dylan heard the movement outside the door and saw Regina. He wasn't sure how long she had been there, but Booger was next to her. Neither of them came closer. Maybe she was observing him to see if he was going to screw this up. Booger was trying to see if he could chew the heel off Regina's right shoe. Dylan ignored both and focused on Corbin.

"Are you okay, buddy?" Dylan asked.

Corbin nodded, but he also wiped his eyes with the back of his hand. Dylan had seen him do that when he was tired, but this looked to be more from the threatening tears than fatigue. He nearly asked Corbin if he wanted some ice cream, but that probably wasn't a good way to handle sadness. Though Dylan might try some on himself just to see if it worked. It broke his heart to see Corbin like this.

"What happened?" Dylan whispered to Jordan. "What brought this on?"

"Adele used to play chase with him."

Dylan's first reaction was to think—no more chasing games—but he'd seen how much fun it had been for Corbin. So maybe the way to deal with this was head-on. "Your mommy can't be here right now, but Jordy and me will take good care of you. And Grandma Regina will, too," he added.

Corbin stared at him. An "I'm giving this some

thought" kind of stare. "O-tay." He hugged Jordan and then Dylan.

The kid sure had a whole lot of trust in them, considering they were all still just strangers to him. And Dylan wanted to make sure that trust wasn't misplaced. That meant he needed to do something.

"I'll call and see when we can take Corbin in for a visit to see Adele," he said. "Then, I…*we* need to work on something more permanent for his bedroom."

Dylan didn't mind sleeping on the floor next to Corbin, but the boy needed a bed that was geared to his age.

"I can take care of his room," Regina offered.

He nearly told her no, but that was a knee-jerk reaction to her screwing things over with the custody. Plus, his mom would be a lot better at that sort of thing than he would.

"I can call about getting us in to see Adele," Jordan said.

No knee-jerk reaction that time, though there was a reaction when Dylan glanced at the front of her shirt. Or rather he glanced in the direction of that navel ring.

"Maybe we can also talk about Corbin's ring bearer suit," Regina added, getting Dylan's attention off what it should have never been on in the first place.

Dylan looked at Jordan to see if she knew anything about that, but she shook her head. "A ring bearer?" Jordan asked his mom. "You mean for Lawson and Eve's wedding?"

His mom nodded and came closer. "The wedding's just a little over a week from now, but I thought it'd be cute if Corbin was part of it. Lawson and Eve agreed."

Dylan suspected there was some coercion involved in that. Both Eve and his brother wanted everything low-key, but maybe they'd all decided that it would make Corbin feel more like a part of the family.

"Eve mentioned it to me," Jordan explained. "When she invited me to the wedding."

Again, more coercion. It'd started with his mom, but now it would ensure that Jordan was at the ceremony. Dylan didn't mind. Eve and Jordan were old friends, but he didn't want this to be too much for Corbin.

"I can order him a little cowboy suit to wear," his mother added. She held up a tape measure. "I just need to make sure I get the right size."

"What about it?" Dylan asked Corbin. "You want to be in the wedding and help carry a ring or two?"

Corbin probably didn't get all of that, but he nodded. "We'll ride de horsey?"

Dylan had to smile. "Yep, we can do that afterward. And there'll be cake at the reception."

You would have thought he'd just offered Corbin the sun, stars and a moon or two because his whole face lit up. This time his nod was a lot more enthusiastic.

Jordan stood Corbin on the floor, and the boy went to Regina, who was motioning for him to come to her. Corbin did, but only after Jordan and Dylan walked in that direction with him. They stayed back a little though, so that they weren't hovering over him.

"I'm sorry about last night," Jordan whispered to him.

Dylan had wondered if she was going to bring that up. "Don't worry about it. You helped me with my vow of celibacy. I had trouble walking this morning when I got up."

Jordan gave him a funny look. Then, glanced down at his zipper region. And that's when Dylan realized this wasn't about his sore nuts. It was the birthday suit thing.

"*That* didn't help with my celibacy," he joked.

Her mouth moved a little as if a smile was coming on, but it didn't quite spring to life because his phone rang. When he took it out of his pocket, he saw Melanie's name again on the screen. Two calls from her in the past ten minutes.

"Go ahead. Answer it," Jordan insisted, stepping away from him and heading toward Corbin and his mom.

Since his time had already started with Corbin, Dylan almost declined the call, but maybe he should just go ahead and tell Melanie that he was busy and would have to get back to her. But he didn't get a chance to say anything to her because Melanie started the moment he answered.

"Don't be mad at me, please," Melanie begged. "Everything just sort of happened."

That was not the way he wanted any conversation with anyone to start—especially from a woman who kept trying to marry him. "What are you talking about?" he asked when he stepped away from the others.

Melanie made a sound, dread mixed with frustration. Yet something else he didn't especially want in conversation. "I was out gathering up those bingo cards for Abe. He said you wanted the game to stop."

"*You* gathered the cards?" Dylan clarified.

"Yes. And FYI, I think it's a stellar idea that you're finally putting a stop to that stupid game."

Apparently, he needed to have a little chat with Abe about subletting his bingo-collecting duties, especially since Abe had gotten paid for it.

"Anyway, I was on one of the card missions," Melanie went on, "when I ran into Theo at the Longhorn. You know, Jordan's boyfriend."

"I know him. You mean you ran into him yesterday before he left?"

"Oh, Theo didn't leave. He's still here in town. He's staying at the inn."

Well, that was a surprise, and he wondered if Jordan knew that. If so, she hadn't said a peep about it. Nor had she shared Theo's room because she'd been at the ranch the whole time.

"Theo was drinking," Melanie went on. "And he started telling me things. I swear, I didn't mean to hear what he said, but he wouldn't shut up."

Again, Dylan had to ask, "What are you talking about?"

"Theo." Melanie stopped again, and it sounded as if she'd gathered her breath. "He said that he'd slept with Adele a few years ago and that he thought he might be Corbin's father."

CHAPTER ELEVEN

GOAT SNOT. WORM PISS. And toad puke.

Jordan had heard those words often. They'd been some of her mom's favorite *terms of endearment* for men who'd seemingly done her wrong. Which had happened much too often. Obviously, when it came to insults, her mom had preferred to pair various critters with their disgusting bodily fluids.

She didn't want to put Theo into that "done her wrong" box. Mainly because he wasn't her actual boyfriend. But he had been once. And until Jordan talked to him, she didn't know if his boyfriend status had overlapped with his sex with Adele. Or even if sex had actually happened with her cousin. It seemed like too much of a bad coincidence that Adele had been with not one but two of Jordan's exes.

Theo and Adele knew each other, of course, and shortly after they'd met, the three of them had spent that "interesting" evening together when Theo had bailed Adele out when she'd gotten arrested. Maybe that had created some kind of bond between Theo and Adele. A bond that had led to sex.

While Dylan drove them to San Antonio to the jail, Jordan tried to call Theo for the umpteenth time to get his side on what Melanie had told Dylan. No answer.

That could be because he was on his way back to Germany or else he was avoiding her. Avoiding Dylan, too, since he'd also tried to call Theo a couple of times, as well.

"I think Melanie's dead wrong," Regina said. "Either she misunderstood Theo, or maybe she said that so she could get Dylan back. If he's not tied up with raising Corbin, then Melanie might think it'll improve her chances of mending their relationship."

It was a repeat for the umpteenth time of variations of what Dylan's mother had already said. Regina had insisted on going with them to the jail to talk to Adele, and she was in the back, next to Corbin, who was sacked out in his car seat. Jordan doubted anything good could come from Regina accompanying them, but the woman probably couldn't make things worse, either. Things were already pretty rock-bottom in the emotion department.

At least that's how Dylan felt.

She had seen that look on his face before. When she'd told him that their marriage was over and she was leaving. He'd looked crushed, just like now, and while he'd clearly gotten over their breakup, this one might not be so easy to get past. Band-Aid sex fixed broken relationships, temporarily anyway, but nothing could fix losing a child that you loved. And she had no doubts that Dylan loved Corbin.

"I don't think Adele would have lied about me being Corbin's father," Dylan mumbled. That, too, fell into the umpteenth time repeat category.

Jordan wanted to believe that. Adele could be impulsive and irresponsible, but she wasn't a liar. Well, except she hadn't mentioned her previous arrests to Jordan. Or Corbin. So maybe Adele had slept with both Dylan and Theo and didn't know the father of her child. Of course, she had named Corbin after Dylan so maybe there was no uncertainty about paternity in Adele's mind. That's why she had to talk to Adele and find out if Theo had any chance of being part of Corbin's gene pool.

"I know this is going to be a hard visit," Regina went on, "and Adele will want to see Corbin. But it's best if there's no conversation about daddy-hood in front of him."

Finally, they all agreed on something. Jordan wasn't sure how much of this Corbin could actually understand, but they couldn't take the risk of upsetting him. Especially since the boy did indeed call Dylan *Daddy*.

"You two can go in and talk to Adele first, and then I can bring in Corbin after I'm sure there won't be any more yelling," Regina added.

Again, they were in agreement, though Dylan only voiced his with a grunt. He hadn't said a lot on the drive from the ranch, but then there wasn't much to be said until they spoke to Adele and Theo.

While Dylan pulled into the parking lot of the jail, Jordan tried once again to call Theo. Still nothing. Too bad because she would have liked to get his side of the story before this visit even started. Maybe, just maybe, Theo's comments were just said by a man who'd had too much to drink.

Dylan gently hoisted a still-sleeping Corbin out of his seat, and with the boy resting against his chest and shoulder, they went in, making their way through the rungs of security. Jordan had called ahead to get the paperwork started, but it still took them a good fifteen minutes to get back to the visitors' section. Once they were in the waiting area, Dylan brushed a kiss on Corbin's forehead and handed him to Regina.

"Remember the safe words that we had when we were together?" Jordan asked him as they walked toward the visiting room.

Dylan glanced at her and frowned.

"Not *those* safe words," she amended. "These didn't have anything to do with sex. They were for when things were getting too heated between us during an argument. We thought it would keep us from saying plenty that we might regret." Which had happened way too often when they were nineteen. "Yours was—"

"*Sasquatch*," he provided, "and yours was *Popsicle*."

It was surprising that he remembered them after all this time. Even more surprising that he didn't verbally object to using them now. After all, they hadn't worked so well back then. They'd still argued, and the escalated arguments had led to their split-up.

When they went into the visiting room, Adele was already there and seated at the table. She smiled, but that quickly faded when she saw their expressions. "Did something happen to Corbin?"

"He's fine," Jordan assured her. Dylan and she sat across from Adele. "You'll get to see him in a few minutes, but for now we need to talk about Theo."

Jordan had held out hope that Melanie had been totally wrong about all of this, but one look at Adele's face, and she knew there was at least some truth to it. Dylan figured it out as well because he groaned, and

Jordan felt every bit of his pain in that sound. That's why she threw some caution to the wind and gave his hand a quick squeeze. Dylan didn't pull back, but his muscles were so stiff that it was like touching a rock.

"Do you need any questions from us to get started on an explanation?" Jordan prompted when Adele didn't say anything.

Adele shook her head. "I guess Theo told you that we slept together."

Dylan muttered some profanity, and since he looked ready to do more than mutter it, Jordan gave him the safe word. "Sasquatch."

Of course, that caused some confusion to go through Adele's eyes, but Jordan didn't bother clarifying. Not when it was Adele who had a mountain of clarification to do.

"Why did you lie about Corbin?" Dylan growled.

Adele's eyes widened a moment, and her attention volleyed from Dylan to Jordan. "Did Theo tell you he was Corbin's father? Because he's not. I swear, he's not," she repeated to Jordan.

Jordan didn't feel any relief yet. In fact, she wasn't sure what she should feel. It didn't matter who Corbin's father was—the boy would always be her cousin. But she hated the idea that Adele could have been yanking Dylan's chain about fatherhood.

"I slept with Theo, sure," Adele went on, "but that happened months before I got pregnant with Corbin."

Finally, she felt Dylan's muscles relax, and he quit with the under-the-breath profanity. Jordan, however, wasn't anywhere near the point of relaxing yet.

"Any reason you didn't tell me that you'd had sex with my boyfriend?" Jordan asked.

"The same reason I didn't tell you that I'd had sex with your ex-husband. You weren't with them at the time. You'd broken up with Theo months before that, and he called me when he was in San Antonio. And as for Dylan, well, that was long over between you two."

Her mind promptly reminded her of the very recent memory of the barn kiss. And Dylan being on her bed. Heck, the nonrecent memories came back, too, causing Jordan to mumble her own round of profanity. Some of it wasn't mumbled, though.

"Popsicle," Dylan said to her.

In that moment, she hated safe words. Hated Adele. And Jordan especially hated memories that were messing with her head.

"And FYI," Adele went on, "I didn't plan to sleep with Theo. It just sort of happened."

Had this been any other person, Jordan could have argued that sex didn't just happen, but this was a woman who'd stolen flip-flops and Twizzlers. Adele's life had seemingly been a string of things that'd "just happened" or else really stupid things that she'd planned.

That didn't stop this from stinging, though. And it riled Jordan that it stung. She should be past these feelings, and she was with Theo. He'd only been her boyfriend, but Dylan, well, he was a different matter. It was that damn kiss again. Her being next to him didn't help, either.

"I'm sorry," Adele said to her, and after she paused again, she opened her mouth as if she might say more.

She didn't. Adele seemed to change her mind when she glanced at Dylan.

"Are you doing okay with Corbie?" Adele asked him. "Is he being a good boy for Jordan, Regina and you?"

A muscle flickered in Dylan's jaw. Maybe because Adele had included his mom and her in that question. Or it could be because Adele didn't seem as bothered as she should about all of the lives she'd disrupted. Of course, it was hard to feel too disrupted because Corbin was also in that equation. At the very center of it. Without Corbin, there would be no safe word strong enough to keep Jordan from venting about what Adele had done.

"He's being very good," Dylan answered, his jaw still twitching. "Now, why didn't you tell me about him before you landed in jail?"

Adele lifted her shoulder. "I didn't think you'd want to know."

Oh no. Definitely not the thing to say to Dylan. Yes, he was a player, but he didn't shirk responsibility. That's why he still ran the family ranch when some of his other siblings had long moved on.

"Sasquatch," Jordan whispered to him before he could get out a single curse word.

Adele smiled as if there was actually something to smile about. "Is that some kind of lover's word you two are using?" Her smile widened. "And are you two getting back together?"

There was nothing flatter than the flat look Jordan gave her cousin. "No and no," she said, answering the question. But then something occurred to her. Something that might make her need the safe word, too. "Please tell me that you didn't mean for this custody arrangement to be a way to play matchmaker for Dylan and me."

"No," Adele jumped to say, but her next pause had Jordan bristling. "Well, it wouldn't be the worst thing, would it? I mean, I always thought Dylan and you should have given it another try."

"Yet you had sex with him." Jordan regretted that the moment the words left her mouth. She sounded jealous. She wasn't, but since she didn't know what she was, she waved it off. "Quit playing with our lives. With Regina's, too. Did you think she would help with your matchmaking?"

No smile this time. Adele's face bunched up. "No, I told her she could share custody because she was threatening to take Corbie. And Walter Ray was egging her on to do it." She turned to Dylan. "I definitely don't think Walter Ray wants Jordan and you back together. Did you know he's trying to pair you up with his daughter?"

Dylan beat Jordan in the flat look department. "I knew," he grumbled. "So, you only included my mom in the custody because she pressured you. Well now I'm the one who's pressuring you. Regina's about to come in here in a few minutes, and you can tell her that the shared custody deal is off. I'm Corbin's father, and I should be raising him."

Dylan stopped and looked at Jordan. "Sorry, but it's how I feel," he added.

Jordan hadn't doubted that. But she didn't want to be booted out of this arrangement, either. She was about to tell Adele that, too, but her cousin held up her hand.

"I want to keep things as they are for now." Adele definitely wasn't using her flighty voice, and she spoke directly to Dylan. "Regina can be stubborn, but Corbie needs a grandmother. He needs family, and that includes a father and someone who can stand in for me as his mother. That's why I wanted Jordan to be part of this. Temporarily, anyway. I figure a month is all she'll be able to take in Wrangler's Creek before her wanderlust kicks in."

Normally, Jordan could have easily seen that happening. But "the hole" had changed her. Heck, Corbin had changed her.

"I've been thinking about getting out of the Air Force," Jordan threw out there. "*Seriously* thinking about it. In fact, I'm going to the base first thing next week to see what I'd need to do to make that happen." She had gone over it so many times in her mind that she hadn't realized it would be a surprise to Dylan and Adele.

Still no smile from Adele. Definitely not one from Dylan, either. That's because they didn't believe she could do it. This was like Dylan ending his womanizing ways. Obviously, no one had a lot of faith in either Dylan or her. For a good reason, too.

Because Jordan herself wasn't sure she could pull it off.

Even now, she could feel the tightness in her chest and the flood of old memories. Not just those of her not being able to make a go of it with Dylan, either.

Plenty of those memories involved her mother and her need to call men those vile names. There'd been chaos and neglect. No safety net. And while it wasn't exactly something others might understand, all of that had gotten rolled into being in Wrangler's Creek. She'd always thought if she could just get out, that the bad stuff would fade enough for her to forget it.

Most days, anyway.

It had, too. The memories had faded. The fear of having no safety net had lessened. Until those men had put her in the hole. Then, it had all come crashing down on her and was still crashing. Smothering her. Making her want to run to try to find another net.

"Jordan," Adele said, her voice doused with concern. "Are you okay?"

That's when Jordan realized she was breathing too fast, and judging from the way Dylan and Adele were looking at her, they thought she might be on the verge of a panic attack. Which she probably was. It certainly didn't help that she was locked into this place and this room.

"It's probably time for Adele to see Corbin," Dylan told Jordan as he helped her to her feet.

That's when Jordan realized something else—that she actually needed help to stand. She cursed, and even though it was pretty raw, Dylan didn't scold her with a safe word reminder.

"I'll come back for another visit so we can talk," he added to Adele.

Adele gave a shaky nod as if she wasn't looking forward to that or maybe the nod was just because she was worried about Jordan. Jordan knew how she felt because she was worried, as well. It'd been a too-extreme reaction.

Dylan kept his arm looped around her while he

walked Jordan to the door. "I was just thinking about that time we were having sex in my truck, and you accidentally kicked the gearshift."

Jordan frowned. She'd expected words of comfort. Words that probably wouldn't have helped, but this certainly wasn't helping, either.

Why the heck was he bringing that up now?

It reminded her of something Theo would say that he thought would make things better but never did. Remembering the gearshift incident definitely wouldn't make this better. Because when she'd kicked the truck into gear during the throes of foreplay, they had ended up rolling into the creek.

They'd gotten out just fine, but Dylan's truck had been ruined and their clothes and phones had washed away in the swift rain-bloated current. Dylan had still had on his jeans and boots, but she'd been butt naked. He'd given her his wet boxers to wear, and she had used his socks for a makeshift bra so they could walk to get some help. Or rather he'd walked and carried her since her flip-flops had floated away, too.

And that's how his brother, Lawson, had found them.

Lawson had given them a ride—after he'd snapped a picture that her mother and half the town had ended up seeing because Lawson hadn't been especially careful about showing it around.

"One of the squares on the Dylan Granger Bingo Sex game is to wear my boxers while being carried by me," Dylan added. "There's probably a sock-bra one, too, but I haven't seen it yet."

It was such a ridiculous thing, and that's probably

why it made her smile. A ridiculous memory as well, but it eased away the other stuff, and Jordan no longer felt as if she was in that hole or on the verge of a panic attack.

"Thank you," she said.

Dylan also smiled, and as usual his was a lot better than hers. "Anytime. If you need another distraction, we can talk about the time you put me up against a tree, and I ended up with a poison oak rash on my ass."

Yes, that would indeed be a distraction since she'd ended up being the one to doctor his butt with calamine lotion. It was a distracting memory and a smile all rolled into one. Jordan was still smiling with Dylan's arm still around her when they walked back into the waiting room.

And Theo was there.

Jordan was so stunned to see him that she froze. And, yes, she did that while still smiling. Something that Theo definitely noticed. Ditto for the hold Dylan had on her. Regina also noticed because she got to her feet while she had Corbin in her arms.

"I'll just take Corbin in to see Adele," Regina said at the same time Theo said, "I'm sorry."

Dylan wasn't staying quiet because he spoke right in sync with them. "Corbin's not your son."

Dylan's comment caused Theo to snap toward him. "But I was with Adele."

Regina mumbled a repeat of her going to see Adele, and she took Corbin out of the visiting room. Probably because she thought things were about to get heated. They weren't.

"Adele said you weren't the father," Jordan stated

as plainly as she could. The plainness involved some anger, though. She couldn't imagine how much worse the anger would have been if she'd actually been in love with Theo.

Theo shook his head. "She was positive?" But he didn't wait for an answer. "I want a DNA test done. You should want it done, too," he added to Dylan. "Adele might not even know which of us fathered the kid."

Dylan showed a lot more anger than she did. He took one step toward Theo. One very calculated, menacing step that put him close enough to Theo to violate plenty of the man's personal space.

"He's not *the kid*," Dylan said through clenched teeth. "He's Corbin Dylan Rivera. Do I need to explain that to you in a way that doesn't involve words?"

Oh no. Not this. A fight in a jail definitely wasn't a good idea. Jordan compounded that idea with one of her own. Facing Dylan, she wormed her way between them just as they went forward and squished her like a human Oreo.

"I'll get a court order to get a DNA test," Theo snarled.

"Why?" Jordan snarled back. "You've told me countless times that you didn't want to have children."

Theo didn't respond to that. But Dylan did.

"If he has Corbin, Theo thinks he'll get you," Dylan said, and yes, his teeth were still so clenched that his words were a little garbled.

Jordan glanced over her shoulder at Theo to see if that was a possibility. Crap. It was. Worse, Theo was smirking now as if daring Dylan to escalate this pissing contest to the point that it would result in no winners.

Especially not Corbin if there was indeed a long drawn-out custody fight. Theo might not be the only contestant in that fight, either. Regina might not back off.

"I think Adele said you were the dad because you're rich," Theo said, still aiming that smirk at Dylan.

Dylan wasn't smirking back, but his muscles were getting so tight that his eyes were practically pinched together. He wasn't quick to fight, but Theo was testing the limits here.

"Sasquatch," she tried, hoping that would make Dylan back off.

It didn't.

Dylan inched forward, his muscles still reacting to the anger he was no doubt feeling. Anger that would almost certainly lead to a face punching if she didn't do something to stop it.

Jordan hooked her hand around Dylan's neck, forcing him to look down at her. This called for something drastic. Unfortunately, she soon realized that she just wasn't very good when it came to non-work-related drastic situations. But at least she stopped a potential fight with what she said.

She also opened a big-assed can of worms.

"Marry me," Jordan blurted out to Dylan. "And we'll raise Corbin together."

CHAPTER TWELVE

DYLAN HAD GONE thirty-four years without a marriage proposal, and now he'd gotten two in the same week. He'd dismissed Melanie's right off, not giving it any more thought since she'd dropped that particular bombshell. Jordan's "marry me," from the previous week, however, was a whole different story.

It hadn't taken Dylan long to dismiss her proposal, either, figuring it was just another version of a safe word to stop him from punching out Theo's lights, followed by what would have almost certainly been his arrest. But there'd been no dismissing the proposal in his thoughts. It had flicked its way into his thoughts for the past four days, and it was still flicking like crazy. Not because it was a good idea.

It wasn't.

But it sure brought back memories of when he and Jordan had actually been married. Of course, most of those memories were of sex so he supposed that didn't actually count, but it was hard to stop mulling them over.

Outside the window of his office, he saw another crack of lightning, followed by more thunder. The storm was moving in fast, and it was practically dark outside. He checked the baby monitor to make sure the sound hadn't upset Corbin. It hadn't. Jordan and his mom were dressing him in his little cowboy suit so he'd be ready for Lawson's wedding.

The monitor with the camera was a new addition. Or rather, *monitors*. They were scattered all over the house in any of the rooms where Corbin might be at any given time. It cut back on some of their privacy, but it was worth it to make sure Dylan had eyes on him at all times. That hadn't really been an issue, though, since someone was always with him, but Dylan liked being able to peek in on him.

In this case, the peeking also included Jordan.

She was sitting on Corbin's bed while she adjusted the boy's jeans. Regina was playing around with the angle of the red cowboy hat. Both women were engrossed in what they were doing, but Dylan knew Jordan well enough to see the occasional troubled look that would cross her face. She always made sure the look was gone when Corbin turned to her.

Maybe Jordan was blue because there'd been no resolution with the custody. Or it could be that weddings, *any* weddings, brought back memories of their own ill-fated "I do's." If it was either of those, then Dylan figured that was normal. What wasn't normal was the way she'd reacted in jail, right before the blowup with Theo.

It hadn't been merely a troubled look he'd seen then.

Jordan had been on the verge of some kind of anxiety attack. Perhaps from the combination of events, but it could also be from what'd happened to her when she'd been on deployment. He knew it was bothering her because he'd been on the receiving end of the ball-crushing when Dylan had interrupted her nightmare.

Hole, she'd said.

And he doubted she'd been referring to a doughnut or the metaphorical one he'd dug with his argument with Theo. No. That panic-laced word had to do with her being taken captive.

Hell, had they really put her in a hole in the ground?

That thought didn't torment him for long because Dylan looked up from the monitor when he heard the hurried footsteps outside his office. Several moments later, Lawson appeared in the doorway. "We gotta move the wedding indoors so we're taking over the sunroom."

Dylan figured there would have to be some adjustments made since Eve and Lawson had intended for their vows to take place in the rose garden next to her house. That was neutral ground, since his Granger cousins, Garrett and Roman, were at odds with Lucian. Since just about everybody fell into that "at odds" category with some family member or another, it wasn't usually a big deal. However, Eve hadn't wanted it to be an issue because Garrett and Roman were like brothers to Lawson. Actually, they were more like brothers to Lawson than Lucian.

"Eve's living room isn't big enough," Lawson went on. "Neither is the one in my house so we're stuck having the ceremony here."

Stuck said it all. This was probably the last place Lawson wanted to marry the love of his life, but he'd put up with being here because he was, well, marrying the love of his life. Doing something like that canceled out a lot of negatives.

"Need me to do anything?" Dylan asked.

Lawson usually had a laid-back kind of intensity about him, but there was nothing laid-back about him right now. The nerves were firing all through his eyes. "Yeah, you can save my ass."

"I'm not marrying Eve for you," Dylan joked, though he knew that was the last thing Lawson would want.

"I lost the wedding rings," Lawson blurted out.

Dylan had already gotten up from his desk, ready to do some tie tying or whatever it was he needed, but that stopped him. "Rings, as in plural?"

Lawson gave a choppy nod, and Dylan realized this was the first time he'd seen his older brother ready to lose his lunch. "They had to be resized. All of them. My ring, Eve's and her engagement ring. I picked them up from the jeweler yesterday, but now I can't find them."

Yeah, definitely unnerved. "They'll turn up, I'm sure. In the meantime, I'll find something you can use for the ceremony."

Lawson gave another of those choppy nods and headed off, probably to try to fix whatever else had popped up with this change of location. Dylan headed off, too. Upstairs and to his bedroom.

He passed Corbin's room along the way, but Jordan and Regina didn't notice him because they were working to get on Corbin's cowboy boots. At least Regina was. Eve and her daughter, Tessie, were now in the room with them, and Jordan was fiddling with Eve's dress while Eve read something on her phone.

"Lawson can't find the rings," he heard Eve grumble.

Dylan didn't wait to hear how the rest of that conversation would go since he had a fix for the ring issue.

He went to his bedroom but didn't bother to turn on the lights. No need. He knew the exact location of what he was after since he looked at it probably more often than he should. And there it was—beneath a layer of boxer shorts and some condoms.

His wedding band.

It was possible that Jordan would recognize it and wonder why he'd hung on to a relic from their failed marriage. The answer to that was simple: Dylan didn't have a clue why.

He took the ring, shoving it into his pocket, and he was about to make his way downstairs when he heard the movement in the doorway. It was Jordan. She was turned away from him and backed into the room. Dylan was about to say something to let her know he was there, but then she hiked up her dress, and he saw something that stunned him to silence.

Jordan had a penis tat on her lower back. A huge penis, too, on a skinny little stick figure body. It was butt ugly. And speaking of butt—it was aimed at hers.

Dylan was betting alcohol had been a major factor in her decision to get that done. As he well knew, alcohol and lust often led to unwise choices.

She yanked the dress up even higher, and while Dylan couldn't see exactly what she was doing, Jordan was tugging at something. Making soft sounds of discomfort, too. Actually, he was making some of those same sounds because despite the ugly penis staring at him, he was also getting a view of Jordan's backside. A view he shouldn't be getting because he shouldn't be staring at her. He cleared his throat so that she'd know he was there.

And Jordan yelped as if he'd gutted her.

She followed that yelp with some garbled words about him scaring the bejesus out of her and never, never, never doing that again. It didn't take long before his mom and Eve came running. Corbin, too, but thankfully Eve held him back when she saw Jordan with her dress pulled up to her waist.

"What happened?" his mother immediately asked, and she took note of the dark room. Of Dylan's questioning, lurking pose. Of Jordan's exposed stomach. "Oh, you have a ring there."

"I was trying to get it out so that Eve could use it for the ceremony," Jordan mumbled. "I was going to sterilize it," she added when Regina made a face.

Actually, his mom made a face at the ring itself. God knew what her expression would be if she saw the inked penis.

Regina nodded, paused, nodded again, and then she ushered Eve and Corbin back into the other room.

"Need some help?" Dylan asked Jordan. He hadn't intended to sound so cocky, but he'd figured she could use some humor right now.

But she apparently didn't see the humor in it because she scowled, reached for the light switch, and then gasped. That was likely about the time she realized what he was seeing on the backside view because Jordan yanked down her dress.

"How much did you see?" she snapped.

"Nothing." The lie would have been much more believable if he hadn't snickered, but he couldn't help himself.

Her scowl would have been much more effective

if her mouth hadn't twitched, threatening to smile. "I know. I want to have it removed, but I'm embarrassed to show it to anyone."

"It's not that bad," he lied again.

Jordan lifted her head a little, their eyes connecting, and it seemed as if the air changed between them. It got a lot hotter, and that was no easy feat after seeing that tat.

"Why were you in here?" she asked.

Uh. That was his cue to get moving. Hot air and recent memories of Jordan's partial nudity were not a good time for him to tell her that he'd kept his ring after all these years.

"I was getting something for Lawson." After two back-to-back lies, he'd wanted the truth. Well, the "keeping it vague" truth anyway.

Dylan started for the door, but she caught onto his arm. He was pretty sure this was going to fall into an unwise choice category. And yeah, lust could easily get involved.

"I proposed to you because I didn't want you getting in a fight with Theo," she said.

He didn't say "duh," but that's exactly what he was thinking.

"Theo's a martial arts expert," Jordan went on. "It wouldn't have been a fair fight."

"Ouch. If you're trying to smooth over my battered ego, you're not doing a good job."

"There's nothing battered about your ego," she mumbled.

Well, there was now.

"Anyway, we were all upset that day." Jordan glanced

away from him, and she began to study the door hinge with the same intensity as if it were a prized painting. "I know what Adele said hurt you. The part about her thinking that you wouldn't want to know about Corbin."

Yeah, that had been a deep dig, one that played right into the other thing that was pissing him off—that no one in his family seemed to believe he was capable of changing and becoming someone who, well, someone who didn't sleep on a woman's naked butt.

"I'll prove Adele wrong," he said, and then he added to himself, "I'll prove them all wrong."

Dylan again started to leave, but then he realized he'd only fixed half of Lawson's problem. He tipped his head to her stomach. "Any chance you'll be able to get out that navel ring, or should I see if Mom has something Lawson can use for Eve?" He touched the gold chain around her neck. "Or maybe we can just have Lawson wind this on Eve's finger."

Jordan froze. A deer-caught-in-the-headlights kind of freezing. "Maybe."

It was the most lukewarm agreement in the history of lukewarm agreements.

That possibly meant that it was special to her as in maybe a gift from Theo. Of course, she hadn't exactly shown a lot of warmth and fuzziness to Theo so it could have some other sentimental value.

"I'll talk to Eve about some options," Jordan said, heading in the direction of Corbin's bedroom.

Dylan followed her so he could check on his son before he went in search of Lawson—who was probably about to bust a gut right about now. Corbin was all dressed in his cowboy suit and was looking at himself in the mirror. Apparently he approved because he was smiling.

"'Ook, Daddy," he said. "I a towboy."

Dylan wondered if he would ever be able to hear that word, *Daddy*, and not feel the emotional punch that came with it. Talk about warm/fuzzy overload. But Dylan knew he'd never grow tired of it even if he heard it at two in the morning when Corbin sometimes woke up.

"You're a good-looking cowboy," Dylan told him, and he shifted his attention to Eve. "Standing next to a fine-looking bride."

"Really? You think so?" Eve immediately asked. "Is this dress okay?"

"The dress is great," Dylan and Jordan said in unison. And it was. It was pale pink lace, and it skimmed those curves that Dylan was certain would make Lawson truly appreciate it.

Because Eve's nerves were showing just as much as Lawson's, Dylan went to her and brushed a kiss on her cheek. "It's about time you made an honest man of my brother," he whispered to her. "You've made him a happy one, too. Well, except for this whole losing the rings thing. If we can't find something, I'll make you one from aluminum foil," he added with a wink.

Dylan kissed Corbin, too, scooping him up so he could see how they both looked in the mirror. Pretty damn fine, if Dylan had to say so himself.

His mom came hurrying out of the adjoining bathroom, and she had a wad of Q-tips in her hand. "Corbin needs his ears cleaned," Regina explained.

When she got close to the boy, Corbin immediately

took one of them, but he didn't go for his ears. He put it in his mouth and swirled it around.

"Like Nunk Luc-shen did," Corbin said.

"Nunk Luc-shen," Regina repeated. "That's what he calls Lucian. Isn't it cute?"

Maybe. But it wasn't cute that Corbin was swabbing his mouth.

Eve, Jordan and Regina all looked first at Corbin, then at Dylan as if he had an explanation for what was going on. Dylan didn't know, but he soon came up with an answer.

One that Dylan didn't like.

Hell.

Dylan hurried out of the room to look for Lucian, and he was reasonably sure there'd be nothing warm and fuzzy going on in the next couple of minutes.

CHAPTER THIRTEEN

"DID YOU KNOW Jordan Rivera's got a dick tat on her back?" Grady Tanner asked.

That wasn't a question that Lucian had ever gotten before, and he was reasonably sure it didn't have squat to do with the info he actually wanted from the private investigator who was standing in front of his desk. Grady and his father, Elwin, had been on Lucian's payroll for years, and it wasn't unusual for Grady to stray off the subject, but this was a big-assed detour.

"Is Jordan's dick tat connected to Corbin or Adele?" Lucian countered, and yes, he barked it, adding a scowl, too. Over the years, he'd found that people cut through the bullshit faster when they were facing him when he was in one of his unpleasant moods.

Which was about 95 percent of the time.

Grady lifted his shoulder. "No, but I thought it was interesting. Wanta know how I found out?" But he didn't wait for Lucian to say he didn't care a rat's ass how he'd come by that tidbit. "Her boyfriend got drunk at the Longhorn and mentioned it to one of the waitresses."

Theo might as well have taken out a full-page ad in the local paper because there was zero chance that info like that wouldn't be gossiped about. But it did make

Lucian wonder why she'd chosen a tat like that. Jordan might have crushed his baby brother's heart way back when, but she didn't seem the dick tat sort.

Since he wanted to make sure Grady stayed on topic, Lucian stood, staring the PI down and repeating the scowl. "What'd you find out about Adele? Is she running some kind of scam on Dylan?"

Grady smiled, obviously not as intimidated as Lucian would have liked. "Adele," he repeated. "Now, there's a piece of work. Her arrest record reads like stuff a stand-up comic would use. Did you know she once got arrested for peeing on a CEO's car? She was protesting the way he treated his employees."

Lucian made a circling motion with his finger for Grady to continue. "Before you say anything, though, ask yourself if it gives me any info that I paid you to get. If it doesn't, then keep it to yourself."

"Sure. Right, boss. Will do." And then Grady went silent for a couple of moments. He shook his head twice, obviously ruling out some useless drivel that he'd been about to dish out. "Okay, so I didn't find anything about Adele running any scams. Still, she's a thief and a troublemaker so there might be something that I'm not seeing."

"If there's something to see, then see it ASAP," Lucian ordered. He didn't want anything connected with Corbin or Adele to come back to bite them, and he had a bad gut feeling about this.

"Will do, boss," Grady repeated. "Want me to go out the same way I came in, through the side door?"

Lucian nodded, though no one would have any suspicions about Grady being in the house. Especially since the sunroom was currently in chaos while it was being set up for Lawson and Eve's wedding. Which was only an hour from now if the ceremony happened on time, that is. Too bad that he had a gallon of work to get finished before then.

Which might not happen.

Just as Grady made his exit, there was a soft knock on his office door, and a woman poked her head in. Bianca Turley, the judge's oldest daughter. Bianca was the woman he was currently seeing and also his date for the wedding. She was a half hour early, but Bianca went straight to Lucian and kissed him. If he hadn't been so annoyed at her being there already, he might have enjoyed it.

Or not.

Bianca and he had been seeing each other almost a month, which meant they were at the tail end of their relationship. Dylan might have sex bingo cards, but Lucian knew that his poker buddies had running bets as to how long he stayed with a woman. His record was thirty-four days. Bianca was at twenty-nine.

"You're put out because I didn't show up at the last minute," Bianca said, obviously picking up on his tight body language. "Sorry, but the storm's going to get worse, and I didn't want to drive in a downpour."

She kept her tone and expression pleasant. It was what he liked best about her. Very little drama, and she was well aware that things weren't going to last between them.

"It's okay," he assured her.

Bianca smiled. "No, it's not, and that's why I'm going to drop off these things and go mingle with whomever I can find." She set her purse and wet umbrella on the floor next to his desk.

The bending down motion caused him to notice her dress. Snug, pale blue and with a little shimmer. The mile-high heels she was wearing managed to look slutty and proper at the same time.

Bianca had once told him that two things had helped make her who she was. Her daddy's money and her grandma's pearls. She was wearing those pearls today, and her daddy's cash had likely paid for the dress.

"FYI, I thought you should know," Bianca said. "I stopped by Arlo's gas station on the way in, and he was prattling on about something he'd heard about Jordan. That she has a penis tattoo with balls and everything. And by everything I mean a place for that penis to be inserted."

So the gossip had already reached the embellishment stage. Hardly fitting for Jordan, who was a military hero.

Maybe a damaged one, though.

That was something he had Grady's father working on. Lucian wanted to know just how much being a captive had hurt her. Then, Lucian might be able to figure out what they'd be up against if it did come down to a custody battle. If Jordan was a mental mess, then she shouldn't get custody of Corbin. Of course, that was assuming the Grangers had a say in Corbin's future. They might not if Adele was trying to pull something.

The talk about Jordan's tat must have reminded Bianca that he, too, had *balls and everything* because she kissed him again and ran her hand from his belly to the front of his jeans. Four weeks ago, that would have caused him to clear out a spot on his desk and take her there, but today he held back. Good thing because there was another knock at the door, and Karlee came in.

Karlee took one look at the close proximity of Bianca's hand to his balls, and her right eyebrow came up. "Do you two need a minute?"

Bianca blushed, dropped a quick kiss on his mouth and headed for the door. Karlee didn't blush, probably because she'd walked in on too many instances similar to that one. Once, she'd walked in on desk sex. That had taught Lucian a lesson: lock his door before unzipping. When he'd mentioned that to Karlee, she'd had it needlepointed on a pillow that was now hidden in his closet.

"Oh," Bianca said, turning back around. Not to face Lucian, though, but Karlee. "Wow, you look really nice."

That caused Lucian to give Karlee another look, and he agreed. A green dress and high, sex-against-the-wall heels like Bianca's.

"I brought my business partner, Malcolm Day," Bianca added to Karlee, "and I want to introduce him to you. He's someone who's pulled himself up by his own bootstraps."

Shit. Bianca was matchmaking, and while he figured her intentions were good, Karlee would silently bristle at the bootstraps remark. Because it was a reminder that she'd had to do that after her mother had run out on the family.

Of course, it was a reminder, too, for Lucian since the running out had been with his own father, Jerry. Even though that'd happened years ago when Lucian and Karlee were teenagers, folks still gossiped about it. Despite that, though, Karlee and he had managed to put it behind them and work together just fine.

"Thanks," Karlee said. Her voice was cool, but Lucian doubted anyone would notice but him. "I already have a date, though." She checked the time. "He should be here any minute."

"Oh." Bianca's extreme surprise would cause Karlee to silently bristle, too, along with causing Bianca to look embarrassed. "Oh," she repeated. "Good." And this time she finally headed out.

"Since you're leaving for your business trip right after the wedding, I wanted to go over some things with you," Karlee said the moment Bianca was gone. She put a blister packet of meds on his desk. "An antihistamine," she explained. "You'll be in a meeting on Monday with Helen Jenkins, and her liberal dousing of Chanel number whatever always makes you sneeze."

It did, and it was something he never remembered until he was in a closed room with the woman.

"I've loaded all your notes and reports on your phone," Karlee went on. "Remember to eat a big lunch on Tuesday because you're going to the Watersons' for dinner."

He groaned. The Watersons were business associates who had tons of money to spend on catering or a chef, but yet they insisted on cooking inedible meals that they served to their guests. The last time they'd served what he was certain was boiled shoe leather with a side of greasy grass.

"Tessie's bringing her new boyfriend to the wedding. He's a hand at the Granger ranch so don't scowl at him," Karlee added. "Lawson will scowl enough, and the kid already looks spooked."

Lucian appreciated the update, but he'd still scowl. Tessie was his nineteen-year-old niece, and Lucian wanted the guy to know that there'd be consequences if he dicked around with her.

"You want me to round up Bianca and have her come back in?" Karlee asked. She wasn't smiling, or scowling, but Lucian got the feeling that she might want to do one of those things. With Karlee, though, he never knew which thing it was.

"No. I wasn't going to have sex with Bianca," he assured her.

"I figured as much. It's her twenty-ninth day. The consensus with the Lucian pool is that you'll end things with her today. Which brings me to something else. I ordered roses to be delivered to her on Monday. It's her birthday. And the card just says Happy Birthday. If you want to cancel the order or have it say something else more intimate, the number for the florist is in your phone."

He'd cancel it. Because Karlee and the Lucian pool were right. He would be ending things with Bianca today, and then Karlee would automatically send the woman a second batch of flowers to signify a parting of the ways.

"Do you really have a date?" he asked.

"Yes." Karlee frowned. Don't you dare look as surprised as Bianca. His name is Chad Preston, and he's the owner of—"

"The new feed supply store we're using," Lucian finished. He didn't actually know the man because

Dylan was the one who'd been dealing with him. Apparently, Karlee, too. But Lucian would make a point of meeting him today.

Karlee gathered up some of the signed contracts and proposals that were on his desk, and she started for the door. Just as Dylan stormed in.

Jordan and his mom were right behind him.

"We need to talk," Dylan snarled. "Now."

That appeared to be code for *I'm mad and want to bust your ass*. There definitely was nothing wedding-ish or festive about their expressions.

"Did you do a DNA test on Corbin?" Dylan demanded the moment Karlee was out of the room. Though Dylan spoke so loud that Karlee and half of Kansas would have heard the question.

Lucian fully intended to answer him but first he went to the door and made sure Corbin wasn't there. He was in the general vicinity. Tessie had him in her arms, but she was taking him toward the sunroom, and Karlee was following her. Though Karlee did shoot Lucian a warning glance. Later, she'd chew him out for this, but the first chewing would come from Dylan. Then Jordan and his mom. They were all clearly pissed, and it'd been a while since Lucian had seen that many flared nostrils in one room.

Lucian shut the door and turned back around to face them. "Yes, I did do a DNA test. Yesterday morning. It's at the lab now."

Both Dylan and Jordan cursed. Regina attempted it, but it came out as sputtered anger with some syllables thrown in. Lucian thought he caught the word *asshole* in the mix.

Since this wasn't going to be easy for any of them to hear, Lucian got started. "Adele has an arrest record, and she's not exactly a beacon of credibility. She lied to the cops on four occasions," he quickly added when the trio opened their mouths to protest.

"She wouldn't lie about this." That was from Jordan, but Dylan and his mom said variations of the same.

That was a nice sentiment, that Adele would be truthful when it came to her son's paternity, but Lucian preferred to get some backup proof. He was just funny that way.

"It's important that we know," Lucian went on. "Just in case the question of custody goes to court. You don't want Theo coming forward to make a bogus claim on the boy."

Or a legitimate claim after Dylan had put every ounce of emotional investment into fatherhood. Lucian suspected his brother had already come close to doing that, but if he could stop the floodgates, he would.

Maybe.

Dylan leaned in, putting his fisted hands on the desk that was in between them. "You're way out of line on this. *Way out.* If and when I want a DNA test done, I'll be the one to make that decision. Cancel the test." He didn't shout them this time, but that only seemed to make his words stand out even more.

Lucian huffed. "The test is being processed." Probably. The lab had said it would take a week or so, but he didn't want Dylan calling this off. "What harm would it do just to go ahead and get the results?"

"The harm is that you stuck your nose where it didn't belong." That didn't come from Dylan but rather his mother. She put her hands on his desk, too, and leaned in. "You run the family business, but that doesn't give you the right to run Dylan's personal life."

Lucian wasn't sure who looked more surprised at his mom sticking up for Dylan—Jordan, Dylan or Regina herself. Dylan was usually their mom's whipping boy, mainly because he was the only one who would let her do it. Or maybe because Dylan thought he deserved it.

"Call off that test," Regina added, "or so help me, your dad and I will move back here permanently, fire you and take over running the family business."

Now, Lucian was sure he was the most surprised person in the room. It was true that his parents legally owned the majority share of not only the ranch but also the collection of companies that were part of Granger Enterprises. But neither of them had shown a thimble's worth of interest in stepping up to be in charge of anything.

And he was certain they wanted it to stay that way.

What he did was way too much work for them, so that meant this was a bluff.

His mom just didn't want him to ruin the fantasy family she was building in her head, and her possible fantasy grandson was at the center of it. Still, he knew when to call a bluff and when to fold. This was a folding the cards kind of moment. Or at least his idea of it anyway.

"All right," Lucian finally said. "No test results."

There were no loud breaths of relief and certainly no thank-yous. Lucian just got a trio of glares and some under the breath mumbles that he didn't catch. Didn't want to catch, either.

He hadn't totally lied to them. The three of them wouldn't get any test results on Corbin.

But Lucian would.

KARLEE SAW THE look on Lucian's face when Regina, Jordan and Dylan came out of his office. Whatever Lucian had done, he must have convinced them that it hadn't been as big of a deal as they'd thought.

Or else Lucian was covering up something.

She sighed and started toward him so she could get to the bottom of whatever was happening, but then she saw the familiar face coming toward her.

Her youngest brother, Mack.

What now?

Sadly, that was always her first reaction when she saw him. That question, followed by a boatload of memories that Karlee didn't want. Her other brothers had managed to find success or at least an even keel in their lives, but Mack hadn't quite managed it.

She blamed herself for that.

That's the reason she didn't point toward the door and tell him to get out.

Mack had been just three when their mother had run off with Lucian's father, Jerry. It hadn't helped that her mom had taken most of her "old money" with her. Overnight, they'd gone from being respectable to being poor and the family that everyone else gossiped about. Mack had grown up believing that he'd somehow been the cause of what had become the tawdriest scandal in the town's history. Since Karlee had been thirteen years old when it'd happened, she knew the truth.

That the blame was solely on their mother's and Jerry Granger's shoulders.

However, Karlee had never managed to convince Mack of it. That's why she'd gone through life believing that she owed him. Along with feeling plenty sorry for him.

Their mother certainly hadn't tried to convince Mack of that no-fault responsibility. Once things had fizzled out between Jerry and her, she'd remarried one of her old money family friends and had cut her children out of her life. Karlee's father, Whitt, had ended up dying a short time later.

That hadn't helped to fix her kid brother, either.

It'd been a little over a year since she'd last seen Mack. That's when he'd shown up on his twenty-second birthday to ask for five grand to pay off what he called a "bad loan." Even though that still riled her, it was hard to totally give up on him. After all, he was her baby brother despite the way he was throwing away his life.

"I didn't know there'd be a wedding going on," Mack greeted.

Then he hadn't been anywhere near Wrangler's Creek, since everyone in town knew that Lawson and Eve were finally tying the knot.

"You look really nice," he added. "A definite wow."

It should be a *wow on steroids* considering how much she'd spent on the dress and shoes. Definitely splurge items. Stupid ones. Because in the back of her mind, she'd thought that since Lucian would be winding down things with Bianca that he would finally notice her as something more than just his assistant.

He hadn't.

Lucian had mentioned her *date*. Briefly mentioned it anyway. But he'd had no reaction, which was probably for the best since it wasn't a real date anyway. When she'd been talking to Chad about a feed order invoice, he'd asked about Lawson's wedding, and she'd invited him as her plus-one. Mainly because Chad was new in town and this way he could get to know folks.

She certainly hadn't bought this outfit for Chad.

And now she was in a dress that required body-shaping underwear and wearing shoes that sardined her toes. She really needed to rethink her choices when it came to getting Lucian's attention.

"I know you're busy so I won't keep you long," Mack continued a moment later.

Since she didn't want to spoil the day for anyone, especially Eve and Lawson, she motioned for Mack to follow her to Lucian's bedroom. It was the only room on the bottom floor where they were certain not to run into any arriving guests.

"I'm not giving you any more money," Karlee told him right off.

He nodded as if he'd been expecting her to say that, and he gave her that lopsided smile that always made her love him a lot more than she should. It was his little boy smile, the very one he'd used to get his way out of some situations that she didn't want to know about.

"I'm not here for money," Mack answered. "I need a job."

She had to shake her head to that, too, because Karlee had once gotten him a job here at the ranch, and he'd quit without notice after just a week. "Lucian and Dylan won't hire you again."

Another nod, but it wasn't so much of a smile this time but a slight wince. "Yeah, I really messed up, and I figured they wouldn't take me back. It's the same for our brothers. They won't hire me, either."

Karlee hadn't needed him to add that last part. Unlike her, their brothers had indeed washed their hands of Mack.

"I was hoping, though, that you knew somebody else. Somebody who might take a chance on me. And before you say anything—this time I promise I'd try very hard to make it work out."

It was a knee-jerk reaction to point out that he'd said "try" instead of a stronger word to let her know that he was serious, but she'd already lectured Mack enough that she was no doubt the voice in his head. The one that kept harping on him to do a lot better than he had been doing.

"I'll talk to Garrett Granger," she finally said.

That got him smiling again, and he went to her and put her in a bear hug. Mack was a big guy with plenty of muscles so he had no trouble twirling her around. Something that Karlee wished he hadn't done because her shoe went flying and smacked into Lucian as he was coming through the door.

Lucian wasn't alone, either. Bianca was right behind him, her hand sliding over his butt. Lucian wasn't the sort to have a quickie right before his brother's wedding, but there was a first for everything. This definitely looked as if it might turn into a first.

Mack took his time standing Karlee back on the

floor, and despite the slight dizziness she was experiencing from the twirling and the breath-robbing underwear she was wearing, she saw the disapproval in Lucian's eyes. He knew what a pain in the ass Mack had been. Also knew that she'd shelled out plenty of cash and favors over the years.

Karlee stopped her own disapproving look from appearing on her face. She hoped. No way did she want Lucian to see that it bothered her that he was with the likes of Bianca Turley.

But it did.

God, it bothered her.

"Is everything okay?" Lucian asked Karlee.

Karlee put on a smile. It wasn't charming like Dylan's or Mack's, but it was effective enough. And just in case it wasn't, she hooked her arm through Mack's and got them out of there as fast as her toe-vising stilettos would carry her.

CHAPTER FOURTEEN

DYLAN STOOD BACK and watched Jordan "dancing" with Corbin. She had him in her arms and was twirling him around, causing the boy to laugh.

Regina was right there on the makeshift dance floor, and she was snapping pictures along with the photographer. Eve and Lawson were dancing, too, but their moves weren't as robust as Jordan's. They were swaying to the music while gazing in each other's eyes because they were caught up in the moment of just having said their "I do's."

Dylan was caught up in a different moment.

And he could blame Lucian for part of his mixed shit bag of a mood. His brother had really stepped in something he shouldn't have been stepping anywhere around. But even if Lucian hadn't pulled that stunt about the DNA test, Dylan figured that other blue memories would be playing into this.

For the past fourteen years, any wedding he'd attended came with memories of his own. Jordan had danced that day, too. With him. And they'd been just as wrapped up in each other as Lawson and Eve were now.

Of course, there was one huge difference between today and that past wedding. No one was glaring at the newlyweds, but there'd been plenty of glaring going on at his and Jordan's celebration.

The general consensus that day was they had rocks for brains and that it wouldn't last.

The consensus had been right.

But in that moment Dylan had thought it would be like this forever. That's why the consensus was right about the rocks-in-the-head part, too.

When the song ended and a new one started, Jordan handed Corbin off to Regina so she could have her turn dancing. Jordan immediately glanced around the room, and the glancing stopped when her attention landed on him. She managed a smile. Not a good one, though. It was the kind of smile you gave someone who'd lost a race. An unspoken "oh well."

Jordan gave Corbin another look before she started toward the bathroom. Dylan was about to go closer to his mom and Corbin so he could have the next dance with his son, but then he saw Eve making her way toward him. Dylan made sure he put on a big smile for her.

"Lawson and I are about to head back to my house so we can get ready to leave for the honeymoon," Eve said. She brushed a kiss on his cheek and looked back at her groom, who was making his goodbyes to Regina and their cousins, Roman, Sophie and Garrett. "No family feud today," she added in a whisper.

No. The feud had preceded the nuptials and hadn't involved the cousins but rather Lucian. Dylan kept that to himself, though. No need to put any kind of damper on this day for her.

"Lawson said I should give this back to you," Eve went on. She handed Dylan the wedding band that he'd lent his brother. "And if you don't mind, would you please give this back to Jordan?" Eve pulled off the ring she was wearing and handed it to Dylan.

Dylan hadn't gotten a good look at it during the ceremony, but he sure looked at it now. And recognized it. It wasn't Jordan's navel ring but rather the wedding band he'd given her fourteen years ago.

"Yes, it's the same one," Eve said with a knowing little smile. A smile that smacked of all sorts of things—like *are you surprised Jordan has kept it all this time?* And—*why do you think she did that?*

You're dang right he was surprised and wanted to know the answer to both of those unspoken questions. Jordan had not only kept it, she'd had it on her when she'd come to the ranch.

"My advice?" Eve said when he started to walk away and find Jordan. "When you ask her about the ring, use your charming voice. It might make her remember why she accepted it from you in the first place."

It was hard to be charming when he was confused and mad. Yes, mad. If the ring had meant anything to Jordan, then she should have told him. He made it two steps before he realized how stupid that sounded. Their marriage had ended ages ago, and maybe the only reason she had the ring with her was so she could return it to him. It could mean nothing.

Hell.

Now he was riled about that.

Despite his flip-flopping mood, Dylan went in search of Jordan, but he ran into Abe along the way. The timing couldn't have been worse, but Abe pulled out several of the bingo cards.

"Sorry," Abe said, "the rain got to the top one, but I figured you'd still pay me for it anyway."

Dylan huffed. He would have paid him even more if all the ink on all the pages had been illegible. "I'll write you a check for them later," he added, stuffing them into the inside pocket of his jacket.

"Are you about to check on your crying girlfriend?" Abe asked.

Dylan had already started to walk away, but that stopped him. "Jordan's crying?"

Abe's forehead bunched up. "Is she your girlfriend?" He shook his head. "Never heard a man call his ex-wife a girlfriend. Say, is it true that she's got a…dick tattoo on her backside?"

Dylan was sure his forehead bunched up, too. "How'd you know about the tat and who's crying?"

"Gossip and the judge's daughter," Abe answered. "Judge Walter Ray Turley's daughter."

He considered pressing Abe as to which gossip had gleaned him that info about Jordan's ass, though he doubted he'd learn the origin, but it meant someone had gotten a rather intimate peek of Jordan. Later, he'd find out who that was, but for now the crying woman was the issue. Then, questioning Jordan about the ring.

"Which of the judge's daughters is crying?" Dylan pressed. He glanced around the sunroom. It was packed, but other than Bianca, he didn't see another Turley. And Bianca definitely wasn't crying. She was hanging close to Lucian's side as if he were the solution to world peace and calorie-free premium chocolate.

Abe shook his head. "Sorry, I can't tell 'em apart,

but it's the one who was just here. Not today but not that long ago."

Hell, Abe would have to get more specific because both Melanie and her sister Misty had been at the ranch in the past two weeks. Dylan tried a different angle. "Where was this crying Turley?"

"Parked in her car just up the road. Maybe she was upset about not getting an invite to the wedding."

That was possible. Dylan vaguely remembered Eve asking him if he wanted her to invite Melanie, but he honestly couldn't remember what he'd told her. All of that seemed a lifetime ago what with Corbin's arrival.

Dylan took out his phone to call Melanie to check on her. No answer. So he continued his search for Jordan, and this time he found her before he could get interrupted again.

Jordan was coming out of the kitchen, and she immediately took hold of his arm and pulled him into the powder room. All right. That saved him from telling her that he wanted to go somewhere private where they could talk. Obviously, she wanted privacy, too, because she shut the door.

"Did you tell anyone about my tat?" she asked.

Oh, that. "Nary a soul, but since Abe knows about it, someone blabbed."

"Abe knows about it?" Jordan practically howled. "The housekeepers do, too. So does Bianca Turley and the caterer." She paused a second, her expression going a little dark. *"Theo."*

Dylan thought his expression might have darkened, too. Of course, Theo would likely know about the tattoo. After all, he was Jordan's ex-boyfriend, but it bothered Dylan more than he wanted to realize that Jordan had had sex with that guy. Not nearly as much as it bothered him, though, that Theo might have spilled something like that to anyone, much less to someone in Wrangler's Creek.

She took out her phone, probably to call Theo, but Dylan wanted to settle something else with her first. He took her hand and dropped the wedding band into her palm. "Eve wanted me to return this to you."

And he waited.

And waited.

But Jordan just shrugged and slipped the ring into her pocket. What she didn't do was offer any explanation whatsoever. So Dylan reached in her pocket to take it out so he could open up the discussion.

Something he wished he'd given more thought.

The pocket was small. His hand wasn't. Also, the pocket was on the side of her dress, angling from her hip to the front of her body—an area he definitely shouldn't be touching. That's why he quickly tried to draw back his hand, but because of the small size/big hand thing, he ended up doing some jiggling. It seemed like some sort of foreplay, and Dylan nearly cheered in victory when he finally managed to get his fingers on it.

He didn't cheer for long, though.

That's because Jordan started jiggling his wrist, maybe an attempt to stop him from touching her, and in the process she grabbed his balls again. Or rather she knocked into them with the back of her hand. That didn't put him on his knees, but he did sink in that general direction, and he grabbed onto Jordan to break his fall.

And that's how Bianca found them when she threw open the powder room door.

"This isn't how it looks," Jordan immediately said.

Dylan didn't even attempt an explanation. He had hold of Jordan by the waist/buttocks. Her hand was on his balls. And at that moment, the wedding ring that he'd worked so hard to retrieve pinged to the floor and bounced a couple of times. It landed right next to Bianca's shoe.

"Oh my God. Did I interrupt you proposing to Jordan again?" Bianca asked.

"No," Jordan answered. Good thing, too, because Dylan was still having some pain management issues because of the ball knocking. He needed to start wearing an athletic cup around Jordan.

Jordan reached down, scooped up the ring and shoved it back in the very pocket that had already caused too much trouble. "Eve borrowed the ring, and Dylan was returning it, that's all. No proposal involved."

Yes, returning it along with having some questions about why she still had it. Questions that were going to have to keep, because it was obvious he needed to deal with Bianca because she didn't look as if she was buying Jordan's non-proposal claim. She wasn't a gossip like so many others, but he didn't want her leaving with the wrong idea.

"If there is something going on between you two, then my advice is to try to keep it quiet for a while," Bianca said. "You don't want this getting back to Melanie or my dad. He's already mad about what happened at the bachelor party, and he'll get madder if Melanie is upset. I don't want him to take it out on you if Theo and you have a custody showdown in Daddy's court."

Dylan had to mentally repeat everything Bianca had just said. "Theo? Custody?"

Jordan did some repeating, too. *"Daddy's court?"*

Bianca nodded to all of those, and she must have thought a nod was enough of a response because she turned as if to walk away. Jordan stopped her by stepping in front of her.

"Theo is actually considering a court showdown?" Jordan asked.

Bianca nodded again. "Theo's got to be leaving soon to go back to the base where he's stationed, but he's planning on asking to be reassigned here in Texas. He called Daddy to talk about it. He's actually called a lot of people. And he's been spending his evenings at the Longhorn doing yet more talking." Bianca looked at Jordan. "He let it slip about a tattoo you have."

Dylan was about to curse, but Jordan beat him to it. She also took out her phone and called Theo, but he didn't answer.

"Is Theo bad-mouthing Jordan?" Dylan asked Bianca.

"Not sure you could call it that. He did mention the tattoo and that he's worried about Jordan's well-being. You know, because of…you know."

There was no need for Bianca to clarify that. So, yeah, Theo was bad-mouthing Jordan maybe because he was jealous of them or maybe because he was dead wrong about Jordan being a good mom. Dylan had seen her with Corbin, and she definitely wasn't lacking in the motherhood department.

"Is Theo still staying at the inn?" Jordan asked.

A third nod from Bianca. "But they haven't found one of the snakes yet so Alfred's moving Theo and the other guests from room to room while they keep searching."

Alfred Crenshaw was the owner of the Red Rooster Inn, and while Dylan could call him to ask if Theo was in whatever room he'd been assigned, it was best if he talked to Theo in person. It was obvious that Theo wasn't going to let go of his paternity claim on Corbin if he'd involved a judge who was currently pissed off at Dylan.

"This is why Lucian wanted the DNA test," Jordan mumbled.

That could have been part of it, yes. But Dylan wasn't going to give Lucian any big brother awards just yet because he should have gotten permission for doing something like that. Permission that Dylan wouldn't have given him.

If someone asked him why he didn't want the test, he would stick to his guns about believing Adele. Which in hindsight probably wasn't very smart. Still, Corbin was his, and it didn't matter what the test said.

"I'll drive up the road and find Theo," Jordan said, already heading toward the front of the house. "Could you tell Regina that I won't be able to do the next dance with Corbin?"

"I'm going with you," Dylan insisted. And he didn't give Jordan a chance to argue with that.

As they went to the front door, he texted his mom, knowing that Regina would be in hog heaven because she'd be able to spend more time with Corbin. Still, that didn't mean Dylan wanted to spend any more time with Theo than was necessary to get his point across.

Jordan grabbed her keys from the foyer table, threw open the door, and it was as if a tidal wave came at them. Dylan had known it was raining, but this seemed to be a couple of steps past the mere storm stage. Still, that didn't stop Jordan. She opened an umbrella, which promptly flew out of her hands with a gust of wind. That didn't stop her, either. Pushing the unlock button on her keys, she ran to her car. So did Dylan and he got into the passenger's seat at the same time she got behind the wheel.

There wasn't a single inch of him that was dry.

The rain had seemingly blown from multiple directions at once, and Jordan hadn't fared much better. Her hair was plastered to her head, her makeup running, and her clothes had become transparent.

Something he wouldn't mention. Or try to notice.

Hell. He noticed. Dylan saw the outlines of her nipples.

She turned on the engine and the heater full blast, but Dylan estimated it would be a day or two before they dried out. That didn't deter her from going after Theo, though. Jordan put the car in gear and started driving despite the fact that there was only an inch of visibility. That meant they were creeping along. So slow that it might indeed take that day or two to reach the inn.

"I swear Theo's not usually like this," she grumbled. Then paused. "Well, sometimes he is. He's persistent when he gets an idea in his head even when it's a bad one."

At least she wasn't taking Theo's side. That was something. Of course, Dylan wasn't sure how Jordan would feel if her ex-boyfriend kept up this fight. Or got his new pal, Judge Turley, to order a DNA test. Dylan didn't have to guess how Jordan would feel if Theo continued to push for custody. She'd be as pissed off about that as Dylan was. And Adele would get in on that who-was-pissed-off-most contest because she'd made it clear that Theo couldn't possibly be the father.

"And Theo shouldn't be talking about my so-called well-being to anyone other than me," Jordan added. She glanced at him as if he might disagree with that, but Dylan only shrugged.

And thought about it.

"If you tell me you're okay, I'll believe you," Dylan said. And he waited for her to confirm that "fine" part.

Her silence lasted longer than it took snails to go a marathon. "I'm supposed to take meds, but I don't." Another long pause. "I have nightmares."

"Yeah, I remember." He pointed to his balls and steeled himself up to hear her say that the nightmares were godawful and that they were driving her to the brink. Or maybe she'd say that everything was hunky-dory and that she was tired of people fussing over her.

She kept her attention on the windshield. "I'm not a hero."

All right, that hadn't been one of his steeling-up options, and Dylan wasn't sure how to go with this. If he disagreed and said she was indeed a hero, then it might trigger an argument he didn't want to have with her. Not when it felt as if they were on the same side.

For the moment anyway.

Dylan wanted to hang on to that moment, since it seemed as if whatever they did together would benefit Corbin along with squashing Theo like a bug.

"I'm not a hero, either," Dylan finally answered though it was almost certainly the wrong thing to say. Plus, it was as obvious as her puckered nipples. "Maybe we can aim for something slightly below the hero level and be okay with that?"

Yeah, definitely the wrong thing to say. It sounded like something that a really bad life coach would come up with.

"Maybe," Jordan whispered, and it seemed as if she was agreeing with him. "I'm almost certain I'll be getting out of the Air Force."

Almost certain. So she was still mulling it over. Perhaps even wondering if she could get reassigned nearby as Theo might do.

"You're getting out because of Corbin?" he asked.

The fact that she didn't jump to answer that told him loads. That maybe this non-hero label was playing into it. "Uh, we need to talk about something else," Jordan insisted.

That was fine by him, but Dylan figured this was a subject that might come up for a while yet. There might be more nightmares. More of those unsettled looks. Since there was nothing he could do about that, he went with changing the subject. Unfortunately, it wasn't a pleasant one.

"Bianca won't tell anyone about what she thought she saw in the bathroom," Dylan threw out there. "Well, no one other than Lucian. But it's probably a good idea for you to clarify to Theo that we're not together. He could be putting up this bad idea of a fight as a way of trying to hang on to you."

She made a sound of agreement. Angry agreement. "I'll clarify a lot of things to Theo."

He figured Theo wasn't going to care much for those clarifications, but it needed to be done with the hopes that it might get the man to back off. *Might*. Dylan needed to do the same to Melanie with the same hope of getting that *might*. He didn't want her encouraging her dad and Theo simply because she was jealous. And besides, there really wasn't anything going on between Jordan and him.

Well, nothing except he couldn't keep his eyes off her.

Dylan forced his attention off her nipples, and he soon spotted the piece of paper on the dash. Familiar paper since it was a bingo card.

"Oh," she said when he reached for it. "I got that from Arlo's gas station."

Dylan sighed. He'd need to send Abe looking there for any others.

Jordan cursed, hit her hands on the steering wheel, and for a moment Dylan thought she was reacting to the card. But no. The rain got even harder, and their one inch of visibility went to zero. Jordan wisely pulled to the side of the road, stopped the car and put on her emergency lights. She also tried to call Theo again.

Still no answer.

"Maybe the rain will let up soon," she grumbled, looking out the window.

Maybe, and if not, they might have to postpone this little adventure. It bugged him, though, that Theo might not be answering his phone because he was avoiding them. Well, avoidance wasn't going to work. And Dylan should know because he was having no luck in keeping his eyes off Jordan.

Her bra was lace. He could see that, too, and it was one of those barely there garments that caused his groin to tighten. Of course, anything Jordan happened to be wearing would probably have the same effect on him. That's why he tried to glue his attention to the bingo card.

"You got the hard one," he said.

Jordan looked over at it. "It's not that hard. We've done that one." She pointed to the square about making out on horseback. "And that one." Sex on the hood of a truck. "That one, too." A thigh hickey.

Yes, they had indeed done all of those, but he pointed to one block that she couldn't check. "You haven't made out with me in a thunderstorm."

Good timing because at that exact moment, it thundered.

She was still scowling over Theo and this drive, and the scowl stayed in place when she shifted her attention to him. "We're not making out."

"No, we're not," he agreed. "But this is close enough that you can check off the box if you want."

"Close enough?" she challenged.

"I was thinking about making out with you," Dylan admitted.

He figured that was only going to cause her scowl to get a whole lot worse, but it didn't. Jordan groaned softly and laid the back of her head against the seat. Not relaxing. More like surrendering to the fact that she wasn't going to get to yell at Theo while her anger was still at the hissy fit stage. It was going to be more of a cool-down anger. And if her nipples were still showing like that, Theo might get so caught up in the view that he didn't even hear what she said.

But Dylan heard her all right.

"I kept my wedding and engagement rings because it didn't seem right to throw them away," she said. "I thought they might be family heirlooms or something."

They weren't. He'd bought them at a jewelry store in San Antonio, but it was decent of her to think of that possibility.

"So, why did you keep yours?" she asked.

Well, he couldn't play the family heirloom card since he'd been with Jordan when she'd bought his. She'd been basically near broke at the time and had used her tip money from waitressing to get it. Since she wouldn't let him pay for it, Dylan had purposely picked out the cheapest one in the store.

"Ditto on it not feeling right to throw it away," he said. Though he had taken it to the creek a couple of times to do just that. "I guess that's what people do when they're really, really pissed off." Instead, he'd just been really, really hurt.

She looked at him. At the card. And then out at the road. "Maybe I can turn around and we can go back."

He shook his head. "The road's narrow, and we'd end up in the ditch. Besides, I think the rain's letting up a little."

Mother Nature or whoever was responsible for this monsoon from hell must have wanted to give him a little jab because the rain dumped down on the windshield as if someone had poured a massive bucket of water on them.

"Or not," he amended.

Jordan groaned again, but this time it wasn't such an agony groan. It had a touch of sarcastic humor to it.

"So, how many winners have there been?" she asked, plucking the bingo card from his fingers. She was making conversation, that was all. A way to pass the time while the buckets continued.

"Probably too many," he admitted. Again, it was meant to pass the time. "I'm thinking about offering two drinks to anyone who turns in a blank card."

"You mean now that you're celibate," Jordan said. The sarcasm dripped a little heavier with that comment. "I heard about it from your mom."

It took Dylan a moment to remember that he'd sent Regina the video of him making that outrageous promise. Except it wasn't so outrageous. Here it'd been two weeks, and there'd been no sex. A small miracle considering he was right next to Jordan and her invisible clothes.

She looked over the card. And looked. And frowned. And looked some more.

"It's sleazy and slutty when you're just reading it like that," he reminded her. "I mean when the heat's not there to make it seem like wise choices. Of course, a good kiss can make just about anything feel wise."

Jordan was smiling and fighting that smile when she looked at him. For a moment, he thought it was just going to stay a glance and that she would go back to studying that blasted card. But the glance turned into eye contact.

Uh-oh.

Not good. Here they were talking about sex bingo cards, heat and kisses with some sleazy and slutty thrown in. That was a bad combination. So was the single word of profanity that Jordan mumbled. No sarcasm, just a crapload of frustration.

"Dylan, we can't do this," she added.

That was definitely the right thing to say, and that's why it surprised him when she leaned in and kissed him. Apparently, they could do *this* after all. Well, if *this* involved doing the dumbest thing they could possibly do with their clothes still on.

Jordan didn't go for a little peck. She went with the happy birthday/Merry Christmas/big-assed lottery win all rolled into one. But then, they'd never been the willy-nilly type of kissers. The first time they'd liplocked when they were fifteen, it'd been a second-base kind of deal with mouths open and already leaping toward the home run. That's why he'd kept kissing her and only her for the next five years.

And here he was again.

Dylan could have stopped, of course, if it hadn't been for that drenching of pleasure he got from the taste of her. Oh, and the touch. Because Jordan immediately slid her cold, wet hand around the back of his neck. The cold, wet part should have been a turnoff, but since the rest of them was cold and wet, it blended right in and somehow stuck out at the same time. Leave it to Jordan to manage both.

She also managed to move closer, leaning over the gearshift to keep on deepening an already-deep kiss. Even though his mind was fuzzy with heat, he still checked to make sure they weren't going to roll into the creek. Thankfully, the creek was a good quarter of a mile away, but it was possible they could drift in that direction, and neither of them would notice.

"We shouldn't be doing this," she said with her mouth against his.

At least she'd moved on from they couldn't do this. That had already been proven wrong so she was now going with the obvious. No, they shouldn't be kissing, and she definitely shouldn't be dallying with her finger in that spot just below his ear. She knew that was a hot zone for him, but she kept doing it while getting closer.

Since Dylan still had just a thread of common sense left, he remembered the kicked gearshift/creek debacle and decided to do something about that. He pulled Jordan into his lap. No sane man would have done that, which proved just how little that common sense shred was.

Jordan proved it, too, by continuing the kiss and the finger dallying. It was even more potent now because her wet body was pressed against his, and he could feel those nipples that he'd been fantasizing about. It made him crazy. Or crazier than he already was because he sacrificed kissing her tasty devil mouth so he could lower his head and go after her breasts.

She must have approved because she caught onto his hair and pulled him even closer to her.

"I'm not going to be a filled square," she complained.

Because his head was fuzzy and this body was throbbing, it took him a moment to realize she meant the bingo card. Because, yes indeed, there was a stupid square about making out with him in a thunderstorm.

A square that could now be ticked off.

But Dylan didn't want any box ticking. He wanted to get Jordan naked and… He stopped and forced himself to think about this. Did he want to have sex with her in this car while they parked on the side of the road?

Yes.

But did that mean he *should* have sex with her while they were parked on the side of the road?

No.

He repeated that. Sixteen times.

Jordan seemed to be mentally repeating some stuff, too, because she'd stopped kissing him and started staring at him. He couldn't tell if she was planning to put an end to this or ask him if he had a condom.

He did have not one but two condoms in his wallet. And with her body squished against his, it'd take some pretty interesting maneuvering for him to reach back there and get them. It was possible for at least one of them to get an orgasm during the process. But the sound Dylan heard had him dismissing any condom-retrieving/accidental orgasms that might happen.

Because it was the sound of an approaching car.

He took out the *approaching* part when he looked out and saw that the vehicle was already there. It'd stopped right next to them. And despite the rain and all the thunderstorm making out that had gone on, the windows weren't fogged up nearly enough because he had no trouble seeing the driver of the vehicle.

Judge Walter Ray Turley.

Dylan had no trouble spotting the judge's passengers, either.

Melanie and Theo.

And worse, the eyeballing/scowling trio had no problem seeing Jordan on his lap. Dylan was thinking that this was one particular cat that he wasn't going to be able to get back in the bag.

CHAPTER FIFTEEN

DYLAN DOUBTED THE strong smell of horse shit in the air was the cause of the abundance of stink eye he was seeing. Nope. He figured those squinty eyeball gazes were aimed at him.

And Jordan.

He'd been right about not being able to put the making-out cat back in the bag, and it was obvious that everyone attending the Wrangler's Creek Charity Rodeo had heard of the lip-lock between Jordan and him in the car. Since it'd been a week since that happened, Dylan had hoped that talk about it would have died down by now. The stink eye, though, let him know that it hadn't.

That particular facial expression also let him know that the town had sided with Melanie. It didn't matter that it'd been over between Dylan and her; she was the town's darling. The woman from the right side of the tracks and suitable for a Granger. No one other than Dylan had ever thought Jordan had been a just-fine fit.

Not even Jordan herself.

That was probably why she'd been keeping her distance from him. He got that. She was in the middle of some messy things in her life what with Corbin, Theo and dealing with whatever else she was going through because of her being taken captive. Dylan had decided since she was keeping her distance that he would give her space, too. After all, he was in the middle of his messy thing as well, and it was best not to add sex with his ex to the mix. Even if he'd thought that had been a fine idea when they'd been kissing.

"Horseys," Corbin squealed when he saw the broncs.

Just hearing his son's voice chased away any sourness that Dylan was feeling from the stream of stink eyes. Soon, maybe folks would see him as the kind of guy who carried his little boy on his shoulders to the town's rodeo, instead of the one still making out in a car on the side of the road.

"Yep, they're horses," Dylan confirmed.

However, they were ornery ones that would buck the shit out of anyone who tried to ride them, but he kept that description to himself. Especially since he'd be competing in the saddle bronc competition—as he always did. Ditto for Lucian and any adult male with the surname of Granger. Even the nonadult males now, too, since Roman's teenage son, Tate, would be riding today.

The rodeo had basically turned into a pissing/testosterone contest to prove… Well, Dylan wasn't sure exactly what it proved except that his gene pool was stupid enough to climb onto the back of a crazy bronc while people either cheered or jeered for you. Normally, Dylan got cheers, and he'd even won the competition once, but he was betting that wouldn't be the case this year. Either for the cheers or the win. He hadn't done even one training ride to help him get ready for the competition since he'd been spending all of his free time with Corbin.

Dylan kept walking, making his way through the stream of people. Once he got away from the corral and pens, he picked up on some smells other than horse and bull shit. Cotton candy and fried stuff. Any and everything got fried at the rodeo—candy bars, cheese, pickles—so it was impossible to escape the smell of hot grease.

He finally spotted someone not in the stink eye mode. Karlee. She was at one of the booths buying a hot dog, but she smiled, went to them and gave Corbin a goose to the stomach.

"I'm hoping you and me can get a good sugar high while we watch your daddy and Uncle Lucian ride," Karlee told Corbin.

Since Jordan had said she would be the one looking after Corbin during the bronc riding event, Dylan was about to ask Karlee where she was, but he realized she was the woman with her face partially hidden behind a giant cloud of the pink cotton candy. That heap of sugar was almost certainly what enticed Corbin to go straight into Jordan's arms when she reached for him.

She was also smiling when she took Corbin, but that smile turned to a slightly openmouthed gawk when she looked at Dylan. He was already dressed for the ride in his chaps, boots and leather vest, and he hadn't forgotten that the getup had always appealed to Jordan. Cowboy eye candy, she called it. She'd liked it even better, though, when once he'd worn the chaps without the jeans.

Or his boxers.

But it was best if he pushed aside that particular

memory today. It'd be damn difficult to ride with a hard-on. Not to mention downright embarrassing.

"Garrett and Roman are here," Karlee said, tipping her head toward the arena fence. Both were geared up just as Dylan was. "And there's Lucian."

Yep, it was. Lucian was standing off by himself, staring into the arena the way a general would survey a battlefield right before an attack. He looked ready to launch that attack, too, and unlike Dylan, he'd actually trained for this event.

"Good Lord, is that rivalry still going on between the cousins?" Jordan asked when she saw Lucian aim a snarl at Garrett and Roman. The cousins aimed one right back at him.

"It's not merely a rivalry," Dylan explained. "At least not for Lucian anyway. He doesn't like getting beat by Garrett year after year." Which reminded him of something. "I heard Garrett hired your brother Mack."

Karlee nodded, but she definitely didn't seem enthusiastic about that. Maybe because Mack was a known screwup. Which meant Karlee had called in a favor with Garrett to get him to hire her trouble-making kid brother.

They started moving closer to the arena as Garrett went in to do his ride. Eight seconds might go in a couple of eye blinks, but it'd feel like an eternity once he was on the bronc. Plus, he wouldn't be just judged solely on the time in the saddle but also on form. Considering this was a Podunk event to raise money for charity, a whole lot of people, including the judges, took it way too seriously.

The person who wasn't taking it seriously was

Corbin. He was doing exactly what a kid should be doing. He was chowing down on the cotton candy while he got lots of attention from not only Jordan and Karlee but also from anyone who happened to walk by him and notice what a cute kid he was. Thankfully, Corbin got smiles instead of stink eye. Corbin was also getting the sugar goo all over Jordan, but she didn't seem to mind. She laughed when a hunk of it landed on her cheek.

But she stopped in midlaugh.

Dylan turned to see what'd caught her attention, and it was Theo hurrying toward her. Ah, jeez. Not today. But judging from the intense look on the guy's face, he could be here for another round of convincing Jordan to marry him so they could team up to get custody.

"I didn't call them," Theo immediately said to her. "I was getting ready to leave town when I heard they were here. I tried to stop them, but they were hell-bent on seeing you."

Dylan had no idea who the *them* and *they* were or why they were in the hell-bent mode. But he soon saw the pair coming their way. It was a man with a big camera hoisted onto his shoulder, and the other man with him had a microphone. Obviously, they were part of a news crew. Not that unusual since the San Antonio stations often covered the charity rodeo. However, these two weren't looking at the arena where the reigning bronc riding champion, Garrett, was currently getting bucked on the back of a paint gelding. Nope. They were making a beeline for Jordan.

"Major Rivera," the guy with the mike said. "How

are you coping on the two-month anniversary of your being taken captive?"

Jordan seemed to freeze, and Dylan doubted she was merely surprised by the question or the reporter being there. Something had triggered inside her. Maybe a flood of the memories that had been causing her nightmares.

Dylan stepped to her side, and Karlee reached in and automatically took Corbin from Jordan's arms. Karlee thankfully moved the boy away from the camera and to the area where Garrett had just finished his ride. According to the announcer, Garrett had lasted the full eight seconds, and that caused the onlookers to burst into cheers and applause.

But Jordan wasn't cheering or applauding.

She had moved on from the stunned look to swallowing hard. The pink cotton candy looked like some kind of surreal Statue of Liberty torch that she had lifted in her right hand.

"I'm doing fine," she said when she finally managed to answer the question.

Jordan couldn't have possibly sounded any less convincing, and even that went down a notch when the reporter took out a folded newspaper from beneath his arm, and he held up the front page for Jordan to see.

Dylan got just a glimpse of the picture on the front page. A glimpse was all he needed because the image was etched in his mind. It was of a haggard-looking Jordan, her torn uniform and smears of grime and possibly blood on her face. Her expression showed the horror of what she'd been through.

Theo was also in the picture, behind her, his focus

straight ahead, and he was no doubt trying to get her out of there. Not just away from wherever she'd been held but also away from the photographer. Theo was attempting to do that now, too. He stepped in front of her, which meant he went in front of Dylan, as well.

"Major Rivera's just here to enjoy the day," Theo added to Jordan's response, "and she wants to thank everyone who prayed for her safe return. She's recovering and doing well."

It sounded rehearsed, but it was also obvious that Theo still cared about her. This seemed a little more than just being part of the job.

They were gathering a crowd now, everyone hanging on what was going on instead of watching Lucian, who was about to take the arena. Theo opened his mouth, probably to add more of that rehearsed sound bite, but Jordan eased him aside and stepped between Dylan and him.

"Yes, I am here to enjoy the day in my hometown," Jordan said, and she seemed much stronger than she had several moments ago. Though Dylan saw her cringe a little when she looked at the photo that the reporter was still holding up.

"And you're here with Colonel Shaw," the reporter commented. The guy smiled. "Does that mean there's something personal going on that your well-wishers would want to know about?"

Well, shit. Talk about putting Jordan on the spot. Even though Dylan knew it had to be hard for her, she put on a smile and patted Theo's arm.

"Colonel Shaw and I are old friends," she said. "And

I'll always be grateful to him for rescuing me and my crewmates."

The cameraman pulled back to get both Theo and Jordan in the shot. Behind him, Dylan could hear a few people mumbling about the start of Lucian's ride, but he kept his attention on Jordan.

"Now, if you'll excuse me," she added to the reporter. "I'll get back to watching the rodeo."

Jordan was still smiling when she stepped away, moving toward the arena. Theo stayed behind to continue talking with the reporter, but Dylan went after Jordan. He wasn't sure she'd want or need him…

She did.

The moment he reached her side, he realized she was about to lose it. She was blinking back tears and trembling.

"Please get me out of here," she whispered.

"BECKFAST," JORDAN HEARD someone say.

It took her a moment to realize the voice wasn't part of a dream. It was real, and it was Corbin who was talking.

She opened her eyes, yawned and nearly went into cardiac arrest when she saw the bright light streaming through the windows. Her heart didn't slow down any when she realized it was 10:00 a.m. Good grief. She hadn't slept this late since she was a teenager.

"Beckfast," Corbin repeated.

He was at the side of the bed, holding a paper plate with a Pop-Tart. Apparently, he'd brought her breakfast. And he wasn't alone. Regina was in the doorway.

"It was Corbin's idea," Regina said. "I think he was

worried you might be sick or something." She paused. "Are you—sick or something, I mean?"

Regina probably meant her mental state. Or more specifically her mental state considering the week before she'd had a semi-meltdown when the reporter had shown up at the rodeo.

Jordan hadn't completely fallen apart after seeing that picture of herself only minutes after her rescue, but she'd kept it together only because Dylan had gotten her out of there—fast. That meant he'd missed his bronco ride. Thankfully, though, he hadn't complained about it. Lucian was the only complainer in the house, but that was because he'd lost to Garrett once again.

"I'm fine," she told Regina, and she helped Corbin onto the bed.

Since he was looking at the Pop-Tart with much more anticipation than she was, Jordan halved it so they could chow down together. The sharing had been a stellar idea because he grinned and bit into it.

"Thank you for watching him this morning," Jordan added. "But you should have gotten me up to do my shift."

Regina waved her hand to dismiss that. "You know I love spending time with Corbin."

She did. So did Jordan. And so did Dylan. It was amazing how easily the boy had fit into their routines. Of course, Karlee had helped plenty with that. She'd put their appointments into a group calendar to make sure there'd always be someone to watch the boy. It was a lifesaver since Dylan had work, Regina was still doing follow-up appointments with her oncologist and Jordan would need to make a trip to the base first thing in the morning. She hated to admit it but Adele might have had the right idea by giving all three of them shared custody.

"App-top," Corbin said the moment he finished off the Pop-Tart.

Jordan had gotten good at deciphering his words, and she knew he meant laptop and the game that she'd downloaded for him. She took her computer from the nightstand and turned it on for him to play. Dozens of bunnics popped onto the screen, and Regina came even closer to watch him.

"So, are Dylan and you back together?" Regina asked.

Jordan was surprised the woman hadn't asked that earlier, but then they hadn't exactly had a lot of time alone for personal conversation. "You heard about Dylan and me kissing in the car the day of Lawson's wedding?"

Regina patted her hand. "I'm pretty sure everyone in the state has heard about it. According to whichever gossip is telling the story, Theo got really mad and called you a bad name. But, you know, you can never believe what you hear."

In this case, it was mostly true. Theo hadn't called her a name, but he'd cursed, and Jordan knew that the cussing was mostly aimed at her. Though Dylan had gotten some four-letter words thrown at him, too.

However, that was all that'd been thrown because at the moment that Theo had been stating the obvious—that it was over between them—all hell broke loose. Deafening thunder, lightning strikes and golf-ball-sized hail. It had sent the judge driving off, and seconds later,

Jordan had done the same. Dylan and she had gone back to the house where the only saving grace was that no one inside had seen either the kissing or the fallout that followed.

"Is it true?" Regina pressed. "Are you and Dylan getting back together? I'm leaning toward the answer being no because you slept in the bed alone last night."

Jordan had indeed gone solo and would continue to do it. Because now that the heat from the making out had cooled, she remembered something she should have remembered right from the get-go—that her life was already complicated enough without adding Dylan back into the mix.

And speaking of Dylan, he came strolling in, and he didn't look nearly as guilt riddled as she did. After all, the kissing hadn't just caused problems for her in the complication department, it had perhaps sent Walter Ray on a vendetta to screw Dylan over for Corbin's custody.

"Daddy," Corbin said, smiling. "'Ook." And he showed Dylan the bunny game.

Dylan smiled, too, came closer, and he moved as if to sit down on the edge of her bed, but he must have changed his mind in midmovement because he snapped back upright.

Regina saw the maneuver and volleyed a few glances at them. "I think I'll powder my nose to give you two a moment. Does Corbin need to come with me?"

Dylan shook his head. "He'll be fine. I don't have long. I've got a cattle buyer coming in from out of town today."

Regina nodded and went into the hall bathroom

where she could still probably hear everything they said. But there'd be no yelling or anger involved. Not with Corbin in the room.

"I just wanted to say I'm sorry about what happened yesterday." The words just rolled off his tongue as if he'd rehearsed them. They sounded very similar to the words she'd rehearsed and planned to tell him. "We've always had this fire, and I need to be more careful about it."

She was about to agree, but Dylan just kept on talking. "I just make stupid decisions sometimes. *Very* stupid decisions," he amended, "and that was definitely one of them."

Yes, stupid, but for some reason it bothered her that he'd lumped it together with all the other dumb things he'd done. And that he'd added the *very* and *definitely.*

He chuckled, scrubbed his hand over his face. "So, I just need to do better. I need to keep my eye on the prize." Dylan ruffled Corbin's hair.

The prize was custody, but now that the judge and Theo had seen them together, any damage had already been done. If Walter Ray could actually do damage, that is. Jordan had to believe that it all hinged on Adele, and as long as she didn't change her mind again, then Dylan would be a primary part of his son's life.

Now Jordan had to figure out if primary was what she truly wanted, too.

Dylan checked his watch. "Sorry, but I've got to go. See you in about two hours, buddy," he said to Corbin, and he leaned down and kissed the boy. Dylan smiled. "He really has adjusted well, hasn't he?"

Jordan made a sound of agreement. Corbin had indeed adjusted, and even though he still asked about his mom every day, he didn't seem on the verge of tears when they explained that she'd be away awhile longer.

Dylan walked out just as Regina came back in, which meant the woman was probably listening for him to leave. She was also gauging their expressions.

"We didn't have an argument," Jordan told her.

If she was pleased about that, Regina didn't show it, and the deep breath she took let Jordan know that her former mother-in-law was going to explain what was on her troubled mind. She didn't jump right into it, though. She motioned for Jordan to join her in the hall while Corbin stayed on the bed, playing his game.

Uh-oh.

A talk that required privacy from a two-year-old probably wasn't a conversation that Jordan wanted to have. Especially before coffee. But Jordan got up anyway and went to the woman.

"You don't have to remind me that it didn't work out with Dylan and me before," Jordan threw out there. She kept her voice at a whisper so that Corbin wouldn't hear. "Or remind me that I'm mainly responsible for what happened between us."

Regina didn't disagree with either of those statements. "You left before because you couldn't stay here. I understand that." She also whispered, "I'm a wanderlust kind of person, too. But my cancer has settled me down some. Having Corbin and Tessie has, as well."

There was an unspoken question at the end of that. *Did what happened to you on assignment bring on the need to become settled? Or has it only been covered by a thin blanket for the time being? A blanket that could easily slide right off?*

"I need you to ask yourself if staying is something you can do," Regina went on. "I know you and Dylan can share custody with Corbin following you wherever you end up being assigned, but that might not be good for Corbin. Without his mom around, he might need more stability than other kids."

Jordan could definitely see that side of it. In fact, it had been weighing heavily on her.

"When you left last time, it was only Dylan's heart that got broken," Regina continued. "But this time, it could be Corbin's. That's why I have some advice for you." She looked Jordan straight in the eyes. "Either pee or get off the pot."

PEEING OR GETTING off the pot wasn't easy. Jordan knew because it'd been nearly two days since Regina's *suggestion*, and she was still on the metaphorical pot and still hadn't peed. That couldn't go on much longer. She had to do something to end the stalemate.

She picked up the pen, held it over her signature block on the form, hesitated, and then put the pen back down. She'd lost count, but she thought this was the seventh time she'd repeated the process.

The seventh time she cursed herself, too.

Still not peeing, still pot sitting, still stalemating.

Jordan had gone to the base to get this paperwork to start the separation process. It'd taken hours of her time to initiate it, get the forms finalized and then for her to go back to the base to pick them up. She wouldn't have gone through all of that if she hadn't been sure.

Except now she didn't feel sure at all.

Something had to give, and that's why she'd asked Karlee if she could use her office that she'd set up in the guesthouse. Jordan hadn't needed the privacy so much as she had a copier for the separation papers once she'd signed them. The base would give her copies, of course, but she wanted her own before it reached the paperwork processing stage.

Signing it was something that needed to be done. She'd been back in Wrangler's Creek a little over a month now. That meant her leave was almost up, and signing the papers was the next step to moving on with her life. Strange that doing it might keep her in the very place that had once felt like deadweight instead of an anchor.

Regina had brought up her wanderlust problem, but it was more a wander-meh these days. There was no country she wanted to visit. Well, not unless she could see it through Corbin's eyes.

Now, that made her smile.

Of course, any traveling would likely include Dylan and Regina. A month ago that would have seemed like a nightmare scenario but not so much now.

Jordan had just picked up the pen again when there was a knock at the door, and a moment later, Karlee stuck in her head. "Just checking to make sure you found everything you needed."

"Got any extra spines?" Jordan joked. She motioned for her to come in.

"Several," Karlee said without hesitation. "I often need more than one when dealing with Lucian."

Jordan didn't doubt that for a moment. More spines

and something to rein in a temper. Karlee's tongue had to be sore from biting it so much because at best Lucian was just a grouch. At worst, he lived up to his nickname of Lucifer.

"Why exactly do you need a spine?" Karlee asked.

Jordan tipped her head to the papers on the desk, prompting Karlee to have a look at them. "It's scary giving up a life I know for one that I failed at before."

"I'll bet. But it's not the same. Dylan and you were way too young then. Plus, you'll build another life, maybe even work at the hospital here. And if Wrangler's Creek starts to close in on you, you could always get a place in San Antonio. That'd be near enough for you to see Corbin nearly every day."

All very valid points, and Jordan instantly remembered why they'd once been best friends. Friends who talked about their problems and dreams. Since Jordan had been back, though, their conversations had stayed pretty shallow, and there was a huge part of Karlee's life that Jordan hadn't even talked about.

"I should have asked sooner," Jordan said, "but how are your brothers?"

Karlee made a so-so motion with her hand. "The twins, Judd and Joe, are doing great. They have a ranch near Kerrville. And Mack…well, he's still Mack."

No need for Karlee to clarify what she meant by that. Over the years, Jordan had heard about Mack getting in and out of trouble, and as Jordan had done for Adele, Karlee had been the one to bail out Mack. Since that likely wasn't a pleasant reminder for Karlee, or her, Jordan switched subjects. One that would be good for both of them.

“Where’s Corbin?” she asked.

“Making cookies. And Dylan’s going to take him for a ride this afternoon.”

“They’ve been doing that a lot lately.”

Karlee nodded. “It’s all settling into a nice routine. You with Corbin in the mornings so that Dylan can work. Regina takes the middle shift, and Dylan gets the afternoons.” Karlee paused. “Of course that means you’re not spending time with Dylan. Are you okay with that?”

“Sure.” But the moment the answer came out of her mouth, Jordan frowned. “I *should* be okay with it.” She huffed. “I’ve been back a month and have already kissed Dylan twice, grabbed his balls once and I’m thinking about having sex with him.”

Jordan said that last part very quickly, but Karlee still caught it.

“Sex, huh?” Karlee chuckled. “Well, Dylan is hot.” She also noticed the return of Jordan’s frown. “That’s a generic statement of fact and nothing based on experience. I’m the only woman in Wrangler’s Creek who hasn’t bedded a Granger.”

That was possibly a true fact. Lucian, Dylan and Lawson had indeed gotten around. Heck, Lucian and Dylan were still in the getting around stage, though Dylan was taking a hiatus because of Corbin. A hiatus that she could end if she kept fantasizing about going back into his bed.

Jordan’s phone rang, and when she saw Theo’s name on the screen, that put a quick end to the talk about sex with Dylan. Karlee must have seen who the caller was, too, because she said, “Good luck,” and she headed out.

Jordan debated even taking the call. Theo and she hadn't spoken since the thunderstorm incident, and she wasn't even sure there was anything left to say. Well, unless it was to give her a chance to tell him a proper goodbye. Or to tell him that she hoped he'd backed off on his custody quest.

Apparently, she did have something to say after all, and that's why she hit the answer button.

"Remember the time we were in that cave in Peru?" Theo greeted.

That nearly caused her to hang up. "Are you about to remind me of yet another mistake I made? And then use the mistake to prove some kind of point that will benefit your position in whatever argument we're about to have?"

Apparently, that had been exactly his plan because he went silent. "I don't know how else to make you understand that your getting back together with your ex-husband is wrong."

That was almost certainly true, but Theo had riled her, and Jordan doubted logic was going to be her ally on this.

"First of all, I'm not back with Dylan," she snapped. "And no, I don't expect you to believe that after what you saw. And secondly, even if I were back with him, I'm pretty sure this falls into the category of *not-any-of-your-flippin'-business*."

"I care for you—"

"I care for you, too, but at best our relationship is travel buddies or friends with benefits. Or rather, it *was* friends with benefits. We haven't been benefiting like that for a long time now."

"That was your choice, not mine," he quickly pointed out.

"Yes, my choice. And it's one I'm sticking to. Our shared past doesn't give you the right to dictate what you think is best for me. And don't you dare bring up me being held captive because it's not playing into any of this, either."

Oh, that little outburst felt good, and she could almost feel her spine returning. But the good feeling didn't last. Because she never felt good when she lashed out—even when lashing out was the right thing to do.

"Look, Theo," she went on when he didn't say anything. "Let's just say goodbye and wish each other the best."

"I can't do that. I still care for you, and I don't want you hurt. Are you taking your meds?"

She suddenly felt another lashing out coming on. "Goodbye, Theo," she repeated. And she hit End Call before he could say another word.

Jordan also picked up the pen and started signing. Of course, she was pressing the pen so hard on the paper that she was gouging it a bit, but still, she was doing it. And she wasn't doing this solely because of Theo. He'd been just the reminder that this was the right thing to do for Corbin. Somehow, she'd make it the right thing for herself, as well.

She slipped the papers into a folder that she'd need to drop off first thing in the morning at the base in San Antonio. Then, on the way back she could stop at the Wrangler's Creek hospital and apply for a job. She had a decent savings built up, but she didn't have the luxury of a trust fund. Which brought her to the next thing on her to-do list.

A new place to stay.

Maybe she could find a short-term rental somewhere nearby. A house with a yard close enough for her to see Corbin whenever she wasn't working. She hadn't lied when she'd told Karlee that she was considering sex with Dylan, but it was best to establish some boundaries first. Boundaries so they wouldn't be under the same roof if things moved from good sex to a bad falling-out. Besides, having her own space might make her feel less claustrophobic.

Jordan closed down her laptop, ready to go back to the house when the landline on the desk rang. Since Karlee wasn't around, she answered it.

"I need to speak to Lucian Granger," the caller immediately said.

"I'm sorry, but he's not here." Jordan was about to offer to take a message, but the caller kept on talking.

"I'm Larry Larson with Biomeds Labs," he continued, "and I need to know where to send the DNA results he ordered."

Everything inside her went still. "There's been a mistake. Mr. Granger canceled that test."

"He put them on hold, but then I just spoke to him a week ago, and he told me to go ahead and run it."

The stillness inside her didn't last. Lucian had agreed to stop the test. He had agreed to do that to their faces, anyway, but he'd obviously gone behind their backs and done it anyway.

"He wanted me to call him as soon as I had the results," the guy went on, "but he's not answering the number he gave me so I tried this one."

Lucian wasn't answering because he was almost certainly in a business meeting.

"I can tell Mr. Granger the results," Jordan insisted. Not a lie. Oh, she would tell him all right. Dylan, too. And she was certain it wouldn't be a happy conversation when they confronted him.

"It's a report," the man explained. "I usually like to go over these things on the phone, but I'll just send it to the email address he gave me. Let him know I called, though, in case he doesn't see the email."

Jordan assured him she would do that, but before she could ask Mr. Larson more about the results, he ended the call. She sat there, wondering if she should call him back or try to get in touch with Lucian. Or go and tell Dylan or Karlee. But then she looked at the computer on the desk.

Karlee's business computer.

If the landlines were linked between Lucian's office and hers, then maybe the computers were, too. And she soon learned they were when she saw the email from Biomeds Labs load into the inbox.

She hesitated because it was a violation of privacy, but Lucian was guilty of a much bigger violation by having the test done in the first place. That's the justification Jordan used to click on the email and then the attached report. Once she saw Corbin's name, then Dylan's, she couldn't read fast enough.

And then Jordan's stomach went to her knees.

Oh. God.

DYLAN DIDN'T KNOW who or what to deal with first. What was left of the red panties that Booger had apparently dug up, or Abe, who was sitting in a rocker holding a stack of sex bingo cards. Or maybe he should tackle the incoming call from Lucian.

He decided to deal with Booger since eating the rest of those panties could send him back to the vet. Dylan also needed to figure out who'd let the dog escape—again—because Booger was running around in circles in the front yard with the dirt-caked panties clamped in his mouth.

"Excuse me a second," Dylan said to Abe.

Dylan bolted off the porch after Booger. Of course, Booger did his own share of bolting, and the chase lasted more than the *second* of time that Dylan had mentioned to Abe. Actually, it went on for several minutes before Booger stopped in his tracks, turned to the door where Regina was bringing out Corbin. Booger let go of the panties and jetted toward them.

As nasty as the panties now were, Dylan stuffed them into his pocket. If he left them anywhere on the ground, Booger would find them, and there'd be another humiliating chase. He'd already reached that particular quota for the next month or two.

Booger kept up the jetting pace, running back into the house, and Corbin went after him. Regina followed suit, leaving Dylan to move on to the second thing on his to-do list.

"How many this time?" Dylan asked, taking the stack of cards from Abe.

"Thirty-six. But I got some bad news. Somebody printed a new version of the game. This time, it's squares with things that folks think Jordan and you are doing together. Just look at the card on top, and you'll see what I mean."

He did look, and the only reason he didn't curse was because Corbin might come back close enough to hear him. But yes, it was a new card, and yes, it was about Jordan and him. Other than just their names, there was a common denominator.

Dylan and Jordan get caught making out in the barn.

Dylan and Jordan leave the Longhorn Bar to make out.

Dylan and Jordan are seen making out in a car.

That last box was checked, which meant this was likely Melanie's card since he couldn't see Walter Ray or Theo doing something like this. Of course, someone could have brought the new card idea to Melanie, and since she was no doubt angry and hurt, she might have gone along with it.

And that brought Dylan to an eye-opening revelation.

The cards weren't just going to stop being printed. He'd made his proverbial bed by sleeping around, and now he had to lie in that same proverbial shit. It didn't matter that he'd changed his ways. Or semichanged them anyway. He had made out with Jordan in the car and had kissed her in the barn, but he hadn't woken up with any naked women in the month since he'd had Corbin. That was progress, but it was going to take a lot more than that to get folks in Wrangler's Creek to forget.

"I'll write you a check for these cards," Dylan told Abe, "but don't bother collecting any more of them."

Abe frowned. "You're sure?" He was obviously disappointed since he was making a small fortune off this. Heck, maybe he was even the one who'd started the new game so he could continue his cash flow.

"Positive. Maybe the less said about the cards will mean the notion of them will die off soon enough." Hopefully by the time Corbin was old enough to understand what any of those bingo squares meant.

Dylan heard the footsteps from inside the foyer, and he stuffed the cards inside his shirt so that his mom or Corbin wouldn't see them. But it wasn't either of them. It was Jordan, and one look at her face, and Dylan knew something was wrong.

"What happened?" he immediately asked her.

However, Jordan didn't give him an immediate response. She shook her head and kept shaking it until he went to her and caught onto her shoulders.

"Lucian did the DNA test on Corbin," she finally said.

Dylan wasn't able to hold back the profanity this time, and he reached in his pocket for his phone so he could call his brother. Then, he was going to find him and punch him. But Jordan took hold of his hand to stop him from making the call.

"The lab called Lucian's office phone," she went on, "and when I told him he wasn't there, they sent me the results." She shook her head again and said some words that felt as if she'd stabbed him right in the heart.

"Dylan, Corbin isn't your son."

CHAPTER SIXTEEN

"DO YOU REMEMBER when we had that sex picnic in the pasture, and we caused the cattle to stampede?" Jordan asked Dylan.

She'd known before she brought it up that it would cause Dylan to scowl. And it did. But pretty much everything she'd said in the last half hour since he'd learned about the DNA test had caused him to react that way.

As she drove away from the ranch and toward San Antonio, she was doing her own scowling. At Lucian—who still wasn't answering his phone. But she was especially scowling at Adele, who couldn't take a call, which meant they had to drive to the jail to see her. Jordan knew, though, that she had to try to rein in at least some of Dylan's temper before they came face-to-face with Adele.

Which they would do in about forty-five minutes.

So far, Jordan was failing big-time at temper reining—either Dylan's or hers. She wanted to throttle Adele for lying, but she also needed answers. Like why Adele had done this and who exactly was Corbin's father. The test hadn't told them that because Corbin's DNA had only been compared to Dylan's.

God, she prayed that Theo wasn't the father.

That would not only complicate things for Dylan, it would mean a nasty custody battle looming on the horizon. A battle that Theo might try to solve by putting marriage on the table again.

"When we caused the stampede, we were still partially naked, and we had to run like that all the way to the fence," she added.

And again, she failed. If anything, Dylan's scowl only got worse. At least he'd agreed when she had insisted on driving because with the way his hands were clenched into fists, he would have crushed the steering wheel.

"Sorry," Jordan said. She'd lost count of how many times she'd used that word, as well. It hadn't worked any better than the sex mishaps. "I'm furious with Adele, too, but I don't want us to get thrown out before she even has a chance to explain why she lied."

Dylan didn't jump to respond to that, and Jordan thought he was going to continue the silence all the way throughout the entire drive. He didn't.

"Fuck this," he growled. "Fuck Adele."

Dylan wasn't big on cursing, but this was a cursing situation if there ever was one. DNA didn't matter when loving a child—most adoptive parents would say that. But it did matter in this case because Dylan wouldn't be keeping custody of Corbin. He'd only had the boy a month, but that was plenty enough time for him to become Corbin's father.

When she saw that his knuckles were turning white, Jordan touched his hand, causing him to flinch. She'd never seen him this wired. Or this angry. So, yeah, visiting Adele at this moment wasn't a good idea.

Again, Jordan was thankful she was the one driving because she pulled off onto a ranch trail. It was a heavily treed area with no one else around so he could have privacy if he wanted to have an adult version of a temper tantrum.

"No need for you to tell me that you want us to keep going," she said before he could balk at what she was doing. "I want that, too. But this is for our own good."

"The only thing I want to do right now is confront that lying witch and demand to know why she fucked me over like this."

Jordan had zero doubt about that, but Dylan had broken a record in using the *f*-word, and that only convinced her even more that it was a good idea to stop. She pulled beneath a cluster of trees and tried to think of something she could say that would help.

"We could have sex," was what came out of her mouth.

In hindsight, that wasn't a helpful thing to say because Dylan looked at her as if she'd sprouted an extra ear.

"All right. Maybe not sex," Jordan amended.

It was just she'd been thinking about it since her conversation with Karlee, dreaming about it, too, and that's why she'd blurted it out like that. The sex bingo cards had contributed to the raunchy thoughts, as well. Dylan had pulled those from his shirt shortly after they'd gotten in her car, and they were now facedown on the dash. She was betting there were some things in those little game blocks that would distract Dylan enough to calm him down.

Or not.

The look he gave her said there was nothing she

could say that was going to ease his scowl or get his teeth or fists unclenched. That was probably true, but she had to try anyway.

"Adele might have had a reason for lying," she tried again. "Not a good reason, mind you," Jordan quickly added when she saw the angry fire light through Dylan's eyes. "The real father might be a dirtbag. Or maybe she truly thought Corbin was yours. Even you admitted the timing was right, so maybe she just assumed you'd gotten her pregnant."

"Adele shouldn't have *assumed* something like that," he growled.

"No, she shouldn't have, but we're talking about Adele here. Flighty is her middle name." Along with being irresponsible, immature and unreliable. In fact, it was possible that Adele hadn't even had sex with Dylan.

She tried touching him again by putting her hand on his arm. He didn't flinch this time, but his muscles were still rock hard.

"I don't want you to be nice to me." His voice was still a growl. "I especially don't want you to try to smooth this over or feel sorry for me. Just let me seethe and wallow in this shit storm that Adele created."

Okay. She'd go with the wallowing/seething. And hopefully some passing of time. Even a half hour might be enough to cool a little of the hot anger.

She plucked the top card from the stack, intending to use it to make a joke, but then Jordan frowned. "Someone changed the game. It's about us now." And good gravy, it was *about us* in a stupid kind of way.

"Are people really going to be watching to see if you and I have sex on the back of a horse?"

He took the card, and without looking at it, Dylan wadded it up and hurled it into the back seat the way a pitcher would throw a fastball at a batter. Since that seemed to help a little, she handed him another one to wad and toss. Then another. By the fifth one, she could see that this idea sucked. Dylan was just getting madder and madder.

So, she turned off the engine and climbed onto his lap.

Still no cooling of the anger. In fact, it seemed to make things worse.

"I don't want pity sex," he snapped.

"Good. Because I was thinking more like a pity hand job. You used to tell me I was good at those."

The joke fell flatter than the look he gave her. And that's why she went for broke and kissed him. It was a huge gamble. Because of his mood, he could move her right off his lap, say something hurtful and demand that she start driving toward the jail.

But he didn't.

Dylan hooked his hand around the back of her neck and kissed her right back. Except it was angry kissing. Hard and rough. It was as if he was trying to work out some of his frustrations on her, and while Jordan wasn't a fan of either frustration or pity sex, it wasn't a bad basis for kisses. Of course, this was Dylan, so he pretty much excelled at any type of lip-lock.

He'd given her thousands of kisses, but each one felt both familiar and different at the same time. Even this rough and punishing one. Each time, the pressure of his mouth got to her. It melted her, and it was just as effective as if it'd been part of a moonlight-and-roses kind of date night.

His grip tightened on her, and he kept kissing. Kept taking. Until they were going to pass out if they didn't get some oxygen.

"I'm sorry," she managed to say when they broke for air.

He stopped, stared at her, and she finally saw the change in his eyes. There weren't flamethrowers of fury in his baby blues. Not huge ones anyway. But she saw the sadness that came with the realization.

That he wasn't a father.

Corbin wasn't his.

He groaned, the sound of pain coming from deep in his chest. Jordan could feel every ounce of that pain. That's when she knew the distraction kisses weren't working.

"Just so you know," he said, cupping her chin and turning her to force eye contact. "I'm sorry about this."

Not understanding what he meant, Jordan shook her head, but he stopped the movement by sliding his hand into her hair and holding firm. He repeated the "I'm sorry about this," and he kissed her again.

Since Jordan had initiated the first kiss, she'd been ready for it. Not ready for this, though. It wasn't angry, but it was fast. It was as if Dylan wanted to do this in a hurry or else he'd change his mind and stop. Jordan soon realized she didn't want him to stop even though in the back of her mind she figured Dylan was going to regret this. She might, too, but for now she was just in the swept-away mode.

Without breaking the kiss, Dylan somehow managed to push the seat all the way back to give them some room to maneuver. And he used that room to shove up her dress. When she felt his hand on her bare skin, it was like a blast from the past.

Both recent and from years ago.

He'd touched her in the car when they'd made out the day of Lawson's wedding, but there'd been times when the vehicle had become their makeshift bed. Of course, plenty of places had become that. In fact, this very place had when they'd still been in high school. And it was apparently about to become a repeat location.

Jordan didn't try to slow him down to give herself time to think. That's because she didn't want to think. She just wanted to be swept up in the moment and hoped the same would be true for Dylan. Not just because it might ease his body, but it might ease his mind, too.

He certainly seemed to be trying to do just that.

Dylan kept kissing her, kept sliding up her dress while he dragged her tighter against him. He certainly hadn't lost any of his skills in the sex department and had even improved them. Without easing up one bit on the frenzied foreplay, he managed to reach in his back pocket and get out a condom from his wallet. It was a good thing he'd thought of safe sex because Jordan sure hadn't.

It took some more maneuvering for her to get out of her panties, and Jordan ended up ripping the side of them. Dylan gave her a quick look to indicate approval and "I could have done better" at the same time. He probably could have done better because she hadn't remembered any past episode of panty destruction, but the urgency inside her was building, and she wanted him now.

Dylan unzipped his jeans, put the condom on and gave her *now.* He pushed into her and did what he did best. What he'd no doubt learned from years of practice. Practice that had started with her, since they'd been each other's firsts.

That "firsts" thought didn't last long in her head, though. Actually, nothing lasted because he caught onto her hips and started the thrusts inside her that would end all of this too soon. For her anyway. She was usually primed and ready by the time Dylan finished his chrome-melting foreplay, and today was no exception. It didn't take long for Jordan to feel the climax start to ripple through her.

Dylan wasn't rippling, though.

Despite slipping into the oblivion that came with an orgasm, she noticed that. He just kept up the thrusts as if giving her every possible ounce of pleasure. Which he did.

And then he stopped.

Jordan was still in oblivion land so she couldn't actually form words yet. But Dylan managed that just fine, too. Along with moving her off his lap and onto the side of the seat by the passenger's side window.

"I'll drive us to the jail now," he said.

And with Jordan still in stunned silence, he moved behind the steering wheel to do just that.

DYLAN FELT LIKE SHIT. And it was a three-ring kind of excrement circus. He wasn't Corbin's father. That was the biggest reason for this extreme low he was feeling. But he was not only in this crap pit of despair solely because of that. He was about to confront Adele about her lie, but also he'd used Jordan to soothe his frustrations.

Or rather he'd tried to soothe them.

But he was just as angry and tense as before their sexual encounter in her car. Maybe more so. He'd stopped after he'd gotten her off because he'd realized that it wasn't right. He'd been using her. Now he was going to have to apologize until he was blue in the face to make Jordan understand just how sorry he was. She hadn't needed to be his outlet for the anger and hurt he was feeling. Mainly because there was no outlet to help with that. Plus, Jordan had her own worries without him adding sex to them.

"You want to go in alone to visit Adele?" Jordan asked him.

He appreciated that she made the offer, but he could tell she was hoping he'd turn her down. That's because she wanted to be in the visiting room. To hear Adele's explanation and also to try to stop him from saying and doing something he might regret. Jordan wouldn't be able to stop that because Dylan was absolutely certain there'd be some ugliness going on.

"I'll yell at her whether you're there or not," Dylan said to her.

But that might not be true. Despite his feeling so bad about it, giving Jordan an orgasm had actually burned off some of the anger that would have ensured some yelling. Now he wasn't sure what he was going to say to Adele or how loud it would be.

Jordan took hold of his hand, linking their fingers together. "No matter what happens, you don't have to apologize for what went on in the car. I started that. I just wish you'd finished it…for yourself."

He didn't wish that. It'd been rule-breaking enough without his getting off in the process. Of course, the end result didn't matter as much as the act itself did. Attempted sex was still sex. He'd known his vow of celibacy wouldn't last, but it hadn't been smart to break that vow with the one woman who'd broken his heart.

Of course, the heart breaking was so long ago, and it would have been much easier to put it aside if Jordan and he had ended up raising Corbin together. But now that wasn't going to happen. Jordan would probably take Corbin from the ranch. Or maybe Corbin's real father would do that. Either way, Dylan figured he was going to be in that shit pit for a long time yet to come.

Dylan got to his feet the moment the guard came into the waiting room and motioned for Dylan and Jordan to follow him. Adele was already seated at a table in the visitors' area.

"Is Corbie all right?" Adele immediately asked.

Jordan nodded. "He's fine."

Adele studied their faces for a moment before she looked away. "Oh." That told him loads. Even though Jordan hadn't specifically mentioned what this was about when she called to arrange visitation, Adele must have known from their expressions what had happened.

"Start talking," Dylan said when he sat down across

from her. "And during this explanation, you will tell me why you lied."

Adele repeated that "oh" and groaned softly. "You did a DNA test." But she waved that off. "Or maybe Lucian did." She waved that off, too. "I know in your eyes you think what I did is unforgivable—"

"I don't *think* it," he snapped. "It *is* unforgivable."

Dylan didn't yell, and he was surprised that there wasn't more emotion in his voice because he was certainly feeling a lot of emotion inside every part of him. He'd held out a tiny glimmer of hope that Adele would say the test was a mistake, that he was Corbin's father, but she'd just dashed that glimmer with what she'd said.

Adele acknowledged that with a nod.

"How could you do this?" Jordan demanded, and unlike Dylan, she didn't hold back in the emotion department. She was angry and loud, and it got the attention of not only the guard but everyone else in the room. "How?" she repeated. It was quieter this time around, but she spoke it through clenched teeth.

Now the tears came, shimmering in Adele's eyes, and normally that would have brought out his need to soothe her, but nothing he was feeling right now called for soothing.

"I was desperate." Adele didn't dodge his gaze this time. She looked right at Dylan. "I was about to be arrested, and I couldn't get in touch with Jordan. I didn't want Corbie to end up in foster care, not even for a couple of hours. And I knew you'd take excellent care of him."

If Adele truly believed that, then she was the only one, because no one else in Wrangler's Creek had felt he'd be a good father. Dylan had proved them wrong—for all the good it'd done.

"That's your explanation?" Jordan howled. "Because it's a piss-poor one if you ask me." Again, she got the attention of the guards, and since Dylan didn't want them to get tossed out of there before they even finished this chat, he caught onto her hand, hopefully a reminder that she needed to hold it together.

"It's not piss-poor," Adele argued. "I love my son and would do anything for him, and I mean anything."

Since Dylan now had firsthand experience as to what it was like to love Corbin, he could understand that. But no way was he letting Adele off the hook simply because she'd been worried about foster care.

"You didn't have to lie to us," Dylan told her. "You could have just had Corbin sent to me until you worked out something with Jordan. I would have taken care of him."

Adele was shaking her head before he even finished. "Social Services said the only way they could expedite the paperwork was to turn him over to a family member. Jordan's the only family I had, and I couldn't get in touch with her because she was on a flight from Germany."

Obviously, Adele was forgetting that there was one other family member. Corbin's real father. He could have stepped up to handle this. Well, maybe he could have, but before Dylan could ask her about that, Adele continued.

"We didn't even have sex," Adele whispered. "I lied about that, too. Sorry," she added. "You're really hot, but you'll always be Jordan's in my eyes."

If this had only been about sex, that probably would have made him feel better, because he hadn't cared for the notion of bedding Jordan's cousin. But this was about Corbin more than the sex.

"I remember seeing you that night," Dylan pointed out. Though that was about all he could remember about that evening.

Adele nodded. "We hung out, but you were so loopy from those meds you were falling asleep at the party so I got you a hotel room so you could crash."

He had indeed woken up in a hotel and had had to call Karlee to come and get him because he didn't know where he'd left his truck. That explained one thing about that fateful night, but it didn't explain the three-thousand-pound gorilla in the room.

"You named Corbin after me," Dylan reminded her.

Another nod from Adele. "I've always thought you were a great guy, and I liked the name, too. It just seemed to fit Corbin."

"And it didn't bother Corbin's real father that you'd done that?" Jordan again, and she was back to snapping.

"No." That's all Adele said for several moments. "He was already out of the picture by then. Actually, he was out of the picture before I even learned I was pregnant. Even if I had told him about Corbin, I doubt he would have cared."

That caused Dylan's chest to go tight. Because it was a slap-to-the-face reminder that he no longer had a claim on Corbin. No chance of winning this custody battle that had threatened him for weeks.

But Corbin's *real father* could get the boy. And he could whisk him away from not only Wrangler's Creek but also from Dylan. He wasn't sure he was ready to hear who that person was, but he had to know. However, Adele spoke before he could even ask.

"As for Corbin's father," Adele finally continued. "Well, he's someone you know." And now she dodged their gazes again. "Please, just don't be upset when I tell you who he is."

CHAPTER SEVENTEEN

"Mack O'Malley," Jordan heard Adele say.

Jordan made a sharp sound of surprise. If she'd come up with a list of likely candidates for Corbin's father, Mack O'Malley wouldn't have been on it. Heck, Karlee's troubled kid brother wasn't even on her radar for something like this.

Dylan obviously felt that same kick of shock because he didn't say anything. Neither did Adele. She just sat there, obviously waiting for them to absorb what she'd just told them. It wouldn't have been that hard to grasp if Dylan and she hadn't already met their shock quota for the day by learning that Adele had lied when she'd first named Dylan as the father. But this double dose of surprise was too much to swallow. Especially since Adele had already established herself as a liar, liar, pants on fire kind of person.

"Mack?" Jordan finally said, and she made sure that she sounded skeptical.

It was common knowledge that Karlee's brother was a screwup, along with having a police record. Of course, these days Adele had those same labels. But as far as Jordan knew, Adele had never been attracted to screwups like herself. She'd gone more for men like Dylan. Or even Theo. Hot, rich or adventurous. Dylan had the first two. Theo, the last one. Mack met the hot requirement—all of the O'Malley men did—but he was definitely lacking in the money department.

And then there was also the age issue.

Mack was only in his early twenties, five or six years younger than Adele. That meant Mack had been just nineteen or twenty when he'd gotten Adele pregnant. Not exactly a jailbait relationship, but it was close.

"Yes, Mack," Adele confirmed. She then turned to Dylan. "I know you don't think much of me after what I did, but I lied because of Corbin. There's no way Mack's responsible enough to be a father."

"Then you shouldn't have fucked him," Dylan growled. He shoved himself away from the table and stormed out of the visiting room.

Jordan stood, too, not only because she needed to go after him but also because there was nothing else she could say to Adele that would help. Unfortunately, there were plenty of things she could say that would hurt.

"You'll tell Mack, I suppose?" Adele asked.

Jordan stopped in midstep but didn't turn back around to face her. "No. *You* will tell him. Have your lawyer arrange for Mack to come to the jail so he can hear the news from the mother of his child."

Adele probably wasn't happy about that but tough. She'd been the one to make this mess, and she needed to get started cleaning it up. If cleaning it up was even possible, that is. Jordan wasn't sure that Dylan would recover from this. Mack might not, either.

And then there was the really huge problem of how this would eventually affect Corbin.

Jordan hurried out of the visiting area, but her heart

went to her knees when she didn't see Dylan in the waiting room. Heaven knew what he would do so she hurried to catch up with him. Well, she hurried as much as she could, considering that she had to work her way back through the levels of security along with collecting her purse and phone. When she made it out the front, Dylan was already by her car. He was pacing and cursing.

She wanted to do some cursing of her own, along with maybe yelling at the top of her lungs, but it was probably best if only one of them went into the batshit crazy mode right now. Since Dylan had more at stake in this, it was his turn.

"You want to go to a bar and have something to take the edge off?" Jordan asked him.

He didn't answer, not with words anyway, but he did get in the car once she unlocked it, and Jordan started driving, not sure where she should go. Probably not back to the ranch. Not yet, anyway, because she didn't want Corbin to see Dylan while he was this upset. Dylan wouldn't want that, either.

Karlee would need to know what had happened, and Jordan was betting she wouldn't take the news any better than Dylan and she had. But this meant that Corbin was Karlee's nephew. She could have a claim for custody if Mack didn't want the boy. For that matter, Jordan still had a claim, too. After all, he was still blood kin.

But the two people who didn't have any claim whatsoever were Theo and Dylan.

Theo was already out of the picture, and Jordan wasn't even sure if he'd actually thought Corbin was his child. However, Dylan certainly had believed it and so had his family. Actually, everyone but Lucian had, and that's why he'd done that blasted DNA test that had set all of this into motion by uncovering Adele's lies.

Even though it'd only been a month since Dylan had had Corbin, Jordan had no doubts that he loved the boy. And vice versa. For heaven's sakes, Corbin called him Daddy. It was going to be heartbreaking for both of them to be torn apart. That didn't help the anger that was surging through her, and Jordan had to again remind herself to stay calm.

Jordan wasn't sure what to do until she spotted the hotel, and she pulled into the parking lot. At first, she thought maybe they could just sit there for a while and talk this out. But Dylan was still mumbling profanities, still had a white-knuckle grip on his phone, so talking it out might take a while. Like a day or two.

"I need to call Karlee," he said.

"You can do that later. Regina and she won't be expecting us back for a while." Though they would want to know what they'd learned from Adele. That's why Jordan texted Karlee.

Dylan's upset. Will talk to you in an hour or two.

Hopefully, in that hour or two, Adele would make arrangements to see Mack so that Mack could be the one to tell his sister that she was an aunt.

When she opened her car door, Dylan looked up at the hotel as if he'd just noticed it. He shook his head. "I thought you were taking me to a bar."

"I decided sex would take the edge off better than

whiskey." She meant it as a pseudojoke. It would indeed take off the edge. She suspected that's why she was slightly less agitated than Dylan—because she'd recently had an orgasm. But the real truth was that it was only eleven in the morning and too early for most bars to be open.

He stared at her, maybe waiting for her to indicate it was a joke by adding a smile or a wink. She didn't. "All right," he said, getting out of the car.

Stunned to silence, she sat there for a few seconds, and then had to hurry to catch up with him. She got delayed because she had to give her keys to the valet. When she made it inside, Dylan was already checking them in.

It was a trendy boutique place that thankfully had one room available. A suite on the top floor, which meant it was out of her normal price range, but Dylan didn't blink an eye about the pricey rate of not only the suite but the bottle of whiskey he ordered from the room service menu. Dylan had even asked that the whiskey be brought up immediately and had given the clerk a huge tip to make sure that happened.

Jordan figured by the time they made their way up the elevator that Dylan would have decided this wasn't a stellar idea. Or that he would just crash until the whiskey arrived. He didn't. The moment he had them in the room, he shut the door, hooked his arm around her and kissed her. That put an end to the wacky notion she had of them talking this out or Dylan changing his mind.

He definitely didn't talk. But there was more of that intense anger kissing that'd gone on in the car. Jordan just went with it. Better yet, she let herself slide right into the heat of the foreplay—which she figured would be very short. In fact, this might be a sex against the door kind of thing.

Or not.

Just as quickly as he'd started it, Dylan stopped, looked at her and cursed again. "Sorry," he grumbled, and he moved away from her.

Jordan immediately felt the loss of two things. The pleasure from his kiss. That oh-so-nice pressure of his body against hers. But she gained something in his stopping.

A whole boatload of disappointment.

Yes, it'd only been a couple of hours since their encounter in the car, but she suddenly felt very needy in the sexual urge department.

"We don't have to stop," she managed to say.

Dylan obviously didn't feel that way because he went to the massive floor-to-ceiling window, and with his back to her, he stared out. "I've already used you once today to cure what was ailing me. Best to go with the whiskey and a cold shower for this round."

Jordan made a sound that reeked of that disappointment that was still washing over her. The sound got Dylan's attention because he looked back at her.

And her breath flew off to Pluto.

He certainly made a picture there in his jeans and boots and with the sunlight framing him. Of course, Dylan didn't need frames. Actually, he didn't need clothes—but that was the disappointment and her overly aroused body talking.

"There are other things better than whiskey," she

added. That was her overly aroused body talking, too, and she was sending him a big-assed invitation for sex.

Dylan picked up on the invitation. She could tell because the air changed between them. The temperature skyrocketed probably because of the intense heat that was suddenly in his eyes.

“Room service,” someone called out after a knock at the door.

“Come back later,” Dylan immediately told the guy. “This is about a thousand gallons of wrong,” he added in a mumble, but he still went back to her.

And he kissed her.

Not an ordinary kiss. This was the prizewinner of kisses. One that should be a square to tick off on the sex bingo card. Jordan thought maybe he'd melted her toenail polish. It certainly upped her urgency for this to go well beyond the kiss.

Like to the bed.

But Dylan didn't head that direction, a reminder that he rarely did things the easy way, but when it came to sex, he always did it the best way. He'd never left her unsatisfied, and he was already heading in the right direction to keep his record at a 100 percent in that area.

While he tongue-kissed her neck, he reached in his back pocket and took out a condom. Thankfully, he'd had another one. She wasn't sure he would since he'd used one in the car.

“Unzip me and get this on me,” he said, giving her the condom.

For the briefest second, Jordan wondered why he hadn't put it on himself, but she quickly realized that he was doing exactly what he needed to be doing. He had one hand on her dress that he was shoving up, and his other one was on her butt. Since the dress shoving was exposing the lower part of her body, she'd rather have him doing that than taking care of putting on the condom.

It was a little hard to maneuver, but Jordan finally managed to get her hand between them. And speaking of hard—Dylan was. As hard as stone. That made her quest a little easier since that particular part of him was easy to locate. The unzipping was a bit of a challenge, though, especially since he was continuing to drive her nuts with those neck kisses.

Which suddenly went lower.

He got her dress up far enough that he could go after her breasts, and he used his teeth to lower the cups of her bra. She'd once joked that Dylan could undress her with just his teeth, and he was proving that joke had some basis in truth.

Proving, too, that the right kind of nipple kiss could make her scream in pleasure.

Jordan bit back a scream, but her moan was pretty loud.

She finally got him unzipped, and then had to work her way past his boxers. If she could have gotten her mouth down there, she would have tried his teeth trick, but she didn't want to lose this position just yet. Dylan moved, though. Once she had gotten the condom on him, he went lower and did some tongue playing around with her navel ring.

Her next moan was even louder.

She'd never thought of her navel area as being a hot zone, but it was. Oh, it really was.

He flicked the ring with his tongue, causing a ripple of pleasure to arrow straight down to the correct lady part for maximum pleasure-rippling. In fact, it was so good that Jordan thought she would come before she could get Dylan inside her. That's why she latched onto a handful of his hair and pulled him back up to her.

Dylan cooperated with the return trip up her body, but he dropped some of those scalding kisses on the way. Along with ridding her of her panties. Of course, he didn't just take them off. Merely removing them wouldn't have been enough for Dylan. He first slid his hand into her panties, then touched her in the right place, before he shimmied them off her.

Jordan still hadn't recovered from the touching and the shimmying when Dylan hoisted her up, bracing her against the back of the door. And he pushed into her with the same clever nimbleness as he'd done with all the other stuff.

It was heaven. Possibly other things, too. But Jordan soon lost all ability to put a label on what was happening. Basically, Dylan was just screwing her lights out and she was going with it. Going, going and gone. Because no matter how hard she tried to hang on to the pleasure, the pleasure had its way with her.

As Dylan was doing.

The thrusts lined up just right until she felt the second orgasm of the day slamming through her. This one was a two-fer, though, because Dylan came right along with her.

He pushed into her, cursed her. Then, he cursed himself before he collapsed against her, pinning her in place. Thank goodness for that, because if he'd stepped back, she would have fallen on her butt. The orgasm had turned her bones to rubber and her brain to mush.

"Yeah," Dylan drawled with his breath gusting on her neck, "that was better than whiskey."

CHAPTER EIGHTEEN

DYLAN KNEW THAT a shower wasn't going to fix what was ailing him, but he ducked his head under the too-hot water and let it spew over him. Even if it didn't improve his mood, at least he'd be clean for the drive back to the ranch.

Which had to happen soon.

He couldn't put off what he had to deal with—that he was going to lose Corbin. That might have been a little easier to swallow if he weren't losing him to somebody like Mack O'Malley, whose life's mission seemed to be screwing up as much as possible. Yeah, Dylan had done his own share of bungling things, but he was an amateur compared to Mack.

Of course, no matter who Corbin's real father was, this was still going to hurt.

God, did it hurt.

Dylan scrubbed a handful of the scalding hot water over his face. Nope. It didn't fix squat, and now his eyes were burning. That was his cue to get his butt out of the shower and dry off so they could check out of the hotel and leave for the ranch. First, though, he had to deal with Jordan.

He owed her yet another apology for the "help me forget" sex against the wall. In hindsight, he should have opted for the whiskey. Distilled alcoholic beverages could complicate things but not as much as dicking around with an ex-wife. Jordan had been through enough without him screwing her over—and literally screwing her.

He got dressed and went back into the bedroom to start that groveling apology, but anything he'd been planning on saying sort of got lost with his sudden erection. Dylan went rock hard in record time when he saw Jordan on the bed—where they'd eventually landed after having sex.

She was sacked out on her stomach, bare assed naked, with her face turned toward him. The only part of her body that was covered was her left foot, which was under the sheet. In that instant, he remembered why he'd first been attracted to her.

And, no, it wasn't her butt.

Especially now that the ugly tat was so close to her otherwise-perfect backside. He'd first been attracted to that face. More than beautiful. It was interesting with those soft lines, full mouth and the dimple in her chin. Her eyes had gotten to him, too. Cat-green. Jordan could say a lot of things with just those eyes.

Like now.

She woke up and looked at him. In only a blink of time, he saw the slack euphoria that came with good sex. Then the heat that told him her body wanted even more good sex. And finally, the *oh-shit* moment. Those cat-greens widened, and she scrambled off the bed.

The scrambling gave him a good look at her front side, which didn't help soften his erection one bit. But he just reminded that brainless part of himself that he was out of condoms and that he had other things he needed to do.

Jordan must have realized they should leave, because she started hurrying to gather up her clothes that were scattered all around the room. Her panties were dangling from the doorknob.

As incredibly interesting as it was to watch her naked/scrambling, Dylan took a deep breath to get started on that apology/groveling. However, his phone rang before he could say anything.

"Karlee," Dylan relayed when he saw the woman's name on the screen.

Jordan's groan summed up what he was feeling. He didn't especially want to talk to Karlee over the phone, but it would probably cause her to worry if he didn't answer. While Jordan continued to dress, Dylan answered the call and put it on Speaker.

"Don't panic," Karlee immediately said. "Everything is okay."

Hell. That caused him to panic. Jordan did, too, because she gasped, and then froze, her attention fixed on the phone. "What happened?" Dylan couldn't ask fast enough.

"Corbin was running in the sunroom, and he hit his head on one of the end tables. Regina and I brought him to the ER for stitches, but he's all finished. He wanted to talk to you, though."

Dylan's heart was drumming so loud in his ears and the fear was vising his chest, making it hard to breathe, but he somehow managed to answer. "Put him on the phone."

Oh man. Corbin had been hurt. That scared the crap

out of him, but Dylan tried to rein in that fear because he didn't want to upset Corbin more than he already was. It seemed to take eight lifetimes for Karlee to get Corbin on the line, but Dylan finally heard him.

"Daddy," Corbin said, "I got a polly-lop and a boo-boo."

What the hell was a polly-lop? The rising panic also caused his imagination to go batshit because Dylan was fearing the worst—tumors, a cracked skull, parasites...

"He means lollipop," Karlee interjected.

"A reen polly-lop," Corbin interjected right along with her.

At least Dylan didn't go into an emotional tailspin over the "reen" because he knew that meant green.

"Uh, how are you, buddy?" Dylan asked the boy.

"My head hurted so I got *titches*."

Mercy, that tore away at him, and it didn't matter that Corbin wasn't his son. This was a child he loved, and it twisted at his gut for Dylan to think he'd gotten *hurted* while Dylan wasn't there.

"It's me," Karlee said when she came back on. "I swear, everything is fine, and we're heading back to the ranch now."

No, everything wasn't fine. Far from it. But this put things in crystal clear perspective for Dylan. Corbin was his top priority. That meant even if he couldn't be the one to raise him, then he had to make sure that Corbin got what he needed. And what he needed was a responsible parent. One who didn't lie and wasn't in jail. Since that meant Adele was out, he had to deal with Corbin's other parent.

"Jordan and I are leaving now," Dylan told Karlee. “We’ll be back soon.” In fact, as soon as they could safely get there. Thankfully, Jordan was already dressed and had her keys in hand so they headed out the door.

“Uh, how did it go with Adele?” Karlee asked. “Did she tell you about…well, you know what?”

While Jordan checked out of the room, Dylan took the call off Speaker, and he tried to figure out how to answer that. “It didn’t go great,” he finally admitted. Then he paused. “Is there any chance you can call your brother Mack and ask him to meet us at the ranch?”

Silence. For a long time. “You don’t mean… God, you don’t mean…” More silence. “I would say a really bad curse word right now if Corbin wasn’t next to me.”

“I’ll say it for you.” And Dylan did. It didn’t help, though. “Just please see if Mack will come. If not, I’ll go to the Granger Ranch and talk to him.” Though he would like to avoid confronting the man while he was at work.

“I’ll get him there,” Karlee assured him.

“Thanks. Oh, and don’t say anything to him while Corbin’s around. There are some things I want to get straight first with Mack.”

“Of course. I want to get some things straight with him, too.” And that sounded like a threat.

Dylan felt like threatening someone, too. But like the bad word he’d just belted out, that wasn’t going to help anything. The only thing that might make this marginally better was to put the fear of an ass-whipping into Mack if he didn’t straighten up and be a good father to Corbin. That wouldn’t fix things for him, but it would help with the big picture.

A picture that wouldn't include him.

"We could just keep having sex until you feel better," Jordan joked once they were in the car. "Because right now, I'm not coming up with any other way to help you."

He appreciated both the joke and her wanting to help, but right now he just needed to get home. Then he could check on Corbin to make sure he was okay and deal with Mack. In that order. It didn't help the knot in Dylan's stomach to know that Jordan and he had been having sex while his son… While *Corbin* was getting stitches.

"I'd told Adele that she needed to let Mack know he was Corbin's father," Jordan explained as she drove. She was definitely exceeding the speed limit, too. "But I'm guessing you don't want to wait."

Finally, it was an easy question to answer. "No. God knows when Adele will get around to doing that. I want to start fixing this right away."

"Uh, fixing it doesn't include beating up Mack, does it?" And that wasn't a joke.

"No. He might not have even known that he got Adele pregnant."

If so, it meant Adele had lied again by omission. And it didn't matter whether she'd thought Mack would be a lousy father. She should have at least told him and given him the chance to see Corbin and help her take care of him. There weren't enough apologies in the world to fix something like that.

And speaking of apologies, Dylan had his own to give.

"I'm sorry about the sex," he said just as Jordan

said, "Are you regretting you had me instead of the whiskey?"

Jordan glanced at him. "I'll take that as a yes, but no regrets are necessary. And if you say any sort of apology about my possible fragile well-being, I'm going to yell at you."

Okay. He'd take her mental state off the discussion table. However, that didn't mean it wasn't a factor here.

"The sex helped," he admitted to her. "But if you offered it because of my possible fragile well-being, then I'm going to yell at you."

The corner of her mouth lifted. "I offered it because I wanted sex. No other motives involved."

He doubted that, but Dylan didn't consider himself stupid—most days anyway—so he didn't push it. Besides, part of him had just wanted sex, too. It hadn't been solely to ease this heart-crushing ache in his chest.

"When did you get the horse tat on your shoulder?" she asked.

He hadn't even been sure she'd noticed that, but obviously she had. "About four years ago. Garrett was going through a rough time and didn't compete in the charity rodeo that year so I won. I decided to celebrate the moment with some inking."

"You won?" She made it sound like the minimiracle that it had been. "How pissed off was Lucian about that?"

"Plenty. Of course, he said he didn't want to win anyway unless it was against Garrett."

Dylan stopped, remembering that it was Lucian who started the shit storm by secretly going through with that DNA test. He'd left Lucian some profanity-laced, scathing messages, but now he'd have to pull back on that particular outrage. He wouldn't apologize—Lucian had been wrong to go behind his back and do the test. But if he hadn't done it, then months could have passed before Adele told the truth.

If ever.

Dylan would have been in the dark. He could have continued to raise Corbin, continued to believe that the boy was his. He could have continued to be dumb and happy.

So, maybe he'd kick Lucian's ass after all.

The drive back seemed a lot shorter than the one to the jail, but when Jordan pulled into the driveway of the house, Dylan saw something that instantly lifted his mood. Or rather, some*one*. Corbin. He was running around on the porch chasing Booger.

Dylan's mood dipped a huge notch when he spotted the bandage on the boy's head. Hell. He really had been hurt. Not that Dylan had doubted Karlee, but seeing it brought it home.

Both Karlee and his mom were on the porch, too. Both standing and obviously waiting with dour looks on their faces. No dourness stuff for Corbin, though. Once Jordan and he were out of the car, Corbin barreled down the steps, running straight for Dylan. He gave Dylan a hard, long hug as if he'd been gone for days rather than just a few hours.

"I had a polly-lop," Corbin announced, and when he grinned, Dylan saw that his tongue was still green.

"How's your noggin?" Dylan forced himself to

keep it light, and he tapped the unbandaged side of Corbin's head.

Corbin laughed as if that were a fine joke. That was the cool thing about kids. They laughed even at the goofy stuff. "I got a boo-boo. Can I have 'nother polly-lop?"

"Sure. The next time we go to the store."

Corbin clapped, clearly pleased about that. He didn't know it, but he could have asked for the moon, and Dylan would have figured out a way to get it for him.

The boy's joyous mood didn't spread to Karlee and Regina, and as Dylan went closer, he could tell his mother had been crying. With everything going on in his own head and heart, he hadn't considered that this had to be getting to her, too. She no longer had the grandson that she thought she'd had.

Karlee brushed a kiss on Dylan's cheek. Then, on Jordan's. "Mack's on the way here."

That wasn't exactly good, but it was a necessity.

"What did Adele have to say for herself?" Regina asked. Her tone was exactly what Dylan thought it would be. Anger with a side order of bitterness.

"Why don't I take Corbin inside?" Jordan suggested. "Maybe he can have some milk to wash down the polly-lop."

Dylan was thankful when Corbin went right to her, because he didn't want the boy to hear any part of this. He especially didn't want Corbin to be privy to the conversation that would go on once Mack arrived.

"Adele lied because she thought I'd make a better father than Mack," Dylan told Karlee and his mom the moment Jordan and Corbin were out of earshot.

"You would," Karlee admitted without hesitation.

His mother added her own agreement with some rare profanity. "You're damn right."

That made Dylan feel better. Then worse. He appreciated the votes of confidence, but the other side of that coin was that confidence votes didn't mean diddly because Mack was the one with the legal right to raise Corbin. It was ironic that a single sperm could determine that.

And speaking of sperm, Dylan heard the truck approaching, and when it came into view, he spotted Mack behind the wheel. Mack spotted them, too, because his eyes widened with concern. If he knew what shit was about to hit the fan, he might turn around and drive off.

Dylan figured it was a bad thing that he was hoping for that.

Mack stopped his truck, got out and slowly made his way to them. Of course, Dylan immediately tried to pick through Mack's features to see if there was any resemblance to Corbin. Maybe there was. But since Corbin looked so much like Adele, then there weren't any obvious O'Malley genes.

"What'd I screw up now?" Mack asked his sister. It sounded as if he'd wanted to use a much-harder word than *screw*, and he put his hands on his hips in a defensive posture. Obviously, he was used to having to deal with Karlee when it came to the consequences of his actions.

Karlee looked at Dylan, giving him the chance to answer that. "Adele," was all he said.

Mack lifted his shoulder. "I heard she got arrested,

but I didn't have anything to do with that. Contrary to popular belief around here, I'm not the source of all bad stuff that happens in or around Wrangler's Creek."

He was definitely defensive. And Mack clearly didn't have a clue as to what was going on so Dylan took a deep breath and filled him in.

"Adele Rivera had a baby two-and-a-half years ago. A boy. His name is Corbin."

Mack shrugged again. It was still not registering, but then he froze. His eyes went to the size of turkey platters, and this time when he cursed, it was much worse than the *screw* word.

"Yeah," Dylan confirmed. "You got Adele pregnant, and now you have a son."

Mack started shaking his head, but he didn't seem to be denying what Dylan had just told him. The guy was having trouble wrapping his mind around it. Dylan knew exactly how he felt, because he'd gone through something similar a month ago when the social worker had first brought Corbin to the ranch. It hadn't taken that long for the shock to wear off, though, and for him to realize how much he loved the boy.

He still did.

Not sharing DNA with Corbin hadn't changed that one bit.

Mack sucked in some quick breaths and caught onto the porch column to steady himself. "Adele never said anything about it. She didn't tell me. I didn't know."

Dylan nearly filled in that particular blank—to let Mack know that Adele hadn't thought he would care and that whole bad-daddy concern. But Mack would no doubt fill in the blank soon enough for himself.

"Corbin's inside," Dylan said. "Would you like to see him?"

That offer hadn't been an especially easy one to make. Dylan was having to fight the urge to go into flight mode with the boy.

Mack looked at Karlee as if she would give him the answer to that, but she huffed. Only then did Mack nod.

It was hard for Dylan to get his feet moving, but Karlee helped with that, too. She took hold of his arm and led him into the house with Mack and Regina right behind them. They followed the sound of Corbin's laughter that was coming from the kitchen, and when they got there, Dylan saw that Jordan had made *drinking* milk fun. She'd given Corbin a straw, and he was blowing bubbles into the glass. The frothy white foam was high over the rim.

"'Ook, Daddy," Corbin said when he spotted them.

Mack staggered back as if he might have a heart attack.

"He's not talking to you," Dylan assured the guy. "That's what he calls me." Though he would have to do something about that. He'd have to coach Corbin into using his name. And Dylan wondered just how much that was going to sting to hear "Dylan" come out of the boy's mouth.

Probably as much as it hurt to see Mack ogling Corbin as if he were an alien instead of the great kid that he was.

Dylan went closer to the table, hoping that it would prompt Mack to do the same. It didn't. Mack stayed back, and he started the head shaking thing again.

"Shit," Mack grumbled.

Dylan nearly blasted him for cursing around Corbin, but again, he'd been in Mack's place so he held his tongue. Besides, Corbin didn't seem to hear over his bubble blowing.

"Shit," Mack repeated.

That's when Karlee gave him a sisterly poke on the arm, but since she used her fist, it was more than a stern reminder tap to watch his language.

Mack opened his mouth as if to repeat the word, but then he must have thought better of it because he hurried out of the kitchen.

"I'll stay with Corbin," Regina volunteered when Jordan stood.

Good. Because Jordan needed to be part of whatever it was Mack was going to say. Or do. He might demand to walk out with Corbin. And if he did, Dylan wasn't sure what he was going to do.

Karlee, Jordan and Dylan followed Mack, and by the time they all met up in the foyer, Mack was still shaking his head.

"I want a DNA test," Mack said, looking directly at Dylan. "Because I'm not even sure that the kid is mine."

CHAPTER NINETEEN

JORDAN HAD TO bite her tongue to keep from lashing out at Mack. Not only because he wasn't gushing about how precious Corbin was but also because he was basically accusing Adele of lying.

Which Adele had done when she'd told Dylan he was the father.

Adele had lied through her teeth, and that's the only reason Jordan didn't give Mack a piece of her mind. However, she did give him some glares.

"I was only with Adele one time," Mack added.

"That's all it takes," Dylan assured him, and he was glaring at him, too.

But Karlee was winning the contest when it came to giving Mack some freezing-hell looks. Of course, Karlee had a history of that since she'd practically raised her kid brother. A brother who now had a kid of his own. One that Dylan, Karlee, Regina and she had all come to love.

"I used a condom," Mack went on. "And don't ask me how I remember that after all this time," he added to his sister, "because I *always* use a condom. That's the one lesson you drilled into my head that actually stuck."

"I'm glad something stuck," Karlee snapped, "but

condoms aren't a hundred percent effective. That's something else I told you. Is the timing right? Did you have sex with Adele about three years and three months ago?"

Mack's mouth tightened. "I still don't think he's mine." What he didn't do was acknowledge the whole right-timing thing. "Shit, he doesn't even look like me." He stopped, shook his head and mumbled another, "Shit."

Apparently, that was one "shit" too many for Karlee because she took hold of Mack's arm and marched him out the front door. "Excuse me while I have a word with my brother."

Jordan figured it was going to be more than only a word. There would possibly be yelling involved. Maybe more of those arm pokes like the one she'd given him in the kitchen.

"He's mine, isn't he?" Jordan heard Mack ask his sister. He cursed some more, groaned. "Corbin's mine."

"Why don't we take Corbin to the back porch so he can play?" Jordan suggested since they could still hear Mack's profanity. It sounded though as if Mack was at least accepting the paternity. It made Jordan wonder how he would handle it once it'd sunk in.

Thankfully, Dylan didn't argue, but when they reached the kitchen, Jordan thought Regina looked ready to battle someone.

"There's no way Mack O'Malley should have Corbin," Regina whispered. She covered Corbin's ears. "He peed in the gas tank of Mildred Wheeler's Toyota after she fussed at him for being drunk in public. Then, he peed on those feral chickens that are out by Police

Chief McKinnon's house when somebody bet him that he couldn't do it. One of the chickens got mad, jumped on his wiener and spurred him. He needed stitches."

Jordan sighed and hoped none of these were recent incidents. Or that Mack's peeing issues were part of some deeper psychological problem.

"And then there was the time he put a bunch of pigeons in the school building right after Christmas break," Regina went on. "They pooped everywhere."

Again, she was hoping for nonrecent stuff, and just in case it wasn't, Jordan stopped Regina when she opened her mouth to continue the Mack bashing.

"Maybe Mack's changed," Jordan suggested. She didn't actually want to defend him, but she wanted to say something that might soothe Regina's raw nerves. "After all, he's working for Garrett now."

"Only because Karlee called in a few favors." Regina still had her hands over Corbin's ears, but since he had gone back to blowing milk bubbles, he probably wouldn't have heard her anyway. Who knew that blowing into a straw could be so loud? "I can have my lawyer do a restraining order or whatever it is you call it when you stop someone from trying to do the wrong thing."

It might be the wrong side in their eyes, but the law wasn't going to agree with them about that. However, it did surprise her that Regina wanted to hang on to Corbin even though she now knew the boy wasn't her grandson.

"There's no need for lawyers," Dylan told his mom. "Mack probably won't even want custody."

That was true, and since Karlee knew her brother's

shortcomings, maybe she'd be able to reach some kind of agreement with him. An agreement that would get him to sign over all his parental rights to…

She mentally filled in the blank with Dylan's name. But she wanted Corbin, too. Which meant they were back to square one.

"Mack really doesn't want custody?" Regina asked. Finally, there was some relief in her voice, and she no longer looked as if she was holding a live wire.

"Seems that way," Jordan answered.

It was hard not to be angry at him for that, but Jordan reminded herself that Mack was only twenty-three, and he could barely support himself. She wasn't even sure he had a permanent place to stay—hardly the ideal circumstances to take on raising a toddler.

Dylan went to Corbin, scooped him up and blew a raspberry on his belly, causing the boy to giggle like a loon. It was exactly what Jordan needed to push away some of the gloom and doom that'd settled over her since learning about the DNA test and Adele's lie.

Regina didn't follow Dylan and her when they took Corbin out back, but she did pull her phone from her pocket. Probably to do the very thing Dylan had just warned her not to do. But if Regina was indeed calling a lawyer, then maybe it wasn't such a bad idea.

Booger shot out the door with them when they went onto the back porch. It was sweltering hot, but that didn't stop Corbin from immediately wanting Dylan to put him down so he could chase the dog.

"Be careful," Jordan said to Corbin.

"Don't fall," Dylan told the boy at the same time. They sounded like worried parents. For a good reason. Corbin had fresh stitches, and they didn't want him hurt again.

They stood there watching Corbin play, and for a moment Jordan nearly stepped right into Dylan's arms. But he didn't exactly have a "hug me" expression. Nor did he seem to be open for a conversation. Neither would have helped anyway, especially since things were still shaky between them after the hotel sex.

And the car sex.

And the long heated looks they'd been giving each other since she'd been back.

Normally, things like that only built the intimacy between two people, but in their case, it just complicated the heck out of things. Those complications weren't likely to get any better if Dylan and she had to duke it out for custody once Mack excused himself from this. Which led her to something else she'd yet to tell Dylan.

"Before all Hades broke loose earlier today over the DNA test and Adele's lie, I signed my Air Force separation papers," Jordan explained. "I figured next week I'd put in a job application at the hospital and look for a house to rent or buy."

Dylan glanced at her but then nailed his attention to Corbin. "So you're staying." He paused. "You're sure you'll be okay with that?"

That was a huge, multifaceted question. It involved her wanderlust. Her PTSD. And maybe even the sex.

"I'm thinking if things start closing in on me that I can travel," she said. "There are places in the world that I'd like to show Corbin."

He made a sound of agreement. "And the nightmares?"

"Counseling." Jordan didn't have to think about that. She needed it, period. The nightmares were becoming less frequent. Ditto for being on the doorstep of a full-blown panic attack when she thought of the "hole." But that didn't mean things inside her had been stitched up and ready for healing. A green lollipop definitely wasn't going to make things better.

"So, travel and counseling." Dylan made another sound of agreement. "Two fairly easy fixes." He looked at her. "I'm not such an easy fix, though."

No. He wasn't. If she got full custody of Corbin, Dylan would still want to see the boy. And she'd want Dylan to see him. That meant she'd be seeing him, too.

"We could just keep things as is," he went on. "Maybe work at filling up that sex bingo card." He smiled, winked at her.

Mercy, it felt good to see that smile after what they'd just been through, and she did like the idea of more sex. But she also knew that it could lead to other things.

Like love.

Well, on her part anyway. Dylan probably wasn't going to risk a heart-stomping like the last one she'd given him, but Jordan could easily see herself falling in love with him while also falling into his bed.

Before Jordan could even consider how to bring that up to Dylan, the back door opened, and Karlee came out. Mack was right behind her.

"I'm sorry," Karlee said.

Jordan had no idea why Karlee was apologizing, but it sent her nerves into another tailspin. So did that look on Mack's face. It certainly wasn't the defiant expression of denial he'd had earlier.

"Corbin's my son." Mack's voice was a hoarse whisper now. "What I said earlier about him not being mine, I didn't mean it. It just hit me hard, that's all. He's mine," Mack repeated, louder now.

"I tried to talk Mack out of it," Karlee added.

"Talk him out of what?" Jordan asked, and yes, her nerves were soaring.

"She tried to talk me out of doing the right thing. Because she doesn't trust me," Mack spoke up. "All my life people have seen me as a screwup. A mistake. Well, I'm about to fix that. I won't make a mistake with Corbin."

Oh God. Jordan definitely didn't like the sound of that. "Fix it how?" she managed to say.

"By doing the right thing." Mack went to Corbin, scooped him up and kissed his cheek. "I'll be the one to raise my son."

DYLAN WENT THROUGH the motions of signing the invoices and time sheets for the ranch, but for all he knew he could have been signing away his soul to the devil. His head just wasn't on business, though it was something that had to be done. The sooner he finished, the sooner he'd be able to see Corbin and try to come to terms with what had happened.

Of course, he'd had half a day and a full night to wrap his mind around things, and there'd been no coming to terms just yet.

So far what had happened was a lot of whining and attempts at sympathy, and sadly some of the whining had come from him. Others had contributed, though. Dylan had gone through it and heard all the clichés.

The rug pulled from beneath his feet. The wind taken out of his sails. His world turned upside down. Pee dumped on his head.

The last one had come from his mom, and it'd been *their* heads instead of just *his*. Obviously, Mack's bombshell had put Regina in a tailspin, too.

And Jordan.

Her clichés had involved words like *shit storm*, *hell in a handbasket*. Along with that, she'd cursed Adele for setting up the shit storm/Hades hamper situation. Dylan figured the cursing would continue during her visit with Adele, which should be going on right about now. He'd considered going to the jail with her, but there was nothing left for him to say to Adele except maybe "fuck you," and that likely wouldn't help things.

He wasn't sure anything would help.

Dylan had already gone through the anger stage. For him, that meant liberal use of words that caused his mom to make liberal use of scolding him for using those words. Thankfully, he hadn't cussed in front of Corbin. Dylan had waited until his mom had taken the boy inside so that he could try to reason with Mack.

It hadn't worked.

Mack was still hell-bent on taking Corbin for the five years that Adele would be in jail. The same five years that Dylan had hoped to have with him. Of course, he'd hoped for more because Adele had claimed at one time that she wanted him to have permanent custody. Adele's word on that wasn't worth a thimbleful of spit.

However, Dylan had gotten a reprieve. A short one anyway. Since Mack was living at the Granger bunkhouse, a place where he couldn't take Corbin, that meant Mack needed a few days to find not only an apartment or house but also to arrange a sitter for Corbin. Mack probably didn't earn a boatload of money as a ranch hand so Dylan suspected it'd be Karlee who would end up footing some of the bills. Dylan would offer to help, too, but he doubted Karlee was going to let him do that.

His phone buzzed with a call, but when he saw Lucian's name on the screen, he let it go to voice mail. Dylan had talked to him a couple of hours ago, and he didn't want to rehash the argument. Lucian wasn't apologizing for going behind his back to do the DNA test. Considering the outcome, it'd been the right thing to do, but Lucian had sure gone about it the wrong way. He wanted his brother to stew about that for a while before they talked again.

Dylan signed the last of whatever the hell he was signing, and he went into the kitchen where he'd last seen his mom and Corbin having breakfast. No Regina, but Corbin was there with Karlee having lunch.

"Daddy," Corbin gushed.

That was another thing on his to-do list—getting Corbin to call him something else. But maybe he could put that off until tomorrow.

"Ride de horsey today?" Corbin asked.

"Sure. Just finish your lunch first." And it seemed as if he had a ways to go since he was picking at his vegetables. Whatever had been on the other side of his plate, though, was completely gone except for some smears of ketchup.

"Regina fixed him chicken nuggets," Karlee said, following Dylan's gaze.

Dylan should have guessed, since those were Corbin's favorite along with pepperoni pizza and any kind of pasta.

"Where is Mom?" he asked. "And please don't tell me she went with Jordan to see Adele."

"No. At least I don't think so, but she did ask me to watch Corbin while she went to talk to her lawyer."

Dylan groaned. "She shouldn't have done that. You've got work to do. If she pulls that again, come and get me." Of course, there wouldn't be too many chances for something like this anymore.

"It's okay. I needed a lunch break anyway." Karlee paused. "Regina did ask me if I'd help her fight Mack for custody."

Dylan didn't bother groaning again. He'd already done too much of that along with pissing and moaning.

"I'm sure the lawyer will tell Regina that she doesn't have a case," Karlee went on, "but I couldn't talk her out of going to the appointment."

No, Karlee and no one else on the planet could have managed to stop Regina when she had something in her head.

"Ride de horsey soon," Corbin babbled.

And he must have really wanted to go riding because he was chowing down on the veggies while Karlee got up and walked closer to Dylan. Judging from the dark circles under her eyes, she'd gotten just about as much sleep as he had. Which wasn't very much at all. Lots of tossing and turning had been involved.

"Dylan, I'm so sorry."

He'd lost count of how many apologies she'd given him, and she didn't owe him a single one. Dylan hoped he let her know that by brushing a kiss on the top of her head. "Have you talked to Mack today?"

She nodded. "He looked for a place all yesterday afternoon, but there are no rentals in his price range here in Wrangler's Creek. He's going to have to move to my house in San Antonio."

San Antonio wasn't far, but it'd be a commute for Mack to get to work every day at the Granger Ranch. A commute that would mean Corbin would likely end up in San Antonio with a sitter. Dylan had hoped he'd be closer so he could check to make sure he was okay.

"Maybe Mack and Corbin could stay in the guesthouse," Dylan said.

It wasn't exactly an *off the top of his head* suggestion. Nor was it a particularly good one. Because it would keep Corbin at the ranch where he'd continue to think of it as home and call Dylan "Daddy." It would also put Mack right under Dylan's nose, and right now, that wasn't a good place for Mack to be.

Karlee shook her head. "It's a kind offer, but Mack says he wants to try this on his own. Of course, he won't be on his own when he's at my apartment, but he claims that's only temporary. He wants a place with a yard so that Corbin will have his own room and a place to play."

Good. Corbin needed those things. Mack was at least thinking of the big picture. That was more than Dylan was doing. He was still in the heart-wrenching mode of not wanting to lose a little boy that he loved.

"Mack also saw a lawyer yesterday," Karlee went

on, her voice a whisper now. "He's getting a simple custody agreement drawn up for Adele to sign. The lawyer said it'd be ready this morning so it's possible Mack's already picked it up to take to the jail."

Things were certainly moving along. An apartment and now papers. Dylan had thought he might have a couple more days with Corbin, but this might be his last one.

"I'll help Mack and Corbin of course," Karlee added. "Well, as much as Mack will let me help." She paused, shook her head again. "I think I pushed him too hard when I was talking to him yesterday. I told him I didn't think he was up to being a father, and he seemed to take that as some kind of challenge. If I'd just kept my mouth shut..."

Dylan pulled her into his arms. "It's okay."

It wasn't. In fact, it was as far from okay as it could get, but he didn't want Karlee putting this on her shoulders. She'd already done that enough when it came to her brothers.

Karlee moved away from him when they heard the footsteps coming toward them. Not Regina but Jordan. And yeah, she looked just as bad as the rest of them. Except she seemed even more concerned—if that was possible. Her forehead was bunched up and her breath was uneven.

"Have you spoken to Lucian?" Jordan asked him.

"Not in the last two hours or so. Why?" Dylan almost hated to tack on this next question. "Did something else go wrong?"

She nodded, her gaze firing to Corbin. Karlee picked up on the cue and scooped up Corbin. "You've finished enough of those carrots," she told him. "Let's go look at the horses so you can pick out which one you want to ride."

Nothing could have pleased Corbin more unless it'd been the offer for him to get a ride right now. He grinned and went straight to her.

"Nothing's wrong with Lucian, is there?" Karlee whispered to Jordan.

"No, he's fine," Jordan quickly assured her. "This is about Adele. Mostly anyway."

Hell. Considering Jordan's breath gusts and such, Dylan hadn't expected there to be a silver lining in whatever storm cloud was about to hit them, but it was an especially bad mix if Lucian had something to do with it.

"No sugarcoating," Dylan instructed Jordan when Karlee and Corbin were out of the kitchen. "Just go ahead and tell me what happened. Did Adele agree with Mack having custody?"

She took another of those ragged breaths first. "I wasn't able to get in to see Adele because she's in lockdown. She organized a protest over…panties."

Dylan sure hadn't expected that to come out of her mouth. "Panties?"

This time Jordan huffed. "It's not going to make sense to you or anybody else, but it's an Adele thing. She apparently disapproved of the choice of panty material so she put together a protest, but it turned ugly. Since Adele was the ringleader, they charged her with inciting a riot. And assault."

"Assault?" Great day in the morning.

"Adele kicked another guard in the nuts when he

tried to put her back in her cell." She mumbled some profanity. "If it weren't so serious, it'd be laughable. But, Dylan, this is going to add a lot of time to her jail sentence. Since Adele's already on probation, Lucian thinks it could add up to ten years with the five years she already has."

Well, hell. That meant Mack would essentially end up getting permanent custody of Corbin since he'd be nearly eighteen by the time Adele got out of jail. And it might be even longer if she couldn't stay out of trouble.

Dylan had to shake his head, though, at something Jordan had said. "How the hell is Lucian involved in this?"

He could tell from her expression that he wasn't going to like this, either. "Lucian was there at the jail trying to visit Adele when the riot broke out. When he heard about the new charges, he hired Adele a new attorney. A team of them."

On the surface that didn't sound worthy of a bunched-up forehead so Dylan made a circling motion with his finger for her to continue.

"Lucian says he'll try to help Adele get these new charges reduced." Jordan paused. "In exchange, he wants her to sign over custody of Corbin to you."

CHAPTER TWENTY

DYLAN FELT AS if he were about to start an Old West showdown with Lucian. No guns or quick draws at high noon in the center of town. This one would take place in Lucian's office at the ranch where he'd just arrived after Dylan had spent most of the afternoon waiting for him. But instead of bullets, there'd be words.

Some bad ones.

That's why Dylan had had Jordan take Corbin to the barn. They'd already had their ride for the day—a long one since it could be the last one—but seeing the horses would keep the boy occupied while Dylan had it out with his brother.

"Are you trying to win the dick-of-the-year award?" Dylan asked him.

Lucian didn't seem surprised or upset with the question. "According to plenty of folks, I've had that award for some time now." He eased off his Stetson and calmly made his way to his desk before he even looked at Dylan. "I'm sure it's occurred to you that I went to Adele to try to help you."

And that's what made this even more infuriating. "You tried to blackmail a woman in prison. That's a new low even for you."

"It could have gotten you Corbin," Lucian pointed out just as quickly.

Dylan was well aware of that. Well aware, too, that he would do almost anything to keep the boy. But almost anything didn't include browbeating a woman when she was down. Even when that woman had lied to him and torn his life into a million little pieces.

"Call off your lawyer dogs," Dylan warned him. "If Adele wants a new attorney, I'll hire one for her. One that won't come with dick-strings attached."

Lucian lifted his shoulder in a suit-yourself gesture. "Adele turned me down, by the way."

Dylan had figured that. Adele was a nutjob, but she wouldn't have kowtowed to Lucian over something like this.

"I didn't try to do this just for you," Lucian went on. "I did it for Corbin, too. Mack's going to be a shitty father, and you know it."

Yeah, he did. "That's why I'll help him. And Karlee and Jordan will. I wouldn't be surprised if Mom doesn't get in on the helping, as well. Because we all want Mack to make this work."

Man, it hurt to say that, but it was the only choice he had here. Just because Mack had screwed up in the past, it shouldn't mean he didn't deserve to raise his son. And Dylan knew a whole lot about brands and overcoming what folks expected.

"Is Adele still on lockdown?" Dylan asked.

"No. I was able to talk to her, and as I was leaving, she got another visitor. Mack. He said his lawyer had drawn up some papers for Adele to sign."

Custody papers. Dylan had thought—hoped—there

might be a glitch or holdup with that but apparently not. In fact, Adele had probably already signed them. That was a reminder that he needed to wrap up this chat with Lucian and go spend what little time he had left with Corbin.

"Look, I know you thought you were doing the right thing, but stay out of this," he warned Lucian as he headed out the door.

Dylan went toward the back porch, but before he could even make it outside, he saw Karlee and Jordan walking toward the house. Jordan was holding Corbin, and he was sacked out, his head on her shoulder.

Karlee and Jordan were talking, obviously about something that amused them because they were both smiling, but the smiles and whispered conversation stopped when they spotted him. Too bad. Because it was nice to see smiles for a change when there'd been so much gloom. Of course, most of the gloom was coming from him.

"Corbin fell asleep on a hay bale," Jordan said.

The disappointment hit him harder than it should have. Though anything was going to hit him pretty hard right now. Corbin's naps lasted an hour or more, and those were minutes that Dylan wouldn't have with him.

Yeah, he was definitely the gloom generator, and he needed to find out what had caused Jordan to smile so he could maybe get a dose of it.

"Did you talk to Lucian?" Jordan asked. Definitely no smile accompanied that.

He nodded, and that was all it took for Karlee to spring into action.

"Let me put Corbin to bed," Karlee offered, easing Corbin away from Jordan and into her arms. "I've got an errand to run, but I'll have Regina watch him."

Dylan thanked her and brushed a kiss on Corbin's head, but he didn't answer Jordan's question until Karlee had walked away with the boy. "Adele declined Lucian's offer."

She nodded. "I figured as much. Adele doesn't do well with demands like that. Besides, it's probably occurred to her now that she was wrong not to have told Mack about Corbin."

Yeah, it was wrong. In the month that Dylan had thought Corbin was his, he'd blasted Adele for not coming clean with him, and now he would do the same about Mack. Even though it felt like a stick to the gut to stand up for the man who'd be taking Corbin from him.

"What were you and Karlee laughing about?" Dylan asked. In the grand scheme of things, it probably wasn't important, but he was pretty sure a laugh or even a smile would feel good right about now.

Jordan took hold of his arm and started leading him toward the barn. Definitely not the direction he'd go for some levity. Apparently, though, Jordan thought otherwise because she took him all the way to the other end of the barn and threw open the door to the overflow tack room.

"Don't worry," she said. "Corbin didn't see it. And even if he had, he wouldn't have known what it was."

Dylan didn't have to ask what she was talking about because he saw it the moment he looked inside. On the wall next to the calendar from the feed store and a half dozen scrawled notes about what to do/not do and touch/don't touch, there were at least a hundred of the sex bingo cards. Someone had pinned them up as if they had some importance in the daily operation of a ranch or tack room.

He cursed. "I swear, those cards are like rabbits. They keep breeding."

Jordan chuckled. "Abe apparently asked the hands to keep an eye out for them, that he would pay them five dollars each for any they could find."

"Hell. I was paying Abe ten dollars apiece." That meant the cook had been making a tidy profit and probably hadn't done a lick of work to find any of the cards. Still, it showed initiative—something that was rare when it came to Abe.

"Some are the old ones," Jordan went on, plucking one from the wall and handing it to Dylan.

It was indeed one from the original batch, and whoever had owned this card had checked off one of the boxes: have your hands on Dylan's butt.

"Well, that explains why Shayla Conners groped me in the grocery store," he grumbled, still not finding anything about this to make him smile.

"At least half of the new ones are about us." Jordan pulled another one and passed it to him.

Yep. Nothing had been checked off on this one, but it had an interesting center square: Dylan and Jordan have sex in the barn. The top right box was for them to remarry.

Now Jordan laughed again. "All of the new ones are the same so I think Abe or one of the hands must have copied them so they could make a little pocket money."

Maybe more than just pocket money. If he'd still been doing the payout to Abe, there was anywhere from five hundred to a thousand bucks worth of cards held up by all those pushpins.

"You have to admit it's funny," Jordan said.

He still wasn't seeing it, but Dylan got a glimmer of glee when he looked at Jordan. She was smiling, a big wide smile that lit up her face, and it occurred to him that other than Corbin, they hadn't had too many smiling, light moments in the past month. Maybe she'd decided to lower the bar when it came to that sort of thing.

Dylan lowered his, too, and he joined her in the smile. Man, it felt good. It felt even better when she saw his goofy grin and chuckled. Still chuckling, she leaned against him. Probably not foreplay, but whenever she touched him, there was always the possibility that it would feel like that.

Apparently, that was the case when she smiled, too.

Because Dylan leaned in and tasted that smile. Yeah, it was good. Exactly as he thought it would be. Soft and Jordan-scented. He lingered a moment, savoring it and her, but then he eased back expecting to see regret or some other cautionary warning that smooching in the tack room had led to sex when they were teenagers, and it could do the same now.

But no regret.

Which was troubling because he kept going back to the notion of pity sex and making out. He thought that was maybe what Jordan had done when they'd been together. And it had to stop. Dylan would have been the one to stop it, too, if she hadn't hooked her hand over the back of his neck and pulled him to her. Jordan slid her hand over his butt.

"That's one bingo square filled," she said.

Oh, so this was the game. Except maybe it wasn't. Because she kissed him, and it seemed too simple a square just to have a kiss in the barn. Still, what did he know? It was a stupid game. However, it seemed to be leading to a really nice moment here. Maybe some long, slow kisses. A little touching. Something easy and laid-back…

"We have to hurry," Jordan insisted. She started unbuttoning his shirt. "Corbin might not sleep long."

The moment she had his shirt open, she landed against his chest. Now normally, that would have been exactly where he'd want Jordan to land at the start of something like this, but there was a problem.

He didn't know what *this* was.

"Is it just sex?" he blurted out, and wished he'd rehearsed it so that it sounded better.

She pulled back, blinked. "Is that what you want it to be?"

If he knew the answer to that, he wouldn't be standing there with her hand on his chest and his hands on her butt. He would have either been removing clothes or walking away.

Dylan was leaning toward the clothing removal.

But that was his dick talking, and he was pretty sure he could make more sense than that brainless part of him. He'd had sex with a lot of women, but it'd never quite been just sex with Jordan. It still wasn't. Which meant he could end up paying dearly for the orgasm he was about to give her.

The brainless part of him won out. For the moment anyway. And he dragged Jordan back to him. Good thing he'd kept his hand on her butt because it made it a little easier to get her against him again. She didn't protest, either, but she did make a little sound of relief—that immediately got trapped with their next kiss.

Since this was definitely headed in the direction of an orgasm or two, Dylan maneuvered them back to the door. There was no inside lock, which meant anyone could come strolling in for supplies or to pushpin another bingo card into the wall. Best not to have anyone catch Jordan and him filling in one of those squares.

It wasn't easy, not with Jordan kissing him and going after his zipper, but he managed to drag a saddle in front of the door to block it. But Jordan had a different notion about what to drag because she pulled him down to the floor. Floors weren't his specialty, especially wooden ones that could lead to splinters, but his dick was just fine with it.

So was Jordan.

Because she pushed him onto his back and straddled him. She was wearing a little cotton dress that he had no trouble pushing up. The panties gave him some trouble, though, but that was mainly because she was trying to get his wallet from his back pocket so she could take out the condom.

There was a lot of twisting, moving and otherwise grinding of her on his erection. Not good because he wanted this to last more than five seconds. And that's why Dylan took hold of her hips to steady her. And to steady himself by looking at her.

Jordan probably didn't know that she was his Kryptonite and his salvation. Probably didn't know that she was the benchmark he'd held up to all other women, and those other women had always fallen short.

No. She didn't know that. Because at the moment she probably didn't know much of anything. The fire had her now. Which meant Dylan had her. He knew exactly what to do about that, too. He got on the condom, shimmied off her panties, and he pushed into her.

Every time he was with her like this he always forgot just how good it could be. Even pity sex, which this might be, still made her the benchmark winner.

Jordan rode him hard. Fast. And while Dylan was still in the "making it last" mindset, he decided just to let her have her way with him. After all, she was doing a damn good job of getting him off. So Dylan decided to return the favor. Catching onto her hips, he adjusted her just a little so that she was getting the right pressure in the right spot.

It worked.

The riding hard turned into a thrust, then a sultry moan, and Jordan would have collapsed against him if Dylan hadn't held on. He wanted to see her face as he felt her body ripple around him. He managed it, too.

For a few seconds anyway.

Before Jordan caused him to ripple right along with her.

JORDAN WAS NOW certain of one thing. She was too old to be having sex on a tack room floor.

Her knees were bruised and creaky, and somehow she'd wrenched her ankle. It was sore and twinged every time she stepped down on it. Still, that didn't stop her from chasing Corbin, and therefore Booger, around the yard. With each sprint, though, she was reminded that it would be a while before she got to do this again.

Dylan obviously felt the same way because he was in the chase game, too, though there really weren't any rules. Corbin just ran until one of them caught him—which was frequently—so they could get a sloppy kiss.

Jordan let the running go on for a good ten minutes before she slowed things down by scooping up Corbin and taking him to the back porch. She definitely didn't want the exertion to trigger an asthma attack for Corbin. And that was another reminder that she needed to talk to Mack about how to give him his meds and drill home the need to never miss a dose.

"Read to me, Daddy," Corbin said the moment Dylan's and his bottoms were in the porch swing. He pulled a book from the basket that Regina had put there for him. There were at least twenty he could choose from, but Corbin always picked the same one—a picture book about horses.

Dylan motioned for her to sit down next to them, but Jordan shook her head. The view was better from where she was standing. She could take it all in and catalog this moment before the great depression took over. By now, Mack had had plenty of time to take those papers to the jail for Adele to sign.

She heard the movement behind her and saw Lucian when he stepped into the doorway. Dylan spared him a glance, or rather a glare, but he continued to read to Corbin.

Jordan also gave Lucian a glare, but her heart wasn't in it. He'd been thinking of his brother, and she couldn't fault Lucian a whole bunch for that. Of course, she still expected him to give her an apology, which was likely the reason he'd come out to the porch.

"Do you know you have hay in your hair?" Lucian asked. He pulled a piece from the back of her head, showed it to her and tossed it into the yard. "Been spending time in the barn with Dylan?"

Now her heart was in the glare. For a second or two anyway. That was exactly the same sort of thing Lucian would have said to her when Dylan and she were teenagers. Back then, he'd voiced a ton of concern over them getting too involved too fast. Lucian had been right.

But she had no intention of admitting that to him.

"Karlee's not back yet from visiting Adele," Lucian said a moment later, "but when she gets here, could you tell her I needed to leave for that meeting in Austin?"

She nodded for the part about telling Karlee, but Jordan shook her head to the visiting Adele part. "Karlee went to the jail?"

"Yeah, to tell Adele that she was going to help Mack raise Corbin. She figured Adele would be worried about that."

She would be. Adele was a screwup, but she loved her son, and Karlee's assurance would go a long way to helping Adele accept that Corbin's actual father was going to be the one to raise him. Jordan just kept reminding herself that Adele was far from being the most responsible person and she hadn't managed to screw up Corbin. Maybe Mack would be the same way. And if not, then she would be their safety net. Dylan, too.

When Lucian left, Jordan turned to Dylan to see if he'd heard about Karlee's visit. He had, because he nodded while he continued with Corbin. Even though Dylan had read the same book to him dozens of times,

Corbin still continued to hang on every word and picture. And he was still hanging when Regina came onto the porch. She smiled when she saw Dylan and Corbin together, but the smile faded as quickly as it'd come.

"Mack O'Malley's here," Regina said.

Well, no wonder the smile hadn't lasted. Worse, Regina glanced at Corbin as if there was something she wanted to say that he shouldn't hear. Jordan was about to offer to take him inside, but Regina continued.

"So that you hear it from me and not him, I offered him money so that we could keep Corbin." Regina managed to sound confident that it'd been the right thing to do.

It wasn't.

Jordan wasn't sure whose huff was louder, hers or Dylan's.

"Mack turned me down," Regina added.

That actually made Jordan feel a sliver of relief. Mack wasn't the sort to let Granger money sway him, and that showed he had some honor.

"I'll take Corbin to his room to play while you talk with Mack," Regina went on. "But I'm not packing his things."

There was no need for that. Jordan had already done that along with writing out a note for Corbin's meds. Still, it wouldn't hurt for Regina to have some alone time with Corbin while Dylan and she met with Mack.

Dylan stood, giving Corbin both a kiss and the book, before he handed him off to Regina. He kept his eyes on the boy until Regina and he were out of sight. There was nothing Jordan could say to Dylan to make this less painful so she went with the silliest thing she could think of.

"We can x out that bingo square about sex in the barn," she reminded him.

The corner of his mouth lifted. Not even close to that charm-cowboy smile, but it'd do. Later, maybe she could break out a bottle of whiskey for him. Maybe, too, they could tick off more of those boxes. It was a Band-Aid, of course, but it might help them both get through this.

When they went back into the house, they found Mack pacing in the foyer. He had a large manila envelope in one hand and his cowboy hat in the other. Maybe Regina hadn't offered him a seat or maybe he'd refused. Either way, he stopped, his gaze immediately connecting with theirs.

"I know you don't think much of me," Mack started before either of them could say anything. "I don't have a good track record for anything but f-ing up. Hell, I'm just one arrest away from ending up like Adele because I'm on probation right now, too."

Jordan hoped he was about to say that was all going to change, that he was going to be the best father he could be to Corbin.

He didn't.

"And that's why I can't do this." Mack's voice was such a low mumble that at first Jordan wasn't sure she'd heard him correctly. "I can't raise Corbin because I'd just mess that up. I can't do that to the kid."

Everything inside Jordan leveled out and got very quiet. Then, the rush of relief came. There was so much of it that her knees nearly buckled. But then something else came. The realization that if Mack wasn't taking him, then who was?

Mack handed her the envelope. "That's the paperwork I had my lawyer draw up. It's to revoke any parental rights that I have to Corbin."

So that meant this was back on Adele's shoulders. Clearly though, Adele wouldn't be raising Corbin.

"Revoking my rights won't be temporary, either," Mack went on. "I couldn't see the sense in me coming back to get him in five or six years from now. By then, he'd be settled wherever he's going to be settled. I'll let whoever gets him decide if I should be able to visit him. Not soon, though. I'm taking a job up in Montana."

So he'd be out of the picture. Maybe permanently.

Dylan took out the papers, and both Jordan and he looked at them. Mack had indeed put his signature on them. But Dylan wasn't celebrating. She wasn't even sure he was feeling any relief because all of this was still so uncertain. That uncertainty went up even higher when Karlee came rushing in. She looked at her brother, then at Dylan and her.

"You told them about the papers you signed?" Karlee asked Mack.

Mack nodded. "How'd you know about them?"

"Adele. I just came from visiting her."

Mack glanced away, shook his head. "Is she mad?"

"No. She understands and thinks this is for the best."

Good. So Adele was on the same page. Now Jordan needed to figure out exactly what page that was.

"I gotta go," Mack told his sister.

He hugged Karlee, slipped his hat back on, and he walked out without even hinting that he wanted to say goodbye to Corbin. Maybe because he thought it would confuse the boy. Or it could be that Mack truly didn't want any part of fatherhood.

"Is it true?" Dylan asked Karlee after Mack had left. "Does Adele understand?"

Karlee's forehead bunched up. "More or less."

Heck, that didn't sound good. "What does that mean?"

Karlee's bunched-up forehead stayed in place, and she added a sigh. "Adele agrees that Mack shouldn't raise Corbin. She wants Dylan and you to do that, and she's willing to sign over joint custody. But she has a condition," Karlee quickly added.

Jordan had been about to jump for joy, but that nipped a celebration right in the bud.

"What condition?" Dylan asked, and he sounded just as skeptical as Jordan felt.

Karlee didn't simply look skeptical. Her expression was more akin to don't shoot the messenger. "Adele said that since she came from a messed-up childhood, that she's decided she doesn't want Corbin to have the same. She wants him to have 'normal.'" Karlee put that last word in air quotes.

"What's Adele's condition?" Dylan repeated.

Karlee hesitated, her face screwing up even more. "Before Adele will give you two joint custody, she wants you to get remarried. And if you don't agree, then she'll give Corbin to me."

CHAPTER TWENTY-ONE

DYLAN WAS NO longer surprised by anything that Adele did—including her latest demand for Jordan and him to remarry.

But he was pissed off about it.

Apparently, Jordan took the title of pissed-off champion, though, because as soon as Karlee had told them what Adele had said, Jordan had gotten in her car and headed straight for the jail in San Antonio. Dylan had stayed behind because: a) he figured it wasn't going to do any good to talk to Adele and b) he wanted to spend what was left of the afternoon taking Corbin out on their favorite horse.

Dylan wasn't in the mindset of this might be the last ride or the last evening with the boy he still considered his son. Nope. He was just going to enjoy it. It helped that he knew if Karlee did indeed get custody, that there'd still be plenty more days like this. Even if Corbin didn't live at the ranch, Karlee would see to it that Jordan and he would spend time with him.

"Sketti-balls," Corbin announced when he saw the spaghetti and mini meatballs that Abe had fixed them for dinner.

Since they actually looked edible, it probably meant

either Regina had fixed them or else Abe had picked them up from the diner in town. It was Regina, because she appeared out of the butler's pantry with some extra napkins. Which would be needed since Corbin tended to be a splasher when it came to pasta sauce and peeing.

Booger was right on Regina's heels, but when he trotted to the table, the dog positioned himself beneath Corbin's chair. Smart. Because Corbin was a food dropper, too.

"How are you feeling about all of this?" Regina asked him as they sat down to eat.

"I'm okay. Okay *enough*," Dylan added. "You?"

She gave him a smile, but it came with plenty of uncertainty. "Okay enough." She paused. "Are Jordan and you going to get m-a-r-r-i-e-d?"

Dylan wasn't sure why Regina had spelled out the word *married* the same way she did when talking about diseases and the mild profanity she used. Maybe because she'd spelled it, it got Corbin's attention. While sucking a strand of spaghetti into his mouth, he stared at Dylan as if also waiting to hear the answer.

"N-o," Dylan answered. He added a wink to Corbin, who was no longer interested in the conversation. The boy turned his attention back to eating.

"N-o?" Regina questioned. "But why not?"

The answer to that was so obvious that Dylan didn't bother with it. Plus, he didn't want to have to spell out that Jordan and he had already failed at marriage and that he wasn't going to give in to Adele's blackmail.

Even if he'd kind of, semi-wanted to give in to it.

No way, though, would Jordan jump back into another "I do" with him when she was just trying to get her life back together.

"But you have feelings for Jordan," his mom went on. "I know you do because you've been s-l-e-e-p-i-n-g with her."

No, not sleeping. "We had s-e-x." In the car, hotel and the barn. There'd been no sleep involved.

His mother's mouth tightened a bit so it probably hadn't been a good idea to confirm the s-e-x with Jordan part. "But that sort of thing can lead to m-a-r-r-i-a-g-e," Regina pointed out.

Dylan gave her a flat look. "It can also lead to just more s-e-x."

Of course, it could lead to nothing, too. If Karlee had to move Corbin to San Antonio, then Jordan would probably also move there and start a new life. One that would hopefully still involve orgasms with him in whatever new place she chose to live.

And speaking of orgasm recipients and givers, Jordan walked into the kitchen. She was sporting the same mouth-tight expression as his mom. Except coming from Jordan, it was just because she'd climbed onto the pissed-off/disappointment wagon with them. It likely meant she'd gotten bad news when she visited Adele.

Despite the tight mouth, Jordan conjured up a smile for Corbin. "You're eating sketti-balls."

Corbin grinned and nodded. "And spell-y-ing words."

That had Jordan volleying glances at Regina and Dylan, probably because she figured if they were spelling things, then they were likely talking about this situation with Adele. Which they had been in a roundabout way.

Jordan dropped a kiss on the top of Corbin's head before she motioned for Dylan to go out of the kitchen. Obviously, they needed to talk.

Dylan sighed and walked out with her, but apparently this chat was going to require them to put some distance between Corbin and them, because she led him into the sunroom. Abe was there, taking a nap, but apparently this wasn't Jordan's destination anyway. She went out back, and they started walking. Not toward the barn or the guesthouse but up the road.

"Adele has lost her flippin' mind," Jordan announced.

Dylan wasn't certain Adele had ever had a mind to lose, but mentioning that would only delay this discussion. "What did she say?"

Jordan huffed and kept walking except it was more like a marching pace that included some mumbled profanity and kicking at rocks. "She won't budge on the marriage demand even though it's completely unreasonable. She wasn't married when she was raising Corbin, and there's no reason for us to be, either."

So it sounded as if the visit had accomplished exactly what Dylan thought it would—nothing.

"What were you and Regina spelling about in the kitchen?" she asked after kicking another rock.

"S-e-x. Mom apparently believes it leads to marriage."

She frowned. "Or more sex."

"Yes! That's exactly what I told her. But I spelled it out because Corbin was there."

Her frown deepened with each step and new rock kick, but Dylan finally realized where the stepping and kicking were leading. To the creek. Jordan led him off the road and down the winding path that took them right to the banks. And thankfully to some shade trees since it was hotter than hell right now.

It was a pretty spot with wildflowers and the sounds of the water washing over the rocks. It was also the place where during the throes of foreplay, Jordan had kicked the gearshift and his truck had gone into the water.

"Did you bring me here for s-e-x?" he joked.

Jordan didn't deny it, but since she was still frowning, he was getting some mixed signals here. "This has nothing to do with that Jordan-Dylan bingo game," she grumbled.

Now he was even more confused, and he took hold of her arm to turn her so they were facing each other. "I'm going to need a few more details to make sense of this. Is this about sex?"

"I wish. Sex is easy. Well, it is with you anyway."

Most men would have taken that as a compliment, but it smacked a little too close to home in the man-whore department.

"Marriage is what got us into trouble," she went on. "I didn't feel trapped, *really trapped*, until then."

Yeah, he'd gotten that. "And that's why we won't give in to Adele's demand. We can maybe work out something with Karlee so that we're all big parts of Corbin's life."

Jordan nodded, then huffed. "Damn it, you sonofabitch. I'm in love with you again."

That was not a huge shift in the conversation, but it was also the most unromantic declaration of love he'd ever gotten. Sadly, it wasn't the least, either.

However, it was by far the most important one of his life.

Dylan lifted his shoulder, and because he wanted to touch her, he pushed her hair from her face. "Damn, shit and hellfire, I'm in love with you, too."

She groaned. Moaned. Groaned again. "But this wasn't supposed to happen. I wasn't supposed to feel like this again."

"I totally get that." And because he wanted to kiss her, Dylan did that, too.

It only caused her to curse him even more until she finally slipped into the heat—and into his arms.

"Did Adele have a deadline for us getting married?" Dylan asked.

Jordan pulled back, stared at him. "No."

"How about a legal marriage? Or would one of the hippie, barefoot by the creek ceremonies do?"

More staring. "Adele didn't say."

"Then, there's our loophole, our *fix*." And because he wanted to keep kissing her, Dylan moved her back against a tree. He was pretty sure he'd had sex with her against this very tree several times. Equally sure that he was about to add one more sex notch to this patch of bark.

Jordan was out of breath when she eased back from the next kiss. "What do you mean?"

"I mean I ask you to marry me. Or you can ask me. Then, when and if we get around to it, we can come back here to the creek and have that hippie ceremony. No legal commitment. No rings. No talked-out agreements for which way we'll put the toilet paper on the bathroom holder."

Jordan gave her another of those long stares while her breath gusted against his mouth. "No toilet paper rules," she mumbled. It was surprising that she picked that out of the perks he'd just spelled out for her. "How would we do it?"

He was hoping they weren't talking TP placement right now. "We can say 'I do' to each other and consummate the marriage right here. A free spirit like Adele can't argue with that."

Yet another long stare, followed by a nod. Then a slow smile. "It does feel less…stifling without the rules."

Good. Then he was making progress. He didn't especially want to hurry this along… Okay, he did. And Jordan seemed to be of a like mind about that, too.

She groped his hard-on.

"All right," she said.

At least he thought that's what she said. It was suddenly difficult to hear now that the blood had rushed to that hard part of him.

"Let's take care of the consummation first, and then you can propose," she clarified.

By some miracle, Dylan heard that part just fine. And nothing could have made him happier. Sex. Then marriage. Not the order his mom would care much for, but it was the right way for Jordan and him.

"Just remember, this has nothing to do with the bingo game," Jordan said as she dragged him into a scorcher of a kiss.

Nope, it didn't have diddly to do with the game. But Dylan figured in the next thirty minutes or so, he could manage to tick off all the right boxes.

* * * * *

Look for USA TODAY *bestselling author*
Delores Fossen's THE LAST RODEO,
A WRANGLER'S CREEK *novel,*
on sale in July 2018.

And don't miss the previous books in the
WRANGLER'S CREEK *series:*

THOSE TEXAS NIGHTS
NO GETTING OVER A COWBOY
BRANDED AS TROUBLE
TEXAS-SIZED TROUBLE

Available now wherever HQN Books are sold!

COWBOY HEARTBREAKER

CHAPTER ONE

"WEDDINGS SUCK," RYDER CROWLEY grumbled under his breath as he took a long drink of his beer.

He obviously hadn't said his complaint quietly enough, though, because the woman standing next to him, Allie Devlin, poked his arm with her elbow. "I have more reasons to say that than you do. *Five yards of reasons*."

Allie fanned her hand over his "Texas tuxedo"—jeans, jacket, Stetson and boots. Then she fanned that same hand over the "five yards" of bridesmaid's dress she was wearing. The color was what Ryder would call turtle-snot green, and it puffed out in all directions because of the thick gobs of netting that were everywhere, even on the sleeves.

Ryder drank more of his beer and made a sound to indicate she was right, but the dress only confirmed that weddings did indeed suck on several levels. He wasn't a fan of the clashing odors of the too-rich food, the flowers and the sweat being generated in the barn by the wedding guests who were boot scootin' on the makeshift dance floor.

His attitude about weddings was likely heavily influenced by the fact that he didn't consider himself the marrying sort. Of course, he hadn't considered the groom that, either, but there was Curt Mercer, part one of his best friend posse, working up a sweat dancing with his bride, Savannah O'Neil, who he had met on one of the online dating sites.

After the reception, Curt and Savannah would be moving to her family's cattle ranch two hundred and forty-five miles away in Abilene. Then, in about six months, they'd be having a baby that they'd yet to tell their folks about.

Ryder was happy for them and had never seen two people more in love, but he figured he was still allowed to feel the…loss.

Silently feel it anyway.

There was no chance in hell he'd ever let Curt know, but Ryder would miss not being able to call him at any time, any day for any reason. He'd miss their spur-of-the-moment fishing trips. And just hanging out when it was Curt, Allie, him and part four of the "Crab Posse," Ryder's twin sister, Bree, who was on the dance floor, too, with a groomsman.

They'd come up with the word *crab* using the first initials of their names. They'd been kids, only seven or eight, and had thought it pretty darn clever. By the time they learned it wasn't just a dish served at the seafood restaurant but also a nasty STD, the name had already stuck.

Still did.

It was selfish, yes, to feel that loss, but the four of them had been best friends since preschool, and it was hard to let go of nearly twenty-seven years. You couldn't just replace a first-part best friend.

His *second*-part best friend, Allie, gave him another nudge with her elbow—which was suddenly a lot sharper and more poky than he remembered. "Your date's flirting with Dylan Granger. Nothing can go wrong with that."

Ryder automatically smiled at the line the posse often threw around. "Nothing can go wrong with that"—something doled out with both sarcasm and assurance. It was used just slightly more often than their other tossed-around line—"Easy Cheesy cures all."

Easy Cheesy was the brand of canned string cheese they preferred, and the line, too, was often said with sarcasm and assurance. However, it had proved to be their comfort food of choice and gotten them through elementary school and the rough teen years. So, maybe it did cure all.

"Did you hear me?" Allie asked. "Your date. Dylan Granger."

He'd heard her just fine, and Ryder followed Allie's gaze to the cleared-out area by the tack room, where he did indeed see his date, Mindy Franklin, eyeballing Dylan as if he were on the dessert menu. A lot of women eyed Dylan that way, though, since he was rich, good-looking and a Granger.

In their hometown of Wrangler's Creek, Texas, the Grangers were practically royalty, and until three days ago, Curt had worked for Dylan and his family as one of their top hands. Ryder worked at the ranch, too, and Allie was their large-animal vet. Bree was the horse trainer, so even when it came to work, the Crab Posse had been inseparable.

"Mindy's trying hard, but Dylan won't hook up with your date," Allie commented. "It'd be violating one of those man rules. But it'll cause some talk about you not being able to keep a handle on your sweet things."

He didn't want a handle on Mindy, but he supposed it should bother him to have his date openly flirt with someone else. Mindy had moved on from eyelash batting to making sure her right boob bumped against Dylan's arm. However, Ryder couldn't even muster up a grunt of disapproval.

"I wish Dylan would put the moves on her. I'm not in the right mood to take Mindy home. Or have sex with her," Ryder added in a grumble.

He really did need to work on his grumbling skills because Allie heard that, too, and she cut him a glance, complete with a raised, questioning eyebrow. "Really? You don't want sex?"

Like Mindy's flirting with Dylan, Allie's skepticism was a reasonable reaction. Ryder didn't have Dylan's name or money, but he didn't have trouble getting female company when he wanted it. Most folks thought all he did was want it, though, and with mandatory short-term relationship limits to boot, and that was how both Dylan and he had earned the labels of cowboy heartbreakers.

"Really," Ryder verified.

"Careful, you'll ruin your reputation," she drawled, "and folks will think my prudish influence finally rubbed off on you."

Well, maybe it had. Allie certainly didn't have his "quick to bed 'em, just as quick to leave 'em" reputation.

Just the opposite.

She might not know that her nickname was Dr. Good Girl, but it fit her to a T. It was one of the reasons she was so easy and comfortable to be around, despite the fact that she was damn attractive. The issues that could have sprung up with him being a man and her a woman had never surfaced. But Allie never expected, or wanted, more than friendship from him, and sometimes, like now, a friend was exactly what Ryder needed.

Allie grabbed him another bottle of beer from a waiter who was wearing cowboy clothes that had never been meant for a real cowboy. Good Lord. The guy had on skinny jeans. She also took a glass of white wine for herself and, still sighing, they sank down at the nearest table and watched Curt.

"Life as we know it will never be the same," Allie said, obviously not good at mumbling, either, because he heard her just fine. It expressed exactly what he was feeling. "At least he's happy. That's what I keep telling myself. Curt is happy, and Savannah's a great woman."

That was true, but it didn't ease the heavy weight around his heart or the guilt he was feeling because of that heaviness. Ryder immediately tried to change his expression when the Brooks and Dunn song finished and Bree strolled toward them. His twin also grabbed herself a beer and plopped down on the other side of Ryder. She was wearing the same ugly dress as Allie.

"Weddings suck," Bree complained.

Allie and Ryder exchanged a glance, one of those quick silent conversations that often passed between them. When Bree got in on the shared glance, Ryder knew they were all pretty much feeling that same loss.

"I was going to see if I could coax Dylan out of here for some fooling around," Bree went on. "You know, just to blow off some steam, but it appears your date is trying to give him an eye exam and see how many times she can brush her boobs against his chest."

They were indeed doing some deep eyeball gazing and more boob brushing. Again, it was nothing that interested Ryder. However, the man coming toward them—Curt—was of interest, and Ryder immediately tried to put on a happier face. Ryder figured Allie and Bree were doing the same thing.

"Did somebody crap in that wine and beer?" Curt asked, the corner of his mouth hitching with a smile. He took hold of a chair, spun it around and sat, plopping his arms on the chair back.

"We were just talking about how happy you are," Allie provided. As usual, it was the right thing to say. No use dwelling on that whole business of life changing as they knew it.

Curt's smile wavered a bit. Yeah, he was happy, but Ryder knew for Curt to keep hold of that beautiful woman who was responsible for that happiness, he'd need to move and start the life together that both the bride and groom wanted.

"You're the first of the Crab Posse to knock someone up or get knocked up," Bree contributed. "My wedding gift to you is a year's supply of condoms along with video instructions on how to use them."

As usual, it was the wrong thing to say. Bree had a knack for that. But it made them chuckle anyway. For a few seconds. And then the sad faces returned.

"Oh, for Pete's sake. Cheer up," Curt said. "And if you need a visual to help, just take a look in the corner to your right."

Both Allie and Ryder did look, and he spotted the current mayor, Fred Billings, and his secretary, a large breasted woman half his age. They weren't touching, but the sparks were practically flying off them and would be flying even further if Fred's wife, Lucy, spotted it.

"Nothing can go wrong with that," Curt added with a laugh. Like the previous chuckle, his laugh quickly settled, and he turned back to them. He obviously still saw some of the gloominess in their expressions.

"I'll be back for holidays," Curt assured them. He paused. "Hey, remember that time we all got sick when we tried my uncle Buck's moonshine that I'd pinched from his truck?"

It'd been nearly two decades since that'd happened, and Ryder still felt his stomach lurch from the god-awful memory. Judging from the shudders and head shakes from Allie and Bree, they were having a similar reaction.

"We puked, puked and puked some more," Curt added. He flicked the puffball sleeve of Allie's dress. "That's the same color as the puke."

For such a sorry-ass memory, it made them all smile, and they were the Crab Posse again. Ryder had a boatload of memories that were a whole lot better than that one, but it was definitely in the top one hundred for most memorable.

"Green's Savannah's favorite color so please don't mention that puke-dress reference," Curt whispered, glancing over his shoulder to make sure his bride hadn't heard. She hadn't. Savannah was chatting with some wedding guests.

Curt gathered his breath. “I’m gonna miss you guys, but we’ll always be blood brothers and sister. Well, Ryder, Bree and I will be.” He winked at Allie. “You were too chicken to cut yourself, or you would have been our blood sister, too.”

“I wasn’t chicken,” Allie readily admitted. “I just didn’t want to be Ryder’s sister.”

She froze, the glass of wine stopping less than an inch from her mouth, and she got a “deer in the headlights” look before she chuckled. “All right, I was chicken. Call me overly cautious about sepsis and gangrene, but I didn’t like the idea of cutting myself with a pocketknife that you’d used to gut fish and clean your fingernails. Nothing could go wrong with that.”

Allie chuckled at that part, too, but Ryder didn’t. Allie hadn’t said that she didn’t want to be *their* sister, just not his. Curt noticed it, too, and he volleyed some long, confused glances between both of them.

“You two aren’t—” Curt started, then stopped “—crossing lines, are you?”

“No,” Allie and Ryder said in unison, but Allie dodged his gaze. She stared down into her wine as if it held the secrets of the universe.

What the devil was going on?

Ryder tried to look at her face, to see what was in her eyes, but before he could manage that, Savannah came to the table.

“There you are,” Savannah said. She slid her hand around the back of Curt’s neck and kissed him before she studied the three of them. “Oh, I’m sorry. Did I interrupt something?”

“Nary a thing,” Curt said at the same time that

Ryder said, "Nope," and at the same time that Allie said, "No." Bree added, "Does a chicken crap diamonds?"

The four variations of the quick denial—including Bree's oddball one—all added up to making it sound like malarkey. Which it was. Ryder had been on the verge of finding out what Allie had meant and then giving Curt some grief over suggesting that line-crossing thing. He'd never crossed anything with Allie and had no plans to start.

Hell, he mentally repeated that.

Now the notion of crossing lines and starting stuff best not started was in his head. Not that he would do anything about it. Nope, no, nary a thing, and a chicken wouldn't be crapping diamonds. Even if Ryder had been so inclined, he would have to nix the idea because Allie was still his best friend. He could always get a lover, but best friends were in short supply.

"Oh, okay," Savannah said, sounding about as convincing as they had been with their denials.

The silence came, awkward and a little thick before Allie jumped back into the conversation. "Savannah, I want to thank you again for asking me to be your bridesmaid."

"Same here," Bree agreed without adding a smart-ass comment.

"Glad you both agreed. I know how close all of you are with Curt, and we wanted the three of you to be a part of this."

That wasn't lip service. Savannah had immediately agreed with Curt's choice as Ryder for his best man, and the four of them had considered Allie and Bree as honorary best men, too. In the end, though, Savannah had asked Allie and Bree to be bridesmaids and to stand in when needed for Savannah's sister, Linda, the maid of honor—who was seven months pregnant.

"And speaking of being a part of this," Savannah went on, "I need to ask one more favor. Curt and I will be leaving for the honeymoon soon, and the photographer wants to get some shots of the wedding party dancing. Linda has to get off her feet—swollen ankles—but I was hoping Ryder and you would dance together." She tipped her head to Ryder and Allie. "Bree, I was hoping you'd dance with my brother."

Bree jumped right in to do that, probably because Savannah's brother, Trace, was good-looking. Normally, Ryder would have jumped to dance with Allie, too, but that blasted thought hit him again.

I just didn't want to be Ryder's sister.

Now it felt a little off. Obviously, though, he was the only one who felt that way because Allie did some jumping. She got right to her feet, tugging him out of the chair, and they set their drinks on the table while they made their way to the dance floor to Alan Jackson's "Chasin' That Neon Rainbow."

Ryder had never considered himself an especially good dancer, but this was where Allie shined. She'd given both Curt and him lessons before their junior prom, and they'd ended up holding their own with dates whose names Ryder couldn't actually remember.

Allie held her own now, too, as he spun her into a twirl before pulling her back to him for a little Texas two-step. But the fates seemed to be working against him tonight because the DJ switched tempo and put on a slow tune. The kind of song that squashed couples together and aligned parts that he didn't want aligned with Allie.

But an especially stupid part of him started to urge him on.

They were a good minute into the squashing/dancing when Allie pulled back and looked at him. "Please tell me you're not this hard because of me."

Ryder blinked. He didn't have an erection, but the urging on by the brainless idiot behind his zipper had suggested it, what with all the brushing and rubbing Allie's front was doing with his.

"Hard arm and back muscles," she amended, and her mouth quivered a little as if she might smile.

Both the clarification and the smile helped until he remembered there was a question in there. Were his muscles knotted and tight because of what she'd said about the blood-brother thing?

No. That wasn't it.

And Ryder hoped like hell that was true.

He didn't have time to dwell on it, though, or on the groin-tightening dance because the music stopped, and Curt lifted his hand to get everyone's attention.

"Savannah and I want to thank all of you for coming." He kissed his bride during the applause and cheers that erupted, a kiss that lasted long enough to keep the applause and cheers going.

"Get a room," someone called out.

"That's the plan." Curt kept his love-filled eyes on his bride. "Savannah and I are saying good-night and heading off on our honeymoon." More cheers, peppered with some PG-13 suggestions. "Y'all feel free, though, to hang out, dance and have some fun."

Curt stopped by Bree first to say goodbye and hug her before he made his way to Allie and Ryder. More bear hugs that were so tight that Allie looked as if she might puke when he finally pulled back, and just like that, Curt and Savannah were gone.

Ryder immediately felt the loss again, but he pushed it down fast and plastered on the happiest face he could manage. He was doing good. Until his eyes met Allie's. She wasn't crying—Allie wasn't a crier—but there was a shimmer, and she was blinking hard.

"Shit," Ryder grumbled, easing her back to him. Not for a body squash or dance this time but for a much-needed hug.

Between friends.

When he pulled back, her eyes were still shimmering, and she was still blinking hard, but she glanced around the room at Bree, who had obviously set her sights on Trace. His twin had found a Band-Aid fix for her blue mood.

Allie squared her shoulders and looked him straight in the eyes. "Since tomorrow's Sunday and none of us will have to work, want to hand Mindy off to Dylan so we can all get drunk?" she asked.

That sounded like a fine idea…until he realized there could be a big-ass pitfall with it.

"Uh, maybe now isn't a good time," he threw out there, but at best his tone was that of a suggestion. Still, emotions were running high right now, and Bree wouldn't be with them.

Allie being Allie knew just what to say to soothe his

doubts. “It’ll be our farewell to the Crab Posse.” She hooked her arm through his. “Trust me.” And she said the words she’d said to him a hundred times. “Nothing can go wrong with that.”

CHAPTER TWO

SOMETHING WAS WRONG.

Allie got proof of that the moment she opened her eyes. For one thing, she wasn't in her own bed. In fact, she wasn't in a bed at all. She was lying on a blanket… somewhere.

That immediately got her full attention.

She was just a few weeks away from her thirtieth birthday, and not once had she woken up confused about her current location. Allie snapped to a sitting position, instantly regretting the movement because it set off a tornado in her head.

Mercy, where was she?

Despite the spinning and her unfocused eyes—yes, they were bleary—she fired her gaze around the room, only to realize it wasn't even a room. She was in a barn loft, and there were bits of hay poking her in the butt and back.

That got her attention, too, because she realized the hay on top of the blanket was coming in contact with her bare skin and not merely poking through her clothes. She was naked. Or rather, almost naked. She was wearing only her panties and her right shoe, and there appeared to be a hickey or bruise on her ankle.

God, what had she done?

She glanced around and saw the rest of her clothes strewn across the hay on the right. The green puffy bridesmaid's dress and her other shoe. No bra, but there was a deck of cards and an empty bottle of whiskey. Those were hardly enough clues to give her the details she wanted so she shifted her attention to her left. And her breath landed somewhere in the vicinity of her recently pedicured toes.

Because she wasn't alone.

Ryder was next to her. He was sprawled out on his stomach, and there was no *almost* to his nakedness. He didn't have on a stitch of clothing, and Allie had zero trouble seeing his bare butt.

Her mouth went dry. Her heart started to thud, and she wasn't sure it was because she was seeing a lot more of her best friend than she'd ever seen before. It was because of the *quality* of what she was seeing.

Ryder was hot.

Incredibly hot. A real man. Of course, she hadn't needed to see him naked to determine that. Allie had always thought he was scalding in the looks department, but she'd never believed she would get visual proof of it. Proof that would have been a lot more fun if there hadn't been a tornado in her head and hay poking her in places she didn't want to be poked.

Even with all those things wrong with this situation, it occurred to her that she didn't want Ryder to see her like this. It was best if she got dressed, regrouped and found a mirror so she could figure out how bad her remaining makeup was. She was guessing it was bad, and while Allie hated to admit she was vain, she didn't want the image of her like this etched in Ryder's brain.

Especially since her memory would be of his incredible bare butt.

Despite her good intentions, Allie didn't manage to push down the groan she made when she tried to get up so she could locate her bra, and the sound must have alerted Ryder because his eyes flew open. Since his face was turned toward her, Allie saw the same confusion race through his baby blues that she'd experienced just moments earlier.

Ryder looked at her. His attention lingered on her panties and then her bare breasts. That caused her nipples to tighten. It also caused his eyes to widen to the size of turkey platters.

Cursing, or rather attempting to curse, he scrambled to his feet. Since this had already taken a weird turn, Allie decided to try to lighten things up a bit. "So, seen any good movies lately?"

He didn't crack a smile. Blinking and attempting more of that profanity, Ryder kept staring at her until he glanced down at his own exposed parts. Specifically, the male part of him that had garnered her attention. Again, it was impressive.

"Hell, did we..." Ryder garbled out. "No, we didn't. We couldn't have. Hell. Did we?"

Thankfully, Allie had been awake a few seconds longer than he had so her head was slightly clearer. "No. We didn't do that. But we drank way too much, and we ended up here."

He glanced around, obviously trying to figure out where *here* was. It was the hayloft of the Granger Ranch, where they both worked. Until the night before, Allie had never been to this part of the barn, but there was enough recognition in Ryder's eyes now to confirm that he probably had. And that it perhaps involved bringing a lover or two to this place sometime during the time he'd been working for the Grangers, which went as far back as high school.

Ryder cursed again. This time, the words were a lot less garbled, which likely meant this was all coming back to him.

"Damn," he spat out and, wincing with every move, he located his boxers and dragged them on. "We came up here as the reception was winding down, got drunk and played strip poker." He stopped, froze as he dragged on his jeans. "I didn't kiss you or anything, did I?"

He made it sound as if he could have possibly infected her with mad cow disease. Or vice versa.

"No kiss," she assured him. Since the weird was just getting weirder, Allie grabbed the blanket and used it to cover her breasts. "Well, not on the mouth. Shortly before you passed out, the subject of hickeys came up, and I told you I'd never had one."

"Hickeys?" That brought on more cursing.

She understood the reason for this profanity, too. Hickeys weren't an especially good topic for good friends of the opposite sex or for adults. Of course, what had followed hadn't been a good idea, either.

"You called me a hickey virgin and said you could fix that," Allie explained. She stuck her foot out to show him the love bite on her ankle.

He didn't curse this time. Or groan. Maybe Ryder had reached the conclusion that it just wasn't worth any more reactions like that because everything about this situation warranted profanity and groans.

"What else did we do?" Ryder snapped while he searched for the rest of his clothes.

Her memory was still a little fuzzy around the edges, but she did remember nearly melting when his mouth was on her ankle. No way would she tell him that, though.

"We did some flirting," she admitted. Of course, the strip poker told her that. It was basically a game of foreplay, but Ryder had crashed before they'd reached the actually playing stage. "That was about it."

He opened his mouth as if he might ask for details about that flirting, but then he shook his head and started looking around. For the rest of his clothes, she realized, when he picked up his socks.

And her bra.

It was a strapless, barely there strip of white lace that held his attention for a couple of seconds before he must have realized what he was doing, and he tossed it to her. Allie kept the blanket covering her while she put it on, and once it was in place, she got up to gather her clothes and get dressed as Ryder was doing.

"Whose stupid idea was it to play stupid strip poker?" he asked.

With those double *stupid*s in the question, Allie hated to be the bearer of bad news. "Yours. That happened when we found the deck of cards, and you joked that one of the hands had probably played strip poker up here. I said I'd never played…"

She let him fill in the blanks. Ryder had called her a strip-poker virgin and had set out to remedy that. In hindsight, if she'd wanted to have sex with him, she could have lied and told him she was a virgin. But thankfully she'd been too drunk and was too honest to do something like that.

"I'm sorry," Ryder grumbled. "I can't believe I did this—with you of all people."

Until he'd added that last handful of words, Allie had only been caught up in the weirdness and the memory of his protruding male part, not pissed off. But that did it.

"With me of all people?" Allie challenged.

Because they'd known each other for so long, he picked up on the ire right away, and tried to dismiss it with a wave of his hand. "We're friends."

Now he looked at her, and it wasn't an especially good time for it since she was struggling to pull the vomit-green dress over her head. He sighed, went to her and helped, pulling and squeezing like putting sausage in a casing. Once the dress was in place and Allie was cinched in, their gazes met and held.

He opened his mouth but then closed it as if he'd changed his mind about what to say. "I don't want to screw up our friendship."

Allie wanted to assure him that it wouldn't, but she'd never out-and-out lied to him before, and she was worried this might indeed be a whopper. They couldn't have a do-over on this, and she seriously doubted she'd ever look at her ankle again without seeing, and feeling, his mouth on it. She'd never considered that to be a hot spot before, but Ryder had made it one now.

Along with making some memories that he clearly wished they hadn't made.

But now that they had been made, maybe it was time for her to clear the air, even if this was a particular clearing he wasn't going to like to hear.

"Your friendship means a lot to me, too," she said. Paused. Swallowed hard and put on her mental big-girl panties so she could tell him what she'd been wanting him to hear for years. "There's a reason, though, that I never wanted you to be my blood brother. It's because.... well, I'm attracted to you."

Allie steeled herself for him to laugh. Or curse again. Or maybe just leave now that he was dressed. And he might have indeed done one or more of those things if his phone hadn't rung. Ryder didn't especially seem relieved about the interruption, but the ringtone let them know it was Bree.

That realization sent Allie and him following the sound to locate his cell phone under some hay. They found it at the same time, their hands closing around it, which meant they touched, and Allie got another jolt of heat. Not quite as scorching as the love bite, but with her now-clear head, it was almost as potent.

"Whew, you're okay," Bree greeted the moment Ryder hit the answer button. He put the call on speaker, probably so she wouldn't need to stand so close to him to hear.

Allie moved away from him, but their eyes stayed connected. She wished she could crawl inside him and figure out what he was thinking. Or better yet, she wished he'd just kiss her, but she figured they were going to need more of that air-clearing before that even had a possibility of happening. But even if it didn't happen today, Allie wasn't going to take back what she'd just said.

"What about Allie? Is she okay, too?" Bree asked.

Ryder shook his head as if to clear it. "Uh, why wouldn't she be?"

His twin made an "isn't it obvious" sound. "Well, when I left the reception with Trace, you two were doing some sloppy dance moves and talking about getting drunk. Nothing could go wrong with that, I thought to myself." There was more than a smidge of sarcasm in the comment. "With the sour mood we were all in because of Curt leaving, I just didn't want you two doing anything stupid."

Allie had very recent memories of what Bree would consider stupid. Heck, she still had bits of hay sticking to various parts of her body, including a couple that were in her bra.

"Something stupid?" Ryder growled. "Like what?"

Bree laughed. "If I have to spell it out for you, then I'm guessing nothing happened. It's just with emotions running high, I didn't want you to cross any lines with Allie. I know you sometimes forget, but she's a woman, Ryder."

"Trust me, I haven't forgotten," he said under his breath.

"Well, neither has she. Allie's always had a crush on you," Bree added.

Thankfully, Allie managed to contain her gasp, but her eyes narrowed. Bree was spilling a pinky-swear promise that Allie and she had made when they were teenagers. Eighteen or so years ago. And apparently it had still been a secret to Ryder until this exact second.

"Crush aside," Bree went on, "Allie and you have your heads on straight. I know neither of you would risk ruining things. We're the Rab Posse now. Or maybe Bra. Or Arb," she suggested. "Bra," Bree concluded. "Yeah, the Bra Posse works because Allie and I both wear bras, and you get your hands into a lot of them."

Bree laughed as if it were both a fine joke and an equally fine idea. It wasn't. But Allie figured it'd stick as hard and as fast as Crab had.

"Here's to the Bra Posse," Bree continued. "And to all the years we'll keep the posse just the way it is now. Gotta go. I need to call Allie and make sure she got home okay."

Bree added a cheery goodbye and ended the call, and several moments later Allie's phone rang. Judging from the sound, it was somewhere near the scattered deck of cards. She didn't go scrambling for it; neither did Ryder. That was because they still had that eye lock on each other.

"Hell," Ryder said. Her phone stopped ringing, the call no doubt going to voice mail. "What now?"

It was one of the most important questions she'd ever been asked. This was her chance to put a lid on things. Or, as Bree had just pointed out, keep the Bra Posse intact.

Or…

Allie could do something that would change things forever.

She had a quick debate with herself and went with the second choice. Allie slid her arms around Ryder, and she kissed him. Not some friendly peck, either. She went full throttle, down and dirty.

He didn't pull away, but he did grunt, maybe in surprise, and she thought there might be some pleasure mixed in with it, too. There was certainly pleasure for her. His mouth was everything she'd thought it would be. Everything she'd dreamed about for years. Firm, tasty and all man. Just the way she liked the mouths that gave her kisses.

Ryder's next grunt was definitely one of pleasure, and he snapped her to him, deepening the kiss, pulling her even closer and delivering the experience of a lifetime. When he stopped, they were both starved for air. Both looking as if someone had just hit them upside the head with two-by-fours.

He opened his mouth, and she didn't think it was the start of another kiss. No. This was likely going to be an apology where he tried to backtrack. But Allie decided to nip that in the bud.

"If you want to cross any more lines," she said, picking up her purse and phone so she could make her exit, "you know where to find me."

CHAPTER THREE

RYDER SWORE TO himself not to cross any lines. Especially ones that involved Allie.

Of course, he'd sworn to give up booze after the moonshine-puking incident. And sworn not to cut class after getting caught in eighth grade and being grounded for a month. Once, he'd sworn to give up on girls after Juliette Jenkins had broken his heart in tenth grade.

He'd failed on all three of those counts. Plus, plenty of other times.

He couldn't fail with Allie, though. He just couldn't. The stakes with her were higher than puking, detention and, yes, even a broken heart.

That was why this time Ryder had a plan to make sure there'd be no line crossing. Hard work and plenty of it. Cold showers, too. And pinching himself, hard, whenever the image of Allie's breasts popped into his head. The pinching didn't work on the ankle hickey, though. That was because now that he remembered everything in too-perfect detail, Ryder recalled staring up at her panties during the love biting.

He was going to hell in a handbasket for the downright dirty thoughts he had about her and those panties. He was going to a level below hell for the thoughts he had of getting her out of them.

That was why he kept on working, and today was no different. Since he had become one of the top hands at the Granger Ranch, cleaning the tack room wasn't in his job description. That was a task for the newbies, those learning the ropes. Still, he'd volunteered for it, and he welcomed the back-aching chore. Actually, for the past five days since Curt's wedding, he'd been up for any and all work that kept him busy. Anything to keep his mind off what'd happened in the hayloft with Allie.

Too bad the work wasn't, well, working.

He was still thinking about her—about that kiss, too—and about her breasts. The damn panties. And it didn't help that the thinking included the memories of seeing her practically naked.

Sheez.

He should have hit himself on the head then and there. It might have dulled the memories some, and it could have relieved his guilt over what was going on in his mind and body right now. Specifically, he was lusting after his best friend.

Thankfully, in the past five days, he hadn't acted on that lust. Ryder would have liked to take full credit for that, but he couldn't. Truth was, it was just as much Allie's doing as his. There'd practically been a downpour of medical issues with the livestock that had kept Allie working just as hard as Ryder had been. Until today, that work had taken her to another barn, the stables and other parts of the ranch, but that all changed when Ryder came out of the tack room. He saw her in the corral checking one of the new mares.

"She's a looker, ain't she?" Bennie Fredrick said. "I

ain't talking about the horse, either." The ranch hand put a thumb to the brim of his hat, moving it back so that it gave him a better view.

Of Allie.

It wasn't the first time Ryder had heard a hand comment on Allie, but it was a first for Bennie, mainly because the man had only worked at the ranch for a couple of weeks.

Bennie's "observation" bothered Ryder more than it usually would have. Maybe because Ryder's own mind was on the same "she's a looker" track.

"I sure wish she'd go out with me," Bennie went on. "I figure she's an even better looker out of those jeans." He chuckled, and it wasn't a light ha-ha chuckle, either. It was the sound of a man having downright dirty thoughts.

Ryder ignored him and carried some horse collars back into the tack room that Bennie and he had just cleaned. When he came back out, Bennie was still gawking at Allie, and now the hand was leaning against a post.

"I heard she went out with Dylan Granger," Bennie said. "I'll bet Dylan got her out of those jeans."

"He didn't," Ryder assured him. "And they only went out on a coffee date."

Bennie looked back at him as if waiting for an explanation as to how Ryder knew that, but then the man chuckled again. "Oh, right. I heard folks say that Dr. Good Girl and you are friends. No way could I be friends with that."

"That?" Ryder challenged, and he said it a little louder and meaner than he'd intended.

It caused Allie to look in his direction. She didn't keep it at a glance, and she lifted her eyebrow as if to ask him if something was wrong. For just that split second, she was Allie, his best friend, again and he could almost forget that he'd seen her breasts and given her the ankle hickey.

He couldn't forget those panties, though.

"I could use some help moving this tack," Ryder told Bennie, and this time it wasn't mean or loud. It was the tone of a boss, which he was. Well, he was the boss of this shift of hands, anyway, and Bennie was definitely on the shift.

Ryder's phone rang, and he had worked himself up into such a lather that it took him a moment to drag his phone out of his pocket. Bree's name was on the screen.

"Ready for our usual Friday-night beer at the Longhorn?" Bree greeted.

It was the same question he heard most Friday nights, but normally it came from Curt. He'd been the one to bring the four together. Apparently, Bree had taken over that role.

"I'll take that as a yes," Bree said when he didn't jump to answer. "I'll text Allie, and the two of you can meet me there in about an hour. I'll order us some nachos."

Of course, Bree would "invite" Allie, and Allie would probably come. It was her Friday ritual, as well. So, there was potential for beer, nachos, Allie and plenty of scalding-hot memories. There weren't enough places on his body to pinch to help him with that, and that was why Ryder had to do something about it.

"I can't go tonight," Ryder told Bree before she could hang up.

Silence. To the best of his memory, Ryder had never turned down a Friday beer. Over the years, he'd even arranged his dates for Saturday so that Friday would be free.

"Everything okay?" Bree asked.

No, and it especially wasn't okay that Bennie was licking his lips while watching Allie make her way to the barn. Ryder took off his hat and smacked Bennie on the shoulder. "The tack," Ryder reminded him, and this time he added narrowed eyes to the order.

Even with Ryder giving him the stink eye, Bennie took his time hoisting up a saddle, and he still kept firing glances at Allie. Of course, there was plenty to look at. The fit of her jeans, snug in all the right places.

Ryder pinched himself, hard.

"What's wrong with the tack?" Bree pressed as Bennie finally moved out of earshot and from the ogling zone.

"Just busy clearing out the tack room, that's all. I figured you'd be busy, too, with Trace or your current sweet thing."

"Trace didn't stick around. He's back in Abilene. Besides, it's Friday," she reminded him. "Sweet things get put on hold for Friday. That's always been the Crab Posse rule, and I figured we'd keep it up for the Bra Posse."

Yes, it had been, and Bree might be wanting to keep up their rituals as a way of hanging on to Curt. Or rather hanging on to what the four of them had been together. Losing a friend, even because of geography, was hard. It was even harder, though, being with a friend when that friendship had changed because of a kiss.

"You're sure you can't make it? Just try," she added when Ryder didn't respond. "It wouldn't be Friday without Allie and you."

Ryder gave the most noncommittal mumble in the history of that particular form of communication, and he put his phone away just as Allie came into the barn. Her phone dinged with a text. No doubt from Bree, and Allie's forehead bunched up when she read it.

"The Longhorn Bar," she mumbled after she put her phone away. "You, me, beer and memories I can't get out of my head. Nothing could go wrong with that."

So, they were on the same page. And that sucked. Because it confirmed what Ryder already knew. "I ruined things with you in that hayloft."

She gave his arm an exaggerated pat. "There, there. That hickey wasn't so bad. Uneven suction, yes, and a little too big for the surface area, but I give you a ninety out of a hundred." Allie flashed him a smile and wink.

But it wasn't friendly in a friend kind of way. It was, well, flirty. And sexy. Hard to go back to friendly after the things he'd seen and after that kiss. After everything else that'd gone on it the hayloft, the kiss had merely lined his handbasket to hell, but it was a very hot lining.

"Ninety, huh?" he asked. It was really stupid to keep up this flirting. Or talk about anything that involved some kind of love-bite one-upmanship, but it felt good to see her smile again. Like old times. With some heat.

"Okay. Ninety-one." She reached out, touched her finger to the button on his shirt, and Ryder felt tightening in parts of him that shouldn't be feeling that kind of stuff. It was as if she'd touched his bare skin.

Ryder continued with the stupidity. "I used to be a solid ninety-five, but I guess I'm out of practice. The last hickey I gave was back in high school. Plus, when I gave you that one, I think I had a bit of hay stuck on my tongue."

She nodded. "Lots of hay. Lots of tongue."

More body tightening, and it felt like more than bare-skin touching. It was as if she'd unzipped him right then and there.

Where the hell had this come from?

And why was there so much heat?

Ryder wanted to believe it had started at the wedding with that comment about her not wanting him for a brother, but he had to admit that it'd been simmering for a while. It'd obviously just been easier to keep the lid on the heat when they'd been part of the real Crab Posse. Maybe because of the routine of being together. The expectation. But both the routine and expectation were gone now that Curt was no longer in the picture. Their whole dynamic had changed.

Allie smiled at him again, the lids of her eyes a little heavy now, as if she were looking at a lover, and it had an effect on him. A bad one. Because it made Ryder want to continue the flirting, which in turn would only keep teasing parts of his body that were best left unteased.

"I hope my tongue got better than a ninety-one," he drawled. It didn't make sense, and it was a couple of miles past the flirting stage, but Ryder felt a little crazy now.

Apparently, Allie was jumping on that crazy train right along with him because she fingered his shirt button again. “A solid ninety-five,” she said. There was a lot of breath in her voice, and some of that breath hit his face. Now it felt as if she’d unzipped him and taken him into her hand.

A man crazed with lust could imagine all sorts of things. Like voices, for instance.

“Uh, am I interrupting anything?” someone asked.

It took Ryder a moment to realize he wasn’t hearing things, that Bennie was actually there. The hand was out of the tack room, only a couple of feet behind Ryder, and he’d obviously heard more than he should have.

“We were talking about the new mares,” Allie said without missing a beat. She spared Bennie a glance before looking back at Ryder.

“Oh.” Bennie seemed relieved though Ryder didn’t know why. If Bennie had indeed heard the tongue comment, then he knew the conversation hadn’t been about mares. Still, he came closer, as if he might go through with asking Allie out.

Ryder nipped that in the bud. “Why don’t you make sure the new horses are settled?” he told the hand in his best boss tone of voice.

Bennie volleyed a few glances at Allie and him but, shaking his head, he finally walked away. The moment Bennie’s back was turned, Ryder took Allie to the tack room. Not for sex, although that might be negotiable. Because Allie kissed him again.

Better yet, he kissed her.

Like a man dying of thirst, he went after her, pressing his mouth to hers. Tasting her. Gobbling her up. And he did all of that while it occurred to him that this wasn't a woman he should be gobbling. That didn't cause him to rein things in, though. Nope. He just kept on until he was pretty sure his rating for this was going to be more than a ninety-five.

When they finally broke for air, he pulled back, their gazes meeting, and he saw the heat in Allie's eyes. Heat without the hesitation that he was certain was in his own.

"What the hell are we doing?" Ryder came out and asked her.

It took her a moment to gather her breath. "Playing with fire. Running with scissors. Tearing tags off of mattresses." She paused, smiled. "All right, that last one doesn't really fit, but it shows you that I can break the rules even when they're spelled out on mattress tags."

Oh, he already knew all about breaking rules. He'd just kissed the living daylights out of his best friend. If that didn't go against every big-assed man rule, he didn't know what did.

"I need to finish up some work," he said. "After that, if I'm smart, I'll go to the Longhorn Bar and meet with Bree."

"And if you're not smart?" Allie asked.

"The word for 'not smart' is *stupid*, and if I take the stupid route, I'll meet you at your place in an hour."

It was the first time in his life Ryder hoped he would get amnesia. Or kidnapped. Because those were probably the only two things that were going to stop him from crossing this line and jumping right into Allie's bed.

CHAPTER FOUR

ALLIE PACED ACROSS her living room and wondered if Ryder had been kidnapped. Of course, the chances of something like that happening in Wrangler's Creek were slim to none. And she certainly didn't wish for that to happen. Still, it would be one explanation for why he hadn't knocked on her door.

One hour and forty-five minutes.

That was how long it'd been since Ryder had thrown down the sexual gauntlet. Then, Allie had hurried home, showered and gotten ready for what she'd hoped would be one unforgettable evening. She'd even lined up an argument or two in case Ryder was having doubts and showed up to call things off. Even though Ryder had been the one to throw that gauntlet, it was possible—*highly* possible, even—that he not only had doubts, but that he also wouldn't show.

With that thought clamping around her heart like a gorilla's fist, Allie sank down onto the sofa, put her face in her hands and willed herself not to cry. Tears never helped anything, and besides, she'd known it'd been a huge risk letting Ryder know just how attracted she was to him.

A risk that could ruin their friendship.

When she was with him, and the lust was zinging

back and forth, it was much easier to convince herself that sex wouldn't ruin anything. That it would make it better. Yes, better. She had to admit now that lust could talk her into just about anything when it came to Ryder, and the ankle hickey was proof of that.

The hickey had faded, and the heat generated from the flirting and kissing in the tack room was just a memory. A very vivid memory, but still it wasn't happening now, and it might never happen again.

The gorilla fist squeezed even harder.

Allie blinked back those blasted tears that kept threatening, waited several more minutes, and then she got to feet, ready to throw in the towel. There were four pints of rocky-road ice cream in the freezer, but she'd start with the spray can of cheese. It wouldn't taste especially good, but before the Crab Posse had been of legal age to drown their sorrows at the Longhorn Bar, it had become their go-to vice.

Easy Cheesy cures all.

Sometimes, the cure had gotten really messy when it had become an all-out spray-cheese war with Curt, Bree, Ryder and her. That had often resulted in better moods but the necessity for showers and shampoo.

She popped the top of the bacon-and-cheddar-cheese goo and squirted a gob in her mouth—just as there was a knock on her door.

"Ryder," she said on a gasp of breath. Well, she said it as well as she could say anything, considering the massive cheese-product obstacle that was now in her mouth.

With the can still in her hand, Allie ran through the living room, forcing herself to slow down just so she wouldn't look overly eager. But she had to ditch the hope of looking less eager because she couldn't hold back from throwing open the door.

It was Ryder, all right. And he had his own can of spray cheese.

"I was kidnapped," Ryder blurted out. He stepped around her and inside.

Allie waited for the punchline, but it didn't come, and Ryder certainly didn't look as if anything funny had recently happened to him.

"Bree," he continued a moment later. "As I was changing my clothes, she came rushing into the bedroom, threw a pillowcase over my head and said she was kidnapping me."

Allie managed to swallow the cheese. "Why?"

"Because my idiot twin thought I was swimming in a self-pity pit over Curt's moving, and Bree believed the best way to get me out of that pit was to conk me on the head and drag me to the Longhorn for that blasted drink."

"She hit you?"

Ryder leaned down, pushed away some of his thick golden-brown hair and showed her the bump. "Bree did that with this." He held up the can of nacho cheese. "She said it was an accident, that she hadn't meant to give me a concussion, but for shit's sake, it hurt. Still does. So, anyway, that's why I'm late."

As excuses went, that one was a doozy, and despite the injury and Ryder's sour mood, it instantly lifted Allie's spirits. He'd come. And that meant...well, she wasn't sure exactly what that meant yet, but he was here, and that was a start.

He tipped his head to the cheese can gripped in her hand. "Did Bree pay you a visit, too?"

"No." But she probably should have said yes since Ryder instantly knew the can meant she'd been battling the blues. Because of him being late. No way would she eat the stuff because it was actually good.

"Sorry," he mumbled.

Now she tipped her head to his cheese can. "Did you bring that in with you so I could drown my sorrows?"

He shook his head but then shrugged. "I thought maybe we'd need it if I got past being stupid and put a stop to what we both are probably thinking about stopping."

It took Allie a moment to work her way through that wordy explanation, but it sounded like good news. Good news to her anyway. "You didn't get past being stupid," she spelled out, but wished it sounded better than what she'd meant. "I'm glad."

He shrugged again, his eyes meeting hers. "I just want to make sure we've both thought this all the way through." But he immediately added a string of curse words to that when his phone dinged with a text. From across the room, Allie's dinged, too, which meant this was likely a group message. "So help me, if that's Bree I'm going to throttle her… It's Curt," he said when he set aside the cheese can and looked at his phone.

"'Back from my honeymoon.'" Ryder read Curt's message aloud. "'Happier than a bull with two peckers. Got a text, though, from Bree about an hour ago.'" Ryder continued to read. "'She sounded all down or something, but she just texted back to say she was hooking up with Roman Granger. Now I think she's as happy as a bull with three peckers.'"

Allie could understand Bree feeling that way. Roman was a hot bad boy, and the free-spirited Bree was always up for the kind of trouble Roman would be looking to dish out. It lessened Allie's feelings of guilt because of the "all down or something" observation Curt had made about Bree. But Roman wasn't going to be a permanent fix.

Nothing was.

"Things will never be the same," Allie said, repeating what had come up at the wedding. Judging from the puzzled look on his face, Ryder seemed to have a deeper understanding of that now. At least she hoped that was why that look was there, and not because of his head injury.

It was time for her to make the argument she'd worked on before he'd arrived, so she placed her cheese can on the table next to his, and she took him by the hand to lead him to the sofa. With the puzzled look still in place, he sat, and she hurried to get him the bottle of beer that she had waiting for him in the fridge. Because of the hangover from Hades from the week before, Allie stuck with water.

His puzzled look turned to one of suspicion when she sat beside him and picked up her laptop that she'd purposely left on the coffee table. "I want to show you a dirty picture," she said.

He blinked. "Porn?"

"Not exactly." But she had gotten his attention just as she'd planned. Allie clicked on the photo she'd loaded and angled the screen so that it was right in Ryder's face.

"Holy hell." He didn't exactly scramble away from it, but it was close. He moved back as far as he could go and still be on the couch.

That had been Allie's reaction, too, when she'd first found it. "It's a good example of the point I'm trying to prove."

He stared at her at if she'd lost it. "It's a photo of a really old couple having sex." Ryder glanced at it again. "Is that the guy's butt or just super wrinkly boxers?"

"His butt," she verified, but she'd been confused at first, as well. Equally confused why the couple—who were ninety if they were a day—had thought it a good idea to post something like that.

"And the point you're trying to prove," Ryder said, "is what?"

"You can't unsee that, right?"

His agreement was fast and firm.

"Well, I can't unsee what I saw in the hayloft," Allie continued. "You were naked, and I saw every inch of you. *Every. Inch,*" she emphasized. "That means I'll always have that memory with me wherever we go from here."

He stayed quiet a moment. "I have some of those memories of you, too."

Good. She hoped the ones he had were as visually appealing as hers were of him.

Allie looked him straight in the eyes. "Ryder, we can't be just friends. Not anymore."

There. It was all spelled out, and except for the bunched-up face Ryder kept making when he would glance at the old couple, she thought it would soon sink in.

"So, you're saying we're screwed either way we go?" he asked.

Allie would have said yes, a fast and firm one, but she didn't get a chance. That was because Ryder took hold of her, pulled her to him and kissed her.

DESPITE THE FAILED kidnapping attempt, the disturbing senior-sex photo and the strong possibility that he was ruining things with his best friend, Ryder was surprisingly okay with this kiss.

Of course, it was a good kiss, one that dissolved any shred of common sense, so he had to admit that it could be the main reason for the okay feeling. That and he knew it wasn't going to stop at just a kiss.

Nope.

Allie and he had started this a week ago, and they were going to finish it whether it was the right thing to do or not. It certainly seemed right, and judging from that sweet sound of pleasure she made, Allie was in his corner on this.

And speaking of corners, that was where they landed—the corner of the sofa with her arms wrapped around him, pulling him closer and closer until it wasn't possible to get any closer. Well, it was, but it was going to take them getting rid of their clothes to accomplish that.

Allie didn't seem to have a problem with that, either. While the kiss raged on, she squeezed her hand between them to the front of his shirt and started playing with his buttons. It wasn't just the flirty touching that she'd done earlier in the barn; this was actual touching, and it got even better when she undid enough buttons to get her hand in his shirt.

Now her fingers dallied around on his chest. It was nice, very nice, but it got a whole lot better when Ryder returned the favor and turned the dallying tables on her. He slipped his hand beneath her top and into her bra.

Oh, man.

This second-base foreplay already felt like it was only seconds away from hauling her off to bed, but if this did indeed turn out to be a mistake, Ryder intended to make the most of it. He broke the kiss so he could sample what was on the other side of the flimsy lace bra she was wearing.

Allie made more sounds of pleasure and need, which, of course, only fired him up even more. It also upped the urgency inside him, but Allie went for broke in the urgency department when she pressed her hand to the front of his jeans.

Yes, this was definitely going to lead to sex.

That was the last coherent thought Ryder had for a couple of seconds because while Allie kept touching him, she also kissed his neck. And she used her tongue. Talk about hitting his prime hot spot, and she could generate enough heat to melt a glacier with that mouth.

Ryder knew he had to do something, and that was when he went for another round of table turning—literally. He hooked his arm around her neck, shifting her out of the sofa corner. He wasn't quite sure how it happened, but they ended up on the coffee table.

The things that had been on the table clattered to the floor, but they both ignored it because the new position and kisses inspired them to get naked. It went a lot faster than the strip poker had. He had her top off in seconds. Ditto for her bra. He would have gone after her skirt, but her breasts distracted him. He was mindless when it came to that sort of thing, and he had to kiss and taste some more before he could move on.

Moving on, though, was worth the effort because once he had the skirt off, he saw her panties. They weren't the same ones she'd had on in the hayloft, but he knew these would be just as memorable.

So was what was beneath.

He got proof positive of that when he shimmied off her panties. He kissed his way back up her body as she cursed him and tugged at him. Ryder thought she was either trying to make this end way too fast or she was aiming to get his clothes off. Since he didn't want things to go in the too-fast direction, he helped her. Not easily. Because he soon learned that Allie intended to continue those torturing neck kisses while he got out of his jeans and put on a condom.

When Ryder finally pushed into her, he made darn sure he was looking straight into her eyes. That way he could see if there was any hesitation.

There wasn't.

There was only the glow of pleasure, complete with lust-glazed eyes and a gusting breath. It was perfect.

Just as Allie was.

He'd always known that, of course, but this was perfect on steroids.

"Finish it," she whispered, her voice both sweet and hot at the same time. "Easy Cheesy can't cure this, but you can."

Yes, he could. He finished it while one of their favorite mantras pulsed through his head.

Nothing can go wrong with that.

CHAPTER FIVE

WHEN IT CAME to sex with Ryder, plenty went right. Not caring if she got the grammar correct, Allie figured it was righter than she could have ever imagined.

Who knew that there'd be that kind of amazing heat between them? She certainly did—now. And it had only gotten better when they'd had a second and third round, in her bed those times.

Even though she'd known Ryder most of her life and had cared deeply about him for a good chunk of that time, Allie had learned a lot about him tonight. Not just sex related, either. She now knew he was a snuggler, a cover hog and that he could fall asleep minutes after an orgasm. He hadn't overanalyzed things. Hadn't gotten a panicked "we screwed up" look in his eyes. He had simply snuggled, fallen asleep.

And then stolen the covers.

After she'd pulled and tugged most of the night, she'd finally given up and used Ryder for any body heat she needed. All in all, it was an excellent solution because she was touching enough naked parts of him to make her recall in perfect detail what he could do with that nakedness.

She glanced at the clock on her dresser. Already

nine a.m. She rarely slept this late, but then she'd never spent the night with Ryder.

While still nestled in the crook of his arm, she looked up at him and couldn't help herself. She had to brush a kiss on his chin, and Allie wanted to kick her own butt when he stirred. The feeling didn't last, though, when he looked down at her and smiled. Just smiled. And she released the breath she hadn't even known she'd been holding because those blue eyes still showed no trace of regret.

With their gazes locked, the smile still on his incredible mouth, she waited for him to say something. She also steeled herself in case the "something" included a long talk about the complications this would cause in their lives.

"I'm starving," he said. "Let me grab a shower, and then I can whip us up some coffee and breakfast."

Allie was certain she looked shocked because she was. He kissed her, smiled and got off the bed—giving her yet another full view of his body. She figured those doubts and second thoughts would come to him when he was grabbing that shower, but she was wrong about that, too. After he'd been in the bathroom only a few minutes, he came back out and took her hand, leading her back into the bathroom with him. And then into the shower, where he already had the hot water going.

He chuckled. "You should see your face."

She hoped he wasn't talking about smeared makeup or something. "What's wrong with it?" she asked.

"Nothing's wrong. You just look as if you've never showered with a man before."

She hadn't, but she winked. "I've never showered with *you*."

Allie meant to make that sound flirty, but it came out sounding as if she'd attached herself to him and wouldn't let go. Of course, maybe she was overreacting and confused that this hadn't led to the conversation she was certain they would have already had. She might have gone ahead and launched right into the talk, too, but Ryder distracted her with a kiss. Then another. Then another. Until Allie no longer cared if they ever spoke to each other again.

With the water sliding over their bodies, Ryder did some sliding of his own. His mouth still on hers. His hands moving over her. He kept up the touching and kissing. Ryder added some lifting, too. He hooked her legs around him and took her there with her back bracketed against the shower wall.

The climax roared through her, just as the others had, but if she had to rate them, this was the best. Definitely her new preferred way to wake up in the morning.

"You're better than a triple-espresso-shot latte," she whispered, causing him to give her a dreamy post-sex smile and a kiss.

Allie would have probably stayed there, with Ryder still inside her, while the kisses continued. Heck, she would have stayed until their skin pruned. But then she heard the doorbell. Not just one ring but a whole bunch in a row.

Ryder set her on her feet and turned off the water just as the ringing turned to heavy knocks. He cursed, got out and handed her a towel. Allie was cursing, too, when she heard the front door open. There were only three other people with keys to her house. Curt, who was in Abilene. Ryder, who was naked next to her.

And Bree.

"Allie?" Bree called out. "Ryder? What the hell happened?"

FROM THE MOMENT Ryder had kissed Allie in the tack room, he'd known that he would have to tell Bree what was going on. He just hadn't expected the telling to come so soon. This was not the kind of interruption he wanted mere seconds after a very satisfying orgasm.

Allie groaned, huffed and generally looked as if she dreaded this situation as much as he did. Still, she opened the bathroom door a notch.

"I'll be right there," she called out to Bree.

She put on a bathrobe that she took from the adjoining dressing room and looked at him. "Your truck is out front so she knows you're in here. But if you want to keep this just between us, I can tell Bree that you'd had too much to drink and that you caught a ride home."

Ryder appreciated that she was giving him an out, but in that moment, he realized it wasn't an out he wanted. Bree needed to learn the truth.

So did Allie.

He was thinking both of them were going to be surprised with what he had to say.

"We'll talk to Bree together," he insisted.

She nodded, and when they were dressed, she brushed a kiss on his cheek. She seemed uncertain. He sure as heck hoped that uncertainty didn't apply to what was about to happen.

Allie and he went out together, into the living room, where Bree was waiting. She didn't give them the shocked look that Ryder had expected, though. Instead, Bree tipped her head to the two Easy Cheesy cans on the foyer table.

"If you were going to have a pity party, you should have invited me," Bree said. It wasn't sarcastic, either. In fact, there was no clue that she'd come to the conclusion that the pity party had actually turned into a sex romp. And more.

Much more.

Bree sighed and made a beeline for the kitchen. "Sheez. No coffee," she grumbled. "I'll get some started while I tell you all about my dud of an evening. Just as Roman and I were getting ready to head out, he had a family emergency and had to go home. Something to do with his son, so he lit out of there fast. I ended up heading back to my place to watch a documentary on the mating habits of frogs."

Maybe it was his and Allie's silence, but Bree finally seemed to pick up on the clues. Of course, a huge clue was that Ryder had missed a couple of buttons on his shirt, he was only partly zipped and the biggest kicker of all—Allie had a love bite on her neck.

Hell.

He didn't remember marking her up like that, but then he'd spent a lot of time getting familiar with her neck. Along with the rest of her. It was possible there was a hickey or two around her inner thigh region.

Bree had already grabbed the coffeepot to fill at the sink, but she stopped and eased the pot back onto the counter. Her attention was nailed to them.

"You two had sex," Bree finally concluded. She repeated it three times, groaned and sank down onto the floor while she pressed her hands to the sides of her head.

"It wasn't planned," Allie said. "Okay, that's a lie. It was. I invited Ryder over, and he came after your failed kidnapping attempt. But I hadn't planned anything before a week ago."

Bree volleyed glances between them, maybe hoping this was a prank. Then her shoulders dropped when she likely realized that it wasn't.

Ryder didn't say anything, not yet. He just gave Bree some time for things to sink in. It didn't sink in especially well. His twin got up, went back into the living room for the cheese cans and sprayed some from both into her mouth.

"Start explaining," Bree snapped. At least that was what Ryder thought she said. It was hard to tell through all the cheese. She swallowed before she continued. "We're best friends. The Bra Posse. What the hell were you thinking when you climbed into bed with Allie?"

"I was thinking I wanted to have sex with her," Ryder readily admitted.

Allie made a sound of agreement, causing Bree to take another double squirt of Easy Cheesy. "I've wanted Ryder for a long time now," Allie said. "I've had a lot of fantasies about him, and last night a few of those fantasies came true."

That made him want to smile. He didn't. Ryder figured a smile of any kind wouldn't go well with all that cheese Bree was guzzling.

"We'll still be the Bra Posse," Allie went on. "Crab

Posse," she amended. "But I want to keep on living out some of those fantasies with Ryder. If that's what he wants, that is."

Oh, it was exactly what he wanted, and if they'd been alone, he would have asked for some details about those fantasies. Maybe even some show-and-tell. But first he had to soothe things over with Bree.

"This changes things," Bree said. "Again." He thought that was the right interpretation anyway. The words were a little garbled through the cheese hits.

"Yes," Ryder had to admit. "I hope it does anyway. Let me explain," he added when Bree went stiff. "I love you. You're not just my sister, you're my friend, and even I'm smart enough to realize that's a good thing."

Now here was the hard part. Not hard for him but it could come as a big-assed surprise to Bree. Maybe to Allie, too, if she hadn't figured out how things really were between them.

"My feelings for Allie aren't all of the friend variety," he said, "and they run deep."

He waited for Bree's reaction. But there wasn't one. Not a verbal one anyway. Bree headed straight for the front door and stormed out, leaving Allie and him standing there. Ryder started to go after her, but he knew Bree well enough to know this wasn't a situation where talking things out would help.

Hell.

Allie grumbled something similar and sank down onto the sofa. "I should have handled this better. You know, eased Bree into this." She looked up at him. "Maybe we should just cool things between us for a while to give her time to adjust."

Ryder mentally repeated that *hell*, and he added a lot more profanity to go with it. Twenty-four hours ago, he'd never thought he'd be in this position. After all, he had been trying to keep this attraction at bay. But if he'd actually wanted to do that, he would have never shown up at Allie's house. He'd known what was going to happen when he'd walked in the door.

"Is that what you want?" he snapped. But he didn't want her answering that in case she said yes. "Because it's not what I want."

She kept staring at him, then gave an uncertain nod. "But Bree… If you lose her friendship, you might lose her as a sister, too."

Allie was right, and that put a huge knot in his stomach. Still, there was a bigger problem here. "If I quit seeing you, then I'll resent it. I'm talking big-time resentment. That's going to play into how I feel about Bree."

Man, he had the idea of their friendships all going down the drain. They'd all been such a big part of each other's lives, and now that might be over.

"Just how deep is deep?" Allie asked.

It took him a moment to realize she was responding to the comment he'd made about his feelings for her. "Deep," he assured her. And to prove it, Ryder pulled her to him and kissed her. It wasn't one of those scorchers that would lead to sex, but it was plenty hot enough to let her know just what she meant to him. Just in case, though, he spelled it out for her.

"I care for you. *A lot.* And I'd like for that lot to be a whole lot more." He frowned a little, wishing he'd practiced that or used a thesaurus for a better variety of words, but she got the point because she gave a little smile and a larger kiss.

Allie's mouth was still on his when the door flew open. Bree. His sister stood there, bearing some resemblance to a gunslinger in the Old West. Instead of guns, though, she had cans of Easy Cheesy in each hand.

"I keep spares in my car," Bree mumbled when she followed his gaze to the cans. "You know, just in case of a crisis."

After the weird kidnapping attempt, Ryder wasn't sure what Bree intended to do with the cheese, but he considered she might throw them at him. She didn't. Bree squirted some from the first can into her mouth and then did the same with the second one.

"It's too early for tequila shots," she added after she'd swallowed the stuff. "So, this will have to do."

She came in, still moving a little like a gunslinger, but her appearance was somewhat diminished by the yellow goop on her lips.

"I'm not giving up Ryder," Allie told her. "My feelings for him run deep." Allie looked at him. "Sorry, I couldn't come up with a different description without coffee or a hit of that cheese."

He shrugged. *Deep* worked for him just fine because it meant this was just the start. And Ryder couldn't wait.

"And I suppose you're not giving up Allie," Bree said, shifting her attention to Ryder.

"No." Then he did some more waiting.

Bree had a squirt of cheese first, taking it the way she would a tequila shot. She still had on her tough expression, but it faded by degrees with each volleyed glance they gave her.

"Crap," Bree finally said. "All right. Go ahead and fall in love. Just remember one very important thing."

Ryder frowned. "Nothing can go wrong with that?"

Allie frowned, too. "Easy Cheesy cures all?" she tried.

Bree gave them a flat look. "Sheez. No originality from either of you. I was going to say have sex until your legs buckle, and when you come up for air, give me a call so we can get some nachos."

That knot in Ryder's stomach loosened a little. "You mean that?"

Bree huffed, and her flat look morphed into a shrug. Then a nod. "Just promise me that the Bra Posse will live on."

Allie went to her, brushed a kiss on Bree's cheek. "It will. Friends forever."

Bree made an exaggerated roll of her eyes, but the smile was genuine. "Forever," she said softly to Allie, but her gaze wavered a little when she looked at Ryder. "And what about you? Are you in on this friends-forever stuff?"

"Yeah." When Allie stepped aside, Ryder went to his sister and pulled her into his arms. "I won't even object to the *Bra* part of Bra Posse. Not much anyway," he added in a mumble.

Bree stared at him. "I can't lose you. Either of you." Her voice cracked a little, and cursing no one in particular, she slung an arm around Allie, dragging them all into a group hug.

"You won't lose me," Allie assured her.

"You won't lose me," Ryder echoed. It was the truth, but because Bree was also his sister, he had to add the brotherly jab of "Well, unless you try another half-assed attempt to kidnap me. Or squirt me with those cheese guns."

Bree was smiling again when she pulled back to face them. "Well, then. The next attempt will just have to be full-assed." She winked, squirted them both on their mouths with cheese and, laughing, she headed for the door. "Don't forget the part about calling me after you recover from your leg-buckling sex."

Ryder slipped his arm around Allie as they watched Bree leave. He felt as if everything had suddenly moved into place. Not the old familiar grooves that'd once made up his life. But new ones—that still involved Allie, Bree, Curt and, yes, even Easy Cheesy. All in all, these new grooves were darn good.

Perfect, in a new "looking forward to this" kind of way.

"Well?" Allie asked, staring up at him.

"Bree had some sage advice." Ryder smiled. Licked the cheese off her lips, and he kissed her. "Let's see if I can really make your knees buckle."

An hour later, Ryder proved that he could do just that.

* * * * *

USA TODAY bestselling author

DELORES FOSSEN

returns to her wild _Wrangler's Creek_ series

February 2018 | May 2018 | July 2018

"Fossen creates sexy cowboys and fast-moving plots that will take your breath away."
—*New York Times* bestselling author Lori Wilde

Order your copies today!

www.HQNBooks.com

PHDFWC18

Injured and trapped in a foreign country, Reese Brantley will need the help of a SEAL to stay alive...

Read on or a sneak peek of
ONE INTREPID SEAL,
from New York Times *bestselling author Elle James's all-new suspense-packed series,* ***MISSION: SIX***.

Reese Brantley held on to the frame of the window as the Land Rover bounced wildly over the rugged terrain. "Slow down!" she shouted to the driver.

Mubanga, the Zambian guide, seemed not to hear her. More likely, he completely ignored her as he leaned to the left to look beyond the obstruction of a pair of legs dangling over the windshield from a perch on the roof of the cab. He followed the racing leopard across the ground, heading north into the rocky hills, determinedly keeping up with the beautiful creature.

Ferrence Klein, Reese's client, who'd paid over one hundred thousand dollars for this hunting expedition, clung to his rifle from his position strapped to the top of the vehicle.

"He's not even supposed to be shooting leopards, is he? I thought there was a ban on shooting big cats? What the hell are you thinking?" Had Reese known Klein was coming to Africa to bag a leopard, she'd have told him no way. Her understanding was that he was there on a diplomatic mission for his father, the secretary of defense.

She wasn't playing bodyguard to an endangered-animal killer. If they weren't traveling so fast and furious, she'd have gotten out of the vehicle and taken her chances with the wildlife, rather than witness the murder of a magnificent creature.

The leopard jagged to the right and shot east into the rocky hills.

Rather than turn and follow, Mubanga kept driving north.

"Hey!" Klein yelled from the front of the vehicle. "The cat turned right!"

Mubanga completely ignored Klein and increased his speed.

The vehicle jolted so badly, Reese fought to keep from being thrown from her seat. The seat belt had long since frayed and broken. If she wanted to keep her teeth in her head, she had to brace herself on anything and everything to keep from launching through the window.

Klein flopped around like a rag doll on the front of the vehicle, screaming for the driver to stop.

"Stop this vehicle!" Reese yelled over the roar of the engine. She reached for the handgun strapped to her thigh. Before she could pull it from its holster, Mubanga backhanded her in the face so hard, she saw stars.

Reese swayed, her fingers losing their grip on the door's armrest. A big jolt slammed her forward, and she banged her forehead against the dash. Pain sliced through her head, blinding her. Gray fog crept in around the edges of her vision. She fought to remain upright, retain consciousness and protect her client, but she felt herself slipping onto the floorboard of the Rover. One more bump, and she passed out.

HIEJEXP0518